BRUTES FOR KIN
BY BOB GILLESPIE

BRUTES FOR KIN
By Bob Gillespie

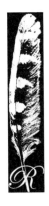

La Remige Publishers

Brutes for Kin (Rewritten from The Angry Sky: first published in 2012)

La Remige Publishers
www.laremige.com

UK Legal Deposit Libraries Act, 2003: British Library Cataloguing in Publication Data; Data applied for.

ISBN UK-English Paperback Edition 978-1-9997639-0-9
ISBN UK-English e-Book Edition   978-1-9997639-1-6

THIS BOOK IS DEDICATED TO SYLVIE,
IN EVERY WAY, MY CONSTANT COMPANION

Readers write: -

"A true thriller, which kept me gripped right through to the conclusion. The story gave a wide and interesting overview of the US and Soviet security apparatus during the cold war period, which taught me a lot. Character description excellent. Thoroughly recommended."

"I read the book with great pleasure: it is rhythmed, well written, and has the suspense to keep you on edge!"

ABOVE HIM NOW THE ANGRY SKY
AROUND THE TEMPEST'S DIN;
WHO ONCE HAD ANGELS FOR HIS FRIENDS,
HAS BUT THE BRUTES FOR KIN.

The Dream of Gerontius
John Henry Newman

FICTIONAL CHARACTERS
THE AMERICAS
Aguirre, Major Carlos: Colombian infantry
Catanzaro, Don Carlo: Chicago Mafia boss
Coombes, Fred: Air-traffic Controller
Corbin, Leroy: CIA domestic operations task force on John
  Glenn
Curry, Jim: FBI Deputy Assistant Director
Davies, Joe: Federal Drug Enforcement Authority Officer
Duval, Ed: CIA Case Officer
Friedman, Dr: Chicago Pathologist
Garcia: DGI, Cuba Officer; KGB correspondent
Glenn, John: CIA Analyst
Hailsham, Don: CIA Director of Central and South American
  Operations, Langley, Virginia
Jones, Bill: CIA Graphological Laboratory
Lebeda, George: FBI and Viet Nam veteran
Levine, Ephraim: Mossad guest at Israel Investment and
  Export Authority, Chicago
Macpherson, John (Bugs): CIA Case Officer; specialist in
  terrorism; secretary, Carol; wife Jenny (Jen):
  Endocrinologist at NIH
McKinley, Florie: Hospital inmate at Golan Memorial
  Hospital
MacTavish, Mike: FBI agent
Muñoz, Carmen: the name is an alias
O'Grady, Pat: Police Officer, Central District, Chicago;
  Corinne O'Grady: Pat's daughter
Rosen: Mossad, Asuncion, Paraguay
Sanchez: DGI, Cuba; field agent
Sinclair, Gary: US DEA resident in Bogota, Colombia;
  secretary Juanita
EUROPE and MIDDLE EAST
Al-Othman, Fatima: Palestinian-born terrorist
Balaian, Victor: anarchist intellectual; claims to be Armenian:
  the name is an alias
Cagnotto, Genaro: small-time mobster from Turin
Cremante, Pino: Mafia lieutenant; GRU agent; code name
  MILK

Ferraresi, Paolo: Red Brigades terrorist; prisoner at Ascoli
  Piceno jail
Glavina, Nino: *Carabiniere* Colonel; wife Edda
Langeac, Brigitte de: Swiss Investigator
Sereni, Lucia: Red Brigades terrorist
Terni, Elio: Red Brigades terrorist in Ascoli Piceno jail
SOVIET BLOC
Antonov, Kimon: Agricultural Secretariat General, Moscow
Berzin, Yuri: Moscow boat keeper
Botev, Traicho: Agricultural Directorate, Sofia
Budhakin, Leonid: Major General KGB: Area Department
  Director at First Chief Directorate
Demicheva, Tatiana (Tanya) Nikolayevna: KGB
  Communications operator; Eighth Directorate; daughter of
  Kirill Fedorovich Demichev, First Secretary of the Central
  Secretariat
Dobrynin, Igor: State-Security Officer, Passport-Office, Sofia
Fedorenko, Ilya: KGB Executive-Action Illegal
Kapalkin, Captain: Cipher Officer Russian Embassy, Rome
Kevorkian, Captain George: KGB Communications Cipher
  Officer; Eighth Directorate; Armenian
Khotulev: KGB Russian Embassy Resident, Rome
Kostov, Nicholas: stolen passport name
Mischa: KGB Executive-Action Illegal: the name is an alias
Nikolaev, General Felix Pavlovich: GRU–Military Security
Nikolaev, Vassily (Vassya): Lieutenant: KGB First Chief
  Directorate; father, Felix Pavlovich; code name SNOW
Ovarev, Colonel: GRU Russian Embassy Resident, Rome
Petrovic Anatoly: General Secretary, Bulgarian Agricultural-
  Products Trading Commission (BAPTCo); wife, Galina
Potanin, Valko: BAPTCo gardener: stolen passport surname
Promyslov, Ivan (Vanya) Dmitriyevich: Colonel: KGB First
  Chief Directorate: wife Olga (Olya) Sergeyevna
Puschner, Dr: Swiss Neurologist
Ryabov, Aleksandr (Sasha) Mikhailovich: Lieutenant: KGB
  First Chief Directorate
Shkoder, Mehemet: Professor of Political Philosophy at
  Tirana, Sofia and Moscow universities; author of *Albania
  Shall Conquer*
Shkoder, Ahmet: Mehemet's son; anarchical youth leader:
  KGB Executive-Action Illegal

Strugatski, Konstantin (Kostya): Central Committee Member; friend of Promyslov
Vladimir Vasilevich: Cabinet Secretary at the Kremlin
Volkov, Marshall Sergei Borisovich: Politburo Member

ACRONYMS

ATC   Air Traffic Control, USA

BAPTCo   Bulgarian Agricultural Products Trading Commission

CIA   Central Intelligence Agency: civilian foreign intelligence service of the United States federal government; called 'The Company'

DEA   Drug Enforcement Administration of the United States federal government

DGI   Direcciòn General de Inteligencia, Cuba

FBI   Federal Bureau of Investigation: the domestic intelligence and security service of the United States federal government; called 'The Bureau'

GRU   Foreign Military Intelligence Agency of the General Staff of the Armed Forces of the Soviet Union

KGB   Soviet Committee for State Security: the chief government agency acting as internal security, intelligence, and secret police. Headquartered at the Lubyanka in Dzerzhinsky Square close to the Kremlin.

M19   Colombian guerrilla movement tracing its origins to allegedly fraudulent presidential elections of 19th April 1970

NIH   National Institutes of Health, USA

PROLOGUE

I have made many mistakes in my years: spending so much time among the young and the clever, you can't be too careful. They are alive with the ideals of youth: they see life simply, where we, the old, come to see it as an exercise in politics, in the elusive art of the possible. I had thought as they once; all appeared so linear; knock down the system and put up a better one. In Albania, Enver Hodja had thought that too when he decided to align with Mao Tse Tung and to join the Chinese way in 1975, but I had cried out against his idea, writing how it would already be hard enough to reconcile an Orthodox Christian culture like that of our Russian friends with our own Islam, even before complicating things by importing a foreign socialism separated from the fatherland by a whole cultural context of Buddhism and Tao.

My book sold well after it was published in Bulgaria: its words developed common ground between Islam and Marxism and echoed down through Albanian society, but for my people, "Albania shall Conquer" had to be published clandestinely in a Tirana backstreet. I was probably foolhardy to dedicate it to my son, but he had been such an admirable youth leader before leaving for his studies in Bulgaria.

My boy, my poor ambitious boy, so young then, was almost destroyed by my collapse of status. He had not yet completely discovered the power of language, but that part of his education occurred instantly: his talent as a speaker during his doctoral years in Sofia quickly matched my own, in fact, it was better.

We fled Albania like thieves in the night. Our hours of freedom were counted. They could come in the night at any moment and drag us from our beds. The trek fleeing Enver Hodja was long. We arrived like refugees in Sofia, where we found our son, and thankfully, my political orthodoxy found me back in academia, but it was too late: my boy, my dear son, had turned: despite his new-found gift for language, he became taciturn, bitter. With his desire to reclaim his birthright and our honour, his opinions hardened, his

1

humanity weakened: he became angry at our differences with the West, we as Albanian Moslems. As he grew distant from us, we were surprised to find how much his Russian was improving: soon he was more involved in sporting activities: his frame grew muscular; he befriended Russians in his university and, just after presenting his thesis, my son said goodbye and disappeared: just like that. The last we heard, he had left for Moscow. He sent us a postcard, only once, from, of all places, Italy!

I applied and got in to the University of Moscow as a lecturer, more than anything else, to find him. I never did. His mother was heartbroken and I taught and wrote books. She left us four years ago, without ever seeing him again and now in my golden prison I pine after my boy.

LATER, IN OCTOBER 1985

Chicago political tradition leaves little room for the aspirations of a Republican President, but any visit from such an eminent guest warms the hearts of the most headstrong Democrats and encourages the city's struggling electoral minority.

Outside the new wing of Golan Memorial Hospital, at the corner of Michigan Avenue and Clark Street, the camera crews waited for hours in the cool October air to complete their live coverage of the visit.

The President, attended by the Secretary of State, whose uncompromising posture on national security issues had won him few friends among the more conciliatory factions of Congress, was there for the opening of the new wing. In his own view, the Secretary of State's position had helped to halt the slide of American influence abroad, caused, he claimed, by previous *laissez-faire* administrations. He was satisfied he had reinstated an effective barrier to the growth of Soviet influence in Central America and was intensely mistrusted by diplomats from socialist countries invariably forced to pass through his office to reach the more pragmatic ears of the President himself.

Before entering the wing, the President made a short speech on the coming summit with the Soviet leader. He strongly defended the policy of countering the expanding role of Communist advisors in Central America and retraced the progress of Russian national frontiers since the times of Catherine the Great: he claimed that the Bolshevik Revolution had been little more than a hiccough in the historic progress of Russian imperialism. Of course, the speech had been written by the Secretary of State.

There were hecklers in the crowd, but their words were drowned by cheers.

The President and his entourage entered the wing: the Secretary of State followed in a smaller, separate party. Bystanders dispersed within minutes leaving the police and a few diehards to await the reappearance of the President for his departure in a sleek, black Lincoln waiting outside.

The ground-floor ladies' ward gave onto a small garden. Sunshine streamed in through the glass doors.

Accompanied by two senior members of the hospital staff and two bodyguards, the Secretary of State had been chatting with bedridden women for five minutes, when, alarmed by a sudden commotion and the sound of a shot in the garden, he sent a bodyguard to see what was happening. Leaving only one bodyguard to protect him was against procedure, but the guard had gone anyway.

The terrorist was dressed in a white coat. He entered quickly from a corridor perpendicular to the ward entrance. The women who saw him first thought he was a medic coming to check the noise.

The first bullet entered the remaining bodyguard's left eye at point-blank range. The force of the 9 mm. Parabellum threw him onto a bed, a second bullet embedding itself in the wall behind.

No amount of training could have matched the terrorist's effect of surprise, but the second bodyguard, who had left the ward, might have brought him down.

Blood and bone shards spattered the stunned Secretary of State. He reacted quickly, his reflexes already attuned to an attempt on his life: he had often rehearsed such moments in his nightmares. He dived under a bed, bumping heavily into one of the two staff members guiding his party through the hospital. Covering his head with his hands, he tried to roll to safety. He thought he should be praying, but panic crowded out all thought except survival.

He rolled into a wall.

The P.38 Walther spat two bullets through his hands into the base of his skull.

The patients' shocked silence exploded into screams.

The terrorist's calm was uncanny. He had waited for his man to stop rolling to get an accurate shot, like a spider spinning its prey into immobility before bestowing the kiss of death. He disappeared into the corridor before the second bodyguard reappeared in the ward.

Instants later, through the din of screaming women, a Chicago policeman entered from the corridor and strolled up to the victims. He looked quietly down at them and went to the window to look outside. He went back to the door, where he met another waiting for him.

'That way!' said the first pointing down the corridor and the two ran off together.

The President had been in the next ward. Hearing shots from the garden and hallway, his bodyguards, pistols drawn, huddled around to protect him.

Setting an example for the budget cuts, the Secretary of State had not thought it necessary to use more than two bodyguards, especially when attending the far more seductive target of the President himself.

In his Georgetown apartment, Bugs Macpherson was drowsily watching live coverage of the hospital opening on national television when the reporter announced trouble inside. The television crews waited in the open for a glimpse of the President leaving the prestigious new building: their audience was to get a more exciting performance than it had bargained for. Bugs watched the defensive formation around the President moving quickly towards the limousine yards from the hospital entrance.

A motorbike broke through a police barrier. The camera swung erratically onto two leather-clad motorcyclists firing on the police. One jumped onto the roof of the President's limousine and fired on his entourage. Within seconds, they killed two policemen and two bystanders.

Bodyguards rammed the President behind the cover of a protruding wall. Two broke off to tackle the assassins. Both were shot down.

With fanatical persistence, the two motorcyclists rushed firing at the President's group. They were shot down by police and the surviving bodyguards. The President himself escaped serious injury but was severely shaken. Tears came to his eyes as he was hustled past bloody corpses lying on the ground around his limousine.

Hundreds of millions of viewers saw television repeats of the massacre. Many bystanders, officers and bodyguards were killed or wounded before the motorcyclists' suicidal attempt to assassinate the President was stopped. Ever since his return from Europe, Bugs had been convinced that such a scene might be played out one day to a US audience on its own soil. Terrorism was Bug's area.

He grabbed his jacket and an overnight bag and raced down the steps to the condo's underground garage. Blue lights flashing, he wove his pool Ford through the traffic towards Washington National airport, his siren wailing ominously as he speeded by stopped vehicles. Over the radio, he asked for a reservation on the next flight to Chicago O'Hare and for someone to pick him up: just as he pulled into the sidewalk by the departures lounge, the operations room confirmed that Jim Curry of the Chicago FBI would meet him personally. It would be nice to see Jim again. Bugs thought him to be one of the Bureau's finest.

Two hours passed before Florie McKinley, one of the inmates of the chaotic ladies' ward, was interviewed. 'I tell you, young man, I saw his face very well indeed. I always remember a face', claimed the old lady.

'Just trying to get this straight, Ma'am. You say the cop waiting at the door for the other cop to check the ward after the shooting looked like the killer.'

'Yes, officer.'

'....and you don't think it was just a coincidence?'

'No, certainly not. It was him.'

'....and you think the cop who entered the ward right after the killer left looked like him too.'

'Correct, officer, very much like him, almost a twin, but it wasn't him, you see.'

The police officer scratched his head and continued to type the old lady's deposition finger-by-finger.

'....and remember what I said about the gloves, young man', scolded Florie.

'What was that again, Ma'am?'

'He was wearing gloves and it was so warm inside.'

'The killer?'

'No! Not the killer: the officer who came in after him. You know, you really ought to listen to what people tell you.'

He eyed the ceiling in despair.

Federal agents found a white, blood-spattered medic's coat in a laundry room across the corridor from the ward. They took it away for analysis by the Quantico Research

Centre. A little later, in the corridor a few yards from the ward entrance and lying on a windowsill overlooking the garden, they found a Walther P.38. They left it untouched awaiting the arrival of forensics staff.

The medical staff and police officers on duty in the wing were made to file before Florie McKinley and two other ladies. The parade included officer O'Grady, under arrest for causing the initial stir in the garden. Then Florie was taken to look at the grey faces of the dead policemen in the morgue: she claimed that none of the physicians on duty, nor any officer, dead or alive, was the terrorist assassin, nor his supposed look-alike.

Pale-faced, crying softly, the old lady asked to be wheeled back to her ward where her daughter was anxiously waiting to console her.

On their way to the morgue, Jim Curry and Bugs Macpherson discussed the German-made P.38 found on the windowsill. 'I don't see why he left it there', said Jim.

Bugs was confused too. First, the P.38 was a favourite weapon of European terrorists, but not commonly owned in the U.S. 'And if the killer was a cop', replied Bugs, 'why would he carry a P.38; and what kind of killer leaves his fingerprints over a murder weapon, then leaves it at the scene of the crime, anyway? It's not carelessness: there has to be a reason, I'm sure of it, Jim.'

Jim strode on, scowling. His staff rarely saw him without a smile. He had the blue eyes and aquiline nose of the all-American male; looks that had served him well in college, when his success with a pretty cheerleader had led to an early, but disastrous, marriage. Now the fine features and the athletic figure still attracted attention, but his tastes had matured into a love affair with his job. In contrast with Bugs' taste for unbuttoned collars and sports jackets, Jim's smart appearance in large, polished shoes, pressed trousers and tie gave him the bearing of a corporate executive.

Reporters overran the main hospital entrance. Police refused them access to the morgue, itself overcrowded with relatives weeping around the poor corpses of innocent victims: grim-faced police took a last look at colleagues, and hospital attendants wheeled cool, blood spattered bodies into refrigerated cubicles. The Secretary of State's corpse was taken to a theatre table where his face would be re-sewn before the arrival of his family from Washington.

A Pathologist walked over. 'Good evening, I'm Doctor Friedman.'

Jim removed an official wallet from a back pocket. 'Hi, Doctor, I'm Jim Curry, FBI and this is John Macpherson: he's a specialist in terrorism.'

Friedman eyed Bugs' open collar and led the two men to his office. 'I've said nothing to the press about the two motorcyclists.'

'It's not the right time', said Jim

'The FBI took their clothes and I have put the bodies in the examination room.'

'Of course,' said Jim, 'I'd like to see them, Doctor.'

Friedman led them to a stark, neon-lit room walled with white tiles. Four porcelain slabs stood side by side in the centre of the room. Two were covered with stained shrouds. The pathologist unceremoniously pulled them back to reveal the lifeless forms of two women. Both had sleek black hair. The features of one were disfigured beyond recognition by the explosive impact of a bullet inside the motorcycle helmet she had worn.

'Handsome women', said Friedman. 'The features seem Mediterranean: the one on the right is in her late twenties with possibly Semitic features. The one on the left was in her mid-thirties: possibly Hispanic. I could try to reconstruct her features, but there's little point: they wouldn't be recognisable: the bone structure of her face is beyond repair.'

'We'll let you know if that's useful.' Jim turned to go.

'I'll join you outside', said Bugs. 'Doctor, may I take a closer look?'

'Please do', answered Friedman.

Bugs looked at the women's teeth and fingernails, noting that the nails of the older, unrecognisable woman were filthy. *Rigor Mortis* had not set in. He rolled the bodies gently, searching for identifying marks or tattoos. Bloodless bullet holes reminded him of Europe, where so often had he seen corpses of innocent men and women fallen prey to the arms of terrorists.

'Our report will be thorough Mr Macpherson', remarked the physician with a barely masked air of annoyance.

'Yes, of course, Doctor', answered Bugs absently. 'A sample of the grime under the fingernails of the woman on the left ought to be sent for analysis.'

'I'll see it's sent to the Chicago Crime Lab, Mr Macpherson: we work with them all the time.'

Bugs walked out into the bustling street where Jim was waiting for him at the crowd barrier.

Pat O'Grady sat with his head in his hands. As a Chicago cop, he had often been the questioner: never had he been the questioned: this was humiliating. Lieutenant Salvaggio continued unmercifully, mixing sarcasm into his questions to vent the anger he felt that one of his own men should be a traitor to the hitherto unblemished tradition of the precinct. 'So, this guy just comes up to you two weeks back and says he's gonna find your daughter if you do like he says, right?'

'That's how it happened, Lieutenant.'

'What colour pumps was he wearin' O'Grady?'

'Brown.'

'You say he talked funny. How'd he talk?'

'With an accent.'

'What kinda accent?'

'I told you, I don't know.'

'So, you reckon a nut with brown pumps and a funny accent can do a better job findin' Corinne than the whole fuckin' Chicago Police Department. Then you do him a nice favour and get half the fuckin' White House killed. Cosy, isn't it. It's so cosy, O'Grady, I don't believe it.'

'He said he'd find my girl.'

'So, what're we doing, you dumb bastard? We got the whole city lookin' for her.'

'We've been lookin' for two months now and not found anythin'. Then this fella appears sayin' he knows where my Corinne is.' O'Grady's eyes filmed over.

'How come you didn't tell us about this nut?'

'He said he wouldn't help if I did, an' anyway, he said other cops from the district were in on this thing. I wasn't goin' to ask any dumb questions.'

'What'd he look like?'

'Dark hair an' eyes, 'bout five foot ten, hundred sixty pounds.'

'Would you recognise him again?'

'Maybe'

'Did he give you any other instructions?'

'No'

Salvaggio detected an uneasy pause in O'Grady's reply. 'Listen, dumb ass, didn't you think there might be something wrong with someone tellin' you to run around, shoutin' an' shootin' in the air with the fuckin' President of the United States next door?'

'Sure, Lieutenant, but I didn't figure anyone was goin' to get hurt. I just thought it was one of them demonstrations.'

'Since when do cops demonstrate against the President of the United States?'

'He said other cops were demonstratin' too. Another cop was gonna signal me from the window. I figured this guy was in cahoots with half the district.'

'So, you say this cop signals from the corridor window.'

'Yeah.'

'What kinda signal?'

'Just a wave, Lieutenant.'

'Are you sure he was a cop?'

'Yeah!'

'That's kinda strange', said the officer: '.... he couldn't see into the ward from the window, so how did he know when to signal?'

'What's that, Lieutenant?'

Salvaggio thought it pointless to pursue his line of thought with O'Grady. He changed the subject. 'What did you do then?'

'That's when he said I had to run around and shoot in the air.'

'Did you say you recognised the cop who signalled you?'

'No, Lieutenant, it was sunny an' he was inside an' I couldn't see him too well.'

'But you said earlier he looked like the guy who promised to find Corinne?'

'I can't say for sure, Lieutenant.'

Salvaggio raised his eyes in despair. 'OK, O'Grady, that's all until the Feds arrive. Get changed outa your uniform and give it to McCook here: you'll probably never need it again. We're lockin' you up.'

O'Grady arose unsteadily and followed McCook to the cells.

That evening, an attorney visited O'Grady's wife. 'A client of mine has authorised me, Mrs O'Grady, to offer you $110,000 of the $125,000 bail needed to get Pat into the comfort of his own home tonight. You might like to chip in the extra $15,000 yourself.'

The woman dried her tears. 'Pat's a good man: he's never done anyone no harm.'

'If you don't have the extra $15,000, maybe Pat has a few friends who could help out.'

Mrs O'Grady sobbed, 'Anythin', so he can come home.'

She thought of O'Grady's colleagues and picked up the phone directory. Thumbing the pages, she asked the attorney, 'Who's puttin' up all that money?'

'I can't tell you, Mrs O'Grady, your benefactor wishes to remain anonymous.'

'.... but all that money!'

'It is bail, Mrs O'Grady. No one expects Pat to disappear: your benefactor will get his money back, you know.'

She lifted the phone and called around.

His police friends contributed the balance: they felt sorry for Pat: Corinne O'Grady's disappearance had left her father a shadow of the man he had been. No one could blame a man who doted on his daughter for trying anything to find her again.

Later that evening, at home with close friends and a few beers he admitted he had been willing to be fired from the force to find her: he had not expected violence, otherwise he would never have agreed to help the stranger. O'Grady insisted on walking the dog. 'I may never get to walk the pooch again:' he said, 'she's gettin' old now, and they could lock me up for a long time.' He looked upset: his wife put it down to the shock: walking the dog may do him good, may calm his nerves.

'It's so late Pat. It's eleven already.'

'I'll tell you later', he said with a wink and left slamming the door without so much as a kiss.

Pat's wife was afraid to cause more trouble. She waited until 2 a.m. before calling the district, hoping he had met a friend on the street and gone for a very late beer.

EARLIER, IN JANUARY 1985

The January wind blew bitterly: it was so cold, it almost hurt to breathe. Botev raised the scarf to cover his nose: moisture froze on the wool, shrouding it with a white crust. Winter this year had been too long, too cold.

He trudged under the lintel of a baroque archway marking both the entrance to the Trade Commission and a long-forgotten decadence. He arrived scowling in the atrium. Rarely had anyone seen him look so gloomy: Party comrades exchanged puzzled glances.

Usually, Traicho Botev loved the deference his position in the Agricultural Directorate inspired in others, and his good nature showed it. Long, unquestioning devotion to the Party had secured this lucrative position and a mention among the lower ranks of Sofia's coveted nomenklatura, but this morning he didn't notice the staff's polite good mornings: the prospect of calling Secretary Antonov in Moscow had upset his bowels and his otherwise secure little world.

Anatoly Petrovic, the General Secretary of the Bulgarian Agricultural-Products Trading Commission wanted Traicho to call Moscow himself. Talking to Antonov could be construed an honour: it could also be dangerous: last year's shipments had been catastrophic.

He grumbled biliously all the way up to the top floor.

Sitting at his desk, warming his hands around a small cup of mint tea, Traicho waited diligently. One minute before the appointed time, armed with a notepad, and trying with no success to control an unprofessional flutter in his throat, he scolded the switchboard into hurrying a confidential call to Comrade Secretary Kimon Antonov of the General Agricultural Secretariat in Moscow. He swung nervously from side to side in the ancient chair he had chosen from the basement. His stomach tensed: he sighed in anticipation of the nervous cramp he was going to suffer.

His gut leaped at an angry peal from the phone. He lifted the handset. 'Hello, I'd like to speak to Comrade Secretary Antonov, please.'

'Speaking.'

Good grief! The old buffer had answered his own phone. 'Uh...., Comrade Antonov, Secretary! This is Botev at the B....'

'Botev? .... Ah yes, Botev. Shipments weren't good last year, were they?'

'No Comrade Secretary.'

'Explanation?'

'Well, Comrade, I....'

'Well? Not well, Botev: very poor; very, very poor!'

'I think....'

'I think too, Botev, but it's not enough: you need help.' Kimon Antonov paused; then, carefully enunciating each word, he continued, 'Petrovic made a mistake appointing you to a post with so much responsibility.'

Traicho paled.

'I am sending you somewhere they will buy your miserable seeds: it may help you keep your job.'

'I....'

There came a laugh. 'I'm going to help you to appreciate the true fruits of socialism.'

'Where .... ?'

'America, Botev. You're booked on LZ 129 to Paris on April 19th: it's a direct Air France flight to Chicago from there. A Party aide will escort you to special rooms at a hotel near the Exhibition Centre. There you can peddle your little seeds at the International Agricultural Commodities Fair. It's the opportunity of a lifetime, Botev. I expect results.'

'Yes, Comrade Secretary?'

'I'm taking special measures to protect you while there: beggars surround the hotel and approach foreigners for money: sending you with an escort is costly, but I'm happy you'll be in good hands. Think of your companion as a guardian: he's a Russian: no sense of humour, but he's the best I can do, and he's very committed to the Party.'

'I appreciate your concern, Comrade Secretary.'

'Incidentally, I have sent your boss, Petrovic a sealed envelope you must personally give someone attending the exhibition on the twenty-first. Get it from his office on the way to the airport. He'll instruct you on the details. Questions?'

14

'Uh....I don't think so, Comrade Secretary.'

'Prepare your trip well, Botev. Keep me informed of your plans. Don't talk about the envelope to anyone under any circumstances at all. Is that clear?'

'I think so, Comrade Secretary.'

'You think so? Botev, a mistake, even a trifle, in delivering the envelope will result in your dismissal, certainly from the Second Directorate and probably from the Party.'

The handset clicked. Botev replaced the instrument in silence.

In Moscow, Kimon Antonov lifted his finger from the hook and dialled Anatoly Petrovic himself. The line wheezed and crackled.

A woman's voice replied, 'Comrade Secretary Petrovic's office.'

'Antonov in Moscow, pass me Petrovic.'

'One moment please, Comrade Secretary.'

Kimon Antonov lit an American cigarette, his first of the day. He inhaled deeply. A Bulgarian posted to Moscow to crown a dazzling career in the Party, he profited assiduously from the perks mother Russia provides her more talented children. One day he would return, an elder statesman, to Sofia and live out his retirement in total comfort.

'Good morning Kimon', came Petrovic's voice.

Kimon detected a tremor and relaxed. 'Good morning Anatoly', he answered brightly, 'I've just given Botev his instructions. He'll do as he's told: he's terrified.'

'So he'll come here to collect the envelope?'

'Yes, on his way to the airport: that was our agreement, was it not?' Kimon Antonov waited in silence for a reply.

When Petrovic did reply, it was to change the subject: 'Kimon', he began, 'what about the reputation of the Second Directorate? Could anything go wrong?'

'Nothing.'

'Since the Agca case, Simeonov's office has been relocated to the broom closet. He could lose his pension.'

'Stop fussing, Anatoly. No one is going to link Agca to Bulgaria or to you. You should feel honoured I've chosen your people. Think, when it's over, your career will leap to new heights.... but you must succeed, I wouldn't have chosen you otherwise.'

Anatoly Petrovic nibbled fretfully at a fingernail, while Kimon Antonov marked time taking a long draw at the cigarette hanging from his fingers: he went on condescendingly, 'My dear Anatoly, I'm asking you to do this for a just cause: loss of revolutionary zeal among young socialists in the West must stop: it's too dangerous. The theme has come up at every Party congress since the late seventies: we must continue to win the lion's share of their support, so, from time to time, we help things along a little.' Kimon chuckled, 'We Bulgarians are faster politicians than our Russian cousins.'

His voice a pitch higher, Anatoly Petrovic interrupted. 'Have you seen this Freedom Fighter's Manual, Kimon? It could have been printed in a Saigon alley! I never thought the Americans would teach resistants in Central America to make Molotov Cocktails.'

'The Cubans are beside themselves since those Washington hotheads started this 'fighting-terrorism-with-terrorism' nonsense. If the heads of young Western socialists are filled with reactionary ideas now, the International Party's progress could be set back forty years.' Kimon rolled the American cigarette between a finger and thumb. 'We must strike at the source of reaction in the West's chain of command: we must strike at the top, and few can do this better than our own countrymen.'

'But why me, Kimon? Our job is agriculture: we are not equipped....'

'Nonsense, Anatoly, for the little I have asked the Directorate to do, first in Switzerland and now in America, you are as well-equipped as anyone. Don't you owe me this favour? Besides, embassy people are always followed, and State Security is overrun with lumbering idiots.'

An embarrassed silence followed. Kimon hastily added, 'No one else has your cover. Agriculture is, by definition, peaceful.'

Anatoly was impressed with Kimon's overwhelming confidence. He had never heard anyone speak this way about the State Security over a telephone. Kimon had to have the clout to be that confident. 'Very well', he whispered, 'our Agricultural Trade Commission will bow to the great cause of socialism.'

'Excellent! Make arrangements to pay the funds immediately.' Kimon Antonov's lips in Moscow folded into a grin of irony. 'Here we are haggling with the Italians over who tried to kill their Pope, and at the same time, mounting this thing with their own criminals. Their's is surely the most democratic political system outside the socialist world.'

The voice disappeared in laughter, and the click in Anatoly Petrovic's phone confirmed that Secretary Kimon Antonov had said all he wished. In Sofia, Anatoly Petrovic trembled violently.

In Moscow, through a thick cloud of smoke, Antonov leaned forward in his chair and cursed his own stupidity: he rarely talked so foolishly, but he had had to get Petrovic to act: there was no time now for another trip to Sofia. He hoped the 'lumbering idiots' had not been listening: maybe those fools at State Security would dismiss the comment as sarcasm. He relaxed: surely, they wouldn't notice, and the remark had been useful to focus Petrovic's attention.

The listener at the Moscow international switchboard put down her earphones, removed the tape and marked it for the special attention of State Security.

The American wouldn't stop talking! Traicho Botev had never met a trader with so much to say and so little to talk about. He stole a surreptitious glance at his watch: two minutes were all that remained to deliver the letter and both the trader and his omnipresent guardian, had him locked in shallow conversation. He tried to weigh the chances his burly Russian chaperone would stay cool in an exhibition hall filled with foreigners: it might, after all, be embarrassing if he showed he was there only to hound Botev. Traicho was sure it could work: he just had to walk off. His Russian guard's arrogance irritated the Botev, yet he could appear so polite with imperialist foreigners despite his smelling of stale cabbage and sweat.

Traicho Botev couldn't wait any longer: nothing was worth the risk of losing his position on the District Conference. He gasped a quick, 'Excuse me, please' and strutted off towards the toilets, leaving the Russian gaping after him in mid-sentence. Botev had seemed so submissive that the guard was taken completely by surprise. He had thoroughly instructed his charge in the correct procedure for leaving a conversation, and this was not it. He abruptly apologised to the confused trader and chased after Botev: little more than fifteen seconds separated them.

Traicho's guard burst into the washroom. A closet door opened and a dark, keen-eyed man walked out, hands in his pockets. The man walked to the exit door looking sternly at the Russian guard, who would dearly have liked to collar him, but Chicago was forbidden ground, and that look! He could recognise that piercing look again.

Seconds later, Traicho Botev walked out of the adjoining cubicle. The Russian grabbed his sleeve. 'Are you mad? What are you up to?'

Botev gave a frightened grin and tossed his head at the closet door, 'Something you can't do for me, Comrade.'

The Russian stared stupidly at the toilet, then his face brightened. He leered at the Bulgarian clerk; 'You haven't pulled the chain, Botev: I can do that for you.'

Botev almost fainted in panic.

The guardian looked into the bowl. 'Well, well', he sniggered, 'we haven't used the toilet at all, have we. What else were you doing in there I can't do for you?'

The Bulgarian glanced involuntarily at the opening under the panel separating the cubicles through which, seconds earlier, he had passed a sealed envelope.

The guard smirked. He rushed to the door and looked outside. 'The bastard's gone' he growled. He grabbed Traicho's lapel and drew his face so close that the Bulgarian could smell the rancid breath. 'Who's less fortunate, Botev: you for being caught with your pants up when they should be down, or I for missing the crime, but seeing the criminal?' He tightened his grip. 'We go back to the hotel; you will tell me everything. Your day's over here; your trip's over; I suspect your career's over too. You'll always remember April in Chicago as the date of your downfall.'

They knocked while he was reading by the dim light of a flickering bedside lamp. He peered short-sightedly at the alarm clock on the table and grunted in annoyance. Hell, It was almost midnight.

Galina Petrova awoke. She gave him that frightened look she had in the dacha each time she was sure she had heard burglars downstairs. 'The door, Anatoly.' The knocking continued. The frightened woman pulled the bed cover high over her shoulders.

Anatoly Petrovic shrugged and grunted again, feigning a calm he didn't feel. He slipped on the dressing gown the kids had given him on Labour Day and shuffled off down the corridor. The caller thumped noisily. 'He'll wake the whole fucking building up', complained Anatoly. He started to feel cross. 'All right, all right, I'm coming!' Reaching the door, he called, 'Who's there?'

'Security. Open up!'

Anatoly hesitated. He shivered: it was so cold. 'What do you want?'

Amid a flurry of thumps at the door, the caller shouted again, 'Open up, Petrovic! Now!'

They hadn't been polite; it was surely State Security. Galina would throw a fit. The neighbours would talk. He opened the door.

Two were in uniform, the third wore the flat, short-brimmed fedora and dark-blue raincoat of KGB plain-clothes men: he seemed in command. 'You Petrovic? Anatoly?'

'Yes, Comrade' stammered the first secretary.

'Come', said the plain-clothes man, handing over a yellow sheet headed, 'Warrant.'

'I'm not dressed', he protested.

'You'll do.'

'Identity! I want to see your identity', objected Anatoly.

The plain-clothes man, glanced at the two uniformed officers and jerked his head at the Secretary of the Bulgarian Agricultural Products Trading Commission. They stepped forward: one pinned his elbows while the other slipped handcuffs around his wrists.

Galina rushed, screaming from the bedroom. The officers pushed Anatoly towards the steps leading to the street.

He struggled to see Galina, but she was blocked by the burly frame of one of the security police. Tears rolled down his cheeks. 'The children', he shouted, 'call my brother!'

The neighbours' doors remained stubbornly closed. In the street outside, only the black Volga's purring engine disturbed the calm of the night as it drew away, leaving Galina sobbing bitterly, alone at the door.

Traicho Botev's Russian, cabbage-smelling guard worked in a vast pastel-pink complex close to the radio tower on the M38 out to Beskudnikovo. The main building was covered with a forest of masts and satellite dishes with good reason, for this was the centre of the Ninth Directorate of the KGB. Here, many of the guards lived with their families inside the compound, a short walk from offices housing hundreds of thousands of files on foreign individuals and expatriates thought to be, for good reasons, or for bad, important to the Soviet Union. He had spent three days searching photographic archives and was beginning to suffer from a twitch in his right eye; this was no place for a man of action. Just one more drawer and he would have finished all the archives. It was locked. 'Shit! Who's got the key to this thing?'

A bespectacled clerk lifted his head and ran a precious hand across his brow: he disliked this bull of a man who took himself so seriously. 'That, Comrade, is the classified section; no names on the photographs, just numbers. The chief of the archives said you should go to him for the key if you hadn't found your man yet.'

The big guard strode to the chief's office, his aura of sweat making the clerk cringe as he passed within a few feet of his sensitive nose. He knocked on the door and marched in. 'I need the key to the last drawer.'

The chief of the archives sighed. 'Are you absolutely sure you haven't found your man?'

'Look, you've been through the school and so have I. When I saw this character, I used all the tricks to remember his face: association, colour, shape; the works! Now give me the key, or get on the phone to the Centre, where they'll tell you the same thing.'

The chief of the archives sighed, opened a drawer and handed over the key.

Eighteen minutes later, the clerk nearly collapsed with fright at the guard's whoop of joy. 'I've found the bastard! His eyes!' Two shots, full-face and profile, each with a serial number and a red line traced across one corner showed the man the guard had seen leaving the toilets at the agricultural fair in Chicago.

Thank heavens, thought the clerk.

The chief of the archives appeared at his office door. 'The phone; it's for you: take it in my office.'

'I've found the bastard in your lock box.'

'Let's see him, then, while you take your call.'

Intent on getting to the phone, the guard didn't notice the look of surprise on the archive chief's face. 'Yes?' bellowed Traicho Botev's guard into the mouthpiece.

'Dobrynin here in Sofia. I've been questioning Botev.' Igor Dobrynin was the State-Security Officer at the Passport-Office in Sofia who was the guard's contact at the Bulgarian end.

'Yes.'

'He's totally incoherent; he keeps babbling about this being the end. The man's petrified; what did you do to him?'

The thick, Bulgarian accent put the Russian at ease; he had no reason to fear these foreign cousins. 'I frightened him a little; I thought it would make your work easier.'

'It's made it harder and anyway, he knows nothing: he was only a courier.'

'So there's no problem.'

'And the man in the toilets: have you found who he is?'

The guard thought of the photograph in the archive chief's lock box and leered at the wall. 'No', he replied. 'And if you want information, use the channels, not me.'

The line went dead. The guard walked out into the office.

The chief of the archives was on the clerk's telephone and the clerk himself, on his feet, his look of preoccupation matching his boss's faltering voice. At length, the phone was put back into its cradle and the two solemnly faced the guard.

'What's up?'

'You may go', said the chief. 'The Centre will get in touch with you if it needs any more information.'

'Now wait a minute! The photograph.'

'It's back in its place, where you found it and locked up. This time you don't get the key; the Centre has just confirmed this.'

'What's going on?'

'You have done what was necessary; now it is for others to take matters in hand from here.'

'But who was he?' faltered the guard.

'Who?'

'The man in the photo?'

'What photo?' asked the clerk.

The guard's face turned scarlet.

The chief of the archives walked to the door and opened it. 'You have five seconds to get out. Any aggression and you will get trouble; think of your family.'

The burly Russian smashed his great fist into the side of a filing cabinet. 'You pompous, bureaucratic bastards!'

'Get out', commanded the chief and Traicho Botev's guard strutted out, knocking the clerk's chair over as he went.

In Sofia, Igor Dobrynin ran a trembling finger along one wing of his pencil-thin moustache. He was still smouldering after this call with the Russian moron they had sent to America with Botev. Dobrynin's small, dark eyes flashed up, from a desk piled high with paper, at the handcuffed man being led by an officer to the stool in one corner of the glass-partitioned office. The officer left the prisoner sitting there and silently walked out, shutting the door behind him.

Dobrynin thought he heard the prisoner sob. That would be useful.

From his corner, his wrists aching, his head swimming from lack of sleep and confusion, Anatoly Petrovic, General Secretary of the Bulgarian Agricultural Products Trading Commission, looked up at the weasel-faced security officer contemplating him from behind a pile of documents.

Dobrynin thought a soft approach would get better results than the louts in the basement claimed; this was the intellectual type; open to reason; used to the politics of expediency; terrified of losing his creature comforts. He would pose no problem.

'A cigarette, Comrade Secretary?'

Petrovic's eyes showed sudden relief. 'I don't smoke.'

'It might help if you do: it calms the nerves. I have some excellent black Balkan; of course, it's difficult for us to get those American brands Comrade Secretary Kimon Antonov is so fond of in Moscow.'

Petrovic shivered.

Dobrynin twitched his weasel nose and inhaled the pungent, yellow fumes. 'You sure?'

'Perfectly.'

'How would you like to be out of here in a few hours, a free man?'

'But I'm guilty of nothing.'

'Wrong, Comrade: you are in very deep trouble indeed, and you are too intelligent not to realise it.'

'What have I done?'

'You know that better than anyone.... for the moment, but soon, we shall know better than you.'

'And the charges?'

'Treason, Petrovic.'

'Preposterous!'

'Is it? Look at the facts: one of your office workers secretly contacts Western Intelligence in America in a Chicago toilet; you personally authorise the payment of millions of dollars in currency by the Bulgarian Agricultural-Products Trading Commission to an unknown individual abroad; you enter into treasonable conversation with another Bulgarian, a Party official in Moscow, who is known to be highly critical of the State: need I go on?'

'Look, officer, there is an explanation for these facts, none of which is treasonable. Everything you have said concerns an operation mounted by the highest authority in Moscow to revive the interest of Western youth in the international mission of socialism.'

'Rubbish!'

Petrovic warmed to his questioner. 'If that's the reason I'm here, I must admit, I'm relieved and, in proof of my good faith, officer, I will, of course, cooperate in giving you absolutely all the information I can.' The Weasel said nothing and drew on his cigarette. 'Kimon Antonov is a great man and a great patriot. You will see; when he returns from his posting in Moscow, he will accede to one of the most powerful seats in Bulgaria.' Petrovic waited for the effect of his words to show, but the tiny dark eyes remained in a permanent smoke-induced twitch: the air was thick with it, making Anatoly Petrovic's own eyes water.

Petrovic went on, 'Look; this is all very embarrassing! I am expected, in my position, to keep confidence with people who hold the key to our future in their hands. I shouldn't be saying this because he is such a great father to our state, but everything you are accusing me of, everything, arises from a mission I am undertaking for Moscow under Comrade Secretary Kimon Antonov's personal instructions.'

'Then you have nothing to worry about, Comrade Secretary.'

'Of course.'

'But, you see, I need more than this, don't I.'

'It's all confidential.'

'Yes, of course.'

'And Comrade Secretary Antonov is Executive Chairman of the Commission.'

'Making him your boss.'

'Yes.'

'And he lives in Moscow.'

'Exactly.'

Dobrynin wondered how on earth Kimon Antonov had swung that one. 'Well, I have a choice.'

Petrovic waited.

'I can either put you in the cells now and wait for my colleagues in Moscow to question Comrade Secretary Antonov, which will certainly take time; or I can hand you over now to our specialists, for whom there are no secrets, and tell Moscow that, even if Antonov is in good faith, we had to act fast to provide them with facts. You may get home during the night, but the convalescence will take months: my colleagues in the basement are more interested in information than in its source if you follow. They are not humanists, but technicians. To them, you are, so to speak, a problem to be evacuated.'

'Is this a threat?' asked Petrovic, massive weakness looming through his defiance.

The Weasel laughed. 'Unfortunately, no: it's plain fact.'

'So what can I do?'

'There's nothing you can do. You could try telling me all, but there's no guarantee, you see.'

Petrovic sighed and brought his manacled hands up to his brow.

The Weasel walked out of his office and returned with another officer holding a notepad. 'This man, Petrovic, is a witness and will note down the facts as you state them. You will sign the deposition when it is finished, and the State Prosecutor will decide tonight whether to let you out on bail, or to leave you behind bars, or to question you more…carefully. I don't believe an intelligent, family man like you could make any choice other than to speak frankly and openly. Telling the absolute truth, Petrovic, is, from this instant, the only guarantee of your survival.'

The note taker cleared a corner of the desk to write on and the Weasel switched on a tape recorder.

'Now', said the Weasel, 'please be so kind as to talk Anatoly Petrovic, and we shall listen.'

Anatoly Petrovic sighed. 'He had a document to deliver. Botev, at the Directorate, was instructed to pass a very strictly worded order acknowledgement issued by my Commission to someone at the Chicago Agricultural Commodities Fair.'

'Go on.'

'It was Antonov's idea. At an exact time, Botev was to walk into a specified toilet in the men's toilet area at the exhibition hall and to pass the envelope under the right partition providing the individual in the next compartment had left a single ten-dollar bill on the floor between the two toilets. Botev was to stay inside long enough for the individual to leave unrecognised.'

'An order acknowledgement?'

'Yes, for sunflower seeds, but the wording had to be precise down to the very last comma.'

'Why?'

'I'm not sure, but I think it provided some kind of identification.'

'And the cash?'

'It was paid on Antonov's instructions.'

'Written instructions?'

'He is the Chairman of the Commission!'

'Written?'

'No!'

'How much?'

Anatoly Petrovic's face went white. 'All our foreign currency reserve.'

'Please answer the question.'

'Five million American dollars.'

'How?'

'By a revolving letter of credit confirmed by a Swiss bank to holders of one Italian and two Bulgarian passports. I gave all those documents to a young, arrogant, Russian officer wearing a brown uniform.'

'A Russian?'

'Yes, in uniform.'

'Petrovic! Is this a joke? Are you claiming the Russian Military is involved?'

'I can only say what happened.'

'What can you tell me about this...officer?'

'Nothing, except that my gardener almost throttled him.'

'Who was the beneficiary of the letter of credit?'

'I told you, holders of one Italian and two Bulgarian passports.'

'Come on, Petrovic.'

'That's all.' Anatoly Petrovic glanced up at the Weasel, but the he was staring through the glass partitions marking the frontier of his office.

'Ah yes', said the Weasel, 'Bulgarian documents but Italian too.'

The white-tiled room in the bowels of the Lubyanka, the Moscow headquarters of the KGB, looked like a hospital operating theatre at the turn of the century. The structure in the centre was of stainless steel and looked for all the world like an operating-theatre table. A large trolley was the only other piece of furniture: it stood against the wall, covered with a large white cloth.

Secretary Kimon Antonov, a member of the most senior Bulgarian nomenklatura, sweating like a pig and babbling profusely, was strapped naked to the steel structure.

The interrogator, a specialist from the First Chief Directorate's Eleventh Department stood over the trembling Bulgarian. Looking at a chart hanging from the chair, he checked the last dose of caffeine that had been intravenously administered to the subject. He was vaguely bothered that his heart would not hold and instructed one of the two guards to telephone up for a medic and a defibrillator.

Antonov had gone on and on about his importance in the Bulgarian Party and how only the Military had any right to question him. He complained of capitalist-sponsored terrorism in Central America during his delirium; but now the effects were wearing off, he was becoming progressively more coherent and exhausted. Perhaps the defibrillator would not be necessary.

'No right to question, no right at all,' said Kimon Antonov.

'Who am I, prisoner?'

''Committee.'

'What Committee?'

'Security.'

'So, I have the right.'

'No right at all.'

'What comes first? The individual or the State, prisoner?'

'State.'

'And you are?'

'Individual.'

'And I am?'

'Security.'

'So, I have the right.'

'But military.'

'You are not military, prisoner.'

'Sergei Borisovich said....'

The interrogator listened, surprised. There followed Antonov's first silence since the injection.

'Sergei Borisovich who, prisoner?'

'Marshall.'

The interrogator turned to the two guards and the medic, who had just walked in with the heart equipment. 'Wait outside.' The door closed behind them.

'What Marshall?'

'Sergei Borisovich.'

'The family name, not the patronymic, prisoner.'

'Volkov.'

The interrogator's own heart thumped: here was a discovery indeed. Should he go on? Trouble of this calibre was not his department; but Antonov was ready to talk now, and another dose like the last could destroy this frail, smoker's cardio-vascular wreck.

He walked to the wall phone and dialled the Kremlin.

CATANZARO

Some thirty minutes from downtown Chicago, the old Sicilian eased himself into his vast, leather armchair. The door closed on the young man who had just abused thirty minutes of his precious time. 'Insolent sonofabitch!' he grumbled. He picked up the small red book the visitor had left on a corner of his desk and reread the inscription. 'Bullshit!' he coughed and dropped it into the wastepaper basket: 'Chinese bullshit!'

A fire burned in his stomach. He shuffled to the door and opened it a little. 'Francesca, get the consigliere on the house line and get me some bicarbonate and tell the cook to put less *pepperoncino* in the *salsa alla diavola*.'

'Right away, Zio', came his niece's voice.

The phone rang. Don Carlo Catanzaro picked it up. 'How much for the October contract?' he barked.

'You net about four million, Don Carlo.'

'In advance?'

'Like you said and in Switzerland.'

'You found a courier to run the cash?'

'Yes....I can still stop the contract.'

The old man remained silent for a few moments. 'No, we go on, but no one talks no more to the client till we finish the job, or I say so. OK?'

'OK, Don Carlo.'

'The guy they picked is an arrogant sonofabitch.'

'I heard in Maicao he's stuck up. You know his woman runs dope? Cremante's seen him; confirms it's the right guy: still full of his own damned importance, he said.'

The old Sicilian grunted. 'He gave me the order: it's the same as the copy they gave Cremante in Milano.'

'I'll have it checked, Don Carlo.'

'Checked? You think I'm too old, huh? You think my eyes don't see no more?'

'No, no, Don Carlo. I just meant....'

'Shut up and listen: I pay you to listen. He wants Cremante. I said we have better, but he don't listen, just like you. Why don't no one listen anymore? So Cremante does it with him, understand? You keep that asshole this side of the Atlantic. You settle him somewhere nice: he goes back late fall. 'Cremante still collect passports?'

'Yes, Don Carlo.'

'Hey, you know who he looks like?'

'Who does who look like, Don Carlo?'

'Like Cremante, that's who he looks like; insolent bastard looks just like Cremante: they look like twins: confuse the shit outa anyone who sees them. You find cop uniforms too; you find a cop and a safe house, somewhere nice, you understand, maybe near Northside. Fix him up with a broad we know. I need a cop.'

'Why a cop?'

'Don't ask questions, asshole: I say you find a cop, you find a cop, OK?'

'We don't have clout in the district right now, Don Carlo.'

'Then get some! What the hell I pay you guys for? You got money coming outa your ears and you sit on your fat duff all day. You get out there and....'

The old man coughed violently. He dropped the handset on the desk and tugged at the handle of a desk drawer. He clutched a small brown bottle. Fumbling urgently with its lid, placing two white tablets on the tip of his tongue, his jowls folded into a grimace of revulsion. He gulped the contents of a carafe of water and lay back in the chair choking.

The coughing subsided slowly, leaving him pale and frightened.

A light knock came at the door. Francesca opened it, 'Your bicarbonate, Zio.'

'Get outa here', he wheezed.

The woman backed out and closed the door.

Minutes passed before he noticed that the phone was still off the hook. He picked up the handset. 'You still there?'

'Si, Don Carlo.'

'Then get to work, asshole! You got bucks to burn? You got time to burn, my time maybe?' He slammed down the handset.

'Sonofabitch!' he growled.

He stumbled over to a couch in the corner of the study and lay down.

The profit on the contract was good, but Don Carlo Catanzaro felt uneasy about the assignment: he didn't like politics; he mistrusted politicians, and passionate young men took dangerous risks. Their man's repeated assurances hadn't impressed him at all. Laundering the Swiss cash through one of his casinos didn't please him either: it seemed too risky by far.

High in the Val d'Aosta, the little alpine town of St. Charles had been the playground of rich of Turin and Milan since the regal years of Piedmont. Its height guaranteed mountain breezes to cool the troubled brows of these city dwellers in summer, and its plush, old hotels provided an elegant base remote from the vulgarly overcrowded ski slopes in winter.Alert to every whim of this well-off clientele, the locals thrived on the restaurant trade and on expensive boutiques of all kinds: small, lucrative businesses sprouted continually around the base of the hill. Above, in white-marbled splendour, stood the true patrimony of the town; St. Charles's renowned casino and the closer a boutique was to it, the more its owner could count on select and profitable patronage.

Its white towers gave the nineteenth-century building the appearance of a wedding cake when viewed from the cars speeding along the autostrada following the valley North West to the Mont Blanc tunnel and to the French border.

Over the years, the original owners had profitably sold their investment in the casino to a new breed of faceless men whose gaming acumen and cash, far outmatched their own. Then the clientele had changed. Exotic, gilded ceilings which previously overlooked the play of a rich aristocracy, now glittered above wealthy shopkeepers and dour, nervous professionals. The gentry disappeared, attracted by the glamour of Monaco or the financial stability of Switzerland and a middle class arrived unsuccessfully trying to copy the lifestyle of its predecessors who no longer trusted the Lira or Italian politics. The new owners subtly downgraded the service to make their new patrons feel less uncomfortable: gone was the mandatory evening dress; gone was the service in white gloves; gone were the French chefs. Unlike those golden times, the *habitués* now rarely saw the truly rich gambling the equivalent of years of earnings of ordinary souls.

However, on one May evening, a man entered the gambling hall and sat at the roulette table amid a murmur of excitement. Dressed in a tuxedo, he was followed by a waiter carefully carrying a heavy tray of chips just purchased at the cashier's desk.

He placed $100,000 of chips on the seventeen to win.

The casino was not air-conditioned and springtime in the fragrant Italian valley had been warmer than usual. While many sweated, he looked cool in his Tuxedo. Some said he was Swiss.

'*Rien ne va plus*', said the croupier, closing the bidding, a conspiratorial flicker dancing in his eyes each time they met the newcomer's calm gaze.

The ball swirled around the hardwood bowl and dropped by golden lozenges towards the spinning wheel. The manager came to join the spectators. He would have to pay more than $3,000,000 if the Swiss won. The ivory ball rattled against the slots of the spinning wheel. A hush fell upon the watchers. The small white sphere chose its slot and sped around until the croupier placed his finger on the spindle.

The crowd moaned with disappointment. '*Le huit; pair; rouge; manque*', said the croupier.

Not the shadow of a frown clouded the gambler's brow. The casino manager ordered Champagne for the gallant loser, and onlookers smiled patronisingly. The manager confirmed with a smile, '*Monsieur continue.*' The crowd rallied.

The cashier was summoned and $900,000 of chips were neatly stacked in front of the gambler. He seemed not to notice: he took a smug sip at his flute of Dom Perignon. The croupier announced, '*Messieurs, Mesdames, faites vos jeux*', drawing many from adjacent tables. Elegant couples moved close to watch the game. The manager took a strategic position between the croupier and the gambler.

The crowd sighed again as the gambler placed $300,000 on the seventeen to win. The croupier closed the betting and re-launched the wheel. '*Vingt cinq; impair; noir; passe.*'

He lost again. A hush fell. Few remained at the other tables: most had come to stare at a man prepared to lose a million dollars without batting an eyelid. He lost for the third time, doubling his bet and placing his final $600,000 on the seventeen.

He arose to applause and ambled across to the cloakroom, refusing another flute of Champagne. The Swiss had not spent more than fifteen minutes at the table. He shook the manager's hand and left the gaming hall through its ornate doorway. As he did so, one of the couples split; the man in casual pursuit of the gambler; the woman opening her purse to activate a small transmitter inside.

The Swiss gambler strolled down the marble steps into the fragrant night air. He called to the doorman to hail a cab.

The intercom in Colonel Nino Glavina's car crackled into life. 'He's leaving now', hissed a woman's voice. 'I've got him', replied Nino.

The gambler's cab left followed at a distance by the unmarked Alfa Romeo. The Alfa responded enthusiastically to its driver's touch: in the mountain pass, there were few other roads a car could take, and many years of alpine driving for the *Carabinieri*, Italy's paramilitary police, had made Nino's driver one of the finest. The taxi sped down the hill towards the autostrada: once through the toll, it turned towards the Mont Blanc Tunnel and the French border.

Nino was unauthorised to cross to the French side, but a three-car team of *Douaniers*, the French customs police, was assembling to continue the pursuit at the other end of the tunnel if necessary.

The cab made its way through the mountain city of Aosta and stopped a few kilometres from the frontier in front of a small ski hotel in Courmayeur. While the Swiss was paying the cabbie, Nino ordered an all-night watch of the hotel: then he crossed the dark street to the doorway. He walked into the lobby in time to see the doors of an elevator close on the man he was following: the dial showed him getting off at the third floor.

Colonel Nino Glavina walked up to the receptionist wearing his most winning smile. 'I've just recognised a friend of mine, Walter Buscaglia; the man who just came in wearing a tuxedo. Could you call him and say I'm here?'

'Yes, of course, Sir. What's your name please?'

'Buscaglia. He was here just a few seconds ago, wearing a tuxedo', answered Nino.

'Uh...yes, that was thirty-four', said the receptionist, his nose buried in the register, '.... but his name doesn't seem to be Buscaglia, Sir.'

'Are you sure?' asked Nino.

'Positive, Sir, that's not the name I have.'

'Strange! I'm sure it's Buscaglia. Maybe he's playing a joke, or having some fun, eh?' Nino winked at the receptionist. 'What name did he give?'

''Can't tell you that, Sir', replied the receptionist with a priggish look.

Nino suppressed a burst of laughter at the man's conceit: the badge in his pocket would have loosened his tongue. 'Yes, of course, I understand.' he replied soothingly, 'Thanks for your help anyway.' He returned to the car and lifted the microphone from the radio. 'He's in thirty-four', he said. 'I want a plainclothes watch and a tap on the hotel line: now! Get an officer from the local barracks to look over the register for his name: use someone they know at the hotel: make it look like a routine check: don't take his passport, even if it's still at the registration desk. Tell the French they can relax, but they should be ready to move quickly.'

The gambler made no movement during the night hours. Nino and his driver watched the hotel and the parking lot until two officers, a man and a woman posing as a married couple, registered into the hotel. Another unmarked car from the local *Carabiniere* barracks stopped ten metres down the road. The driver extinguished his lights, lit up a cigarette and began his long vigil.

Nino took a room in a nearby inn to get a few hours' sleep.

The couple radioed they had managed to get room thirty-six. They heard little except the sound of snoring next door. They claimed they could do nothing now to improve surveillance without entering the gambler's room.

The next morning the local *Carabinieri* confirmed that a Swiss rental car in the parking lot belonged to the man in thirty-four. They checked the hotel books during the village patrol: he had registered as 'Genaro Cagnotto'. A man of that name answering the gambler's description was a small-time hood in Turin with suspected links to organised crime.

The telephone tap on the hotel was authorised too late to be of any use: Cagnotto had had all the time he needed to make his calls in privacy and, during the rest of his stay at Courmayeur, the listeners picked up nothing. Eating alone in his room, watching television, he seemed a man of frugal habits, strangely inconsistent with the image of a big spender. This man, who had lost $1,000,000 in fifteen minutes, did not move from his room for three days. He checked out swiftly the morning of the fourth. He strode from the room, settled his bill in cash and, within minutes, was speeding towards the frontier. He paid no heed to a car following him driven by a grey-haired gentleman beside a woman in her fifties.

At the mouth of the tunnel, Italian financial police checked the passports. The queue moved at a snail's pace. From time to time a vehicle would be taken out of the line for a search.

Genaro Cagnotto broke into a cold sweat. The customs officer eyed him carefully noting the beads of sweat streaming down Cagnotto's forehead: ''Hot today', he remarked.

Cagnotto nodded, afraid to speak lest he should croak with fear.

'Anything to declare?'

Cagnotto shook his head.

'Currency?'

'No.'

'Live in Switzerland?'

'Business', replied Cagnotto.

The customs officer handed him back the passport and drew his face close to Cagnotto's. 'You're being shadowed by half the fucking *Carabinieri* in Piedmont you stupid bastard. They can't follow you to the other side, so pray they haven't talked to the French.'

Thunderstruck, Genaro Cagnotto drove through, switching on the headlights at the dark mouth of the tunnel. The daylight he would find some thirteen kilometres away would be French. It hadn't occurred to him the Mob had people even in the customs. He opened the window to the roar of the tunnel. Tears in his eyes, he yelled again and again at the hissing black walls, 'The bastards have been watching me all along!' He struck the seat back next to him with his free fist. 'Bastards! Bastards!' He calmed down a few kilometres later: after all, the money had been good: he would return to Turin to resume life slightly on the margin of society; nothing dangerous; less lucrative, but a lot safer. Besides, driving out of Italy was easier than driving in: this way they had nothing on him; the other, he would have to explain each time why his case contained $1,000,000 of undeclared currency. The cash made him nervous and he was relieved that the next time would be his last. This had been a difficult assignment. He was tired, and he felt uncomfortable in the big time. Playing the part of the Swiss gambler satisfied his ego; thrilled him...but was he playing authentically? How could a gambling loss of $5,000,000 in a matter of as many weeks not attract attention? They had told him it would be all right: they had said they would handle any problems.

The grey-haired gentleman and the woman followed at a distance.

The French *Douaniers* were dressed as tourists. They had posted one car with a Belgian number plate at the exit and another two on the valley road, one pointing towards Geneva and the other, inland, towards the French Alps. Whichever way the Italian turned, one would follow and one would drive on ahead. The third car would turn to join them, once Cagnotto had chosen his road, and relay with the other two all the way to his destination. With luck, he wouldn't notice he was being followed.

The *douaniers* radioed Cagnotto's appearance at the exit: the middle-aged couple made an illegal turn in the tunnel and went home.

At the foot of the exit ramp, Cagnotto turned right towards Geneva. Their fears that he would head for the Swiss frontier had been, after all, well founded: without hard evidence the Swiss police refused to cooperate with anyone and the *douanier's* file on the average Italian hoodlum was, to say the least, slim. Hot on his scent, they crossed into Switzerland as private citizens. With them was an attractive woman, who, as a registered Swiss investigator could intervene if a national was needed.

Cold and blue below the splendour of its alpine garland, Lake Geneva, known locally as Lake Leman, sparkled in the afternoon sun. Cagnotto relaxed, unaware that his was one of four cars speeding along the autoroute towards his own destination. He inclined his seat a fraction more and stretched his arms: the window was wide open, warm air tousling his hair, the radio blaring the latest sedate sound to sweep the French cantons.

He liked the clean village communities clustered around the foothills: proudly kept chalets adorned the lakeside roads leading up to the granite masses above. He respected the speed limit, amused that he would never have dreamt of doing so in his native Italy: he had to avoid attracting attention in Switzerland. They had said they couldn't help him if he got caught the other side. He veered off the autoroute at the Lausanne exit. The car in front continued East and the two behind followed him down the ramp into the outskirts of the city. Cagnotto drove to the Place de la Gare and returned his car to the rental agency.

The *douaniers* waited outside with their Swiss detective. Minutes later, Genaro Cagnotto came out into the street and, suitcase in hand, walked two hundred metres to the Hotel de la Gare. He stayed in his hotel room throughout the weekend. The *douaniers* moved into rooms across the corridor and kept a rotating watch from the lobby.

On the Monday, he walked into a branch of the Federal Union of Swiss Banks and, glancing at an attractive young woman who had followed him in, apparently to apply for a job at the bank, presented the cashier with his passport and a magnetic card. The cashier left to call the manager, leaving Cagnotto waiting at the window with an Italian passport open on the counter. Standing next to the Italian, the young woman memorised its number and listened carefully to the exchange of words as the manager led Cagnotto obsequiously through the security doors to the entrance of the bank vaults.

Brigitte de Langeac's family was one of the few to successfully flee to Switzerland during the French Revolution. Raised in the canton of Vaud, she had inherited her mother's coquettishness and the perplexity of her Catholic forebears with the Calvinist values of her neighbours. Bright, very pretty and fascinated with crime, at twenty-two she opened her own investigation agency after graduating from the prestigious École Polytechnique in Paris. The day she told her mother about her plans, the woman suffered from extremes of emotion, ranging from concern for her daughter's safety to serious doubts about her sanity. Despite opposition from her family, Brigitte's business flourished. Only top mathematical minds got into the École Polytechnique and she was very good with numbers and solving riddles.

The bank manager saw her straight after that gauche Italian who appeared every few weeks to open his safe. He asked her to sit in one of the low leather armchairs he used for important clients. He was so overwhelmed with her, that he offered her a job there and then.

'When can you begin?' he asked.

'Now'

'There are formalities.... papers. Maybe it's best Monday.'

'I have my papers here. I'd rather start today'.

'Very well', he said: 'you begin today. I'll ask Madame Mangin to find you a desk and tell you about the job.'

Brigitte stood.

He arose to shake her hand. 'I like to get to know our people from the start, Mademoiselle: we could discuss your background over dinner.'

Brigitte preferred younger, more vigorous stock: she almost burst out laughing, but breeding took control. 'Yes, I'd like that', she answered; 'you could tell me about the bank over dinner. It would be nice to meet your wife.'

'I'll ask her if she's free', he mumbled.

The days following the interview were a drudge: she took shifts at the cashiers' desks; she spent hours at the computer terminals. She learnt how to access the journal and set about reviewing dollar-denominated withdrawals over the past months: the agony finally ended one Thursday evening with the conclusion that no large Dollar movements had been entered. It looked like a first failure.

Mme Mangin, an elderly clerk, had worked her entire career in the Lausanne office: she knew all there was to know about the paperwork and more than intended about the clients. Unanimously detested by the staff, the unsuspecting beneficiary of the sobriquet 'The Dragon', Madame Mangin was the all-powerful keeper of the vaults. The manager had 'every confidence' in Mme Mangin and the Dragon remained fiercely loyal and wholly discrete in return. She refused to open the safe and even sent clients she knew packing for failing to produce the recognised proof of identity. Driver's license in hand, irate customers complained continually about her to the manager: she had seen them all many times and didn't need ID's at all, but she stuck to her guns.

Brigitte discovered that the Dragon's filing system was based on numbers alone: if a client didn't show the correct ID, she would have to search the entire file, and the Dragon wasn't going to do that for anyone, especially now she didn't see as well as she used to. Theoretically, at least, the manager was the only one with access to the names of the lock-box users, and he kept their files in his own desk under lock and key.

One hot day the Dragon called to say she was sick. 'Never ill', she had said, it was something she had eaten the previous day: she wondered whether Brigitte, who had eaten with her, had been ill too. The manager told the Dragon to stay in her lair, though much of the staff was on vacation, leaving only Brigitte and two other women. Brigitte offered to stand in for the Dragon, and the manager accepted, inadvertently launching a swell of muffled fury against her: the seniority of the other two gave them unwritten rights over the newcomer: the Dragon had the plum job: the vaults were cool, and nothing moved down there during the summer months.

Brigitte made an early start on Mme Mangin's file cards: she found one within minutes showing Cagnotto's passport number and made a photocopy: it showed he had accessed his lock box on five different dates. In the margin under a handwritten code, a note stated that funds would be supplied as required by a revolving letter of credit lodged with the manager. A small identity photo was stapled to one corner: the rest of the card bore numbers but no words or names. At last, now, she had something to justify the exorbitant fee she intended charging the *douaniers*.

The Dragon eyed Brigitte suspiciously for days after returning from her sick bed: the newcomer's lunch conversation had been too clever by far. That pretty face hid trouble, but the Dragon didn't yet know what kind: it also belied a dangerous competitor if it was true she had been admitted to the inner sanctum in precedence over the women at the cashier's desk. These two shunned Brigitte, acutely aware of her sexual hold over the boss: their hostility suited her perfectly, leaving her the time to search without interruption. She found it more difficult hiding from the manager, who took the faintest opportunity to position himself where he could see her: Brigitte obligingly turned to face him each time he tried.

She studied the photocopy of Cagnotto's card again and again to find some clue. A number in the top right-hand corner had no obvious explanation: it was not in the Dragon's handwriting but in the manager's. It might well have referred to the letter of credit. There were two numbers, that may have come from other passports. She memorised them all hoping to find one in the reports that crossed her desk from time to time. If it was true that the manager had his own codes for the bank's clients, she would have to get into his office.

By the end of the month, the manager had begun to stay late, finding urgent things for her to do at the end of the day. Her chance, she knew, would come soon enough, especially because he still hadn't honoured the dinner invitation.

'Do you know how to use the word processor', he asked one evening.

'Yes', she lied.

'I need to send an urgent circular to twenty or so customers and my secretary has left: could you type them? Call her at home if you need help.'

'Of course.'

'Punch in these numbers, and the machine should type out the names and addresses. It's very confidential: pretend not to read them and give me everything back to sign. I'll mail the documents myself.' He gave her a slip of paper with twenty hand-written codes on it, each showing a similar sequence to the one she had memorised from Cagnotto's card and in the same handwriting.

He hovered around her for some minutes finding pointless things to do and finally disappeared into his office.

Brigitte called the secretary: by seven thirty she had finished the twenty circulars and added an extra one using Cagnotto's code. She folded the last one, slipped it beneath her blouse and took the others in to be signed.

She sensed immediately this was going to be the night: he stared obsessively at her from behind his desk, perspiring and pale. They were alone: he had never posed a threat to her with others around, but now her dancing, ironic eyes assumed a look of vigilance. He arose as she walked into the room and circled the desk to face her.

'Oh! You don't have to get up', she stammered; 'you can sign these at your desk.'

'Brigitte, thank you for staying behind like this: I am so grateful.' He stumbled towards her, arms outstretched.

She threw the papers on his desk and stepped back. 'That won't be necessary, Monsieur.' She put her hand over the red panic button by the door. 'When the police come, I'll tell them you raped me.'

The manager stopped, shocked, cringing under the imagined consequences of her threat. Moments passed: from his frown, she saw he was coming to his senses. 'Of course, Mademoiselle, I'm so sorry: there must be a misunderstanding.'

'In view of your attitude towards me, Monsieur and of others in this bank, I made the wrong decision coming here. I want to leave and look elsewhere. If Mme Mangin could prepare what you owe me, I'll take it in the morning and leave.'

The manager stared stupidly as Brigitte glided finally out of reach.

Later that evening, sitting in a silk robe and combing out her hair, Brigitte sat contemplating the circular letter in front of her. The manager's words were banal, concerning only the closing dates for the vacation season. The name and address, however, on that twenty-first letter filled her with excitement: the *douaniers* would be delighted with her work and she would have earned every Franc she intended to charge them. There was no doubt she had made a valuable discovery. She wondered what the letters stood for and what this information was worth.

She read the address again out loud: 'BAPTCo, 1 Orlov Square, Sofia, Socialist Republic of Bulgaria....what could BAPTCo stand for?'

It was Ferragosto in Turin; August fifteenth, the feast of the Blessed Virgin. The city was deserted; stores were closed, and only a few bars in the squares surrounding the railway station were left open, the owners hoping to serve those tourists willing to brave the scorching sun. A heat haze lay over the city, whitening the horizon and blurring the outline of the wooded hills overlooking the mighty river Po's valley. The *Torinesi* themselves had long since taken to the Ligurian coast in search of wives and children they had sent to the seaside at the end of June: a few had taken to the pre-Alpine hills, searching for the relief of cool mountain breezes, but they normally migrated South in summer, the hills being reserved for winter sports.

Genaro Cagnotto was among the few in town on this national holiday. He had driven his mother to church that morning, taken her back to her humble cottage by a vineyard and spent the rest of the morning walking the cool arcades of the old quarter in search of friends in the bars. By noon he was back in his apartment boiling a saucepan of salted water for his pasta. He had not met the new people in the flat across the corridor: they were strange. Searching for his keys at the top of the stairs one morning, he had heard footsteps from their apartment. A shadow had floated in the sunlight beaming through the crack under their door: someone had watched him through the spyglass for many seconds and walked off. Placing the key in his lock, Cagnotto had looked again: the shadow had moved. The event worried him. He was tempted to write it off as bad manners: new neighbours were always nosey. It wouldn't be the first time neighbours had complicated his life and it wouldn't be the last.

The phone rang just after he had thrown the spaghetti into the boiling water. He swore softly; turned down the gas; tried quickly to separate the long, brittle sticks without breaking them and rushed into the bedroom to answer it.

'Hello....Hello!' he repeated.

'Cagnotto?' came a man's voice.

'Yes'

'You owe us.'

Genaro Cagnotto glowered. 'Call back later: I'm eating.'

'Damn your lunch. The Berettas: you have them?'

'I....I don't know what you're talking about', he stammered.

'Get wise, Cagnotto. Do you have them?'

'Maybe.'

'In ten minutes, you give two of them to a man at your door. He's dark, about a metre seventy-eight. He'll be holding a suitcase: he'll ask for Cathy Fabbri: say she's in, then let him in. Understand?'

'But who's going to .... ?'

'You understand?' interjected the voice.

'Yes, but....'

The line went dead.

Cagnotto scanned the newspaper; walked back to the kitchen and prodded the sullenly bubbling water in the saucepan. He tried to run the prongs of a fork through the coagulated spaghetti lurking under the boiling surface, sighed in exasperation and threw the white mass into the toilet in the bathroom. The visitor would come soon: he didn't care to break bread with the individuals they sent him. He didn't want to share his pasta: besides, his sauce was spicy: not to everyone's taste.

He urinated over the clump in the toilet bowl and pulled the chain: water rose dangerously to the rim and gushed onto the bathroom floor.

Someone knocked at the door. Cagnotto groaned. He crossed the apartment and shouted, 'Who's there?' There was no reply.

'Who's there?' he repeated anxiously.

The knock came again.

He opened the door a fraction and looked into the hallway. A dark-haired man stood there, a suitcase in his left hand: he didn't move and volunteered no words: he just stood there staring. Cagnotto swung the door open.

'Is Cathy Fabbri in?' asked the visitor.

'Yes', answered Cagnotto.

The stranger brushed past, and Cagnotto closed the door.

'The assault rifles', said the visitor, his 'r' guttural and un-Italian.

'Wait here', said Cagnotto and returned to the bathroom, where the Berettas were hidden. He slipped in the puddle on the floor and frowned at the toilet bowl. Soaking the knees of his trousers, he knelt to remove a panel covering the side of the bathtub.

He noticed his flies were undone and moaned in exasperation. He wished he had gone to the coast like everyone else.

When Cagnotto finally returned with the two weapons, the visitor was standing calmly in the hallway, his suitcase open on the floor. Cagnotto handed over the two automatic assault rifles, searching for some tell-tale flicker in the stranger's eyes that he had seen the open fly. Instead, the dark eyes glittered at the weapons. The stranger put one in the open case and carefully stroked the other. So absorbed was he, that Cagnotto might no longer have been standing there. He removed the empty shell clip; checked the smooth action with military familiarity; peered down the barrel at the window; unfolded the stock and sprung it back again. Then he picked up the other and repeated the procedure.

Cagnotto stared, admiring the newcomer's confidence. The stranger's eyes lifted and met his, their intensity draining rapidly as if Cagnotto held absolutely no interest. He nodded and said, 'OK', then closed the case and faced the door waiting to be let out.

Cagnotto suddenly regretted not having invited the visitor to lunch: he felt he needed to know this person who was so much in control, his eyes so piercing and intense, so competent: how much Cagnotto burned to have such qualities, but he said nothing. He opened the door and let him out.

The transfer of arms had not taken ten minutes.

Cagnotto stared at the closed door contemplating the strong, silent creature who had just walked away with two of his most valuable assets. He ambled hungrily back to the kitchen and cursed remembering the mess in the bathroom: he would eat first and clear it up later.

Genaro Cagnotto was still mopping up an hour later when another knock came at the door. Maybe the stranger had returned. He dried his hands and checked his flies. He walked up to the door and shouted, 'Who is it?'

'*Carabinieri*. Open up!'

He rushed whimpering into the kitchen. He looked into the courtyard: uniformed officers, their pistols drawn, peered up from behind parked cars. He ran to the front window: he saw three squad cars, blue lights flashing. Passers-by had been stopped at the end of the street.

The knocks came again, this time with a threat to break down the door if he didn't open it.

He wanted to call. They would be displeased. He clutched the telephone. They had promised to get him out of trouble: their reach was long: they protected their own: they had to help. He was trying not to panic. Why did the phone dial take so long to travel around?

The lock flew off the door. It swung violently open to reveal four *Carabinieri* pointing their rifles at him.

Cagnotto dropped the handset, buried his face in his hands and sobbed loudly. What would he tell his mother? It would break her old heart.

IVAN

Each time Ivan Promyslov, Colonel at the KGB First Chief Directorate, walked into his boss's office, he felt like a schoolboy in short trousers. Leonid Budhakin, Major General and an Area Department Director, was obnoxious to the point of utter rudeness towards his staff, and Ivan was certain that Budhakin had taken a special dislike to him.

No sooner had Ivan walked in than Budhakin barked, 'Contact Executive Action, Promyslov; get their best man and send him to Havana. I hear Fedorenko's good. I want him to bring in Ahmet from wherever he is on the American continent; you'll find his file in Department Victor. Keep in touch through Garcia. That's all.'

'But General....'

'And, Promyslov....'

'Sir?'

'That's all.'

'General!'

Budhakin virtually shrieked. 'That's all, Promyslov, get out!'

'Antonov is a damned fool!' exclaimed Promyslov.

'Rather! Kimon Antonov could have retired as Secretary of the Bulgarian Central Committee. Can you imagine such stupidity?'

'He isn't a likeable character anyway.'

'I doubt you people like anyone', laughed Konstantin Strugatski, a member of the Soviet Central Committee, and Colonel Ivan Promyslov's guest.

'Will this cause trouble at the Kremlin?'

'Oh yes, the Personnel Directorate has asked for a list of 'appropriate' transfers for the culprits. The decision was taken by the General Secretary himself.'

'Anyone in the Politburo involved?' asked Ivan.

'Now, Vanya, you know I can't answer that', replied Konstantin with a grin, 'but pour me another shot, and pass me another of Olga Promyslova's excellent zakuski, and I may tell you a secret or two.'

The KGB colonel laughed. He retrieved another bottle of export Stolichnaya from the crate in the freezer outside. He returned to the dacha and walked into the warm, pungent smell of the log cabin. He poured the clear, syrupy liquid into two empty glasses and offered his guest one of the small *blinis* covered with salmon and fresh cream. Olga had taken special care: it was rare her husband entertained such an influential Party comrade, even if he was such an old friend.

'I think it's common knowledge that Marshall Volkov was absent from the last Politburo meeting: Vanya, I'd be surprised you didn't know that too.'

'I had heard something.'

'Strange Dzerzhinsky Square hasn't been more involved', remarked the guest, 'I would have expected the KGB to be buzzing.'

Ivan Promyslov felt the need to qualify his guest's statement: 'Maybe at a higher level than mine, Kostya.'

Konstantin Strugatski picked up his glass and looked Ivan in the eye. 'Na Zdarovje', he said solemnly. 'Na Zdarovje, your health', replied the Colonel.

The two men threw back their heads and emptied the shots of vodka. They replaced their glasses on a small ivory-encrusted table Promyslov had brought back from Uzbekistan, close to the Afghan border, and he picked up the bottle to refill the glasses.

'What did Antonov say during the investigation at the Lubyanka?' asked Konstantin.

'I understand he went on about inhibiting capitalist-sponsored terrorism in Central America. It took an interrogator from the Eleventh Department time and patience to see through him.'

'Did he name any accomplices?'

'At first, he claimed to be under instructions from the military and said that State Security had no mandate to question him. He hoped I suppose, the military would bail him out. Very much later, he tired and gave names. The interrogator cleared the room and continued alone: Antonov felt less threatened that way. The matter was taken out of the Eleventh's hands once the report had been sent, and no one else in the First Chief Directorate seems to have heard anything more until the arrival of this latest instruction.'

'...and that's when you called me?'

'Yes, Kostya: that's when I called: if I send an illegal to risk his neck, I want to know why. Fedorenko's one of the best people in the Executive-Action group: he gets things done, but he asks questions.'

Konstantin Strugatski hesitated for a few moments, then spoke: 'What I have to tell you, Vanya, is just between us, *dusha-dushe*, heart-to-heart, agreed?'

'It's been that way since our school days, Kostya, *dusha-dushe*.'

The Central Committee member settled into his chair and stared at the empty hearth, collecting his thoughts before speaking. 'Rumour has it there's been tension between the General Secretary and Marshall Volkov. The old soldier disagrees strongly with this policy of re-launching détente. He intensely dislikes so-called modern pragmatism and thinks it will destroy the Party and our country. He caused considerable embarrassment in the Politburo saying that a leader who had lived the Glorious Revolution through the history books and had never defended Russia as a soldier was unfit to lead.'

Ivan whistled.

Konstantin went on: 'It's rumoured the Marshall wants some international tension to reduce the chances of a successful summit with America. His intentions are thinly disguised!'

'....and he uses the Bulgarians?'

'Certainly! He can't use Russian apparatus, Vanya, your people would be down his neck in two minutes.'

'Couldn't he use the military?'

'Using Military Intelligence would be too risky: one way or another his plans would get back to the Kremlin, probably even through State Security: your people and the military GRU spend vast resources riddling each other's corridors with informers. Kimon Antonov was a clever choice: he was Volkov's Party protégé and able to control money flows in Bulgaria, far from Moscow: he had access to funds, and absolute control over a politically naive organisation in Sofia.'

'He spoke during questioning of some Directorate for Agricultural Produce.'

'He had them salt away a credit for five million US dollars in Switzerland to pay for some work.'

'Good grief!'

'You probably don't know either that the work has been contracted to Italian organised crime.'

Ivan Promyslov grinned impishly. 'You have to admire his cunning: there are no loyalties in the capitalist world; anything can be done at a price, and the International Party is cumbersome when we have to work fast.'

Konstantin admonished his childhood friend in a steely voice: 'The International evolves at the same speed as Society, Vanya. Socialism has all the time in the world. It will triumph in the end: we know that capitalism cannot last.'

The KGB colonel refilled the glasses.

Konstantin Strugatski continued: 'Initiative is commendable when one works for the good of the state and according to policy, but reprehensible in a case like this. These people have not just thwarted the General Secretary but acted against the interests of the Soviet Union itself. They will be severely punished.'

Ivan decided to move to more comfortable ground. 'If the work has been contracted to Italian organised crime, why do I have to send Fedorenko to bring in Ahmet?'

'Because Ahmet was chosen to create the incident, and he knows the Italians. Heavens knows how Marshall Volkov managed to find himself a KGB Executive-Action agent and to get him to go underground. Ahmet worked with Italian organised crime and with Italian anarchists extensively before his flight to Colombia. Besides, I understand that when the Bulgarians asked, the Italians refused the job but promised, for this exorbitant sum, only to provide support.'

'What confirmation do we have that Ahmet really is involved, Kostya?'

'Now I understand how badly information circulates in State Security! He's one of your people, Vanya!'

'We all like to keep our little secrets', said Ivan with a frown.

'A guard from the Ninth Directorate just missed seeing Ahmet get his letter of introduction to the Italians in

Chicago....' Konstantin laughed. '....'seems it happened in a toilet.' He paused to drink from the small glass, and went on, 'He recognised Ahmet from our photographic archives. So, your boss, Budhakin, is sending Fedorenko in to get Ahmet; a wise choice.'

Ivan frowned at the fire. 'He's starting the search from Havana. He may arrive too late to stop the damage, leaving us with egg on our face.'

'On your face, Vanya', corrected Strugatski, 'and certainly on Fedorenko's too.'

The look of cosy comfort left Ivan's eyes. 'Has the Kremlin tried to stop the job through the Italians?'

'All contacts have disappeared into thin air. Despite repeated attempts the Bulgarians have failed to reactivate lines of communication existing up to only a short while ago. It's very strange: as if someone had given explicit instructions to break with us. Now they have our money, we have no leverage.'

'Our only recourse is to stop Ahmet ourselves if we can find him.'

'.... using our Cuban allies, of course: that's why the Direccion General de Inteligencia has been briefed.'

Ivan Promyslov stared gloomily at the wall.

As if reading his mind, Konstantin reassured him, 'Never mind, Vanya, you will have done all you could. I'll see this is known at the Central Secretariat, and, of course, being in State Security, you are to some extent protected from the opinions of minor Party officials.'

'That's not the point, Kostya: my only concern is to avoid national embarrassment and to bring Ahmet and Fedorenko in safely.'

'Of course, my friend', replied Strugatski. 'That fiftieth year looming larger and larger, eh? It makes a man turn an eye to the achievements of his past and to the comfort of his future. You know, now is the time to be rewarded with a posting abroad. Moscow is so dull: it's impossible to get anything here. Have you ever asked for a foreign transfer?'

Ivan's eyes narrowed slightly. He disliked being patronised and had always felt a twinge of jealousy over their unequal career growth since school. His brown, Russian eyes lifted to meet Konstantin's. His friend had political talent and enormous clout in the Kremlin. He ran his fingers through his dark hair. 'Once or twice', he answered.

Konstantin acknowledged with a grunt.

Ivan Promyslov's frame had gained weight in recent months despite the heavy training sessions with the Lubyanka rowing eight. Konstantin looked slim, ascetic, and infinitely dangerous. There was the excuse of Olga's superb cooking, yet those extra kilos expressed dissatisfaction with the way his career had reached a plateau.

'You've gained weight too, my friend', said Konstantin. 'You shouldn't: it's out of fashion in the Kremlin to be overweight.' He paused. Ivan said nothing. 'I'd like to help you, Vanya, and I think I can through the Party. I'll work on getting you a posting abroad if I can.'

'I appreciate your concern, Kostya, but....'

Konstantin went on heedless: 'The quality of the posting would be linked to your success in Fedorenko's mission: the status of a Resident in Paris is very different from that of one in Addis Ababa.'

Ivan opened his mouth to voice an objection but Konstantin raised his hand. In the superior tone that so irritated Ivan, he said, 'I don't want to hear any more, my friend: I know you don't want to put me to any trouble, but I take a personal interest in your well-being, and, of course, in Olga's.' With that, he looked at his watch and rose to his feet. The motor of the black Chaika outside purred into life, and Olga opened the door to a uniformed guard from the Ninth Directorate holding Konstantin's coat and hat.

Lieutenant Aleksandr Mikhailovich Ryabov was one of a new generation of talented young bloods to assume an important post in the First Chief Directorate of the KGB. He had jumped at the offer of a job in the Lubyanka building before even knowing that he was to become an intelligence officer at the Italian desk of the Fifth Department. He would have preferred something more 'Anglo-Saxon' in the First or Third, but he found Italy a fascinating, complex country, and full of potential. His goal of a good position was accomplished: he would be happy for a few years, and, being in Moscow, he would be with Tanya. A posting abroad now would have torn through his difficult courtship of her influential family, now he had won her heart.

As Ivan Promyslov walked into the office, Aleksandr Mikhailovich jumped smartly to attention, formally clicking his heels. ' 'Morning, Coach', he grinned.

'Stop clowning, Ryabov', retorted Ivan.

'Yes, Coach', laughed Aleksandr Mikhailovich, and sat down.

Ivan pulled over a chair and sat astride it. 'I need your help.'

Aleksandr Mikhailovich leaned forward on his desk, clasping his hands. 'How can I help you, Ivan Dmitriyevich?'

'Have you heard of an agent from Department Victor called Ahmet? He may have worked in Italy.'

'Yes: he disappeared some months ago: he's probably gone underground. I don't know who runs him now. Has the Executive-Action group lost him too?'

'Yes, and I must find him, quickly!'

'You looking for recruits?'

'When you've been around a little longer you'll learn not to ask crass questions, young man.'

'OK, Coach.'

'I want you to get me your dossiers on any agent in Italy likely to know Ahmet and able to help me search for him.'

'We've got a lot of recruits in Italy, mainly ex-terrorists, but few heavyweights able to do a job like that. With Ahmet's training, he's far too skilled.'

Ryabov walked to his safe, pulled a key chain from his pocket, and unlocked a drawer inside. He opened it and drew a file. 'This is as heavy as you'll get, Coach, but I don't trust him. He knows Ahmet all right: he even knows Nikolaev, who ran him in Rome.'

'Nikolaev?'

'Yes, Ivan Dmitriyevich, your ambitious young Lieutenant Nikolaev', confirmed Ryabov. He passed the file to Ivan: the front cover was marked with the code name, 'Milk.'

The KGB colonel began to read the file. 'Why don't you trust 'Milk'?' he asked distractedly.

'I don't understand how we paid him nor what we paid him for. Nikolaev set up such a complicated system in the Embassy in Rome that it's impossible to find what Milk actually produced.'

'Have you asked him about it?'

'He claims he doesn't remember Milk very well. I think he's lying.'

'What's in the accounts?'

'Payments for prison breaks, arms deals, negotiations with local radicals.'

'This 'Milk' sounds like a crook.'

'He is a crook. He's paid on commission: perhaps there have even been local services not registered here at the Centre.'

'I don't like crooks as agents either', mumbled Ivan.

'Maybe Milk wasn't working for us at all', commented Ryabov. But Ivan's attention was elsewhere, and Ryabov concluded he had not heard his comment and said no more.

He continued to read the file. 'Anyone else we can use?'

'It's the best I can do, Ivan Dmitriyevich: despite his weaknesses, Milk does know Ahmet personally.'

'Fair enough', said the Colonel. 'I may use him.'

'If you can find him, Coach.'

'Stop playing games, Ryabov. What are you talking about now?'

'Well, Milk hasn't been in contact with us in Rome for months: I hope he'll re-appear by the time you decide to use him.'

Ivan sighed, picked up the file and walked to a desk in the corner of the office to read it.

The Russian told Sanchez to stay in the Jeep. He loped across a small clearing and squatted by one of the stilts holding the cottage clear of the floor of the Colombian jungle. He listened: there were no voices; no footsteps on the wooden boards above his head; no patter from a radio. Only shrill sounds of the jungle, which were nonetheless sweet to KGB Executive-Action Illegal, Ilya Fedorenko's ears, filled the air. A damp fragrance and a racing pulse returned him to silent missions in the swamps of Indo-China.

He circled the cottage and crawled up the steps to the veranda. He peered through the windows and tested the door handle. The place seemed uninhabited. His tension draining, careful to avoid the line of sight of the cottage windows, he crossed to a hangar at the end of the jungle airstrip. Oil drums were stacked at one end: a bent propeller slouched against a far wall: greased mechanical parts lay around the floor on scraps of newspaper.

He returned and mounted the veranda steps: the search would be simple, yet he felt uneasy despite the remoteness of the clearing. Prying eyes along the road from Maicao had left him sure his visit had been noticed. The Cubans hadn't had time to ensure him safe transit through these perilous domains, and he doubted Sanchez's good sense allowing a search like this with insufficient preparation.

He went back to the Jeep. Sanchez suggested it should stay parked there under cover of the jungle, a short sprint away in case of trouble.

They searched with method, breaking everything hollow. He didn't know what he was looking for: Ilya was counting on leads.

He watched Sanchez from the corner of an eye: the Cuban was in his glory, breaking everything in sight. The Russian didn't want him looting: when he saw Sanchez fingering women's garments drawn from a closet, he barked, 'If you take anything from here, I'll break your dirty neck.'

Sanchez glared up from the soft, silken nightgown he had meant to purloin, a murderous lust in his eyes. He snatched a switchblade from his sleeve and threatened Ilya. 'I'm sick of you Russian bastard', he hissed.

The Soviet agent drew his pistol: the Cuban backed off towards the bedroom. Overcome with greed, Sanchez had forgotten his own firearm in the Jeep. Ilya advanced grimly.

The Cuban tripped over a step, crashing heavily to the floor. Aware he was about to be shot, Sanchez howled. He looked up expecting to see the Russian's burly frame, but he had disappeared. The Cuban came shakily to his feet, rubbing the back of his head where it had hit an upright of the steel-framed bed.

That Russian bastard was cool: it would be better not to provoke him. Sanchez stumbled off to the comparative safety of the hangar.

Ilya Fedorenko had not noticed the step up to the bedroom until the Cuban had obligingly tripped over it. Leaving Sanchez half conscious, he had run out to look under the stilts: there was no step up in the under frame between the bedroom and the other rooms.

Seeing Sanchez disappear into the hangar, Fedorenko walked back up the veranda steps, taking a crowbar from the equipment case.

He knocked on the floorboards: years in the tropics had taught him what dangers lurked in cool, dark spaces: he searched the floor on his hands and knees, looking at each slat for signs of wear. One seemed loose: he jammed the tongue of the crowbar into the crack at one end, intending to pry it up.

Sanchez rushed into the room.

Ready to kill, Ilya leapt over the bed his pistol drawn, and aiming at Sanchez, rolled heavily onto the floor on the other side.

'We go!' yelled the Cuban, and sprinted back out.

Ilya was suddenly focussed on a heart-stopping beat that had once struck terror into his soul among the sounds of the jungle. He ran after the Cuban, reaching the edge of the clearing just as the helicopter began its final, spiralling descent onto the airstrip.

Sanchez had started the Jeep and was tugging at the gear stick. 'You think they see us?' he hissed, ashen-faced.

'Of course'

'You try to kill me!'

'Go to hell!' The wheeze of the craft's turbines grew louder: it advanced towards them. 'Get moving!' yelled the Russian.

Sanchez crashed into reverse gear, backed into the undergrowth, and shot forward into a barely distinguishable track. He accelerated off with no idea of the direction he was taking. Ilya gripped the windshield frame careful to shelter his knuckles from the whiplash of green shoots in the speeding Jeep's path. They bumped over exposed roots and thick vegetation, hoping the jungle's green umbrella would cover them from searching eyes in the helicopter above.

Sanchez drove for five minutes before Ilya felt it was safe to stop. The Cuban cut the engine so they could listen. They strained to hear the ominous beat above the cacophony of forest birds, but there was no more sound from the helicopter.

Ilya wiped grimy sweat from his forehead. Sanchez, hands trembling, lit a cigar butt.

They drove to a hill overlooking the valley. Ilya searched for the clearing through binoculars while Sanchez squinted at the surrounding hills through his compass sight. The cottage lands had been perfectly chosen: they were completely hidden from view. 'Nice work, Comrade', Ilya whispered: 'even in the Colombian jungle you apply your lessons well.'

Sanchez walked over, pointing triumphantly at a cross on his map. He traced his finger along a track leading them back to the road North-East to Maicao. Ilya had humiliated him, but the Cuban seemed not to care: in fact, he had become inexplicably cooperative. They stopped only once during the long drive back to empty a can of gasoline into the tank, while Sanchez urinated over the front wheel on Ilya's side.

They reached Maicao during its short twilight. Sanchez returned the rented Jeep to the small garage, and they went back to their dingy rooms by the fishermen's docks.

Colonel Ivan Promyslov invariably had trouble sleeping in the top-floor apartments. It was cold too: the October winds had brought the polar air back to Moscow.

It was no fun to spend the night in the Lubyanka officers' quarters: he would have preferred to be home listening to Olga's gentle breathing.

He tossed about in the slim bed, thinking over his tiresome day.

He had spent the morning listening again and again to Kimon Antonov's taped telephone conversations with Bulgaria. Overwhelmed with the man's fatuous ego, Ivan concluded that Antonov deserved everything coming to him: if he was lucky, he might survive to live the lifestyle of an interned lunatic. Marshall Volkov's fate, however, could be very different: Ivan was not willing to bet on his survival once the old soldier was brought to heel and charged.

The KGB had kept Traicho Botev in Lefortovo prison since his extradition from Bulgaria: the unfortunate had been sent over to Moscow following his questioning by Dobrynin in Sofia. He was small game, hardly worth the trouble of hanging on to, but he had to be kept at hand as a witness until judgment was passed on Antonov. Botev might get off with a severe reprimand and a discharge from the Party. Ivan had disagreed with Dobrynin's refusal to inform Botev's family of his whereabouts after all these weeks, but this was an issue of national sovereignty, and he had no authority to overrule the decision. Interviewing Botev between his fits of tears had been tedious. Ivan was now perfectly convinced that the man was useless to the investigation: he hadn't even seen Ahmet's face while passing him his credentials for the Chicago Mafia.

He had spent the afternoon trying to keep Galina Petrova's influential Kremlin friends off his back, too: Anatoly Petrovic had had the good taste to marry into a Russian family, and the good sense to choose one well connected with Moscow's nomenklatura. Petrovic's complicity was marginal too, if undeniable, but the KGB was not going to get a free hand in dealing with him: the Bulgarians would have to handle Petrovic themselves, and Ivan had already begun to draft his recommendation as such.

He had been preparing to go home when young Lieutenant Vassily Nikolaev knocked at his door accompanied by the five members of the finance department's audit committee. They had finalised their report on the loopholes through which five million US dollars had passed out of the Bulgarian treasury into the hands of capitalist criminals, and they needed his advice on how to continue. The meeting had taken hours.

Olga had gone alone to the reception in honour of the new Austrian ambassador. Ivan had called his wife to tell her that he would either see her at the reception or at home later that night. The meeting had continued past midnight, and he had finally called to say he would stay overnight in the Lubyanka at Dzerzhinsky Square.

Nikolaev had been insufferable, refusing vodka and contradicting the accountants sitting around Ivan's office table: Ivan disliked such behaviour, seeing it all the time among insecure young officers who dealt in fear to get results. Nikolaev had no skill of subtle persuasion: the machine had moved on since the times of Stalin, but Nikolaev hadn't noticed.

When he had first read through the lieutenant's personnel file, Ivan had been attracted by his rich background, and immediately accepted him as his assistant. At the interview, Vassily Nikolaev had orally completed the information on his file describing how he had been fascinated as a child by a procession of circumspect men through his parents' house in Berlin: they minded their tongues and their manners in a way he never saw at the homes of his friends: either profound fear or profound respect motivated their reserve, and, with no way of understanding the source of his father's influence, he became intoxicated with the idea of power. An officer and a Russian, the elder Nikolaev had maintained his military status on being awarded the coveted senior position for Aeroflot in the German Democratic Republic.

Vassily's respect for the Party was carefully nurtured through repeated service in the Komsomol, the party's youth movement. His opinions matured within accepted guidelines, out of phase with the rest of his Beatle-loving, gum-chewing generation, and his need to see strict order in Russian society hardened into a code little removed from Stalin's: he became a hard-line conservative, devoutly opposed to reform.

Vassily graduated from the prestigious Military Diplomatic Academy long before he understood his father's true profession: once a serving officer, he was told by his father of the dark link between Aeroflot, the jugular of Soviet Military Intelligence, and the GRU, the Military Intelligence Corps itself. Little by little, the weight of his father's vast influence as an officer of the GRU became apparent to the young man.

A talented young infantry officer, conscientious and politically aware, Nikolaev was removed from the mass of his comrades in his regiment and directed to serve senior staff as a liaison officer. He became personally known to top military brass and exposed to the discussion of issues usually intended to fly over the heads of lieutenants.

The file didn't specify how or why his potentially brilliant military career had come to such an abrupt halt: Nikolaev claimed it was because he preferred the problems of national security to 'playing soldiers.' One day he arrived as a trainee in a KGB school, and a few months later he was appointed as Trade Attaché in the Russian Embassy in Rome. The speed of his ascent in the KGB left the other trainee officers reeling in his wake.

The years in Rome were active: Nikolaev foiled two attempts at defection by embassy employees and found locals able to supply the GRU Resident with information on NATO air bases operating F-104 Starfighters on the Adriatic. His tendency to spend more time on issues involving military intelligence irritated his KGB boss, but Vassily was left his head and played an active role on the perimeter of the boiling criminal and terrorist underworld of the Italian peninsula.

The Rome posting over, Nikolaev returned to Dzerzhinsky Square, where he became Ivan's assistant. His progress was now only a question of time: he was still young and new at State Security. It would take Ivan's recommendation to 'rubber stamp' his promotion. However, Ivan had doubts: he felt faintly suspicious of his assistant's star status, and he disliked his pretentious self-assurance. He struggled to overcome his aversion to Nikolaev's personality, recognising the quality of his work and searching for sparks of humanity in the young lieutenant's brash manners. On the face of it, Nikolaev was perfectly promotable: underneath he was ill-mannered and ruthless, but none of these weaknesses would be held as such in his evaluation. Ivan, conceding that the machine would adapt slowly to the will of the Party's new pilot, had welcomed the breath of change sweeping through the dark corridors of Dzerzhinsky Square: yet this young lieutenant, a representative of the Russian state's future, appeared to be more Stalinist than Ivan's own father had been. Who said the young cried out for change? Maybe Nikolaev was an exception. Maybe he was just cocky because his father was a very big wheel in the military.

He turned for the hundredth time, opened his eyes, and stared at the streaks of light on the wall projected by the street lamps of Marx Prospekt. He tried to concentrate on the pattern of the beams to slow the swirl of his mind. He turned on the bedside lamp. Had he been home, he could have wandered off into the front room and read a book: here, he had nothing at all to read. The bedroom was bare, not in the same style as the lavishly appointed officer's club. He lay back, crossed his hands on his belly and stared at the ceiling.

Then he got up.

The hallway guard uttered an embarrassed greeting: he had been fast asleep, his dark, Mongolian eyes pleading with Ivan for a break. Ivan asked for his name and number and noted it on a sheet of paper. He said he would give the boy's serious transgression some thought, and decide what to do with him over breakfast: he advised him to stay awake in the meanwhile, the best way being to stand to attention until the arrival of his relief at 6 a.m.

Ivan took the stairs to his office wondering how on earth a Mongolian had got himself a job in the Lubyanka building.

Telegraph machines clattered behind the locked doors of the Communications Directorate, the operators working all night to ensure daylight coverage of the American continent and Pacific basin. He smiled at a pert, uniformed woman looking up in astonishment at him from the counter: officers rarely appeared during the darkest hours of the night. She stood up, her blue eyes wide with apprehension.

'I'm not a ghost', laughed Ivan. 'Please sit down.'

'Thank you, Sir', she stammered.

'I'm Colonel Promyslov. Do you have anything for me?'

'I....I need to see your identity card, Comrade Colonel, and you must sign for whatever you take.'

'That's normal: I'm glad to see the rules are applied. Now, if you please, my messages.'

The woman disappeared into the cipher room. She returned with two sealed envelopes in her hand and lifted her eyes to meet his.

'My messages?'

'Your identity, Comrade Colonel: please!'

'Ah, yes', said Ivan, and drew out his wallet.

The first cable was from the Direccion General de Inteligencia, the DGI, in Havana asking him to call as soon as he got to his desk in the morning: Fedorenko had been dissatisfied with arrangements for the Colombian trip, and the Cubans wanted to explain. 'If Fedorenko's got something to complain about, he's probably right', mumbled Ivan, and strolled off to his office.

He lit the desk lamp intending to catch up on his reading until the officer's restaurant opened to serve breakfast. He opened the second envelope.

'Oh no', he groaned. He left his office, walked to a room operated by the communications staff, and switched on a television set in time to watch a US satellite broadcast of headline news covering an assassination attempt in Chicago on the US President's life. At the end of the broadcast, he sat back and put his hands moodily in his pockets: doubts and worry about the assassination attempt coursed through his mind: this was a bad time for an international incident if talks on normalisation between the Soviet Union and the United States were to progress. He found the slip of paper with the name and number of the young Mongolian floor guard asleep in the corridor upstairs: he crumpled it up and threw it into a wastepaper basket. 'Fifty-three damned republics to shepherd in our Soviet, and only one of them Russian', he fumed: 'sometimes I wonder how we manage....and over the other side they say our system can't work. Just look at theirs!'

Nikolaev arrived for breakfast in the officers' club, that morning's *Komsomolskaia Pravda* newspaper carefully folded under his arm. The Colonel winced: strong coffee and the young officer's precious conversation taken together would give him heartburn. He tried to hide behind his *Izvestia*, but Nikolaev intruded anyway and started a tedious monologue on his favourite subject, himself. Promyslov mentioned he had slept badly, but Nikolaev was not to be deterred: 'I sleep so much better in the outskirts, Comrade Colonel: I live beyond the Tretyakov Gallery, you know. Travelling is such a waste of time when you live that far out....'

Trying not to yawn, Promyslov muttered agreement.

'.... of course, Comrade Colonel, I don't yet merit the privilege of a driver.'

Ivan sneezed violently. Not wanting to draw out the conversation, he said nothing about Chicago: the lieutenant would find out soon enough. Throughout Nikolaev's soliloquy, Ivan tried to think of a way of getting feedback on the assassination attempt. He would have to be ready for the fallout when the Kremlin heavyweights called for their intelligence digest over breakfast. He had to call Havana too.

Respite came with Nikolaev's black bread and sausage. 'It's a habit I picked up as a child in Berlin: those Prussians really know how to eat!'

'True', mumbled Ivan: he had never been to Berlin.

'But my favourite's still a croissant with a cappuccino: I used to breakfast on nothing else in Rome.'

'You've been around, Lieutenant.'

'My father says a man has to travel before settling down, Comrade Colonel.'

'Of course.' Ivan had not travelled much and viewed others who had with faint envy.

Nikolaev bit heartily into his black bread and sausage.

The colonel stood and walked back to his office.

He yawned in weary anticipation of the interviews with Kimon Antonov's unfortunate accomplices imprisoned in the cells below. He would repeat the same questions he had asked twenty times before: it left no scars, and the unwary invariably trapped themselves sooner or later in their stress and despair. That was the only thing he enjoyed about interrogation; the intellectual satisfaction of discovering crime through inconsistency; but questioning physically weakened prisoners always left him in anguish. His stomach had never hardened to the conditions of the cell block, and though the distress never showed on his face, his disgust with such inhumanity became more and more difficult to hide.

He called Havana. Communicating with Garcia was no easy task: the Transatlantic link was often down, and even on the lucky days when he got through, his correspondent's voice was barely audible against the background mush: then, Garcia's broken Russian always added confusion.

'....and we're.... about the chopper.... sent by local drug....
who own the.....'

'Chopper? What chopper?'

'.... ought you knew.... opter! Th.... ased by a hel....'

'Is Fedorenko safe?'

'....at?'

'Is Fedorenko safe?' bellowed Promyslov.

'.... Maicao.'

'Is he alright?'

'OK'

'Take him to Chicago.'

'.... checking the....'

'Take him to Chicago, now!'

'.... ight.'

A single chime of the telephone bell cleared the line.
Garcia, willing or not, whether he had understood anything
or not, had disappeared.

'What the hell! If he wants me, he can call back.' Ivan
slammed down the handset in exasperation.

He drafted a note in baby Russian to Garcia asking him to
move Ilya Fedorenko as fast as possible to Chicago. If this
assassination attempt was the work of Antonov's Bulgarian
connection involving Ahmet, Fedorenko would have to get
Ahmet out before the Americans got him. As an
afterthought, he added a few lines to Fedorenko himself:
maybe he was on Ahmet's trail in Colombia, but that wasn't
good enough now that probable damage had been done: Ilya
Fedorenko would recognise Ivan's style. At the top of the
sheet he wrote that copies should go to Fedorenko's and
Ahmet's superiors in the Executive-Action group: this team,
affectionately known as the Department of 'Wet Affairs',
fielded the killers, the illegals who got things done, and Ilya
was the best: today, Fedorenko was the Soviet Union's only
hope that detente at the next summit with the Americans
wouldn't be compromised by any suspicion of Soviet
involvement in Chicago: indeed, Fedorenko's success was
probably the only hope of keeping Marshall Volkov's old
guard off the new, young General Secretary's back. It was
risky having to confide a US penetration to the Cubans, but

Fedorenko was good and experienced enough to ensure his own safety: besides, he spoke some English.

Ivan buzzed his secretary twice before he realised it was too early. He checked his watch: if the cables were sent straight away, Garcia might see them before leaving work, and organise Ilya's transfer into U.S territory during the following Russian night.

The colonel took his despatches personally to the desk at the Communications Directorate. He was disappointed by the presence now of a matronly figure in uniform sitting at the same desk.

'I expected to find the person who was here on the night shift.' He tried to sound matter of fact.

'She left at six, Comrade Colonel.'

He felt stupid. 'Ah, yes, well, maybe you can do something for me.'

'Of course, Comrade Colonel.'

'Please send these cables immediately to Colonel Garcia at the Direccion General in Havana.'

'Right away, Sir.'

Ivan had promised to coach the rowing team before going home.

Water swirled around the concrete tank while he worked up a sweat carefully watching his stroke in the large mirror facing him. Despite his age and weight, he felt he could out-row any one of the three younger officers struggling on the sliding seats behind him, trying desperately to follow the shattering pace he was setting as stroke.

The gymnasium held none of the charms of the silent floodplain waters of the Dniepr, where, as a student, Ivan had loved to skull alone to restore nerves frayed by keen competition. He had never lost his love of rowing and had been delighted to discover the forgotten concrete practice tank at the officers' club. A little gentle persuasion had revived interest in others too, leading to the appointment of a team with him as its coach.

'Halt!' he gasped and left his oar to float back in the swirl. Behind him, the others stopped rowing, and folded in exhaustion. 'We're still too far under thirty strokes a minute

.... if we can get to thirty for long enough, we'll field the team.'

The others panted, unable to speak.

He stripped, showered and leapt into the pool. Tepid, silky water melted away the ache in his limbs. He swam a few leisurely lengths, climbed out and dried himself off. An attendant handed him a white robe in Armenian towelling, and poured him a beer from the gymnasium bar.

Aleksandr Mikhailovich came and sat beside him. 'I don't know how you do it, Ivan Dmitriyevich! We're going to have to find someone less zealous than you as stroke, otherwise we'll end up in hospital long before the season opens.'

Ivan laughed. 'You look fit enough to me, Ryabov, and we still have a long way to go if we intend to compete.'

Lieutenant Ryabov, also of the First Chief Directorate, spread his legs, and reclined into the soft chair. 'You made quite an impression on a friend of mine last night.'

'You should tell him to keep awake on the job! Tell me how, as a Mongolian, he ended up in Moscow.'

'I'm not talking about a he, but about a she!'

'A she?'

'Yes, Tatiana Nikolayevna Demicheva: she's in the Eighth Department: Communications: from the Ukraine, but Kirill Demichev's daughter.'

'Quite a family! A blue-eyed woman?'

'I always said you're good at recognising talent!' laughed Ryabov. 'She was shocked to meet a full colonel: at night, she only ever sees a secretary or two, or at times, Nikolaev.'

'Colonels need their sleep, and that's no way to speak about a fellow officer, young man.... does she see Nikolaev often?'

'That boy works all the time: talk about ambition! Maybe you should choose him as stroke.... or maybe not: he'll wear us out too.'

'Is this serious between you and your friend?'

'We're getting married in May, Ivan Dmitriyevich'

'Congratulations! How do your people feel about you wedding a Ukrainian?'

'My mother loves her: that's all that matters.'

'Bring her to dinner on Saturday.'

'We'd love to, Ivan Dmitriyevich, but she's working; it's her *subbotnik*. Your dinner would be her breakfast before she leaves for an all-night session at the Komsomol building.'

'Then, we'll make it a week on Saturday.'

A glow of pride suffused in the young officer's eyes as Ivan walked off to change.

Sanchez booked the jeep and insisted they be on the road by 4 a.m. He had promised to knock when all was ready downstairs so that Ilya Fedorenko would just have to carry his gear down to the vehicle.

It was almost 5 a.m., and the Russian was dozing fitfully in a chair when the knock came. He arose irritably and opened the door to the dirty bedroom. 'You're late!' he barked, making no effort to conceal his anger.'

'The plan has changed', announced Sanchez.

'The hell it has: I have to finish searching that cottage.'

Sanchez suppressed the desire to knock his guest's annoyance down his throat, and calmly said, 'No.' He watched Ilya's frustration rise to crimson pitch, and slipped an envelope into the Soviet agent's hand. 'Read that', he spat.

The message was worded in terse Russian. He read it and sat on the edge of a couch on which he had spent his uncomfortable night. 'Too late', he muttered.

'Eh?' said Sanchez.

Ilya frowned at the floor.

The Cuban walked over to the window, and drew back the thin curtain to reveal a warm, rising sun burning through the gently swaying masts of the fishing boats.

Ilya rose to his feet. 'Contact your people', he said: 'tell them to get me to America.'

'A boat is already waiting,' sneered Sanchez.

'What made you take up auditing?' Colonel Ivan Promyslov asked the middle-aged Lithuanian woman.

'We all have to make a living, Comrade Colonel', she answered. 'As a child, I showed talent in arithmetic, and I was lucky enough to pass the state economic examinations very well. They say my skills are prized among the capitalists.'

'They are prized in State Security too, Comrade Auditor: the difference is that money buys everything among the capitalists, but no amount of money will get you, or them, into Section 100 of the GUM emporium, or a dacha in Zhukovka.'

The woman frowned as if she didn't know what the Colonel was talking about.

'Come now, Comrade Auditor, we can speak freely among ourselves', Promyslov laughed.

She looked relieved. She leaned towards him, coming at him with practised hesitation.

Promyslov had seen the act before. 'What can I do for you, Comrade Auditor?' he asked.

She took a deep breath. 'I am a servant of the Party and of the State, Comrade Colonel: loyalty forces me to speak to you about my concern.'

'Of course, Comrade. Your job is not an easy one, I know: we have to help each other, and it is gratifying that our future is in the hands of loyal Russians such as yourself.'

She crossed her legs and leaned closer. Her hands clutched the cheap bag on her knees: her eyes were wide open. 'It was when we wanted to liquidate the documentary credit and to close the Swiss account: I was surprised by the instruction not to.'

Ivan Promyslov had assumed the account closed long ago, straight after the discovery of Kimon Antonov's Bulgarian connection with Italian crime. 'Why was that surprising, Comrade Auditor?' He listened attentively.

'The documentary credit is revolving, Comrade Colonel: it can still be used to draw funds, and we still don't know who can access the BAPTCo account. Leaving such avenues open seems a risk.'

'Who told you not to close it?' asked Ivan.

'This is why I came to you. Though you are from the First Department, I understand you are the investigator in this Bulgarian affair, and you do outrank the person who gave the order.' The woman hesitated.

'Comrade Auditor, this is the moment when you show your loyalty to the State and to the Party: please don't let me down now.'

She took a deep breath. 'It came from Comrade Lieutenant Nikolaev: I wanted to verify with you personally that he is following instructions.'

Promyslov's face showed none of the surprise he felt. 'Of course, Comrade Auditor. You did the right thing coming to see me: leave the matter in my hands, and kindly speak to no one else about it. Any one of several departments can issue such an instruction: I will check it. Don't worry yourself any longer with this question.'

'Very good, Comrade Colonel.'

'I shall, of course, inform your superior of your assiduity in this matter.'

The woman arose to leave the office, a smile of evident relief on her face. She was shown out by a guard.

Promyslov thrust his hands deep in his pockets, and walked to the window to look down at the crowds staring up at the Lubyanka. He had a shrewd understanding of their awe.

What on earth was Nikolaev up to? The Swiss side of the Antonov affair was none of his damned business, and he had no authority to give instructions to the auditors, especially without Ivan's own approval. He picked up the telephone and called Nikolaev's superior at the Personnel Directorate's Officer Training Centre. 'Good morning, Mstislav, tell me, have you given young Nikolaev any instructions or advice I should know about concerning his assignment to me?'

'None.'

'Would anyone else counsel him?'

'How about his mother? What do you want to know, Ivan Dmitriyevich?'

'He's showing initiative. I was wondering whether it's his own.'

'An astute fellow, Nikolaev', replied Mstislav Shigaev, 'he'll go far.'

'Oh yes, he'll go far', replied Ivan, 'especially if he continues what he's just started.'

Ivan was answered with a confused silence. Nikolaev walked in just as he was replacing the handset.

'I thought you would like to know I'm drawing a few details of the Antonov case to a close, Comrade Colonel. If you have no objections, I will go to Switzerland myself to tie up some loose ends.'

Ivan looked sharply up at the young officer. 'That will not be necessary, Comrade Lieutenant, I'm sending qualified auditors from State Security to do that: I need official confirmation that not a trace of this affair is left intact outside the Soviet Union. Local embassy staff will chaperone them.'

Nikolaev taunted, 'What are you afraid of, Comrade Colonel? You have no confidence in your fellow officers?'

Ivan struggled to control a sudden flush of anger. 'I have made my decision, Lieutenant Nikolaev: I am not prepared to discuss my reasons.'

Nikolaev took a step forward. 'This affair could have wide repercussions. You can't send the auditors alone.'

'I will be the judge of that, Lieutenant, and I don't like the way you are questioning my order!'

Nikolaev spun on his heel and strode to the door. He turned to face the Colonel for an instant. 'Be informed that I intend to see the General about this.'

Promyslov stood rooted to the spot, enraged. Major General Leonid Budhakin, Area Departmental Director at the First Chief Directorate, remained Ivan Dmitriyevich Promyslov's direct superior and of no concern to Nikolaev.

Nikolaev slammed the door behind him.

'Nikolaev!' shouted Ivan, but it was too late to stop him. He stormed to the door. 'Which way did he go?' he snapped at a corridor guard.

'He took the stairs, Comrade Colonel.'

'Up or down?'

'I don't know, Sir.'

No sound came from the stairwell. Ivan cooled, and turned back to his office. He toyed with the idea of filing a complaint of insubordination with Mstislav Shigaev, Nikolaev's superior officer at the Officer Training Centre.

Instead, he sat down and fumed quietly. 'What is the matter with that boy?' he hissed.

This had to be more than just disappointment over cancelled foreign travel, a perk which officers at State Security so loved, and hated to lose. No, it was more than that: Nikolaev's whole attitude had been tense and contradictory from the outset, but this was the first time Promyslov had seen him act like an arrogant prima donna: it was out of keeping with this young star's so-called reputation, upbringing, and training.

Ivan rapped his fingers moodily on the desk, drumming out the nervousness he felt. It was one thing to deal with the public; it was quite another dealing with a fellow officer, even one of junior rank. Nikolaev could drag the argument into the open: Promyslov's position had the advantage of rank, but the accusation of failing to reasonably trust a fellow officer carried passions in Dzerzhinsky Square's closed community and Major General Leonid Budhakin, didn't care for his direct subordinate, Colonel Ivan Promyslov, finding him uncommunicative and too clever by far. There was a risk too of exposing the Lithuanian auditor as the informer.

Chit chat in the officer's club that evening concerned the disappearance of Marshall Volkov from the Politburo. Everything was not well at the top, and small groups sat around the tables in the mahogany-furnished room exchanging gossip.

Ivan saw Nikolaev sitting in a corner with another young officer. He walked to the table and sat down with them. Nikolaev shot him a hostile glance, not bothering to make the introduction. The other officer glanced in embarrassment at Ivan, who nodded, and introduced himself, bringing a touch of warmth to his frosty reception. The young officer plucked up courage, and said, 'Vassily Nikolaev and I were in the same regiment, Comrade Colonel....the one Marshall Volkov got his first stripes in', he added with a wink.

'Yes', added Nikolaev, 'but I wasn't there for long.'

'That's a Motor Rifle regiment, isn't it?' asked Promyslov. 'You must have spent time exercising in the Urals.'

Nikolaev was about to add something when his friend cut in laughing. 'It was certainly the case for us, but our resourceful Vassily found himself a very easy number, didn't you, old friend.'

Nikolaev stared furiously at his comrade. 'It wasn't that easy: I was kept running all the time.'

The table moved, and the other officer slid into a startled silence.

Ivan looked Nikolaev in the eye, 'With that build up, you should tell me what you were doing, Lieutenant.'

The friend stood up and mumbled something about a chess game, clicked his heels at the Colonel and left.

'The same regiment as the Marshall, eh! Why didn't you want him to tell me?'

Nikolaev forced a smile, 'What makes you think that?'

'You kicked him?'

'He's a loud mouth. It's of no importance. I was attached to staff as liaison, that's all. I met a few people who might have been good for my career had I stayed in the military, but I didn't: I left and joined State Security, that's why I'm here.'

Promyslov ordered two vodkas from a white-gloved waiter. 'You know, Lieutenant, I've thought a lot about our conversation today, and I see you could be offended by my position, but no offence was intended, and I certainly don't want any misunderstandings to hinder your career at this stage: my decision to send the auditors alone is perfectly justifiable. You must understand.'

Nikolaev's eyes narrowed as if he did not understand, and had no intention of doing so. 'Of course, Comrade Colonel.' The moments of defiant silence that followed made it clear that Nikolaev had no intention of apologising for his outburst in the Colonel's office.

The vodka arrived, a welcome break to those tense moments. Promyslov lifted his glass, fully expecting Nikolaev to do the same, and look him in the eye. Nikolaev looked stubbornly the other way.

All right my lad, thought Promyslov, we have the ground rules laid, let's get on with the game.

A cold, polar wind licked the roofs of Moscow. Clear evenings had given way to the blue-grey light of a Russian mid-season: the air was mistier, the humidity bothersome to the old.

Tatiana Demicheva and her betrothed lieutenant arrived to a warm welcome from Ivan and Olga. Tanya had expected the evening to be formal and stuffy, just like the corridors of the Lubyanka: instead, her hosts took care to make their young guests feel relaxed. Besides, Ivan enjoyed Aleksandr Ryabov's company, and, after all, his fiancée was Kirill Demichev's daughter, as Olga told her lady friends over and over again the following day: in fact, Olga was so impressed with the woman that she allowed her to leave with her ancient recipe for borscht, hitherto a jealously guarded family secret.

The men disappeared to the cellar after dinner in search of a bottle of Mukusani Krasnoye, an export-only Georgian vintage Ivan had boasted about at the table. They reunited to finish the bottle around a Scandinavian teak coffee table that was Olga's pride and joy.

'It must be very tiring for you, dear, to work at night like that and try to lead a normal life.'

'Very, Olga Sergeyevna, but I love the job and the advantages of working in State Security.'

'Now you've held this position in communications two years, you could request a promotion quite soon, Tatiana', commented Ivan.

'I'm afraid to do that, Comrade Colonel.'

'You can call me Ivan at home, Tatiana.'

Tanya smiled, and blushed at Ryabov. 'Thank you .... Ivan Dmitriyevich, and please call me Tanya.'

'Why are you afraid, dear?' asked Olga.

Tanya looked pleadingly at Ryabov.

'We can speak freely, Tanya', he said.

'I'm trying hard to improve our service, Olga Sergeyevna', started the woman, 'but with the complaints I've had, it's not the right time to ask for a promotion.'

'Complaints? What complaints?' asked Promyslov.

'We used to get regular radio messages from an agent called 'Milk' operating in Italy....'

Ivan glanced at Ryabov: the young intelligence officer from the Italian desk was watching him closely.

'.... then', continued Tanya, 'Milk took a transmitter with him to America, and continued trying to transmit in the same way he used to, but you can't do that: it's too far: he should have taken a more powerful set operating on a satellite waveband: procedures are completely different. His transmissions are garbled, and I can't risk a request for a retransmission on his frequencies: I'm not even sure he would receive me. Heavens knows how much information we've lost.'

'Can't the embassy or a consulate pick him up over there?'

'They use different wavelengths, Comrade Colonel, and no one has authorised Milk's transmissions locally. Even the cipher he uses is weird.'

'Weird?' asked Ivan.

'But, this isn't your fault, Tanya', interjected his wife.

'That's how I feel, Olga Sergeyevna, but he won't listen, and he says I'll lose my job if I don't solve the problem.' The woman was close to tears.

'He? Who says that?' asked Ivan.

'It would not be right to tell, Comrade Colonel.'

'Is it an officer?'

'Yes, Sir.'

'He speaks to you personally?'

'He's always there at nights, Comrade Colonel: there are few other officers around.' She burst into tears.

'I can't do anything to help you, Tanya, unless you tell me who he is.'

The pretty Ukrainian sobbed into the rich, ruby wine in her glass. She looked up tears in her blue eyes. 'I can't do that: I've already said more than I should.'

The conversation gave a sombre tone to the rest of the evening. Tanya was terrified she had stepped out of line by reporting on an officer, even a nameless one.

Later that evening, Ryabov followed Ivan to get the coats from the bedroom. 'Thanks, Ivan Dmitriyevich. Don't worry about Tanya: she knows you mean well. She talked because the wine went to her head: I was surprised.'

'If only I knew who it is, I could get the misunderstanding cleared up. Whoever sent this agent to America without a proper set and ciphers should be talked to anyway!'

Aleksandr Mikhailovich hesitated a moment, but only a moment. 'Ivan Dmitriyevich, why do you think I call Nikolaev a creep?'

The small boat bobbed lightly to a stop against a rickety wooden pier. Ilya could barely distinguish the shoreline in the dark. The oarsman whistled softly trying to sound like some obscure aquatic bird: it was just another low whistle to Ilya. They waited in silence. The oarsman whistled again, a little louder this time.

There came a sound of cracking twigs some yards away: Ilya prepared to slide into the dark water. A flashlight advanced drunkenly towards them along the jetty. The oarsman and the owner of the flashlight exchanged a few Spanish whispers, and a strong hand was thrust down towards Ilya. 'You come with me, señor.' He grasped it: it was dry and calloused, a working hand: he climbed out. The oarsman passed up his belongings. Ilya had changed into American-made clothes and underwear in the fishing vessel that had brought him across the ocean. He would buy the rest of his wardrobe as he needed it. Everything else lay at the bottom of the Caribbean.

He followed the pool of light along the jetty to dry, sandy ground. The world was swaying and the darkness didn't help his sense of balance.

'Welcome to Florida, señor. Is this your first trip?'

'Thank you, no', he replied, feeling far from welcome. 'Do you have the documents?'

'We have for you green card, Finnish passport, Illinois driver's license, dollar, ticket to Chicago. Tomorrow we go to Orlando: you catch plane. You buy warm American clothes.'

'It's not often that we in Staff are invited to the officers' club, Comrade Colonel.'

'You have done me a service: it is normal.'

'Only my duty.' The auditor dabbed daintily at the corners of her mouth and took a cigarette from somewhere inside her voluminous bag.

He struck a match and bent forward to light it for her.

She inhaled the first wisps of smoke luxuriously: it was a sensual gesture for Ivan's benefit, but the auditor's girth and drabness quelled any desire the 'come-on' look in her eyes might have tried to provoke. She exhaled slowly and placed her fleshy elbows on the table.

The waiter asked whether they wanted another Turkish coffee.

'I've reviewed the decision to leave those Swiss financial instruments open: I've decided to reverse it, Comrade Auditor. You must implement the measures originally requested by the Directorate.'

'I'm relieved, Comrade Colonel: it's a wise decision. Is Lieutenant Nikolaev coming with us to Switzerland?'

'I'll let you know before you leave.' He detected anxiety in the woman's voice. 'In the meanwhile, I'd like you to do something for me.'

'How can I be of service?'

'I understand we maintain separate journals for clandestine services abroad.'

'Yes: we keep individual accounts for major contributors.'

'Do you have access to those journals?'

'Only with authorisation.'

Ivan frowned: Italy had been of key importance to Ahmet, to Milk, to Kimon Antonov, the fired Bulgarian Agricultural Secretary-General in Moscow, and even to Nikolaev. He needed to know more about what they were up to, but he had to avoid attracting attention at the Italian end of the investigation in case Nikolaev discovered he was under investigation, and anyway, Italy was outside Ivan's area of authority.

'Could you be more specific, Comrade Colonel?' asked the woman.

'I need a record of payments made to one of our agents, code-named Milk.'

'Oh, yes, of course, Milk.'

'You have heard of him?'

'We take elaborate security measures in paying our agents and illegals abroad: for Milk, they are twice as elaborate. One of my colleagues spent three weeks setting up the circuit.'

'Why?'

'No idea: you'd have to ask the Italian desk.' She gave Ivan another come-on glance.

'Can you help me?'

'For another invitation like this, Comrade Colonel, let me think about it.'

'Then let's meet here again in three days' time, for lunch.'

She smiled coquettishly and left.

The Promyslov dacha provided a warm haven from the frozen, steely winter outside. July was long-forgotten, although, only months previously, Ivan and Olga had sat together on the veranda during long, warm evenings waiting for the stars and listening to the birds.

The dacha was one of many in a park owned and maintained by State Security, and Ivan's colleagues who rented others in the park respected an unwritten rule of total discretion. Here, the Promyslovs felt secure and at home. Softly shaded by the trees, the garden afforded total privacy in the summer: as winter approached, and the leaves fell, neighbouring dachas loomed through the branches, and the inmates scuttled like wild rabbits from their gardens; then the days shortened rapidly and from the windows warm orange lights glowed, timidly at first, through the flat, grey light. The neighbours disappeared once more behind a white foliage of the first, tenuous snowfalls, and, as winter tightened its grip, anonymity prevailed once more in the park behind a curtain of mist and snowdrifts.

In the afternoon half-light, Ivan could barely distinguish the skyline. He rubbed the condensation from the glass and put his face closer to the pane: there was no mist outside, yet no outline appeared in the garden: nature had painted a dull canvas. He turned and looked contentedly at the little wooded room. He loved this place, and it cost him a song:

the rent was a mere formality, and no amount of money could assure anyone else the privilege of using it.

His status cut him off from his fellow Russians, and he found he had less and less in common with them as each year passed. Ivan could not identify himself anymore with those solemn masses trooping twice daily through the streets of Moscow: they were like Lemmings rushing through a pointless life to a certain and forgotten death. He was afraid he would soon learn to despise the great Russian people, as did most of his colleagues in State Security. He had read Pravda in the back of the car that morning as the driver sped along the exclusive Chaika lane to his weekend with Olga: he wanted to convince himself he had read to catch up on the news, but he knew it had been to avoid looking at the faces, expressionless like the flat winter light, waiting forever in line for some bus or, outside a shop, for some commodity. When he looked, he saw hostility and fear in those dark eyes staring back at him in his speeding, black official car. A world separated him from them now. He felt secure because he personified security, but out there, with them, he would be defenceless. He did the best job he could: if the Party condoned privilege, who was he to question it? He thanked his stars that neither he nor Olga had to spend hours each day waiting in line clutching a string bag as inseparable from the average Muscovite as his or her underwear.

The yellow Zhiguli in the driveway had surprised him: ownership of a car like that showed clout and money, and one parked within the compound implied a KGB pass into the dacha park. Walking in through the door, he broke into a wide smile as Tanya's striking eyes greeted his. She was sitting on the sofa having tea with Olga. The woman's soft voice and candid conversation provided a restful introduction to the two days ahead in these unstirring, snow-covered grounds.

They spent the evening discussing Tanya's plans for her upcoming wedding. Absorbed in details of colours and furnishings, Olga hadn't noticed the time pass and had felt duty-bound to invite their young guest to dine before returning to Moscow. Tanya phoned her parents to announce her late arrival. Her beloved Sasha had left for a week's course in the Ukraine: there was no point in rushing home.

Knowing that the woman wanted to speak to Ivan, Olga didn't invite her into her kitchen, and, little by little, alone with the Colonel, Tanya found the courage to broach the subject tormenting her so much.

Ivan listened, deep in concentration: at the end of her account he arose and walked to the window to peer outside. He still had his back to her when he started. 'Surely, my dear, they taught you at the KGB school that all cables must go through the Cipher Room to be recorded first.'

'That's why I feel so bad, Comrade Colonel.'

'Ivan!'

'.... Ivan Dmitriyevich.'

'.... and you think Nikolaev has the rank to rescind a standing order like that?'

'Not exactly, but once I started, I saw no point in stopping. He said he would take the entire responsibility.'

'Why were you so ready to break the rules for Nikolaev, yet so insistent on seeing my identity the night I asked for my cables?'

Tanya blushed deeply. 'I thought you were only testing me: no one makes that kind of mistake with a senior officer.'

'So if the rank is low enough, you are ready to turn a blind eye!'

'No!' She tried to sound convincing. '.... but he's so threatening. There are never any officers available to overrule him when he comes at night, and his rank is senior to mine: if I call the Guards, they'll obey him, not me.'

'.... and you have never informed your superior officer.'

'No: I'm afraid of being fired: I broke the rules the first night I gave him a cable. The harm had been done.'

The irony amused Ivan: how could a Demicheva, daughter of one of the most powerful men in Moscow, believe her position to be so weak. She was so young: she had so much to learn. He wondered whether such lack of guile suited her for a career in State Security. Had she ever ventured near the Lubyanka cell block? 'Yes, my dear, I see', he answered absent-mindedly.

Olga bustled, smiling, into the room with a tray of china. She saw two faces deep in thought, left the tray on the table, and scuttled back into the kitchen with a frown.

'I'm surprised Aleksandr Mikhailovich didn't insist you go to your superior.'

'Sasha knew nothing of this until two weeks ago. It was his idea I come to you.' Her large eyes glistened: she was close to tears.

Ivan sat with his chin in his hands, staring at the floor in silence. 'Tanya', he said, 'always follow the rules: know them and be as white as the snow outside. Had you been more experienced, you would have realised you could have refused Nikolaev's requests from the outset: even if his rank is superior to yours, you can force him to escalate his demands. Don't underestimate the power of your directorate: few people hold sway over Communications Officers in State Security.'

'I understand that better now.'

'Let's review what happened, Tanya. First, how did you recognise Milk's cables if they were all in code?'

'Lieutenant Nikolaev gave me Milk's sign-on cipher. He ordered me to keep all cables with that sign-on for him.'

'He instructed you to tear them, including the carbons, from the printer, and you did so: you kept no copies anywhere else?'

Tanya blushed again, and whispered, 'No.'

'So we have nothing to work on if we wanted to decipher them.'

'I could make more copies.'

The colonel looked up in irritation. 'It's a little late for that.'

'The printer generates punched tape. I keep the rolls in my locker: I can't take them out of the building: I'm always searched.'

This was more serious than he had expected. 'Tanya, my dear, you must remove them from your locker first thing on your return: leave them on my desk in a doubly-sealed envelope addressed to me, and be careful!'

A large tear rolled down the woman's soft cheek.

'I want to avoid arousing Nikolaev's suspicions for now. I will make a back-dated report giving some reason why you came to me instead of to your superior. In the meanwhile, stop fretting, and continue to give Nikolaev his messages.'

Tanya blew her nose. Olga walked pointedly in with a steaming dish, and, seeing Tanya's tears, scowled at Ivan. The woman jumped up to help set the table.

Ivan felt tired: he had looked forward to a trouble-free weekend, but Tanya's peccadilloes had done nothing to help.

The auditor had put on a floral print dress and enough makeup to open a drug store. Promyslov thought she had lost weight. Still no sex bomb, she made a better-looking luncheon companion than last time. She sat looking at him after the cigarette-lighting ritual. 'I'm leaving for Switzerland next week, Comrade Colonel: I'm grateful for your mediation.'

"Doing my job', answered Ivan, distantly.

A moment of silence passed: Ivan Dmitriyevich Promyslov was not given to idle conversation. He was awaiting information on Milk: that was the deal; this was not a free lunch.

For her part, the auditor felt embarrassed by her failure to attract Ivan's attention on any basis other than pure business. She sighed a cloud of blue smoke and reached into her capacious bag. 'I did get a chance to draw Milk's file: it happened quite by accident. I copied information I thought may be useful.' She handed him two neatly handwritten sheets listing dates and Swiss Franc deposits paid into an account in a Lugano bank.

Ivan relaxed: he almost smiled at her. He took the sheets and read through them carefully. Meanwhile, the auditor glanced carefully around the club, trying to catch the eye of officers at other tables: the potential was enormous.

At length, Ivan asked, 'What's this code?'

'It means an agent is paid only when he contributes information: it requires an embassy countersignature. The vouchers arrive by diplomatic bag, and we check before we pay.' She pointed to a column of initials: 'There, for example, you can see that Comrade Lieutenant Nikolaev signed many of the vouchers in Rome himself. Isn't that a coincidence?'

'There have been no payments for months: not since about the time Nikolaev left Italy.'

'Maybe Milk's not producing, Comrade Colonel: that happens when an agent runs out of sources. The Italian desk should be aware of what's happening. There's not very much more I can do.'

'This is more than enough, Comrade Auditor, now let's enjoy our lunch.'

The brown envelope on his desk that morning contained a dozen rolls of tightly-wound punched tape. Tanya had included a copy of a cable received the previous evening with a note claiming that the sign-on was indisputably Milk's. The message was obviously incomplete. Ivan looked for some moments at the coded groups. Only someone in communications might be able to recreate the text. Maybe George could do it: Captain George Kevorkian was an Armenian and a Cipher Officer in the Communications Directorate. Enormous and jovial, he rowed number three on the team, and Ivan considered him a fine sportsman: he might help, and he would be discrete.

Ivan locked the tapes in his safe, pocketed Milk's cable, and took the stairs to George's office.

George's reactions were predictably sceptical. 'You're not meant to have those damned tapes, Coach: where did you get them?'

'I can't say, George.'

'It's too dangerous, Ivan Dmitriyevich, even if you are a friend: I have a career and a family to look after.'

'George, if there's any trouble, blame it on me.'

George laughed. 'Come on, you know it's not that easy!'

'Can't you decipher the cable as a special favour?'

'Shit, Coach, you're going too far.'

'Look, George, these tapes are linked to an important investigation: you have to crack that cipher for me: I'll make my request in writing if it makes you feel any more virtuous.'

George squinted at the text under a reading lamp. 'Some groups are missing.' He removed a folder from his desk and leafed rapidly through its dog-eared pages. 'Strange', he mumbled.

Ivan peered over his shoulder.

George ran his finger down the page and looked back over his shoulder. ' 'You sure this came from State Security, Coach?'

'I believe so, why?'

'If I'm right about this cipher, we have an outside guest using our own equipment. Damned cheek!'

'What are you talking about, George?'

'Come back after lunch, Ivan Dmitriyevich: if I'm right, I'll tell you then.'

At one-thirty, Ivan rushed back to his office to call George Kevorkian: there was no reply. He called again at two, but, again, no reply. At two-thirty he took the stairs.

Kevorkian's office was empty: the desk was clear, and the safe was locked. George played by the book: Ivan was sure he could be trusted to remain discrete about the cable. He appeared at the door. 'There you are, Coach. I've been in the cipher room since you came to me about your tapes. Your little puzzle has kept me guessing most of the morning, but now I've deciphered it, I'm only going to give it to you on my conditions.'

Ivan frowned and said nothing: he had expected something like this to happen.

'I keep a copy', continued George: 'in two weeks I'll give it to my boss with a report. If you disagree, I'll destroy what I've done right now, and say nothing, but you'll have to find someone else to play your game.'

'Give me a month, George, and we have a deal.'

'One month it is, then.' George's fine teeth sparkled into a grin below his moustache. He drew a sheet of paper from his pocket. 'Before I give you this, know that I only managed to break the code because we borrowed an old deciphering machine from the GRU, and forgot to return it.'

'So that's why you said we have a guest: this cable uses a Military-Intelligence cipher and not one of ours.'

'Whoever sent this to us, prepared it using a GRU cipher we cracked years ago. It was the grouping that aroused my suspicions.'

'Would anyone from the KGB use a GRU cipher, George?'

'Never! .... and the correspondent who sent it needs his head examined and a refresher: the cipher's outdated, and the gaps indicate his transmitter is far too weak.'

Ivan unfolded the sheet of notepaper George had handed him. 'I hope the risk you're taking, Ivan Dmitriyevich, is worth it! Incidentally, I've had it translated from the Italian....confidentially, of course.'

The cable read:

...SNOW...NOT FOLLOW INST... OWN SKIN...WOMEN KILLED...HIS JOB...THINKS YOU...MISTAKE...KEEP ON TRYING...EVIDENCE OF PASSPORT...MAY RETALIATE AGAINST ME... PERMISSION NEUTRALIZE AND ABORT. MILK.

'One month from today, then', said Ivan refolding the sheet.

'Affirmative.'

'....and if I bring a few more of these.'

'The deadline stays, Coach.'

'You're a hard man, George.'

'That's why I'm in the team.'

Ivan laughed and walked away.

He read and reread the intriguing message during the afternoon.

What did it mean? It was early in the season for snow! An instruction was not followed, and women were killed. Someone had tried to save his own skin. Nikolaev was probably the 'you:' he had made a mistake. There was a passport. Milk was going to keep on trying, but was scared: he wanted to shoot first and to get out.

At five-thirty Colonel Ivan Dmitriyevich Promyslov knocked at the door of his superior officer, Major General Leonid Budhakin, to request a pass to visit the Russian Embassy in Rome. He was left standing.

'Granted, Promyslov, it will do you good to see how the rest of the world lives: you've not worked in an embassy before, have you?'

'No Comrade General.'

'Hmm. How's young Nikolaev doing.'

'He's intelligent: a little intense.'

"Father's a very big noise in the Military: we must take good care of this boy. Groom him, Promyslov. I want you to make him into an officer who could replace you in time.'

'When Comrade General?'

'That depends on you, Promyslov. That's all.'

Ivan turned on his heel and left the General's office.

THE DESERT AIRSTRIP

Almost home, Corinne O'Grady stepped onto the street from the rapid transit station. She walked along the sidewalk leading to her parents' cottage on Chicago's Southside. The warm mid-August evening filled her with smiling anticipation of a weekend romp in Wisconsin with her friends. A cool breeze fluttered in from the lake.

A brown-eyed colleen, Corinne drew looks of open admiration from out-of-work men loitering at the street corner, but none ran up in time to stop the brutality of the following moments.

An '81 Oldsmobile skidded to a halt by her. Men leapt onto the sidewalk.

A gloved man in a mask grabbed her by her hair. Another rammed a needle into her shoulder. A third covered the others with a machine pistol while the driver kept the engine running.

The struggling woman was huddled into the car and collapsed into unconsciousness. The Olds sped off.

'Further left of the river bed', shouted Joe Davies adjusting the sunglasses pinching uncomfortably at his nose.

'Change of scenery, huh?' replied the pilot with a sarcastic chuckle over the microphone. He swung the helicopter North of the heading they had followed along the Rio Grande, checked his instruments and peered once more into the canyon.

The sun beat relentlessly on the silent, parched ground; the sky an intense blue above; the rocks a scorched brown. Only the eerie thump of the helicopter disturbed the desert calm.

Joe, a U.S. Federal Drug-Enforcement Agency officer, was ready to turn back. He had had enough; the heat was unbearable. 'Let's go home', he said: 'there's nothing out there. We've been up almost two hours.'

'Not quite a day's work, boss: we've another hour's gas, that's a mile or two more.'

The helicopter continued its course for another minute, Joe wiping the sweat from his eyes, his tanned, eagle-eyed pilot searching the expanse below for signs of…anything. He had begun to sweep a wide arc to bring their heading back to base when he pointed down to his left. 'Look at those marks: the flat stretch between the rocks.'

It looked like a landing strip, almost indiscernible from the sandy ground except for tire marks dark enough to be recognisable from the air; but no strip was registered in the area.

'We're ten miles South of the Interstate', said the pilot looking at his map, 'I guess you could make it to this plateau in a four-wheel drive.'

He landed the craft in the shade of a rock a few hundred yards from the site. The pilot shut down the turbine and stayed with the machine while Joe Davies, removing a pistol and a loaded clip from a case by his feet, left alone to look at the site.

In the heat outside, the silence seemed oppressive.

The airstrip was situated on a plateau of bedrock fifteen hundred feet long: it was barely enough for a small aircraft to take off in such hot desert air.

There was no one around. Sweating profusely, Joe breathed a sigh of relief, flipped back the safety latch and pocketed the Government Colt. He found a hut under one of the two rocks overlooking the runway: hidden at the foot of the rock face, it was invisible from the air. A sand-coloured makeshift wind sock perched limply over its roof. Joe put on his gloves and tried to open the door with a knife, but, not the finest of lock pickers, he gave up. There was no point in frightening off suspects with a sloppy break in: he would leave that to the experts. The inmates of the desert refuge might return, and he wanted to avoid arousing suspicion.

He strolled across to look at the runway, giving a thumbs-up sign to the pilot as the waiting helicopter came back into view.

Concealed landing lights, impossible to see from any aircraft except from one landing in its axis, skirted the strip. At one end of the runway, Joe almost fell over a pile of rocks: a few tumbled to reveal a small, wooden box and a wire hoop.

He returned to the helicopter and climbed into the right seat. 'Would you call this a dangerous place to land an aeroplane?' he asked.

'Yep', replied the pilot, 'there isn't much room for mistakes, even in a light single.'

'This strip's being used at night. There are lights hidden down each edge, and what looks like a radio beacon at the end of the runway.'

'They're mad! You couldn't get me to land a plane here by day, let alone in the dark! The only way down is on visual: you need an altimeter setting and the wind direction: there's no one down here to tell you what they are, Joe. Between those rocks it's suicide.'

'A tough strip for weekend pilots, huh?'

'For any pilot! No one in his right mind would land here, especially at night.'

The turbine whined up to speed and the helicopter gently lifted off. Once airborne, the pilot wrote down the navigation radials pinpointing his position on his knee pad. On the way back, Joe made some notes he would later complete, as his report.

Joe Davies's report on the desert airstrip was released to the FBI.

The Bureau sent George Lebeda, a Viet Nam vet, to investigate the site. Everything was to be left as it had been found: the Bureau did not want traces of a search to alert its users: it would anger them if they were private citizens, even if this seemed unlikely.

While another federal officer worked carefully on the hut's lock, George Lebeda went down on his hands and knees. He brushed loose sand gingerly aside in the early-morning sunlight and quickly found the cord tied to the base of the door.

'For the love of heaven, look at this! Get behind those rocks. Don't come back until I say.'

They walked away and crouched behind a boulder.

George ran his forefinger gently along the cord, following it around the side of the hut: half way along it was knotted to another length buried in the sand. He untied it carefully and followed the remaining length to a hole drilled through the hut's wooden wall. Then, satisfied it was safe, he called the others back.

'Lucky for that Davies guy he flunked breaking and entry!' His wry humour was greeted with quiet nods from the others: George's nose for trouble was legendary: no one could match that 'Nam experience. He opened the door gently and fingered deftly around for more trouble, then he put his gloves on and entered.

Early-morning light flooded into the hut.

They traced the throat-catching smell inside to warm acid in the bank of powerful lead-acid accumulators clustered against the far wall.

The booby trap had been set on the floor to the left: the can held about five pounds of explosive, the detonator attached to the cord that George had untied minutes before. He picked up a discarded bag. Reading the label, he raised an eyebrow in surprise, folded the bag carefully and put it in his pocket. 'Semtex! I'll be darned. That stuff's made by the Reds. There isn't too much of it sitting around in the U. S. of A.'

'You say something, George?'

'Huh? .... sure, Jerry. You should sweep out our footprints before we leave',

Jerry nodded.

To the right stood a wooden bench. Inside its drawer, he found large, black adhesive numerals and letters with the same backing paper as the crumpled pieces littering the work top. He flattened them out: the same numbers and letters had been used repeatedly.

'These people are crazy: they're changing the plane's registration!'

'Crazy!' grunted Jerry in agreement, and got on with his sweeping.

They met to compare notes in the belly of the Army helicopter, which had ferried them and their equipment a few hours earlier.

'What've you found, Sparks?' George asked the radio engineer.

'Quite an installation, George', he chuckled: 'real sly! The strip lights and beacon are activated by a one-sixty megahertz signal. A plane not more than ten miles off could light up that strip using its transmitter.'

'You guys find anything?' asked George turning to the others.

'Fritz found tire marks going North into the desert. I found landing marks and oil stains both ends of the runway: it means the pilot knows which way the wind's blowing between those rocks: I guess that's why that wind sock's over the hut, but it's no use at night, you can't see it, even if it's lit up.'

'What about the batteries?' asked George.

'Fully charged: density's fine: they're maintained. We've sniffed the hut for drugs. Air samples are being taken back to the lab. There's a latrine behind the rocks.'

George said nothing of the Czechoslovakian plastic explosive. 'Fingerprints?'

'Clean', came the reply.

The following moments of silence were broken only by the whine of the craft's systems. The sun beat mercilessly on the green hull.

'Sparks, you have your radio-controlled IR video camera and lamps here?' asked George.

'Sure, Chief, I always have them on a job.'

'Come with me and we'll set it up.'

After ten minutes George and Sparks returned. Lebeda opened a cold soda and drank it before addressing the others in the big helicopter's belly.

'Now here's what we do', he said....

Mike MacTavish yawned waiting for George Lebeda to relieve him for the 2 a.m. shift. Soon he would be able to go back to his room and sleep off six tiring hours in front of the monitor.

He would make one final sweep.

For the entire torrid month, nothing had shown on the screen. A month of boredom, waiting in vain for something, anything, to happen, argued against wasting any more time, but those years of training kept him going against the errors of the casual observer. He adjusted his glasses, doggedly gripped the small joystick, and once more scanned the airstrip from more than fifty miles away in the observation room in Esperanza.

The technical staff had found a winner: even in the pitch darkness of the moonless desert night, the infra-red video camera installed high in the rock overlooking the strip showed it up clearly. A strong infra-red flood lamp provided enough light while remaining invisible at the site.

He traversed to the motionless wind sock and continued to follow the runway towards its threshold.

Something caught his eye. He retraced his scan. There was a grey spot on the horizon North-West of the strip: it seemed too low to be an aeroplane. In his relief at some action, Mike almost forgot to turn on the recorder.

Someone knocked. He jumped up and opened the door for George Lebeda arriving to take the next shift.

'Wait your turn, buddy', called Mike rushing back to his seat.

Sensing his excitement, George drew up a chair to watch the monitor. He glanced at the recorder to check that it was working. 'Have you reported in?' he asked.

'Not yet', replied Mike. 'The show's just begun.'

George picked up the telephone, dialled a Washington number, and was greeted with a noncommittal, 'ID please', from the other end.

'4395 Lebeda, El Paso, with MacTavish in the observation room at Esperanza. Possible clandestine activity.'

'On file at oh-two-oh-five, Sir', came the reply.

'We'll call back later.'

'Are you recording?' asked the voice.

'Affirmative', replied George. He replaced the handset and watched as, adjusting the set to reduce the glare, Mike zoomed in to get a closer look at the approaching lights. They disappeared.

Mike looked at George in disappointment and wearily commented, 'I guess we woke up Ops for nothing.'

They stared gloomily at the screen: a few moments of excitement had filled them with heady expectation in their hunt.

Seconds later, as it turned parallel to the airstrip and stopped by the hut, they saw the white flash of a pickup truck's lights. Mike switched on the sound recorder.

The Feds waited in silence for almost twenty minutes concentrating on the grey outline of the truck.

Mike yawned and stretched sleepily.

'Maybe he's checking wind direction and barometric pressure', said George.

They jumped at the sound of an alarm the radio engineer had wired to detect a one-hundred-and-sixty-megahertz radio signal. The strip landing lights ignited. The screen flashed white. Mike adjusted the glare and traversed to the end of the landing threshold.

George frowned at the sound monitor. He turned up the volume and groaned in frustration. 'The sound isn't working.' He checked the recording: no sound had been registered. 'We only have the video, Mike.'

His colleague frowned in disappointment. A sound recording would have been of immense value: voices carried far into the desert night, and the equipment, had it worked, could have recorded conversations. George returned to his chair by the monitor.

The truck drew up to the end of the landing area. The driver switched his headlights to full beam and shone them down the axis of the strip.

'He's lighting up the landing threshold', said George.

'At last', breathed his excited companion. He scanned the airspace immediately above the pickup: the heat-sensitive camera showed a bright grey circle descending.

Seconds later, a light, single-engine aircraft landed on the area illuminated by the truck's beam. The pilot waited until the very last instant to switch on his landing lights. The landing was perfect, the V-shaped tail brightly lit by the pickup's beam as the aeroplane rounded for the flare and touched gently down.

'A Bonanza', remarked George, 'and that's no trainee flying it.' The aircraft stopped, turned, and taxied back along the strip before veering towards the hut. The picture blackened: the lights had been extinguished. Mike readjusted the brightness to that provided by the infra-red lamp and zoomed in on the cockpit. The hot engine made the picture bright enough to see movement in both the front and the rear seats of the small aircraft. The left door swung open, and the pilot stepped out onto the wing.

'I'll be darned', said George. 'That looks like a woman!'

'Looks like a woman driving the pickup too', replied Mike.

The women seemed to ignore each other. Then the larger figure of a man jumped from the right wing and embraced the pickup driver. The pilot walked towards the hut, and the pickup driver climbed into the aeroplane's right seat turning, it seemed, to talk: was there someone in the back seat?

The man drove the pickup to the left wing and, unravelling a hose from its bed, walked back and forth between the truck and the wing.

'I guess he's refuelling', said George. 'It looks like drums on the truck contain fuel.'

The pilot disappeared into the hut. By the time she returned, the man had finished filling the left wing and had driven around to fill the right. She tore markings off the Bonanza's wings and tail, and replaced them with adhesive numerals she had brought from the hut. Two figures climbed out of the back seat and walked towards the latrine in the rocks behind the hut. The pilot made her way carefully around the aircraft inspecting its skin in the beam of a flashlight. She raised the motor cowl to check the oil level.

Within minutes, the two figures had returned, and the four-seater was ready to leave. The woman, who had arrived in the pickup, stayed aboard, swapping places with the man, it seemed, who was left behind on the ground.

The monitor glowed white again as the airstrip lights came on. Mike readjusted the glare.

The Bonanza taxied off. Little more than fifteen minutes had passed since its arrival. The aeroplane's powerful engine had had little time to cool. Take off was immediate: the pilot aligned the nose, opened the throttle wide, and the aeroplane gathered speed down the strip. It lifted off. The landing gear disappeared into the hull; both the strip lamps and the aircraft's own lights disappeared into the darkness. The Bonanza's hot exhaust became nothing more than a fleeting grey shadow in the sky.

Mike swung the camera back to the hut. The man was standing motionless as if looking into the air. He walked towards the pickup. Mike zoomed in. The man stopped, turned, and stood as though listening. He stared up at the rock, it seemed, into the camera.

'He may have heard the positioner motor', said George, 'but it should be too far away for him to hear it. I think he's nervous: besides, the aircraft's probably still close enough to drown any noise it's making.'

The man got into the truck. He drove it to the hut and stepped down. 'I guess he's going to use the generator to recharge the batteries', said George. 'That would be noisy.'

'He moves slowly like he's nervous, doesn't he', commented Mike.

For twenty minutes, the man walked, pausing from time to time to look around. He closed the hut door, appeared to re-tie the booby-trap cord and to cover it with sand. He climbed back into the pickup and drove North into the night using side lights until he was far off.

Mike stopped the video and checked the recording. 'You can call Operations, George: I'm going to bed.'

'Good night Mike. I doubt there'll be more action tonight.'

George was right. The airstrip showed no activity for more than a month, but next time it did, the event would end in tragedy.

At the National Security Council meeting, the Director of Central Intelligence, head of the CIA, maintained that, for this agenda item, the 'Company' should handle the case. He strongly argued probable international implications with a site so close to the border, especially because samples taken in the hut indicating trace quantities of cocaine pointed to Central America. Even if one of the domestic federal agencies were to intervene, the CIA's foreign resources would be involved sooner or later, and it might as well be sooner. The council weighed heavily in favour of his position, though responsibility for the case seemed borderline.

The Director decided to test the skills of one of his brighter, young analysts on this mission. John Glenn was one analyst it was difficult to keep out of the field anyway. If his work unearthed trouble, the Director would instruct Don Hailsham, the newly appointed Director of Central and South American Operations, to put Bugs Macpherson on the job too. It would be fine experience for young Glenn to work with this more senior officer. Besides, Macpherson and his younger colleague had a lot in common in their approach to getting answers.

A late-August Virginian heat wave enveloped the lush greenery outside. Sitting casually around an oak, board-room table, a group of analysts discussed the airstrip by the Mexican border. John Glenn had called the meeting in the air-conditioned 'bubble', a conference centre facing the CIA office block in Langley.

An official from the Federal Aviation Administration was invited to help to track the Bonanza using ground-control radar. He completed his presentation with an explanation of a 'squawk.' 'It's like a bird in the air', he said: 'if it squawks, you know where to look for it. We need one to identify an aircraft by using its transponder. That's how I can follow your plane on our screens, Gentlemen. It's important: we can't trace a small, low-flying aircraft in that type of mountainous terrain if it's not identified by its transponder.'

The FAA official sat down. A discouraged silence fell over the room: for some seconds, no one spoke, then John Glenn stood. 'If we can't count on the FAA to trace the Bonanza because the pilot is unlikely to use his transponder, there's only one solution: we have to follow him in the air.'

The official laughed: 'Mr Glenn, the FAA is a civilian body: air chases are military business: they're dangerous during the day, let alone at night! Your idea seems out of the question: we can't allow this in our airspace.' As far as he was concerned, the discussion was over. He packed his documents, thanked Glenn for the invitation, and left the analysts with their problem. The door closed behind him.

The silence was broken only by the hiss of the air conditioning. The analysts studied their pens or looked out of the window, anywhere but at each other. John Glenn sighed. 'Look! We have a job to do. We can't let these drug dealers slip out of our hands. If no one has a better idea', he went on, 'mine's the only one: we need a small plane available twenty-four hours a day. The next time they come, we'll follow.'

'How are you going to follow in the dark? asked a colleague.

'If we take a high-winged plane, we can fly close enough. There's no upward visibility from the Bonanza cockpit: we can limit the risk of being seen by flying above them without navigation lights. Then we just need to shine a flashlight onto the tail if we need the aircraft registration: I guess they could notice the beam: that's a problem.'

'At night like that, you could collide.'

'We'll have to rely on the pilot to avoid a collision.'

'How are you going to home on their plane, John? You'll be more than ten miles away.'

'I can fit out a light single with short-range radar. I don't expect problems.'

Bugs Macpherson sat in a corner listening intently to Glenn's plan. His deep-set, grey eyes assumed a look of concern: these tactics could end in disaster. One of the Company's most experienced and successful analysts, Bugs heartily disapproved of the project but listened on in silence. He ran his fingers through prematurely grey hair that made a strange contrast with the youthful lines of his face. He was the only person in the room not wearing a suit: Bugs had acquired a penchant for loose collars and tweed jackets during his field assignments in Europe. He drew a sheet of paper from his pocket and made a few notes: he had no better ideas, and decided not to stand in the path of Glenn's breakneck methods: he would regret that decision. 'Surely', he said, 'if we can detect their plane using radar, they can detect ours whether above or behind.'

'We'll have to take that risk', said John.

There were no more questions.

'With Mr Hailsham's agreement, I would like to handle the operation myself, and leave tonight for Texas', said Glenn.

Don Hailsham, the Director of Central and South American Operations, was the senior officer. The Director had told him to put Glenn on the case, and he wasn't going to argue the point. If this young blood wanted to kill himself, that was his problem. That was how the young, energetic John Glenn got his clearance and left that same day to live out the final hours of his short life.

A short-range, radar locating device was successfully fitted to the Skyhawk.

As the small aircraft circled the Hudspeth beacon one night in mid-September, George Lebeda was monitoring the strip with the infra-red video. His voice crackled over the radio: 'They're lifting off now. There's a man in the right seat: the woman stayed with the truck. Darned sound monitor failed on us again. Good hunting. Out.'

'Roger', replied the pilot. It was time to close. A white point flashed on the screen. The Skyhawk veered South and started to climb. The pilot picked up his intercom again. 'Golf Charlie to control: course three one zero: climbing to six thousand.'

They saw no sign of their quarry until the pilot noticed a shadow against the distant lights of El Paso. The radar had worked well. The pilot came no closer than two hundred feet behind the Bonanza in the clear desert night.

Reaching the El Paso Terminal Control Area, the Bonanza veered North, and the Skyhawk pilot gave his new coordinates over the reserved frequency.

'I want to try now to get their number', said John.

'I guess it's as good a time as any', sighed the pilot.

He flew in closer, positioning the Skyhawk above and to one side of the Bonanza. Both aircraft had stopped climbing at seven thousand feet, only a few thousand above the peaks of the treacherous terrain below. The pilot gently tipped the wings and applied reverse rudder for a few seconds, enabling John Glenn to shine the flashlight's powerful beam at the Bonanza's tail section.

'Got it', he shouted in triumph, jotting the number down on a notepad. 'I don't think they saw us, but that's a really bright beam!'

The pilot gently righted the plane and announced the Bonanza's number into his microphone. In their moment of triumph, the Bonanza veered off and climbed. Moments later, the Skyhawk skipped. Steel-tipped bullets tore through its cowling, severing wires, and destroying a magneto. The petrol pump flew off in fragments.

They lost height. The pilot announced a Mayday, frantically trying to switch in the remaining magneto. Smoke drifted into the cabin. He cut off the fuel supply.

They were passing through five thousand feet when he announced he was attempting an emergency landing at the base of the Hueco Mountains. The pilot's voice belied fear: he said he could see nothing in the darkness below, and that is why he didn't see the power lines as he veered steeply in to land: they caught a wing in a blinding flash, and the craft cartwheeled into the black rocks below.

Nobody could have survived that pyre of flames.

They met for brunch in downtown Chicago: Jim was due to interview O'Grady that afternoon after psychiatric tests.

Bugs called Washington again. He was in a black mood when he re-joined Jim.

'You look like a thunder cloud, Bugsy!'

'He's putting Duval on the case: he wastes a lot of time: if Hailsham knew the department better, he'd leave Duval in his hole.'

'It's up to Hailsham to choose his case officer, Bugsy. If you want this show, go and see the Director.'

'I did that when Glenn died in the crash: he thinks I've enough to keep me occupied: I doubt he'll give me Chicago against Hailsham's wishes: the Director's not going to challenge his judgement so quickly after his promotion.'

'Fine, so now you know, quit griping and eat your burger.'

Bugs munched slowly, thinking of John Glenn. Everyone in the department had been shocked by his violent death, not least Bugs, who had gone to the Director of Central Intelligence straight after the funeral to ask for the case. He had agreed, sensing that Bugs had seen something of himself in his bright, young, dead colleague. Bugs had admitted to the older man his guilt for not having killed Glenn's wild idea about a night flight over the desert.

'Anything else biting you, Bugs?' asked Jim through a sly grin.

Bugs laughed: the joke had been cracked by family and friends since his devotion to the collection of insects had earned him his strange sobriquet as a boy. At first, the nickname had embarrassed him: now he took its use by others to be a sign of friendship. 'No, just thinking about Glenn.'

'Poor kid: 'hell of a way to die: 'you any the wiser?'

'No: the plane was burnt out: there's nothing recognisable left. The pilot sent out a Mayday at a thousand feet: he didn't see the power lines in the dark.'

'If anyone deserved an unpleasant death, it's the bastard who shot them down....' mumbled Jim. He sipped his coffee. '.... poor guys died for nothing.'

'Not quite, they did radio the other aircraft's registration.'

'You traced the aeroplane?'

'Not yet.'

'I guess they'd change the number anyway.'

'If the pilot's using controlled airports, she may not want to change too often: it could be noticed. We've got a team searching control tower records in Texas. I'm not real optimistic about finding much, but we're still trying, and local feds are helping.'

''Nice to know the Company needs us too sometimes!' Jim grinned.

Bugs put more ketchup on his hamburger.

'She'd have been frightened off', continued Jim, 'she won't go back: she would've heard her registration radioed.'

'John's radio was tuned to a military frequency: my guess is she or a passenger in the plane saw Glenn's flashlight, but we shall never know.'

'Wild project!'

'Yes, and I could have stopped it.' whispered Bugs with a frown.

All there was to be seen in the media was the wild attack on the presidential party in Chicago and the murder of his secretary of state. A blanket order was given to concentrate most of the security forces in the country on finding and detaining the terrorists. A lot of attention was given to the antics of the Chicago cop, O'Grady as the story of the events came out: he was to be a valuable witness.

Jim telephoned that afternoon from the Federal Building on South Dearborn: he sounded tired.

'What's wrong?' asked Bugs.

Jim sighed, 'O'Grady was murdered last night. We'd better forget the meeting', continued Jim, 'I'm going to the murder site with the Violent Crimes Squad: 'no point meeting now he's dead.'

'Poor guy', said Bugs.

'The politicians have been mudslinging at City Hall: the opposition claims O'Grady should never have been released from custody and anyway, policemen with missing daughters shouldn't guard Presidents.'

'Where would politics be without hindsight?'

'.... or without the Mob? Frankly, Bugs, this whole O'Grady case reeks of it.'

'Why, Jim? I thought you'd cleaned up Chicago years ago.'

'It's text-book, Bugs: you kidnap 21-year-old Corinne O'Grady; keep her under cover until you can use her cop father; blackmail him into cooperating; get him out on bail if he's caught, and shoot him before he denounces you.'

'It's sad to see one family suffer all that misfortune.' Bugs sighed. 'I won't stay if Hailsham insists on sending Duval to Chicago',

'Sorry to see you go, Bugsy: if there's anything I can do....'

'No thanks, Jim, ... well, ... maybe there's something: how'd you like to bend the rules some?'

Jim laughed.

'I'd like you to keep me informed', went on Bugs, 'I'm not that enthusiastic about Duval, and I guess Hailsham will cut off communications between us: he doesn't want me around at all. That leaves you as my only real source of information.'

'I'll think about it: no promises.'

'I'll leave in the morning for Washington.'

'In that case, Bugsy, you're coming to my garbage party: it'll get your spirits up, and clear your nostrils for that Washington smog.'

'What are you talking about?'

'Bring a clothes peg for your nose. 219 S. Dearborn at 5. Don't be late. Dress very casually!'

'Jim, what ...?'

It was too late; he had rung off.

Fifty floors above street level, the Streeterville pad overlooked Chicago to the West and Lake Michigan to the North and South. Bugs walked to the wide bay window and gazed at the horizon. The Michigan and Indiana shorelines glistened in the sun. The shining buildings of the city itself dominated by the Sears Tower stood majestically around him. He pressed his forehead against the window pane and tried to look down at the bustling street below.

His folks had lived on the Southside, working hard to scrape together the money to send him to college. There had been conflict and ingratitude. Now they were no longer around to thank for the sacrifices they had made. At the time, he had not understood the financial burden on them of his college years. His dad had been shocked by Bugs' choice of studies: why didn't he want to be an engineer, or an accountant, or a lawyer? Mercifully, he won a scholarship to Northwestern to research for his doctorate in sociology, and the old man's attitude had changed: his son looked successful: soon he would be called 'doctor', and, suddenly, universities were falling over each other to offer him money.

Bugs went to England in 1964 to continue his research: it was over there that the Company took an interest in the young sociologist. He had been invited to lecture for a year at the new University of Sussex and to continue his work on Eurocommunism.

A paper on working-class attitudes attracted the attention of a case officer in London: Bugs was classified as a security risk and summoned to the U.S. Embassy. The case officer satisfied himself that the young lecturer was taking nothing more than a pedagogical interest in his work, and, impressed by Bugs' clear thought, gingerly asked him for information on a known left-wing activist at the University.

Completing his research and publishing his thesis, Bugs had vainly hoped for a teaching job in England, but little money was available for university posts, and there was already stiff competition from local nationals. The case officer had remembered him, however, and Bugs was offered a position as a junior analyst in the Embassy. The choice was easy: either he could go home and face the draft, or join the CIA and stay in Europe: either way he would work in the service of his country: he accepted to work for the Company reasoning that he could continue his doctoral research.

Bugs had never regretted that decision. He had quickly made himself useful as one of the few analysts to know about the roots of European anarchism and to understand local attitudes to left-wing politics. His penetrating style appeared more and more frequently in reports prepared by the Embassy for Langley.

He matured towards field work as he gained experience. He developed and ran a team of bogus American sympathisers working on the fringe of the Irish Republican Army and another trying to penetrate British contacts of the Baader-Meinhoff gang. Thanks to them, lives were saved, and Bugs refined his knowledge of terrorism.

Jenny was completing her residency in Endocrinology at one of the London teaching hospitals. Both far from their American homeland, the two had fallen in love, married in the tradition of young elopers in 1969 at Gretna Green on the Scottish border, and lived their childless marriage with the intensity they lived their careers.

In 1974 his European work for the Company led to a year's assignment in Tel Aviv to study the work of the Mossad in countering Palestinian subversion.

The lock gates opened to allow a small boat to sail into the mouth of the Chicago River. Bugs broke from his reverie. He was just trying to put it off. He lifted the handset. The receptionist's voice was cool: she answered with mid-Western clarity.

He said, 'Pass me Mr Hailsham in Langley, please.' Long minutes, he waited in silence.

'I'll call you back when I have him, Mr Macpherson.' The woman was a model of patience. After fifteen minutes, she traced his superior and passed the call to the desk where Bugs was making notes on the previous day's events.

Bugs so deeply distrusted Hailsham, he had difficulty speaking to him calmly. How could he respect a man who kept his own tail dry while he expected his subordinates to swim in deep waters? Bugs disliked his boundless arrogance and his talent for soft-talking his way out of incompetence.

Yet Hailsham survived: Bugs stuck his neck out every day for the greater glory of this institutional survivor. Bugs lived for his job, and he was apprehensive that dislike for this bureaucratic chief would lead one day to hot-headed words he would later regret. More than just a pen pusher, the Director of Central and South American Operations was dangerous: Bugs had watched him fire a capable colleague; poisoning the opinions of his own superiors against his quarry; reducing the man's responsibilities. He had performed the *coup de grace* personally at budget time with the blessing of a cost-conscious Director on a man broken by boredom and obsessed with self-doubt. Hailsham was not the type Bugs liked to invite home to dinner, but hostility was unforgivable among the reputedly cool-headed analytical staff, so Bugs adopted a policy of minimum contact, and tried to control his dislike on the rare occasions he could not avoid speaking to the man.

Hailsham was terse over the telephone. 'Yes, I'm sending Ed to handle Chicago: you should come back.'

'But Duval doesn't have experience in terrorism.'

'It's too early to say if that's necessary.'

'Here we need a field man, I'm sure of it', pleaded Bugs: 'I really would like to handle the case.'

'I've taken my decision, John, and I'm not changing it. Ed's fully qualified. I'm surprised to hear you mudslinging.'

'I really think you should reconsider.'

'It's too late. I've told the FBI Ed's our man, and he's on his way. You get back to hunting Glenn's killers.'

'That's moving along.'

' 'That so? 'Any results?'

Bugs had uncovered nothing.

Hailsham continued. 'Leave your report in Ed's hands. I don't need a copy at this stage, and Ed may need to make changes before sending it to me.'

Bugs seethed, listening in stony silence to more directives, and banged down the handset when Hailsham had finished. He strode to the window and peered South along Lake Shore Drive past the green splendour of Grant Park towards the stately facade of the Field Museum.

It had been different in Europe: there had been camaraderie, especially during the Italian crises in 1981. The Company had presented a united front, and discretely helped Italy, America's friend, fight the anarchical gangrene in its society.

This work ended in the arrest of Aldo Moro's Red Brigade murderers in the month of March, appeasing, through the efforts of a stalwart *Carabiniere,* General Della Chiesa, public outrage over the assassination of the President of the National Council. Later that year the P2 Lodge scandal awakened long-dormant nightmares by exposing an attempt by powerful right-wing idealists to control Italy's Institutions, and, on May 13, Mehmet Ali Agca tried to kill the Pope, leading to years of research into the extravagant claims made in his defence of links with Turkish terrorists and a shadowy contact with Bulgaria. The American public, awakened by the attempt on the Pope's life was jolted out of its complacency a second time before 1981 was out: on December 17, a United States military officer working with NATO was kidnapped in Verona by Red Brigade terrorists. The disappearance of Brigadier General James Lee Dozier brought the order from Washington to transfer many key American intelligence personnel from all over Europe to help search for him in Italy.

The Christmas of 1981 was a lonely one: Jenny stayed behind in their Kensington apartment in London. The long hours of questioning and analysis had not permitted Bugs the luxury of Christmas with his wife. Nino Glavina, a *Carabiniere* colonel assigned to the investigation, took pity on him, and invited Bugs to his own place, both he, and his wife, Edda, speaking good English. Bugs had even learnt some fair Italian.

Nino spoke of middle-class frustration with these almost uncontrollable forces of Italian anarchism, and of national embarrassment with the pre-war years of Fascism and post-war years of corruption. Deep into that Christmas night, he talked about the role of the Communist Party as a focus of resistance during the war.

Bugs could still hear Nino's lilting Italian voice: 'The Communists, *Amico-Mio*, my friend, have become like the others: all they do is line their pockets and criticise the Christian Democrats: they are as self-seeking, and as greedy, as all the rest! Roman politics are powerless against corruption. How can you expect young, idealistic Italians to trust these incompetent opportunists?'

Many thought that social improvement through the heavy, Roman wheels of state would be slow, and an anarchist fringe appeared among Italy's youth believing that society itself would first have to be destroyed before a new order could be built on its ashes: that was how in 1970, accepting neither God nor master, having preached his nihilist principles for more than two years in his Journal of the Proletarian Left, Renato Curcio established the Red Brigades. His brainchild was to foster more than a decade of urban terror.

The American general's rescue in January 1982 was an intense emotional release for a people who had not felt pride in its institutions for many years: the Italian forces of order had shown that victory against the Red Brigades was possible after all. From that moment on, a new spirit of confidence beset the judiciary, and, one by one, important *brigatisti* fell into the hands of a police community fired up by Della Chiesa's campaign to stamp out the Red Brigade columns: working in Milan, Venice, Rome and Verona, his teams had arrested more than thirty key terrorists by April 1982.

Nino Glavina's group helped pioneer the method of bargaining with the more lukewarm *brigatisti*: after all, they were always so young. The technique was to isolate the weaker personalities and to convince them to trade information for sentence reductions. The information led to raids on hideouts and to the capture, and conviction, of most of the movement's leaders, though a few escaped abroad.

Bugs had interviewed these apostles of anarchism in halting Italian during the January of 1981: he had returned to London a few months later, a dedicated opponent of the urban guerrilla.

He watched a small aeroplane take to the sky from a runway built on the lake shore by the Field Museum. It veered East. He thought of calling Jenny: she would be worried about him now she was back from her night duty at the National Institutes of Health. He lifted the handset and punched in their Washington number. Following him around the world, she had learnt to live with the constraints of his career and his sombre moods.

She walked into the South-side precinct just after 3.30 p.m. She seemed to be in her early twenties. Her expression was vacant. Her clothes, flimsy for the cold outside, were filthy. The duty officer thought she was a vagrant and prepared to walk around the counter to escort her back out the door. 'What do you want, Ma'am?' he asked.

She tried to reply but had difficulty speaking.

He repeated the question.

She looked drugged: her eyes were red with fatigue. 'Please, ... my dad', she sobbed. Tears welled up in her eyes.

A nut, thought the duty officer. 'What about your dad?'

She sobbed for a few moments, and then gasped, ''At the Central District: Pat O'Grady. Tell him I'm here. I'm his daughter.'

They arrived at the 103rd. Street tip at 6 p.m. They parked and walked up the hill towards a small hut amid an overwhelming stench. Jim grinned wryly. 'That's no ordinary garbage, Bugsy: you're about to sift through the offal of one of the richest men in Chicago. As a member of the Company, you are honoured to assist at this, my friend; one of the finest rituals of the Chicago FBI. This is class garbage from a class act. Here comes the truck now.'

Bugs wondered when Jim would stop clowning around.

'You guys from Langley may find this difficult to believe, but the garbage truck coming through the gates is being driven by a Bureau agent.'

'Doesn't surprise me at all', laughed Bugs.

Jim disregarded the comment, and continued: 'To the untrained eye, the men in that truck look like ordinary garbage collectors: false! They are not employed by the city of Chicago, but by the US Federal Government. These two gentlemen risk their necks once a week to collect the elegant refuse of Chicago's richest worm, Don Carlo Catanzaro himself. Your language skills could be of value this afternoon. What do you think of that?'

The question was clearly rhetorical: Jim walked towards the truck, which stopped, and backed over a large plastic sheet on the ground. Hydraulic pumps whined; the heavy bed tilted; refuse poured onto the sheet, and three men in white overalls and face masks appeared at the hut door.

'Bugs, I'd like you to meet Al, Ted and Dave. They come each week from Quantico to assist in this delicate operation. Wouldn't miss it for the world, would you guys?'

They chorused, 'Nope!'

'We thought you'd appreciate using your special skills in this operation requiring high technology and a firm grasp of Italian. Dig in, don't be shy. Whatever it is, if it looks strange, stuff it in one of these plastic bags: we have all sizes....and don't finger anything, Bugsy: wear the gloves, mask and the shoe covers. They do teach you this kind of thing out East, don't they? 'Could be embarrassing to find your fingerprints on broken, mobster soup plates.'

Dave handed Bugs white overalls, a paper hat, thin rubber gloves, a mask, shoe covers and tweezers. Bugs laughed and prepared to help sift through Don Carlo Catanzaro's garbage.

They sat cradling a welcome Scotch to burn out the foul vapours lodged in their throats.

Jim had moved into his Near-Northside flat leaving the house to his children and divorced wife. Tall and athletic, in his mid-forties, He had become a bachelor with severe misgivings: fear of loneliness drove him into bars and clubs at night, and, over the two years since Bugs had seen him in the throes of domestic upset, Jim had cultivated a circle of racy friends among Chicago's growing community of middle-aged divorced people. He bought a sporty car, successfully pursued some very attractive women, and found himself a part-time housekeeper now that the alimony cut into the pie. He spent more time now than he had ever done on a tennis court, and was rebuilding some of his old confidence, but the thought of slipping into old age alone still haunted him.

The news from the Dearborn office had been discouraging: even the dead woman, whose face had been left intact, remained unidentified. The Los Angeles FBI thought they might have a lead, but wouldn't confirm. Jim had sent photos, dental charts and fingerprints of both women to Interpol and to the CIA at Langley, but it would take days to circulate the data, and the chances of success with the international agencies were slim anyway.

The roadblocks set up around Chicago to apprehend the Secretary of State's terrorist killer had been a waste of time: they had been mobilised to appease the City Hall's thirst for action, any action. A banquet in honour of the President's visit had been cancelled after his security service had whisked him back to Washington, and the Republicans were baying for the blood of the Democratic majority.

Jim slumped into the soft armchair. 'They must have known they'd never get out alive. It worries me to see fanaticism close to home: it was just like Jihadi terrorists: you can't defend yourself from the urban guerrilla with a suicidal desire for martyrdom.' He swirled the cool, blonde Scotch around his glass. 'Islamist terrorists! That's what we should certainly look at, Bugs. Are there any other groups that would sponsor such an attack?'

'If you have all night, we can go through the list right now. There are almost two hundred known terrorist organisations world-wide, and none of them on our side.' Bugs swallowed some Scotch and frowned at Jim. 'We do a lousy job selling our ideals. It's easy to glorify socialism; a little class jealousy goes a long way. You try explaining the merits of a healthy economy to someone poor and hungry: he doesn't listen; his worry is getting something to eat. The corrupt rich in developing countries like to have us around, and we need to feel wanted: but we're wrong to back privileged minorities against a whole people. Some violent person on a mission will always be around to harass us in the name of the down-trodden. We don't know how to sell our values to the grass roots. Jim, ours is the most market-oriented country in the world, but it does the worst job marketing its ideals: you'd think that all those talented PR and marketing people would have found an international 'I Love US, waspish Capitalism' package by now.'

'You're exaggerating, Bugs: people are not that stupid.'

'No, they're not stupid, but they need to be talked to and led: we don't make that effort. Throughout the developing world, they're led by opportunism and Marxist thinking. We don't need to talk communism, just the Christian work ethic this country was built on.' Bugs stood to stretch his legs. 'Envy's a powerful emotion: it thrives on empty stomachs, but if a man has work, pride reigns.'

Jim nodded, 'I guess Washington's close to the moon for the average guy.'

'We swim against the tide, then wonder why we're swept away. Lenin understood that the masses triumph in the long run; Mao understood it, and I guess we won't come through as heroes until we understand it too.'

Jim felt uncomfortably out of his field. 'Hey, calm down, Bugsy: you're in the Windy City here; time out!'

Bugs marched to the window. He drew back the curtain and looked outside. The evenings were getting shorter now, and the leaves were changing colour. Soon, Lincoln Park would be a symphony of ochres and russets, and the first polar winds would begin to freeze the lake shore.

Jim broke the silence. 'We've been reviewing videos of the terrorist's actions. We're assuming he and the women acted as a team.'

''Great deduction! One hell of a coincidence if they hadn't.'

'He may have worn a police uniform and packed an SW 357: two outfits were stolen a few hours before from a cop's apartment in O'Grady's district; hats; badges and all. 'Fool cop was playing hooky at the ball game. He said he'd won a free ticket through the mail, but can't remember in what sweepstake. The guy's a baseball fanatic; slim; weighs one-sixty; five foot ten; just like the terrorist. He's got a cast-iron alibi because he went with his cronies, but he got fired. The break-in was clean: the thief only took what he needed: no money.'

'It would have been brighter to make it look unprofessional. What makes you so sure the break-in's linked to the assassination attempt?'

'O'Grady was shot with this same revolver: both slugs were 357 jacketed, hollow-points fired from the SW belonging to this cop.'

Bugs pursed his lips.

'I think he was shot by someone he knew', continued Jim: 'the body was in a neighbourhood he never entered alone. He had to have a reason for going there: experienced cops in rough neighbourhoods keep clear of areas like that off the job.'

'Maybe he was shot first, and dumped there.'

'No, Bugs: one slug was fired real close and bounced off the skull into a wall. The other was fired into his head at close range as he lay on the ground. The body wasn't moved or dragged. The dog was shot too: it was lying by the corpse.'

'O'Grady could have been attacked by hoodlums who had stolen the 357, Jim?'

'So, what was he doing in that alley?'

'Dog chased a cat?' asked Bugs. Jim looked irritated. 'Maybe you're right, Jim, conjecture is useful. Pour me another Scotch so we can make up some more tales to fit the facts.'

Jim removed the cork from his precious bottle of single malt, and they drank in silence for a few moments, each lost in his thoughts.

'O'Grady's daughter turned up today at a South-side district', said Jim, 'dishevelled, but alive. She's in hospital getting over the shock. Doesn't know about her pa's death yet. It's a weird story: she's been chained to a bed for two months under a tent and forced to listen to pop music through a headset. She's begun to go deaf: that has frightened her. She can tell us nothing useful about her kidnappers, but she bit a white arm before she lost consciousness in the car. She didn't see much else, not even when her captors released her this morning.'

Bugs appeared thoughtful. 'Was the tent pitched inside a room, Jim?'

'Yes, she said that.'

'I saw that happen in Italy.'

Jim continued his report. 'We've found the store that rented the women the motorcycle and sold them their gear', said Jim: 'a cash deal, and no questions asked. We have to assume for now that the killer got into the hospital wearing the stolen police uniform. He may have given O'Grady a sign from the window to make some noise in the courtyard, then put on a white coat over the uniform, and entered the ward. I guess he was lucky there was only one bodyguard, Bugsy: with both there, he would never have got out alive. After the murder, he dropped the white coat in the laundry room, picked up the police hat, and pretended he was chasing the killer. Then he left with a cop entering the ward right after the shooting: we haven't found that cop yet, which seems kind of strange.'

'Why would he leave the murder weapon with his fingerprints all over it on the window sill?' asked Bugs.

'I guess he just threw it there not to be caught with it, or maybe he went back to the window to check on O'Grady and forgot it', replied Jim.

'It's the same P.38 used for the killings?' asked Bugs.

'No doubt about it', replied Jim.

'....and fingerprints?'

'Smudged, identifiable, but not on file', replied Jim. 'Maybe that's why this guy's so cool-headed: he probably doesn't have a record, but that's weird too, leaving us his fingerprints. I've asked for an international search, but we haven't any suspects, and without a record, we're baying at the moon.'

'I believe he's cool because he's good at what he does, but well-trained people don't leave evidence lying around like fingerprints on a murder weapon', said Bugs, 'that is, not unless they have a reason…' He pursed his lips and stared at the floor. '....but what could that be?'

Jim's thoughts turned to the evening's forage among Chicago's garbage. 'Why did you want to keep that little red book today, Bugsy?'

'It's a souvenir. Besides, who would have thought 'The Thoughts of Chairman Mao Tse Tung on Peoples' War' would be sitting on a Mob don's bookshelf?'

'The book was in his garbage', corrected Jim.

'And the inscription's too intellectual for a mobster', continued Bugs. He had noted it before the little red book disappeared to the Quantico lab with the torn envelopes, cigarette ends, cracked plates and other snippets of Don Carlo Catanzaro's cosseted life. The lab would analyse the phlegm on the butts, trace the envelopes and lift the fingerprints, check the prints on the broken crockery, analyse any traces of tissue to see if it was human, verify handwriting: in fact, there was no end to the ingenious methods by which the FBI kept tabs on the Catanzaro family. It was all expensive and possibly useful in the long run, but there were no guarantees, and the old Don wasn't stupid: his own security had been honed to perfection through years of experience in dealing with authority. Bugs remembered the inscription in Mao's Little Red Book: *To C.C.: Our means of slitting America's soft underbelly may be one, but our ends will be forever opposed. With thanks, M.*

'A certain M. wrote the inscription. He's a cocky son of a bitch: not expecting Catanzaro to slit his throat, that's for sure! I guess M. wanted to say that the Mob's means are violence, corruption, and so on, and C.C. must be Carlo Catanzaro. Anyway, they seem to know each other. The idea of an American soft underbelly and ends opposed to the Mob give M. a political identity, Jim', said Bugs, 'did you see when the book was published?'

'No, surprise me.'

'It was the first English-language edition of 1967, published in Peking eighteen years ago, and the date of dedication, June 1st, 1985.'

'All that time lost', laughed Jim, 'in Catanzaro getting a Communist education!'

'It's a Mr Ephraim Levine', said the secretary over the telephone.

'Who's he?' asked Jim.

'I don't know: he won't tell me: 'only wants to talk to you.'

He sighed, 'Put him through, Emma.'

The handset hissed and beeped.

'Mr Curry?' came a foreign-sounding voice.

'Speaking.'

'Ephraim Levine, I'm a guest at the Israel Investment and Export Authority in Chicago.'

'What can I do for you, Ephraim?' asked Jim.

'May I call you Jim?'

'Go ahead, Ephraim. What can I do for you?'

'Not for me, Jim: I want to do something for you: we have identified one of the women in the photographs circulated by the CIA last month. The instructions, I believe, were to call you.'

Jim sat up. 'Who is she?'

'I can't discuss this by phone, but I'd be pleased to show you the file in this office.'

'I'll be there right away.'

'Fine', said Ephraim. 'Just show your federal badge at the reception desk, and ask for me personally: 174 North Michigan.'

Jim replaced the handset. 'A break', he whispered.

The office was clean: not a scrap of paper lay on any horizontal surface.

Jim stepped up and shook a sun-tanned hand. They exchanged polite words and sat facing each other.

Ephraim unlocked a drawer and drew out a file. 'I'll pass you the documents one by one. You may take notes, but you may not take any document away or make copies of them.'

'Thanks', said Jim. ''You guys heard of photocopies?'

'That's what I said: not possible.' Ephraim passed him a notepad and a pencil.

'OK', sighed Jim, 'go ahead.'

The snapshot was of a young, tanned face, not the grey skin of the morgue, nor the unfocused stare of the dead. She might have been a young mother with children and a fond husband. Jim returned the photo. Ephraim exchanged it with a résumé of the woman's background. Born Fatima Al-Othman in 1959 at the Shatila refugee settlement outside Beirut, she had emigrated to Syria in 1977 and left Damascus for Libya in 1978. Her parents, Sunni Muslims, still lived in the camp despite crippling Shiite militia attacks in mid-1985.

In the face of a young Israel, they had fled their lands in 1948: afraid of a post-war flood of Zionist passion in Palestine, her father had joined a column of North-bound refugees, taking his wife and young family with him. Settling with cousins in Shatila, he had never found a way in this Christian-Arab, French-speaking culture to shake off his new poverty and shame. Abu Al-Othman had aged quickly, and slid into apathy: in Palestine, he had lived easily, as his forefathers had for centuries: now he was consumed with hatred for those who, he claimed, had snatched his homeland, and he had bequeathed his hatred to his children.

Listening to the elders in the evenings sing and talk of lands and of a way of life, of which she felt cruelly cheated, the young Fatima had made her own a cause the world was trying to forget. Little about her time in Shatila appeared in the Israeli dossier, but there was no need: her story had been told a thousand times in the annals of Palestinian terrorism.

Ephraim passed Jim more documents.

She had been a cadre in the Palestinian Research Organisation, the registry of the claims of dispossessed Palestinians against the state of Israel. She would not have trained as a terrorist. A report pieced together her movements between 1977 and 1979 concluding she was linked to the radical National Front. She had enrolled as a student in Damascus and Tripoli, but the poor quality of her academic work exposed her cover to agents working in the universities.

The Mossad lost contact with Fatima after she left for Libya, but an unconfirmed report dated early 1983 mentioned she might be working in Italy. However, she resurfaced in Santa Ana, California, as a Carmen Muñoz, once more a university student. An Israeli sympathiser working for the airlines noticed the frequency of her trips to Asuncion, where Paraguay remained a key target in the search for Nazi war criminals. Local agents discovered she was trying to obtain funds to finance National Front subversion against Israel. Her attempt had been thwarted by skilful undercover action, and she had been sent home empty-handed not suspecting her cover had been blown. She had been followed on a return trip via Bogota, where it was suspected she had a lover.

A final document recommended that her Colombian stop-overs be notified to the US Drug Enforcement Agency surmising they could be related to drug running. The advice had been struck through with a note saying that there was insufficient evidence to warrant an alert and that Israeli resources alone were preferable in tracking the woman for the time being.

'I understand why you don't want these files to leave your office', said Jim wryly.

Ephraim remained impassive.

'Do you have the dates of her trips to South America?' asked Jim.

'Yes, here they are.'

Jim noted them down.

'For other information, you'll have to see other persons in South America. Call me at this number if you need to, and I'll arrange a meeting.' Levine passed Jim a slip of paper.

Jim walked back along the bustling Chicago sidewalks.

In his office, reading through the notes he had taken, he thought of Bugs but decided not to call until he had discussed the idea with his boss, reasoning that the Bureau couldn't afford to get involved in kitchen-sink dislikes between Company employees. Sooner or later he would inform Bugs anyway about Ephraim's information, but for now, his duty was only to the newly-arrived Ed Duval. He walked down the corridor and knocked at the CIA case officer's closed door, which was also housed, not far from Jim's own office, in the Hoover building on Dearborn.

Duval let him in, a mirthless grin skulking about the corners of his mouth. He was disconcertingly casual about Levine's information and bewildered Jim with his manner of jotting down pointless details. Duval was like a sponge: he absorbed without selectivity and encouraged no discussion. Jim strolled back to his office irritated over Duval's empty conversation: it had none of the helpfulness he was used to with Bugs.

A photograph of the dead Fatima Al-Othman lay on his desk: it reminded him to access the computer file of her alias, Carmen Muñoz, over the monitor. The set crackled into life: he punched in some codes and one-fingered her name. The screen blinked and scrolled an early opinion, sketchily authored by the LA Bureau, that Muñoz was 'into drugs and smuggling illegal immigrants.' It was followed by an extract of a report dated December 1984 stating she might be involved with cocaine peddlers in Los Angeles. A final note added that Mossad agents had searched her apartment in 1985 and had found incriminating material.

He called the operations room to announce identification of the body. Fatima's parents would be notified by the Red Cross and flown out to claim the corpse. Later they would be questioned by the Bureau and flown back to Beirut with Fatima in a box. 'One less burial of an unknown stiff by City Hall', he mumbled to himself, 'and one less terrorist on the streets to shoot at our politicians.'

The Washington Memorial Parkway out to Company headquarters in Langley was free of heavy traffic. Returning from Washington National, Jenny rolled up to the security barrier. It galled her not to be allowed to see where her husband worked. How many times had he visited her at NIH? The block looked like a fortress of grey stone and glass: it was largely hidden from prying eyes by woodland surrounding the site and a small white satellite dish perched demurely between the block and the barrier.

She turned to Bugs in the passenger seat. 'Hurry home spy man.'

Bugs whispered a fond, 'Maybe', in her ear. 'I have to catch up on my papers, honey.'

A Virginia state trooper swung the security bar. Bugs walked off to the 'fortress' waving as Jenny turned and drove away.

The mail waiting on his desk was in Carol's order of priority, with papers needing his signature on the top. Going through the paperwork on his desk would take willpower.

He read that progress in identifying John Glenn's aerial killers was nil. Field personnel from domestic operations were still searching the Southern states for a lead on the Bonanza. The team was working hand in hand with local FBI agents: Bugs intended to continue that policy as far as he could.

He thought again about requesting the Chicago case. He had intended to do so that morning, but he wasn't in the mood for a fight with Hailsham.

Carol walked in with a coffee. Bugs groaned appreciatively. 'Just what I need!'

'You may like to know, Bugs, that Leroy Corbin's in Texas today: he's sifting control-tower records at Addison Field, just North of Dallas.

He eyed the stack of papers on his desk: it was not where his priorities lay. 'Carol, why don't you book me a flight to the airfield right now.' She laughed and stepped back into her office.

Bugs lifted the phone and punched in his Georgetown number. 'Jen?'

'I just got back, honey.'

'Jen, can you prepare my overnight bag: I'm going to Dallas.' There was no answer. 'Jen? Are you OK?'

'Yes, honey, I thought you were coming home tonight.' She sounded husky, disappointed.

'I can't. Jen, what's wrong?'

'Nothing, honey. It's OK.'

He put the phone down.

The Cessna twin alighted on the hot Texan airfield at four in the afternoon. The thermometer had begun its slow path down from the high nineties, where it had stubbornly remained for most of the day.

Leroy Corbin, the senior member of the domestic operations task force, was waiting for Bugs in the small arrivals lounge. He watched from the air-conditioned side of a vast pane of darkened glass as the light twin taxied onto the black apron. The wheels left glittering lines of melted tar in their wake. The plane's door swung open, steps appeared, and Bugs' prematurely grey hair and pursed lips emerged at the top: he stepped down, overnight case in hand, grim, and apparently lost in thought.

In the lounge, Leroy shook Bugs' hand warmly, a big smile on his face, and said, 'You've brought us luck, chief: we've found our number right here.'

'We or the Bureau?' asked Bugs with a sly grin. Leroy cocked his head and wagged a finger. He led him to an office at the foot of the control tower where agents had spent a morning sifting through records.

Bugs recognised a local federal officer and smiled. 'Nice work, Mike!'

Mike MacTavish showed entries for a Bonanza registered under the numbers that were among John Glenn's last utterances during his short life. The plane had regularly visited Addison every month between August of last year and July of this: landing at about 6 a.m., it had been recorded by a controller who preferred to work the night shift. He was at home and ready to answer questions. Mike had telephoned to say that Bugs would want to interview him.

'Mike, do you have your badge?' asked Bugs.

'Yes, Sir.'

'You'd better come with us: this is not our hunting ground.'

Leroy led the way to a hire car outside: the three, armed with the records, clambered aboard, and drove off to interview the controller. They drew up in front of his small, white house minutes later. A man in his early fifties with a look of habitual concern on his face opened the door.

'You Fred Coombes?' asked Mike flashing his identity.

'I am, Sir', replied Coombes. ''Expectin' y'all to call, why don't y'all come in?'

He led the three into a small sitting room dominated by an outsized television set in one corner and invited them to sit down.

Bugs came straight to the point. 'Fred, we're trying to trace the pilot of a Bonanza that used Addison a dozen times up to this summer.'

'If I can help, Sir, I sure will', said Coombes.

'You registered the landings. The plane always touched down shortly after dawn: look .... right here.' Bugs showed Coombes's most recent record made in July.

Coombes squinted at his entries and scratched his head. Then, triumph blazing in his eyes, he looked up and said, 'Why, yes, I remember: foreign gal! Flies a V-tail: 'nice pilot: don't understand English: forever havin' to say again on the radio. 'Prefers Spanish, but I don't talk Spanish.'

'Have you seen her face to face?' asked Bugs.

'Sure: pilots come to the tower to pay the landin' fee.'

'What's her name?'

''Don't rightly remember, but I write it all down at the tower: we can see what I got. 'Real strange license though: ain't American: got a FAA certificate: back pages in A-rab: 'front in English. Log's got A-rab column titles: had to check where you rubber stamp: entries start in the back and the front's the back if you get my meanin'.'

'How do you know it was Arabic?' asked Bugs.

''Gal told me, I guess. She doesn't like questions though; closed right up the first time.'

They drove back together. Coombes found his records at the tower office and pointed proudly at his clear entries. 'That's her: S-i-mona Grassi: that's her license number. 'Sure looks different in A-rab! See here now: issued Tr-i-poli nine'een seven'y six: 'reckon her log must have at least a thousand hours flyin' time.'

'Tripoli Lebanon or Tripoli Libya?' asked Bugs.

Coombes looked at Bugs as if he had just landed from Mars. ''Can't say, Sir.'

'Is her name written on the logbook?'

'Yep', replied Coombes: ''crossed out the A-rab. 'Wrote it in herself: you couldn't identify the owner otherwise if she lost it: 'can't read A-rab in these parts, and a pilot can't fly without a logbook.'

'Does she fly alone?' asked Leroy.

'Yep.'

'....and when she arrives?'

''Calls from Whisky One 'bout ten minutes out to order a limo. I use 'Quality' at Dallas/Fort Worth: I know young Phil who drives for them: real nice young fella. She's always gone when I get back for the next shift. 'Darned fine pilot; kiss landins in that light plane, even in a side wind. 'May be instrument rated: I guess I don't remember.'

Fred closed his records and put them away.

"Strange thing: she doesn't file flight plans. You'd kind of expect one from a good pilot flyin' at night.'

'Why, Mr Coombes', asked Bugs.

'Safety! 'Plan's sent to the destination and check points. If the pilot doesn't radio in on time, we get out a search.'

'Can it be filed after take-off, Fred?'

'Sure', replied Coombes, 'but ATC don't like that.'

'Can you tell us what she looks like, please, Mr Coombes', asked Mike.

"Dark eyes; 'bout thirty-five; dark hair; five foot six, I guess. 'May be Mexican: S-i-mona Grassi a Mexican name?'

'Probably not', said Bugs. 'Thanks for being so cooperative, Mr Coombes.'

'You're welcome. 'Work for the government too, y'all know. We're all in this kinda thing together. What's she done anyhow?'

'Can't say, for now, Mr Coombes. Thanks again.'
Coombes left to walk home, a proud man.

Bugs told Leroy to check flight plans filed by aircraft in flight on the nights the Bonanza was in the air and called Langley for a search on a Simona Grassi, who would put out a world-wide alert to find this pilot. He met Leroy at the airport bar for a drink and talked over their next steps.

Bugs returned in the Cessna light twin to Washington National late that evening and went straight home.

Disregarding shouted offers of transport from hustlers at the dozen or so other limo desks in the hall, Leroy and Mike ambled up to the 'Quality Limousine Service' desk facing the baggage claim area. The 'Quality' desk was staffed by a fat man sporting black-rimmed glasses and a green card-player's visor. A cigarette butt dangled from his lower lip. He squinted up from a cloud of bluish smoke gathering under the visor, and jammed the telephone handset between his left shoulder and a flabby jowl.

'What can I do for you, bud?' he asked Mike. He jotted a street name down on the pad in front of him.

"Answer a few questions', said Mike, flashing his badge.

The fat man looked up. The confident squint collapsed into a suspicious stare. The butt fell from his lips: he stepped on it and put the handset down. 'Aw, shit! 'Bad for business havin' you guys walk up like this.'

'You have something to hide?' asked Mike.

'Hell, no!' replied the fat man. 'Why don't you guys go wait at the bar. I'll be right along: 'soon as I find someone to take the desk.'

Leroy and Mike walked to the bar and waited. They ordered sodas and watched the merry-go-round of aircraft landing and taking off, as they had so often done before in airports around the US.

The fat man arrived a few minutes later and ordered a ginger ale. 'OK, what's up?' he asked.

"Should be asking you that', said Mike.

'Look, fellas, I'm clean now. I've been goin' straight for three years. I ain't done nothin' wrong.'

"Quality' your business?' asked Mike.

'Quality's the name; quality's the game!' The fat man beamed with pride. 'People say that all over this here town.'

'Show me your business license.'

'Now?'

'… and I want to see your reservations books for this year and last year.'

'Aw shit, fellas, give me a break.'

'Right now, and right here', replied Mike.

The fat man waddled out of the bar back to the desk, and returned minutes later, red-faced.

Mike handed Leroy the reservations book and inspected the business license.

'Driver's License', added Mike.

The fat man fished a shiny wallet from a hind pocket.

'Social Security Card', said Mike. The business license was out of date. Mike looked hard at the now crimson-faced individual quivering in front of him. 'Out of date', he growled.

'Look fellas, I can explain.'

'You can do that downtown: you're coming with us.'

Handing the frightened limo operator, a sheet of paper with scribbled dates, Leroy Corbin interrupted: 'You sent a limo to Addison Field on those dates to drive someone around all day. Tell me more.'

'Heck, I can't remember everyone we pick up.'

'Look at the book, remember, and tell me', insisted Leroy.

The fat man frowned and looked vacantly at his own handwriting. 'Aw shit, I don't know.'

'Maybe I can help your memory: you wrote the same here, and here, and...' said Leroy, showing the entries he had made each month since the previous August.

A spark of recognition glimmered in his eyes. 'Well, maybe that's the run Phil gets.'

'Get him', ordered Mike.

'Now?'

'Right now!' said Mike, winking surreptitiously at Leroy.

Admonished that he would be severely dealt with later, the fat man waddled back to his desk to trace 'Phil.'

It took an hour to find the driver. Mike and Leroy slid into the torpor of the duller moments of their job. Mike dozed off, and, for no good reason, awoke with a start twenty minutes later. He ordered a hot beef-melt sandwich.

'What can I do for you guys?' asked a fresh-faced man. Leroy and Mike assumed he was the elusive 'Phil.'

His mouth full, Mike transferred the dripping sandwich to his other hand and fished around in his pockets for his badge. Taking pity on Mike, Leroy addressed the figure standing cockily in front of them. 'You Phil?'

'Yeah.' The young driver fell into a seat and hung a leg over an arm rest.

Mike, his mouth emptier, took over, 'See the dates on this sheet of paper? You picked up a customer from Addison Field on each one and stayed with that person the whole day. We want to know what happened.'

'That's the foreign woman. What's she done?'

'We ask the questions, Phil: you answer them.'

'Yes....Sir', said Phil, evident sarcasm in his voice.

'Where do you take her?'

'Dallas.'

'Be specific.'

'Look, guys, I'm not sure my customers are any of your business.'

Leroy touched Mike's arm. 'Phil's right, Mike: we should take him down to the Federal building and do this thing properly: fingerprints, body search, blood test, and so on. Phil, tell your folks you'll be back tomorrow.'

His attitude changed like lightning: the limousine driver paled visibly: the slouch became a tense perch on the edge of his chair. 'Who pays my hours?'

'Work that out with Mr "Quality" at the desk.'

'Come on guys: you're joking!'

'There's another way, wise ass; an easier way. You just answer the questions', spat Leroy.

The boy frowned, hesitated as if to gather the remaining shreds of his wounded pride, and spoke. 'First I take her to the Marriott for breakfast. At ten I leave her at the American Airlines arrivals door at Dallas/Fort Worth: she's usually out at ten-forty-five.'

Leroy and Mike jotted it down.

'After that, I take her downtown, where she always buys a whole bunch of stuff. She doesn't eat lunch. At three, we go to a clinic on Munroe: she's out by four-thirty, and I drive her back to Addison: I guess she keeps a plane there. 'Tried to talk her into a little action once, but she doesn't rise easily to the bait: she's real quiet.'

'Name?' asked Leroy.

'Didn't ask: 'don't think she'd say. She got money: pays cash in the stores: I watch her through the window count out the notes.' Phil winked.

'Can you drive us along her route?'

'You may just wind up getting a free ride. What did you guys tell the boss? He's falling apart down there.'

In conversation with Bugs, Leroy lay back cradling the telephone while Mike sat by the window listening to the Texas end of the conversation. 'There were no bookings at the Marriott: she could use the powder room to freshen up, I guess, and eat a cash breakfast in the coffee-room.'

'And at the airport?' came Bugs' voice.

'We'll check passenger arrivals between 9:45 and 10:30 on those dates. If we find the same names each time, we may have a lead.'

'That's not enough', said Bugs: 'check the return flights too. When you've finished American Airlines, start on the others.'

'Yes Sir', said Leroy. "Didn't find much at the stores: one jeweller remembers getting cash for a diamond pendant. His description fits well with the limo service's. She's either rich or mad to walk around with that kind of cash, but this is Texas!'

'Why does she go to a clinic?'

'It's a woman clinic. They stonewalled all the way: first, we got excuses about too many dark-haired women coming in to recognise any particular one. The receptionist admitted to a Miss Grassi coming in: Mike certainly didn't make a friend out of her! She doesn't know Grassi's address because she always pays cash. The physician refused to say anything without a court order.'

'Get one', said Bugs.

'Right away, boss', said Leroy.

Gary Sinclair languidly tore the sheet from the tele printer. It arrived every morning from Washington naming Americans stalked abroad by various federal agencies. He breathed a tired sigh: Sinclair never found anyone he knew on the daily alert. He righted a lopsided eagle on his desk sitting on a wooden plinth inscribed with the words: 'US Drug Enforcement Agency.' He loosened his tie, and called out to Juanita for a cold pop, thinking that he would look through the names later.

He ambled over to the switch operating the ceiling fan. It was just 9:00 and already blazing hot outside. Colombia was the ultimate assignment for a dope officer to get ahead, but hell for anyone without a taste for hot weather or a sense of humour.

He didn't get around to the rest of the tele printer sheet until about 11:00. There was just too much paperwork. His eyes scanned the names and paused at one of a pilot being searched for by the Texas FBI: there couldn't be many with a name like that! He yelled for another pop. 'Could be the same woman; same name, Simona. 'Little more than one of those jungle myths. He wasn't even sure she existed and hadn't bothered filing a suspect report with Washington. The idea of a fairy-tale white woman ferrying drugs by plane from the tip of the Andes was ludicrous: dope was a man's world for Sinclair and most consignments left by boat, entering the USA through the Southern tip of Florida.

'Juanita, get me the file on S-i-mona X, and where's my darned pop?'

He had chosen the 'X' because he didn't know where else to put the file: the ineffectual Maicao police, it was his unpleasant duty to contact from time to time, just called her Simona. A substantial *mulatta* waddled into the office. She left the file on Gary Sinclair's desk and waddled out again with a pained expression. Man trouble again. He acidly decided on silence for the rest of the day: life was complicated enough without his secretary's sour sex life. 'Cherry flavour, make sure it's chilled!'

Sinclair sharpened his pencil and waited. Minutes passed: she wasn't going to cooperate: he got up, exasperated, and walked noisily to the cooler. He slouched into his chair to read his sparse, neat notes on Ms S. X. Five minutes later he placed the slim file on the desk and leaned back to stare at the ceiling fan. 'I could either make a fool of myself, or look like a damned hero', he mumbled.

'Did you say something, señor?' asked Juanita from the door.

'Eh? No Juanita, just thinking out loud.'

The woman retreated in a cloud of gloom.

Sinclair devoted his attention once more to the ceiling fan, and concluded that a mistake could impair his hopes of promotion, yet, at noon, he decided to reply, and dictated a cable to Juanita, who spent the rest of the afternoon doing her nails and waiting for a line to Washington.

'Get me the Airline guide, please Carol', crackled Bugs' voice over the interphone. I need the times of flights to Bogota.'

The secretary stepped into the office with the thick volume. Minutes later she left to order the tickets.

Bugs picked up Sinclair's cable and reread the vapid text: he did not sound very sure of his facts; maybe he was just covering his tail; the DEA would normally use heavyweights in Colombia, he thought. The telephone rang. Bugs took the call: Carol was on another line to the travel office. It was Jim Curry, calling from Chicago. "Something you might like to know, Bugsy.'

'I was wondering when you'd get around to calling', laughed Bugs.

'Strictly off the record: agreed?'

'Do I have a choice?'

'No. We've found the identity of one of the women: she was Fatima Al-Othman, a Palestinian.'

'The Semitic features!'

Jim described his discussion with Levine, and criticised Duval's lukewarm reaction to the information. He had exploded on hearing that the CIA man had won brownie points by informing his boss that he had discovered the identity himself. Bugs listened quietly, frowning at his desk.

The conversation turned to Fatima and to her frequent trips to Asuncion as Carmen Muñoz. 'Asuncion! I'll be in Colombia early next week on the John Glenn case. I could take a look. Can you arrange a meeting for me with Levine's contact?'

'I think so', said Jim, 'but I don't want to get involved in squabbles between you and Duval.'

'Don't be an old hen, Jim. Just call me back with the name of the person I have to see. I need the name by Sunday morning. Call me at home in Georgetown.

ROME

The dull grey suit was badly cut: the cloth was harsher than the gabardine of his uniform. They were all so finely dressed here: the women milling about the transit lounge could have been at the Politburo. The woman at the travel desk at the Lubyanka had told him before his departure that Fiumicino airport was used only by the cream of Italian society, and it showed.

A noisy crowd clustered around the customs exit: Ivan was surprised that the guards made no move to maintain order. Two men advanced from the crowd as he walked through the customs gate, one of whom smiled and offered his hand. 'Comrade Colonel, how do you do. We're here to take you back with us to the Embassy.'

Ivan asked to see his identity card and let the other carry his bags to a waiting Fiat.

A fine mist had settled over the road into the city. The land seemed well farmed, but few peasants worked the fields despite the lack of snow. The weather was mild but damp, reminding him of the Ukraine in the late autumn. He asked whether the Italian annual plan allowed for a winter crop: the answer came with the hint of a smirk.

Ivan disliked his reception committee's familiar manners: the two who had met him spoke openly and often, even the driver joining in the conversation from time to time without invitation. He didn't reply to their quips about Moscow weather and sat sullenly watching the countryside of Latium shoot by his window. Two were Russians and the third, the driver, spoke with a strong Baltic accent. All of them were too well dressed for State Security employees and too enthusiastic by far about Rome for Ivan's tastes. He would have a word with the Resident about their behaviour.

Rome appeared less impoverished than he had expected.

The Embassy windows were closed and shuttered along the street front: his chattering companions claimed this improved security. It seemed a shame to stop the weak sun from seeking its way into the enormous, elegant rooms of the building. The courtyard windows were left ajar, making the inner rooms brighter, but not much. An aide gave him a bedroom overlooking the courtyard explaining that it would be quieter: the locals could be quite noisy in the streets of Rome at night. 'Those damned *Vespas*!' he said.

'I suppose the locals line up for their visas quite early', said Ivan, 'I hope our guards do a better job of keeping order than the Italian militia: the airport was a circus!'

The aide shot Ivan a puzzled look and stopped chatting. He left a carefully folded copy of Pravda on the desk.

'When do I meet the Ambassador?' asked Ivan.

'Lunch is at one, Comrade Colonel, in the dining room. Shall I unpack your bags?'

'I'll do it, thank you', he replied, and the aide left, quietly shutting the door behind him.

How strange the staff appeared: first the informality of the officers in the car, and now the aide's sudden evasiveness. He sat on the bed and reread his notes to prepare for lunch: he would unpack later. It would be tactless to walk uninvited and unknown, around the Embassy. At one o'clock he left his room and took the marble staircase in a wide arc down to the ground floor. The Baroque splendour of the entrance hall and the dining room were breath-taking: only at the Kremlin and in the Leningrad museums had he ever seen such delicate frescos and precious marble: such magnificence; such decadence.

Three places had been set with fine silverware around one end of a long, carved mahogany dining table.

'Good day to you, Comrade Colonel.' The voice came from a corner of the dining room to Ivan's right where two men stood at a bar. He turned to face them: one wore an armoured division colonel's insignia and the other the uniform of a KGB colonel. He felt stupid in his suit and wished he had brought his uniform. 'Good morning', he replied, clearly ill at ease.

'Vodka?' asked the State-Security officer.

'Yes please.' He approached them, acutely aware of the military officer's appraising glance. The sultry air in the corner of the room reeked of aftershave.

'Delighted to meet you, Comrade', said the KGB colonel. His tone was frankly cool. 'We're often visited by Dzerzhinsky Square staff, but rarely by a distinguished fellow officer. Ice? The bottle's warm.'

'Please', answered Ivan. 'My name's Promyslov. I was expecting to meet the Ambassador.'

'Yes, we know. The Ambassador has other engagements and cannot attend the lunch: he asked us to assist you. He would clear any information he gives you with us anyway. You fly out tomorrow: is that correct?'

'I can stay longer if necessary.'

'You will find us most helpful. We have no wish to detain you longer than necessary.' The KGB colonel turned his back on him, ostensibly to pour the vodka.

The military man stepped hastily forward and held out his hand. 'I'm Ovarev. How do you do.'

The KGB colonel handed Ivan the vodka. '....and I'm Khotulev. You may have gathered that we're the Residents: I represent State Security and Ovarev, Military Intelligence. The Cipher Officer is away with the Ambassador.' He held out his tumbler. 'Na Zdarovje!'

Ivan nodded and swallowed his vodka. A door opened at the far end of the room. A waiter entered and stood by it. Khotulev nodded at him. 'Lunch is served, Comrade, please come and sit down.'

No expense had been spared: the food was fresh and served with care. Ovarev chose a young Umbrian wine with some ceremony and smiled at Ivan's evident appreciation. 'The vineyard is operated by the PCI, the Italian Communist Party, through a cooperative', he remarked.

'The International seems well established in this country', commented Ivan through a fork-full of roast quail.

'Yes, this is the original land of the *govnoed*', said Ovarev with a knowing wink.

Ivan stared aghast: 'Shit eaters! That's unkind: why do you call them that?'

'Come now, Comrade said Khotulev with an ironic smile, 'your lack of international experience is showing. You should put in for a transfer abroad before you get much older: at your age, and in your position, capitalist culture shock is unbecoming. Take my advice and use your day wisely: go and buy yourself some clothes and shoes in Rome: you can take my car and my driver. We'll handle payment for you in local currency. Get something for your wife. Believe me, you will learn far more in one day on the streets of Rome than you will inside these embassy walls.'

Ivan was still reeling from the military officer's contempt for the Party, and now a fellow KGB officer was patronising him as if he were a Siberian peasant.

Khotulev softened his tone. 'Life is more relaxed in this world, Comrade. We are told the proletariat is poor and exploited outside our glorious land: probably so, but we are not told about the vast middle class flourishing under capitalism. Search for the beggars and the endless lines outside the bakeries. You won't find them: instead, you'll find richly stocked stores; cars; comfortable homes with gardens; travel with minimum restrictions. That's why we call those here who prefer our way, shit eaters: they prefer the empty stores and the endless lines, the tiny flats and Moscow bureaucracy. They are ignorant. Your shock is warranted, but get out there and take a look: we dislike seeing people at our level from Moscow who still have to discover the real world.

Khotulev paused and took a long drink from his wine glass. 'Because life is less regimented out here, Comrade, many of our colleagues feel .... uncomfortable.'

'There are fewer rules, fewer people telling one what to do', volunteered Ovarev.

These were dangerous men: these were treacherous words. 'You are right. I've spent no time in foreign service', replied Ivan, 'but in the teeth of colossal problems, the Party saved our vast people from serfdom, eliminated hunger, and gave us work.' He looked carefully at his two hosts. '.... but such talk is not the purpose of my visit, and we should stop it now before either of you says something you will regret.'

Khotulev and Ovarev became suddenly intent in their food, the mocking lines playing around the corners of their eyes yielding to wary glances. After a few uncomfortably silent moments, Ovarev spoke up: 'How's young Vassya Nikolaev doing? He's a fireball: it's rare State Security gets that kind of talent.'

'He's certainly ambitious', conceded Ivan.

Khotulev forced a grin. 'Nikolaev is tough to pin down: I had all the trouble in the world getting him to keep his mind on State Security, but he loves subversion: that's why

Ovarev thinks highly of him. That's the way with all these military-academy types: heavens knows why he left the army for the KGB; he would have been far more use to the fatherland staying in the GRU.'

'I was ordered to help him, you know', said Ovarev.

'Of course, ... now, Comrade Colonel Promyslov, let's do some sightseeing this afternoon; the Colosseum; the Vatican....'

'No thank you. Tell me about this order to help Nikolaev, Ogarev: did it come from the GRU? That seems strange if the lad was with state security and not with military intelligence' said Ivan.

Ovarev shot a glance at Khotulev, who seemed deeply absorbed by the ruby liquid in his glass. Silence followed.

'Gentlemen', said Ivan, 'remember under whose authority I am here.'

'Naturally, Comrade', said Khotulev. 'Let's retire to the study where we can talk more comfortably. I have an excellent Italian Grappa I would like you to taste.'

Ivan held his ground. 'Later!' He pointed a finger at Ovarev. 'What order?'

Ovarev frowned. 'You may know that Nikolaev was trained at the Kiev Tank School.'

'I know, and the black flashes on your lapels tell me that you were too, Comrade Colonel Ovarev.'

The military officer looked closely at Ivan and went on: 'His father, Comrade General Nikolaev, is also from the school: he happens to head my directorate. You may not have been aware of this.'

'Please tell me about the order', repeated Ivan.

'When Nikolaev arrived, I got a personal call from his father asking me, as a fellow alumnus, to give his son full and unconditional support in his work, even if, here in Rome, he was under Khotulev's authority in State Security, and not under mine in Military Intelligence.'

'On what grounds?'

'No particular grounds, but Vassya Nikolaev claimed many times he was on a special mission.'

'Were you aware of this?' asked Ivan turning to Khotulev.

'I have never met Comrade General Nikolaev', answered Khotulev.

'Were you aware of Lieutenant Nikolaev's mission, Khotulev?'

'You're getting nervous, Comrade, calm down a bit. Ovarev may have mentioned it to me: yes, I believe he possibly did, once.'

'I assume you verified this 'special mission' through our own directorate.'

'Unnecessary. A General of the Russian Army issues an order to my opposite number in Military Intelligence to cooperate with one of my people: why should I check it?'

'Shouldn't you be aware of your subordinates' 'special missions?''

'If I had to check every little detail, I'd have my nose in other people's business all the time instead of doing my job.'

'Didn't Marshall Volkov attend the Kiev Tank School too?' asked Ivan. 'I assume you know that he has been absent from the Politburo for some time.'

'You are very well informed, Comrade Colonel Promyslov', replied the military officer. 'Now I'm afraid I must leave you, Gentlemen, I have an important appointment this afternoon.'

'I will see you another time, Comrade Colonel: I have many questions to ask', said Ivan.

'Of course,' answered Ovarev, visibly irritated. He clicked his heels preciously at his luncheon companions and strutted out of the room.

Khotulev stood. 'I must go too. It has been a pleasure talking to you. I hope we shall meet again sometime, Comrade Colonel.' He held out his hand.

'It seems to me, Khotulev, you still don't understand under whose authority I am here. I have not finished, and I will decide when our meeting is over. Please sit down.'

Khotulev blustered. 'Look, Comrade, if you go on in this unpleasant manner, I intend to call Moscow.'

'Call, now! Whomever you please. Then sit down.'

The KGB Resident gaped stupidly and remained standing to protect his remaining vestiges of pride. He had taken Promyslov for a staff country boy abroad for a good time.

Moscow had told him to answer in detail all Promyslov's questions concerning Nikolaev's career in Rome: Khotulev had wrongly assumed that this was in preparation for the young officer's next promotion. The visitor from Moscow was turning out to be an altogether more sinister figure than the average State Security personnel officer. He sat. 'No need to get cross, Comrade. I can spare another ten minutes.'

'I shall be the judge of that', growled Ivan. He walked to the door and closed it. 'Now I want to know all about Nikolaev's activities here in Rome. Leave out nothing.'

'I need his personnel file, and it's so much more comfortable in the study.'

'Go and get his file, and return here. We need this table to work on.'

Khotulev left sullenly, returning with Nikolaev's file a few minutes later. He read the slim document preciously before beginning his account. 'Nikolaev came to us in Rome highly recommended, and with impressive military training. He returned to Moscow on assignment to you at the beginning of this year after four active years in Rome.'

'Who recommended him for duty here?'

'The KGB school on the request of his old principal at the Kiev Tank School.'

'Why to Rome?'

'It doesn't say.'

'Why did he leave the military?'

'His file says he prefers politics and diplomacy to war.'

'You spoke of his liking for subversion: a GRU skill.'

'That's why he should have never left the army. Nikolaev, despite his age, is the only member of our staff in Italy to have penetrated the Red Brigade movement. He took control of one of our illegals, a Moscow-trained Muslim, and directed him smoothly through some woman into a position of confidence with the *brigatisti*. That's why his passage here was so successful. To have maintained the cover was a remarkable feat of consolidation of GRU and of KGB resources: all was achieved by Nikolaev out of this Embassy.'

'A double achievement', commented Ivan; 'he penetrated a notoriously difficult urban terrorist movement, and somehow got military intelligence to cooperate with state security. Uncannily good: it defies understanding!'

Khotulev relaxed. 'I had no choice but to allow him to continue, and as long as the results were there, his father's instructions to the GRU Resident appeared to be in our best interest. I wasn't going to challenge them!'

'This Muslim illegal was trained by State Security, you say?'

'Yes, Mischa was trained by us. I don't have his file anymore; I believe that Nikolaev sent it back to Moscow. The name Mischa is certainly an alias: his own name was a Muslim one, I believe. Contact with the Red Brigades is the GRU's prerogative, but I wasn't going to quibble about us at the KGB paying a man doing a fine job here in subversion. Thanks to Nikolaev's father's sway over Ovarev, the GRU played a key role in keeping our man operational, and later, even in stopping him from being shot by the *brigatisti*.'

Ivan took a notepad from his pocket and waited silently for Khotulev to go on. Khotulev frowned as if trying to recollect his thoughts. 'Young 'Nikolaev was not very communicative, but, as far as I can remember, the events were these: our illegal, Mischa, got in by being involved with a woman in the Red Brigade movement. He gained trust by gunning down a few corporate executives and getting arms for the terrorists: this he did through one of our local GRU agents. This agent, an Italian, worked also with one of the Mafia crime families: he refused to trade arms with the Red Brigade columns other than through our illegal, Mischa. That was Nikolaev's idea and a very effective one to support Mischa's role. Then, in 1982, our luck turned: Mischa's woman somehow ended up in jail, and, quickly after, Mischa somehow fell into disgrace with the *brigatisti*: he was in deep trouble, and the only one able to get Mischa off the Red Brigades' hate list was the woman herself.'

'....and she was in jail.'

'So, we had to get her out, and that was Milk's job.'

'Milk?'

'You look surprised, Comrade.'

'You said Milk.'

'That was our code name for this local Italian GRU agent handling the arms deal.'

'Do you know anything about him?'

'You'd have to ask Ovarev. Now, Comrade, I must ask for your cooperation: I have some important reports to attend to this afternoon. Please excuse me.' Khotulev stood uncertainly. 'My car is at your disposal this afternoon.'

'That's very kind, Comrade', said Ivan.

Relieved, Khotulev slipped out of the dining room.

The winter sun reflecting off the red brick warmed his back. His shoes crunched their way over the pebbles marking the areas where tourists could wander about the Colosseum, the definitive monument to ancient Rome's brutality. He had invited the Cipher Officer along so that he could talk to him privately. Once inside the arena, however, Ivan became silent: his eyes roamed ceaselessly over fallen pillars and sunken lairs which, two thousand years ago, had formed the foundations of the pit. He imagined the screams of mutilated men and women living through final moments of agony and the roars in the night of wild creatures which lived in hungry darkness waiting for an unequal chase designed to entertain all Rome. It made him think of the Lubyanka prison block, and he took an instant dislike to the place.

'Fascinating, isn't it?' said the Cipher Officer.

'Yes, Comrade Captain Kapalkin', replied Ivan, 'society has improved since Roman bestiality, but not very much.'

The Cipher Officer shaded his eyes and looked up at the stalls. 'They were good engineers: much of the load-bearing structure is still there.'

Ivan grunted an acknowledgement and sat on a bench. Kapalkin joined him, looking almost Italian out of his uniform. Ivan stood to check that the two plainclothes guards sent by Khotulev were out of hearing range, and sat down again.

'Why are you so concerned about getting me alone? I have nothing to hide', asked Kapalkin.

'I don't want Khotulev's people to hear, comrade. I know how he works: we have the same employer.'

Kapalkin laughed good-naturedly. He rested his elbows on his knees and lit his pipe. Like all Cipher Officers in foreign service, his privileged position gave him an air of personal serenity no other official at the Embassy seemed able to aspire to.

'I suppose you worked with Nikolaev while he was in Rome: what do you know of his activities?'

'Not very much, Comrade Colonel. Why are you asking me? He has the same employer as you!' Ivan forced a grin. Kapalkin went on. 'Inexperienced young chap: impulsive! I followed all his inept radio traffic with the Italian agent over getting Mischa's woman out of jail. Now, there's a clever operator: he's a crook, organised, and he's got backing, that Cremante.'

'Cremante?'

'The GRU Resident, Ovarev, thinks the world of him: I never did understand why he passed control of his best agent to Nikolaev, who arrived, after all, as a KGB subordinate. Nikolaev gave Cremante the code-name Milk. The Italian word for cream is *crema*, and instead of calling him, cream, he called him Milk.' Kapalkin drew on his pipe and chuckled. 'Childish! The Italian for snow is Neve, and Cremante got his own back by calling Nikolaev, Snow, heavens know why.'

'Snow!' repeated Ivan: he quoted the wording of Milk's message: '*...SNOW...NOT FOLLOW INST.....MILK...;* so, the cable had been addressed personally to Nikolaev by Cremante from America!'

'What cable?' asked Kapalkin.

'A cable we got in Moscow from the American continent: it was signed 'Milk', garbled, and coded in some outdated military intelligence code.'

Kapalkin's eyes narrowed. He stared thoughtfully at his feet for some moments. 'Well, well', he said softly. 'I suspected him, but never wanted to believe it could be Nikolaev.'

'What are you talking about, Kapalkin?'

The Cipher Officer drew on his pipe for some moments before continuing. 'Shortly before Nikolaev returned to Moscow, he came to me for a transmitter capable of reaching Moscow from the American continent. I told him that a moderately powerful set working on satellite bands would do the job, but that I didn't have one, and wouldn't have given him one anyway without authorisation. He didn't like that.' Kapalkin drew on his pipe again. 'Shortly after, a relatively powerful portable transmitter disappeared from my office along with two small experimental military cipher machines I kept for amusement: they were portable machines for use by agents, but the codes were too easy to break. The transmitter may have been powerful enough to reach Moscow, but only under very favourable meteorological conditions. I suspected Nikolaev, but not having proof, I didn't want to create trouble for one so young: besides, his passions were clearly orthodox, so I assumed the sets would be put to good use if he had stolen them, so I filed a breakage report on them.'

'....and this Cremante could contact Nikolaev in Moscow using this stolen equipment?'

'Yes. It would fit your story well, wouldn't it: Milk in America contacts Snow using an old-fashioned code, but because of the low power of the set, gets only a part of the message across.'

As they spoke, the two guards sent by Khotulev approached. 'I suggest we move on, Gentlemen', said one: ''never advisable to stay in one place too long.'

Ivan stood and walked towards the Fiat, closely followed by Kapalkin.

They turned through a massive brick archway onto the street and strode towards the official car with its Diplomatic plates. It was illegally parked, but the Rome police allowed CD cars to get away with murder: in fact, a *vigile*, one of Rome's traffic police, was standing by it grinning benignly at the oncoming group. He saluted as the four approached, and good-humouredly admonished the driver for the way he had parked.

Traffic sped around the Colosseum. It was almost four o'clock; time for Rome's thousands of government workers to return to their offices from lunch and their *siesta*.

The *vigile* wandered off, leaving the guards behind. Ivan walked to the rear door the driver held open for him.

Two men drove up on a scooter. One, riding passenger, drew a machine pistol from under his jacket and strafed the Russian party. Searing lead hurtled into their bodies, shattered the car's windows, and whined like banshees into the venerable walls behind the group. Two slugs hit Ivan, one found his head: his body slumped against the car door and bounced back onto the ground. Two others hit Kapalkin.

The Cubans were infuriating: after Ilya's arrival in Chicago, they had phoned him every day only to tell him to keep calm and to wait. For what? Then one day the voice changed, and the new caller said something useful. 'You go to address I give you: you watch.'

'What for?' asked Ilya.

'You go. You follow license plate I give.'

'Who are you?'

The handset clicked into silence. Ilya slammed it down.

He unfolded a map showing the outskirts and found Oakbrook. He memorised the Illinois plate number and, relieved at last that something was happening, grabbed his motorcycle helmet, his sandwiches, a small thermos of coffee, and made for the door.

Ilya Fedorenko saw the car with the Illinois plates at the Oakbrook address as the driver stopped at the gate to talk to a guard. A prominent bulge in his jacket confirmed he was armed, and the gate would have looked more in place at a state penitentiary. That was how Don Carlo Catanzaro protected his home.

Crouching behind a hedgerow in a field facing the mansion, Ilya watched carefully through his binoculars. Could it be Ahmet? He looked for the hundredth time at a dog-eared identity photo, his only companion since he left Moscow, and then again through the binoculars. It could be, and yet....

The driver pulled into the street. Ilya Fedorenko kicked his motorcycle into life and rode along a dirt track to catch up at the lights.

The car took the Eisenhower Expressway to Chicago and turned North onto the Kennedy before reaching town. Ilya kept to the blind side and, minutes later, turned off into the Northern suburbs. Sometimes he slowed to increase the distance between them. Twice the driver doubled back and retraced his path, forcing Ilya to dodge into an alley before he was seen.

At last, the car rolled into the driveway of a colonial-style house in Evanston and stopped while the garage door slid open. It disappeared into the garage, and the door closed automatically behind, leaving Ilya watching at the end of the road. He waited until twilight.

For Sale panels swung gently outside adjacent houses on the opposite side of the wooded avenue. He saw lights in an upstairs room of the first. In the dusk, the second house seemed deserted. He went back for his bike. He sprung the lock on the yard door and walked through the house to the front room. Satisfied it overlooked the colonial-style house across the avenue, he took the binoculars from their case. The porch and the yard were brightly lit. Iron bars protected the downstairs windows, and two small video cameras mounted high on the outside walls scanned the door and the pathway. Lamps in the base of the window frames, lighting the outside of the blinds, made it impossible to tell which rooms were occupied.

He took a sandwich from his bag and munched it slowly, sitting against a wall to wait for movement. He slid into a state of calm perfected during countless dreary hours spent watching: it allowed him rest during his vigil. When, finally, around midnight, the garage door opened, he got up and loped through the house into the yard to get the bike. The car made for the Kennedy and took the Eisenhower West as if returning to Oakbrook. Ilya was convinced he could see two heads and not just one through the rear screen. At the tollway, he pulled into a parallel lane, where he could look into the off side.

A man in the passenger seat lit up a cigarette, the light of the gas flame throwing his pale features into clear contrast as he glanced up.

Now, Comrade Ahmet, I've found you, thought Ilya. He paid and followed the car down the Oakbrook exit ramp. At the 22nd Street crossing, the driver gesticulated testily at his passenger. He accelerated away violently and took the corner too fast.

Ilya thought they were returning to the Catanzaro mansion.

The driver braked and swung the car into the dark frontage road they had left earlier that afternoon.

Ilya braked violently. The car had pulled up on the shoulder in the darkness: its lights were out. He turned off his own and coaxed the motorcycle onto its mount. He lifted off his helmet and crept in the dark along the far side of a ditch towards the parked vehicle.

Two men were arguing violently inside, then .... silence. He dropped to the ground. Had they seen him? Then came the crack of a pistol shot: only one. He clutched his automatic. Only one shot! At the Executive-Action school, you always fired two in quick succession: bang-bang! Like that.

A door opened. A shadow glided towards the motorcycle. It crossed the ditch, passing within a few dark yards of Ilya. He followed, walked silently into a circle of light, and said, *Do'bree ve'cher*. The man spun violently on Ilya, his face white, the dark features tense. Ilya had just wished a Russian 'Good Evening' in America's heartland.

Twin red lights pulsated over the squad car. From a distance came the wail of an approaching siren. It was cold and dark, even for October. The first chilly winds of a Chicago winter approached. The ambulance stopped: the state trooper who had found the vehicle by the side of a road in suburban Oakbrook strolled up to the paramedic.

'You're the first: 'better wait inside: I got people coming.'

'Maybe I ought to take a look', said the paramedic.

'Too late, buddy: I need a meat wagon, not an ambulance. There's only half a head left in there: rest's in the field.' The paramedic waited meekly out of the cold.

In the growing dawn, officers from the Springfield Violent Crimes Division made a search of the vehicle before taking the body away: it looked like a case of suicide: the corpse was slumped into a corner of the driver's seat. The revolver had fallen to the floor. The bullet had entered the right temple and blown out the left half of the skull, its force shattering the driver's side window and spraying blood and thick, grey cerebral fluid over the internal trim. Bone and brain tissue sticking to glass were found up to fifteen yards from the car.

Blotches of light leapt at him from the cool grey of the room. His head felt as though it had taken the full impact of a sledgehammer. There was a dull pain in his left shoulder, and he couldn't move his arm to ease it. He felt it gingerly: a cast covered his left shoulder.

He tried to lift his head and to look around: the pain was overpowering, and it hurt to roll his eyes. Beyond the carillon playing in his ears, he could just hear street noise and birds chirping.

The blind had been drawn. He wanted to roll over, but he couldn't move. He lay on his back and drifted again into the release of a troubled sleep.

The next time Ivan opened his eyes, the room was darker. His head ached, but he could move it enough now to look around. A small lamp shone from a bedside table, the grotesque skeleton of an intravenous drip feed etched into its pale light. He traced the clear tube down to his right arm and found a needle stuck in it. It made him want to vomit, but he had nothing to throw up...and the plaster cast was truly there: he hadn't imagined it.

The lamp threw a soft light onto the ceiling. It was surely night: there was no street noise now except for the occasional, distant sound of a *Vespa* scooter. There were no more birds. The IV bottle was half-full and dripping: someone was around. A creature glided in wearing enormous white wings on her head and a grey apron. She smiled, said something he didn't understand and disappeared. The nun reappeared with a man in black. 'Well, Comrade Colonel, what a relief to find you awake! I shall call the Embassy immediately.'

Ivan tried to say, 'Wait!' but couldn't.

The man in black hesitated. 'Yes, Comrade Colonel?'

He tried again to speak. The woman in the headdress said something, and the two left together. Ivan felt weak and frustrated. He stared at the ceiling. His head rolled gently to one side, and he fell asleep again.

Someone was sitting by the bed looking at him. The light was brighter now. Others were in the room. 'You had us very worried, Comrade: we thought we would lose you too.'

Ivan focused on the head: it was too close. He didn't want to hallucinate: it would make him want to throw up again.

The head looked familiar. He closed his eyes. He opened his mouth, but no words came.

'You're lucky to be alive. Don't test providence by making unreasonable demands on yourself. If you can hear me, just nod.'

Ivan nodded and winced at the pain: his brains seemed to bounce like gelatine inside his skull.

'You'll be pleased to know that the police shot the two bastards down. One died right in the street: the other's here in intensive care; he won't pull through. Your driver died on the spot, but the guards escaped.'

Ivan tried to remember.

'It's a bad business, though: Kapalkin died a short while ago here in the hospital, too. A replacement Cipher Officer is on his way from Moscow. They're worried about you over there: quite a list of callers!'

A man in white stood over the other side of the bed. He pressed a stethoscope to Ivan's chest, listened intently, and took his blood pressure.

'This is your fourth day in Rome, Comrade: your visit is, no doubt, longer and more eventful than you expected.'

Ivan tried to speak again.

Khotulev gave him a pencil and produced a notepad. 'Write what you have to say.'

The physician, waiting quietly up to now in the corner of the wardroom, complained about the strain on his patient and tried to remove the pencil. Ivan held on weakly.

Khotulev laughed.

Painfully, Ivan tried to remember. It came so slowly. He wrote: *TELL MY WIFE I'M OK. TELL RYABOV IN FIFTH TO SEND MILK FILE TO FEDORENKO VIA CUBAN DGI. SAY MILK'S NAME CREMANTE. DON'T TELL NIKOLAEV OR MILITARY INTELLIGENCE.*

He left the sheet on the bed. Khotulev picked it up, and read it. 'I know Ryabov: friendly type! Milk, eh? Fast work, Comrade Colonel. I'll call the Italian desk in Moscow myself: I assume they'll know why you want to send Milk's file to Havana.'

Ivan felt drowsy: as his eyelids dropped, he thought, no, the file must go to Fedorenko and fell asleep. His visitors retired quietly, leaving *Carabinieri* and a Russian standing outside his door.

The following morning, Khotulev came back at ten. He loved talking, especially now without interruption from this bothersome individual from Moscow in his hospital bed: now that this peasant guest had been pronounced clinically dumb by the neurosurgeon, the KGB Rome Resident could go on as he pleased despite Ivan's exhaustion. Khotulev translated the neurosurgeon's report into Russian for Ivan's benefit: it said the bullet had not penetrated Ivan's skull, but the violent glancing blow had caused the loss of speech: temporary or permanent? He didn't know. A shoulder bone had been splintered but would mend.

'The *Carabinieri* have been most cooperative, Comrade: we have achieved a news blackout: a significant success in this country! These are police photos of the thugs who shot you: the second bastard died in hospital this morning.' Ivan looked at the mug shots: his attackers were young and unshaven. He pushed the photos back across the sheet.

'Usual record of pimping and drugs: Camorra or Mafia: the *Carabinieri* are not sure which. I doubt we'll ever know what they had against Kapalkin. Nobody knew you were here, so I assume they were after him, and not you.'

Ivan wrote on the pad.

Khotulev read his words and replied, 'I telephoned Ryabov yesterday and again this morning. He said the Cubans have been watching Cremante for weeks, and know exactly where to find him and your man. Incidentally, they are releasing you to the Embassy tomorrow. I have booked your flight to Moscow. Your wife will be at the airport to meet you.'

Ivan closed his eyes. 'I'll return for you tomorrow, Comrade.' Ivan waited for the door to shut. He wasn't tired: he wanted to think. Thinking was all that was left. How would he communicate? He would have to learn to listen, only to listen: it would be hard. Olga would be close to hysteria. Dear Olya: as long as she cared, and as long as he could rely on his pension, what else mattered? And yet.... for a moment, his thoughts turned to self-pity: weakness filled his soul. His career was finished: he couldn't talk. Gone was that precious gift of health he had taken so much for granted:

he would have gladly traded his dacha to be able to speak again. He had counted on illusions to bring him joy: never had he thought of the riches he already possessed, and his health was the greatest of all. If only he had understood.

The night was dark. The blinds were again lit from the outside. A limousine stopped in front. Three youths stepped out and rolled up to the door. One tucked a pistol in his belt. The door cracked open, a slim pencil of light escaping from the slit. It swung violently to a kick, bathing the front yard in a bright flash. The three rushed inside and slammed the door so violently behind them, that Ilya Fedorenko and Ahmet heard the noise across the street from where they were watching in the front room of the empty house.

A flame leapt behind the limousine's tinted glass windows, its driver lighting a cigarette.

'She was expecting me', groaned Ahmet in his accented Russian. 'We toss around a little about now: then she leaves in a cab.'

'Strange company you keep', commented Ilya.

'She has a key: she can get in when she wants. Anyway, she's paid by Catanzaro to watch me.'

'Who's is the house?'

'It's his, I guess; a kind of safe house.' Ahmet sat on the floor by the window.

Ilya was disappointed: Ahmet didn't seem the calibre of man he had expected: he was intelligent, even cultured, but he lacked the humanity to be good, and his piercing eyes harboured the lifeless look of a killer.

'She's lousy company, but she's good in bed: you get bored in there, it's good to have a distraction.'

Ilya continued to watch the house. They would be searching it now, probably beating up the woman, expecting she would know where Ahmet was. 'How long had you known Cremante', he asked.

'Pino and I went back a few years: I knew him in Italy; he helped get my girlfriend out of prison.'

'Wasn't he a friend?'

'My friends don't double cross me the way he did.'

'But you were going to frame him after the shoot in Chicago, you said.'

Ahmet's fist banged down on the floorboards where he was sitting. 'It didn't work out the way I wanted!'

'He looked like you', went on Ilya, 'when I saw him leave the Catanzaro mansion, I thought he was you.'

'That's why I wanted Don Carlo to put him on the job with me: some find us tough to tell apart: the Italians called us *i gemelli,* the twins. I thought he would be easy to frame so that I could get out cleanly.'

'It was a good plan: it's a shame it failed: you could have come home without leaving a trace and left the blame on Catanzaro's people, but that's not what Sofia wanted, right?'

'He left the fucking pistol behind, not me: he wanted to frame me. The hit was political and asked for by Moscow, but my instructions from Sofia said to work with Catanzaro and his people. And then Cremante went mad; he told me I was going to get trouble from the military if I messed with him, can you imagine that? An Italian Mafia thug. Nuts!'

'You've been away too long: you should come home.'

Ahmet lit up a cigarette.

Ilya continued his vigil at the window. 'There's stuff I don't understand', he said.

Ahmet glowered at the floor.

'Why the Secretary of State? You were told to shoot the President.'

'I thought he was the President: things happen quickly! Anyway, Lucia and Fatima were outside to finish the job if I missed. The plan was fool-proof: in a way, it worked!'

A film of scepticism crossed the Russian's eyes. 'How can you not recognise the American President?'

Ahmet leapt to his feet. He grabbed Ilya's lapels and thrust his face forward, his murderous eyes glaring at Ilya. 'Cut the questions, Fedorenko. You got your fucking international incident, didn't you? That's what you wanted from me, president or no president!'

Ilya looked back, now sure of his judgement of this man. He waited calmly for the ugliness to subside. 'Not me, Comrade: I'm just here to bring you back in one piece.'

The noise of a door slamming came from across the street. The thugs walked out, got into the limousine, and sped away.

Ahmet pulled on his jacket. 'I'm going to see what they've done to her.'

'No, you're not', said Ilya. 'It's too risky. You don't give a damn about that woman anyway.'

Strangely obedient, Ahmet slid into silence.

Minutes later, a cab stopped in front of the house. She limped down the path. In the half-light of the street lamps, her face seemed bruised and her clothes stained with blood. She doubled up in pain. The cab driver got out to help.

'Bastards!' whispered Ahmet.

'Did you leave anything in the house?' asked Ilya.

''You think I'm stupid?'

'We go back through Cuba tomorrow.'

'Then tomorrow one of us leaves dead, but if you give me time to finish the job, I'll come quietly.'

'How long?'

'The time to leave as a professional.'

'Is it the woman?'

'She's just a hooker!'

'The pistol?'

'Maybe.'

'That's ludicrous: they have your fingerprints in every police office in this country by now. You don't have a hope without Catanzaro's support, and I doubt he would give it now that you've murdered Cremante, one of his best lieutenants. He's just sent three apes across the road to bring him your skin. If you're counting on his patronage now, you're mad.'

'They saw my face at the hospital.'

'You should have worn a mask. They'll probably think by now it was Cremante if they've found the body and any of his face is left. That's what he was there for, wasn't he? That's why you were happy he looked like you.'

'And the fingerprints on the pistol?'

'Yours! You should have worn gloves, you idiot.' Ilya frowned. 'What are you going to do? Kill all the patients?'

'I couldn't wear gloves, I was making a hit! A little Semtex would help, that's all: I left some in a hut close to the Mexican border: it's only a plane ride away.' Ahmet frowned.

'They're civilians. You're out of your mind.'

'The point is I must clean up. I need a few weeks: you must understand.'

Ilya rubbed his forehead. 'I can't let you without new orders. I had to bring you in before you created this mess: I was too late, now we're both in trouble.'

'Ask the Cubans to get the permission from Moscow Centre: it takes a couple of days, that's all. Say it's my fault. Please!'

Ilya scowled: he would want to make a better of job of finishing too. Ahmet had lost the professionalism he had learnt Executive-Action Group, but he had tried. He had served too long away from Moscow; he had lost his edge; he had to come home, but holding his head high if possible. Ilya felt he owed that right to a brother illegal. 'Don't move until I have an answer.'

'Agreed.'

Ilya looked around the darkened room. 'We need a safer place: houses on sale can be visited at any time.'

'I'll find something', said Ahmet.

'No you won't! I'll do it: too many people are looking for you out there, but they don't know me.'

Before the week was ended, Ivan could stand again without feeling dizzy and read without falling asleep.

Khotulev, the KGB Resident, announced that a Lieutenant Aleksandr Mikhailovich Ryabov, an intelligence officer at the Italian desk of the Fifth Department, would arrive in Rome soon. Ryabov had said something about visiting a coach: Colonel Promyslov would know what he meant. Khotulev added an acid remark about young officers abroad mixing business with pleasure.

For the first time in his life, Ivan felt out of control: he might never speak again. He would feel ashamed of being unable to hold up his end in friendly banter with the rest of the rowing team. He was alone in this foreign country. He understood no Italian, and he was sure he couldn't trust Khotulev.

Young Nikolaev was looming as a greater threat than he had expected: he intrigued in a way he probably hadn't learnt in State-Security manuals but rather in military intelligence, and Budhakin was grooming him. Lieutenant Nikolaev could be sitting at Ivan's desk right now with the patronage of Ivan's unpleasant boss. What use was a dumb, middle-aged staff officer without foreign experience or political clout? Nikolaev was well connected through his father, and he resented Ivan.

Ivan couldn't fast-talk his way out of his problems now: he had nothing left to defend himself with if the dogs of State Security were launched at his heels. A shroud of despair swept over him: there was no safety net: he was too low in the hierarchy to protect himself, and he hated corridor politics. Not even the deity his mother had surreptitiously revived in her autumn years seemed there to turn to.

He drowsed fitfully for the rest of the afternoon, fear and confusion drifting into the release of sleep.

Aleksandr Mikhailovich's voice called from far away. A strong hand gripped his shoulder. A face wandered into focus. 'Wake up, Coach!' The Italian doctor chaperoning Ryabov protested lamely about mistreating his patient. Ryabov smiled and nodded vigorously that he didn't understand.

Ivan forced a lop-sided grin: his face belied nothing of his anguish.

'I know you've got trouble, Coach. Don't say a word. I've brought you a letter from Olga Sergeyevna, and Tanya has sent a few books. We don't have much time, so I'll tell you straight away what's happening. A Swiss therapist, the top brass use, has got your file: he's Russian speaking; he's going to get you talking at his clinic. Then you go back to the office and get on with your job. Easy, isn't it! Comrade General Budhakin says take your time and don't worry about office work because that prig Nikolaev is holding the fort.... he's not the one who called him a prig, I am! How's that for good news?'

Ivan's scepticism showed.

'Best of all, Olga Sergeyevna can join you in Switzerland.'

Aleksandr Mikhailovich looked around the wardroom. 'We might be wired.' He lifted the telephone handset and unscrewed the mouthpiece.

Ryabov's dumb rowing coach reached for a notepad on the bedside table and started writing. He thrust the sheet of paper at Ryabov. *I'M DUMB, POTATO HEAD. WHY WIRE ME FOR SOUND?*

Aleksandr threw back his head and roared with laughter. Ivan tapped irritably on the bedside table with the pencil and resumed his note. Ryabov read. *WAS FEDORENKO SENT MILK'S FILE?*

'I got a call from Khotulev before coming to Rome saying to send it to Havana: I assumed he meant to the DGI: he said nothing about Fedorenko, so, no, he didn't get it, Garcia did.'

Ivan frowned. Senior KGB officers never made that kind of mistake: this was not a simple misunderstanding. Khotulev was somehow involved. Ivan wrote: *I WANT TO SEE THE SWISS BANKER WHO HELD THE BULGARIAN CASH FOR BAPTCO. I WANT TO VISIT THIS AGRICULTURAL DIRECTORATE ANTONOV CONTROLLED IN SOFIA.*

The door swung open. Khotulev's Russian guard, who had been just outside the door, strode in. 'Show me that note, Comrade.' He held out his hand.

Ryabov folded the note and put it in his pocket. 'When you talk to me, you say 'please', and you address me as 'Comrade Lieutenant.''

The guard's hand dropped.

'This note was addressed to me at the Fifth Department of the First Chief Directorate of the Committee for State Security, and neither to you nor to the Embassy. If you want to see it, use the proper channels to ask for a copy. Now, get out, there's a good man! No-one invited you in.'

The guard's eyes darkened in horror. 'I shall report this.'

Ryabov waited a few seconds in silence, and added slowly, '… Comrade Lieutenant!'

Fuming, the guard spun on his heel and strode out.

Aleksandr grinned impishly. He took Ivan's pad and wrote: *MAYBE YOU ARE WIRED AFTER ALL. WHO'S THE POTATO HEAD NOW?*

He fished the folded note out of his pocket, read it. Ryabov replied in writing. *I SHALL ARRANGE A TALK WITH THE BANKER ONCE WE ARE IN SWITZERLAND, AND THEN TRY TO GET US BOTH TO BULGARIA*

Ivan nodded and wrote: *SAY NOTHING TO NIKOLAEV. OLGA MUST STAY HOME*

Ryabov grinned, and said in a soft voice, 'I understand, Coach.' He walked to the window and lifted a corner of the blind. He peered down into the street below. 'I'm going now: they're making up a room at the Embassy, and expecting me for a drink. I came straight from the airport.' He turned to the bed. 'I'll be back tomorrow.'

Ivan looked relieved. Who better than Ryabov to be his mouth in this alien land?

When Ivan Promyslov finally got to see the Ambassador, it was to take his leave. He held few illusions now about the ambassador's position as little more than a political figurehead in the Embassy, but Ivan paid his respects all the same. Neither of the Residents accompanied his ambulance to the airport, and Ryabov deployed Khotulev's guards where they could hear or see nothing. Ovarev sent a note with Kapalkin's Moscow address in case Ivan wanted to call on the family of the murdered Cipher Officer. Khotulev sent a note wishing Ivan good luck in Switzerland.

The flight to Geneva lasted an hour. Ivan wrote down his ideas and passed them to Ryabov, who gave a surprised whistle from time to time. The drive to Montreux from the airport took another hour.

In the hills overlooking Lake Geneva, Dr Puschner had installed his clinic in a large nineteenth-century villa combining traditional Swiss pine with modern clinical comfort: though the sun warmed the crisp alpine air during the day, the nights were freezing. Puschner spoke passable Russian, as Ivan discovered when he saw him alone in his office the first day. 'I am aware of your medical file, Herr Promyslov. I can promise you nothing, but we shall work together for a few weeks to see if we can ease you out of this trauma. By the end of that time, I should have a good idea of the next steps. The exercises are frustrating at first, and this is why I suggest you use your afternoons for relaxation or any other work you have in hand.'

Ivan wrote: *SHOULD I LEARN SIGN LANGUAGE?*

'Surely you haven't given up already', replied Puschner. 'No! First, we must try to get you talking again.' He stood. 'This afternoon I want you to practice making any sound you can through your mouth: anything at all. Practice alone in your room. Tomorrow at nine we shall review together the sounds you have managed to produce and draw up a programme of therapy. *Auf wiedersehn*, Herr Promyslov.'

Ivan found Aleksandr Ryabov waiting outside. He gave a low whistle: it was the first sound he had made in more than two weeks.

Aleksandr Mikhailovich returned beaming from his visit to the Soviet Trade Commission. Ivan, pleased to stop his exercises for a few moments, looked at him questioningly. He had spent the afternoon practising a selection of noises through his mouth, some less elegant than others.

'A piece of luck, Coach!' Ryabov sat astride a chair and leant his elbows on its heavy, carved backrest. 'It's at times like these I understand we have friends beyond our frontiers.' He took a notebook from his pocket. 'Listen to this! In August, a Swiss person called de Langeac was employed at the bank: what the manager didn't know was that this person was there to spy on him. This person found details of an account linked to Italian organised crime which may be linked in turn to the Bulgarian affair, and may be willing to sell us the information.'

Ivan wrote:

CAN'T WE JUST QUESTION THE MANAGER?

'According to our source, Ivan Dmitriyevich, we don't stand a chance in hell of getting anything out of him.'

HOW DID YOU FIND THIS 'SPY?'

'That's what I meant about our friends!' Ryabov smiled broadly: 'One of the officials, who employed de Langeac, holds a Communist Party card: he's a Frenchman: he keeps us updated on customs activities on the French-Swiss border.'

Ivan stared in surprise.

'Yes, Coach, France! French customs somehow got wind of this business!'

WHEN CAN THIS PERSON COME?

'I have a telephone number. I'm going to have to use my rusty German.'

Ivan nodded his approval and returned to his exercises: he saved the inelegant sounds for after Ryabov's departure.

Later that afternoon, blonde Brigitte de Langeac, stood smiling at two men with unmistakably Slavic features, and an unmistakably Eastern-bloc wardrobe. The younger was tall and attractive: the elder looked wizened and a little heavy, but built like a sportsman. Neither managed to hide his shock as the woman walked into the room at Puschner's clinic.

Ryabov recovered quickly and plunged into shaky German. '*Guten Abend, Fraulein* de Langeac. Please excuse me: my German is not so good. Allow me to present you, my colleague.'

Ivan stood shakily and nodded.

'How do you do, *Meine Herren*.'

'Unfortunately, my colleague has lost his voice, Fraulein, he can say nothing: please excuse him.'

'Is that why you're in the clinic?' she asked.

Aleksandr seemed not to hear the question. 'Please take a seat.'

Brigitte sat down. 'You looked surprised when I came in.'

'I was surprised to meet such an attractive woman doing this kind of work, Fraulein; we were expecting a man. Please excuse us if we were a little.... primitive.'

'No! I'm flattered. Are you Russian?'

Ryabov hesitated. 'I can't say, Fraulein.'

'Military?'

'Just officials.'

'Ah yes, of course: now, what can I do for you, *Meine Herren*?'

'We would like to discuss some work you did last summer.'

'I don't discuss the affairs of my clients.'

'But we would like to be a client, *Fraulein*: we wish to employ your services.'

Brigitte reached into her purse and removed a card. 'These are my rates.' She gave it to Ryabov. The hint of a smile softened Ivan's face: she found him a good-looking man despite his age.

Ryabov was stunned. 'These are Swiss Francs?'

'I can't use rubles here', she answered with a laugh.

Ryabov passed Ivan the card. 'Your services are not cheap, *Fraulein*.'

'Then I suggest you use the police: they're free of charge.' Brigitte stood.

Ivan scribbled 'DA' on the card and gave it back to Ryabov.

'Maybe you would accept a cup of tea, *Fraulein*: I can have some sent up, and we can talk over the information we require. We accept to pay your fees.' He took a wad of bank notes from his wallet and counted them out on a desk. 'I need a receipt for this.'

Brigitte put the cash in her purse. 'What can I do for you?'

Ryabov spoke of the information provided by the French Communist Party. He ended, 'We want to know how this information is supported by your work in this affair, *Fraulein*.'

'The French *Douaniers* often use my services', she said. 'I'm specialised in bank fraud. They pay well for this kind of case: they're terrified the savings of the French are going to end up in Swiss banks.' She laughed. 'I got a job at the Federal Union of Swiss Banks office in Lausanne where I found that this Italian thug, Genaro Cagnotto, was laundering large sums through a Mafia casino as a courier between Switzerland and Italy. Trying to find where the funds came from, I managed to photocopy the account card.'

'Where did this cash come from, *Fraulein*?'

Brigitte fingered the bank notes in her purse. 'From Bulgaria', she replied, 'from an organisation called BAPTCo....and there you have it all.'

Ivan, who had been listening intently, catching only a fraction of the meaning of the words spoken in the woman's Swiss-German lilt, wrote a few words and passed them to Ryabov.

'Not quite', said Ryabov, 'we need that photocopy of Cagnotto's bank card.'

'The supply of documents costs extra, *Meine Herren.*'

Ivan threw his head back and laughed a guttural, strangely quiet laugh.

'We shall pay you cash.'

'Then I shall return at four with the photocopy.'

The meeting at four went quickly. The payment seemed excessive. Ivan and Aleksandr Mikhailovich sat staring at the numbers for long after Brigitte's departure.

'That's Cagnotto's passport number', pointed out Ryabov, 'and that's the account number opened in BAPTCo's name: so, what do these two other numbers mean?'

Ivan thought for a few minutes, from time to time running his fingers through his hair, then he picked up a piece of paper and wrote: *CAGNOTTO DID NOT PUT THE CASH IN THE SAFE. HE WAS A COURIER ON THE ITALIAN SIDE. WHOEVER PUT IT THERE SATISFIED THE BANK OF HIS OWN IDENTITY USING A PASSPORT. MAYBE THERE WERE TWO OF THEM. WHY NOT?*

'Of course, Coach! These could be the passport numbers of Bulgarian nationals who brought the funds over in the first place.'

CAREFUL, RYABOV, IF THE FOURTEENTH FORGED ME A BULGARIAN PASSPORT, THAT WOULD NOT MAKE ME A BULGARIAN! BUT LET'S CHECK THE NUMBERS

'I'll drive to the Embassy in Berne tomorrow morning, and get the Resident to check.'

Dr Puschner knocked and walked in smiling. 'How's our student this afternoon?'

Ivan's eyes widened. He glanced at Ryabov, then back at the physician.

'Well?' he prompted.

Ivan opened his mouth. His face reddened a little. Deep in his throat, an ugly noise arose like that of a man in agony. Ivan's lips moved modulating the croak into a barely-recognisable, 'Well. Thank you.'

'Excellent', said Puschner. 'Isn't that so, Herr Ryabov?'

Aleksandr Mikhailovich had heard none of the exercises. He had memories of Ivan's strong, clear voice before the Rome shooting. 'Wonderful, doctor', he said, struggling to maintain his composure. None of his reactions was lost on Ivan.

'And you wanted to learn sign language', chided Puschner. 'A few more months, and we'll have you speaking effectively. In the meanwhile, you must practice and develop confidence in your new voice.'

Ivan stared hard at the floor in concentration, and replied, 'Yes, doctor.' If this was his new voice, he preferred not to use it.

'I wish you, gentlemen, a good evening. We shall continue the therapy tomorrow morning, Herr Promyslov: usual time.' He walked out.

Aleksandr Mikhailovich looked sadly at his friend. 'You know it's still warm enough to row on the lake, Coach. I've found a pair of skiffs if you think your shoulder's up to it.'

Ivan's eyes lit up. 'Da!' he croaked. If only his voice had returned the way his shoulder had healed.

Ivan's phone rang at ten the following morning. It had never sounded in his room before while he was alone. The dismay returned: how was he going to answer it? He let it ring on, three.... four.... five times, before clutching the handset and lifting it to his ear.

He tapped gently on it with a pencil. He thought of croaking, but the sound he would have made would have been so ugly, that he didn't.

Ryabov's voice came as a relief. 'Hello! Coach! That's a good idea, tapping like that on the mouthpiece.'

If he was expecting a croak, he would have to wait.

'Let's see if it's you. How many strokes a minute do you want from the team, Ivan Dmitriyevich? A long pause for the tens and short pauses for the units.'

Ivan tapped three times on the mouthpiece, each tap punctuated with a long pause.

'And what's my department number?'

He tapped five times.

'That's you, Coach!'

Ivan whistled two bars of 'Black-eyed Matle', a raunchy song that they sang in the showers after rowing practice. He heard Aleksandr Mikhailovich burst into laughter.

'I'm calling from Berne. We're in luck. If you disagree with anything I say, tap rapidly on the mouthpiece: whistle if you want to say yes. OK?'

Ivan whistled.

'At training school, I made friends with a Bulgarian, who was posted to Sofia and then to the Kremlin. I called him two days ago, to ask if he could help us. He called back to say that the numbers could well be Bulgarian passport serial numbers and that they correspond to those of documents issued to two Bulgarian residents one, Kostov and one, Potanin. He's leaving tonight for a seminar, so he's introducing me to a fellow called Dobrynin in Sofia, who will arrange interviews for me with these two.

Ivan whistled.

'I assume that means approval, Coach. I'm booked on a flight tonight. I haven't bothered to inform Moscow Centre to tell them I'm off to Bulgaria, but I doubt they'd say much anyway. I'll call you as soon as I find anything useful: I suppose it's a bit early for you to leave your lessons and come with me, right?'

Ivan whistled again. He was disappointed: he would dearly have liked to go with Ryabov. He listened stoically to Ryabov's good-bye and hung up.

Maybe it wasn't such a good idea that Ryabov should travel without informing Moscow, but, after all, he was returning to Eastern Europe. He thought no more about it.

One evening, Major General Leonid Budhakin called Vassily Nikolaev into his office overlooking the square where 'iron' Felix Dzerzhinsky's statue turned his back on his sullen progeny. It was Nikolaev's first discovery of his superior officer, Promyslov's close encounter with death. 'You must handle Promyslov's work yourself', went on Budhakin, 'at least until I know whether he can continue. Can you handle it?'

Nikolaev suppressed a leer of triumph. 'I need access to his safe, Comrade General: I don't know what files he has on hand.'

'When the time is right, I'll have it opened: in the meanwhile, process his dispatches. Here's an authorisation to pick them up.' He pushed a signed form across the desk. 'Tell me, how's your father, Felix Pavlovich?'

'Very well, Comrade General. He sends you his warmest regards', lied Nikolaev.

'A fine man; a fine man! That's all, my boy.'

Nikolaev saluted with military flourish and marched off, leaving Budhakin regretting his other subordinates couldn't salute like that. He ran down the stairs two at a time to Ivan's office and walked in through the open door. Ivan Promyslov, like all his colleagues, closed his documents in a safe before leaving his office: his desk was clear except for a note saying his mail was waiting at the communications centre. Nikolaev put it with Budhakin's authorisation and went to get the mail.

Nikolaev's own office was overpopulated with young hopefuls. He hesitated a moment at its door, then turned on his heel and returned to the privacy of Ivan's quarters. He closed the door, put his feet up, and tore open the envelope. The papers were all labelled either secret or top-secret, there being no other classification within the KGB.

A dispatch brought his feet slamming to the floor. It read: AHMET LOCATED. REQUESTS ONE MONTH TO COMPLETE MISSION. FEDORENKO AWAITS INSTRUCTIONS. AHMET LIQUIDATED MILK. GARCIA.

Nikolaev groaned. Ahmet! That troublemaker: a few cross words with Milk, and he almost destroys years of preparation. He would talk the problem over with his father.

The next morning, Nikolaev penned a cable to Garcia. It would bounce as a spurt of scrambled radio waves off a

satellite between Moscow and Havana. He wrote:
*PERMISSION TO COMPLETE AHMET MISSION NOT
REPEAT NOT GRANTED. INSTRUCT AND ASSIST
FEDORENKO TO LIQUIDATE AHMET IMMEDIATELY.*
He signed the cable: *PROMYSLOV.*

The Cuban had sad eyes and flaccid jowls. He had posted
a boy at the other end of the square with instructions to run
for help and not to intervene if anything happened.

Ilya Fedorenko had thought the square was closer to
Chicago's North Loop. He arrived late. The   Cuban   was
terrified of missing his contacts. When Ilya finally opened
his newspaper, and sat on the park bench facing the fountain,
the Cuban sighed with relief and resumed his normal, pained
expression. 'Good of you to come', he hissed.

Ilya's silence was intended to inform the Cuban that his
sarcasm had been noted but not appreciated. He shelved the
apology, but deeply regretted the lack of professionalism of
his own late arrival. The Cuban was a Party comrade, but he
stank of sweat and garlic: it was difficult to feel any kinship
at all with this brute. 'The answer!' he snapped.

The Cuban crossed his legs and tipped his head in an air
of confidentiality.

Ilya folded the newspaper and looked around. He saw the
boy. 'What's the kid waiting for?'

The Cuban's mouth opened a fraction: the tip of a pink
tongue flicked across his fat lips. Very good, he thought.

'The reply', growled Ilya.

The Cuban reached into his pocket, pulled out a white
box, and slid it along the bench. Ilya opened it, saw the
phial, then pocketed it.

''Just one', said the Cuban: ''not for you, this time.' His
face cracked into a sly grin. 'When you're through, call the
number, and we'll come for the body. You have the balls to
wait twenty minutes, with a dead man for company?'

Ilya rose.

'One more thing', said the Cuban.

Ilya waited, facing the fountain, his back turned to him.

'I have another one for you if you fail: Moscow Centre
won't refuse us that pleasure.'

Ilya struggled to control an impulse to slam his fist into the Cuban's face, then he remembered a new expression he had heard on a Chicago Rapid Transit platform. 'You're full of shit!' he snarled and marched off.

Everything was gone. Ahmet had taken everything. Ilya had wisely kept his money and documents with him, and he was livid. Clearly, Ahmet was not counting on seeing Ilya again.

'Damn you', he said. Ahmet had to die, and this fling would mark his final hours. 'Just the time to find you, Comrade, then your time is up.' He picked a girly magazine up off the floor, 'And maybe I know where to look.'

Aleksandr Mikhailovich Ryabov had never been to Sofia: it seemed a warmer city than Moscow, its Byzantine towers bathing in that same soft pink light that characterised a Russian sunset.

He had changed into uniform during the flight: it would help get past the border guards. An Aeroflot hostess led him to a military and government immigration room, and, by the time he left the airport an hour later, the glowing city he had seen from the air had slipped under the shroud of a moonless night.

The hotel was reserved for official visitors from Comecon countries. A stout woman at reception pushed a key across the counter under an appraising glance. She jerked her head at the elevator. 'It's out of order.' She spoke Russian with little accent. 'The room's on the top floor overlooking the courtyard. It's quiet at night.'

Aleksandr wondered why it shouldn't be: the streets of Sofia were dead. 'I have a visitor at eight: please call when he arrives.'

'I'll send him.' She nodded.

He didn't feel like arguing.

At eight, she rang up. 'Your guest's here.'

The stairs twisted grandly up from mezzanine to mezzanine. After the heavy food of the past week, Aleksandr, suitcase in hand, had appreciated the exercise, but walking down was so much easier.

Dobrynin was a small man with a face like a weasel and a pencil-thin moustache. He forced a smile at Aleksandr, who mistook it, at first, for a grimace of agony. 'Igor Dobrynin at your service, Comrade.' He stretched a humid hand.

'How do you do, Comrade. Thank you for making these arrangements.'

A steel tooth darkly appeared below the moustache. 'Shall we go to the restaurant?'

Regretting he had worn his uniform, Aleksandr agreed it would be better than going straight to the bar. ''Dobrynin a Bulgarian name?'

'My grandfather settled here in 1912. Would you like to see the menu?'

Aleksandr squinted at a badly-typed sheet. Seconds of oppressive silence passed. Aleksandr put it down on his empty plate and looked around the restaurant. Dobrynin continued to read as if the menu were the most interesting document he had seen in years.

Aleksandr Ryabov had often kicked himself for his impulsive conversation: Dobrynin was nervous and should be handled gently: even if this 'weasel' knew why Ryabov was here, he would have to gain Dobrynin's confidence first.

'Your Russian is very good', said Ryabov.

Dobrynin sat bolt upright and crossed his arms. 'Thank you, Comrade: our languages are close enough: it's not difficult.'

'I was delighted when my old-school friend, at the Kremlin, suggested I speak to you about my current work.'

'What do you want from me, Comrade? And where is that waiter?'

'You mean he didn't tell you?'

'No', replied the Weasel. 'He arranged this meeting, and left.' Dobrynin stared over Ryabov's left shoulder waiting for the waiter to appear.

'So you don't know we're working on the same case? My Directorate is preparing a fraud charge against Kimon Antonov', his voice dropped to a whisper, 'and one of treason.' Aleksandr sat back triumphantly.

The Weasel seemed unimpressed. 'Of course, I have heard of Comrade Antonov at the Agricultural Secretariat in

Moscow, but I am only from our passport office over here and I was led to believe you just want to trace the owner of a Bulgarian passport.'

'Two, actually, one of a Kostov and the other of a Potanin.'

Aleksandr heard the kitchen doors swing noisily behind him. Dobrynin's paw shot into the air. 'Waiter!' An unshaven person of fortyish ambled over, order book in hand, his white jacket threadbare and blotched. Dobrynin took his time, carefully discussing each dish before he ordered. He smiled at the waiter, but each time he turned his eyes at Aleksandr they cooled. The waiter disappeared leaving dirty kitchen doors swinging noisily back and forth next to the only other occupied table in the restaurant.

A couple sitting there showed more than just a passing interest in Aleksandr: It felt like Moscow. 'Let me give you some background', he said to the Weasel. Dobrynin looked stonily on from his barrier of crossed limbs.

Ryabov talked for twenty minutes without a break, recounting his understanding of the history of the Antonov case. 'I can't give you anything in writing', he finished, 'but I hope I have convinced you to release that information from your records and to get me an authorisation to interview the people they belong to.' He ended with his most winningly lopsided smile.

Dobrynin's face was white. It took a few seconds for him to spit his venom. 'You come to my country in your fine uniforms and think you can dictate to us. You think your little star and dagger can open any door. Maybe it can at home, uncle, but not here! We're not at your orders. Make an official request.'

Aleksandr had been unprepared for such open hostility, and would have made a dignified exit had not the waiter appeared behind him with a steaming bowl. He slopped brown sauce into their plates, left, and came back with a bottle of vodka to the stony silence between the two men.

The Bulgarian ate noisily, presumably to compensate for the silence. The couple by the kitchen doors watched and listened, and Aleksandr wondered whether he had not made a big mistake coming unofficially. He wondered whether the Weasel's performance had not been more for their benefit.

The meal was finished within half an hour, and so was the vodka, but it hadn't loosened Dobrynin's tongue. Aleksandr sweated profusely. He reached into his pocket for a handkerchief and found the beautiful Swiss army knife he had bought for himself at the duty-free shop leaving Berne: he had always wanted one.

Maybe... 'Here!' he slurred through a faint alcoholic mist, 'I bought this to thank you.' He pushed the knife across the table. 'You might as well have it. You're damned right, I should've followed the rules.'

The weasel twitched. Moments passed. An animal glimmer returned to his eyes. 'A Swiss knife', he whispered. He cradled it in his hand and opened the blades one after another: out came a toothpick, tweezers, scissors, a tiny saw....

'More vodka', Aleksandr told the waiter.

'Coffee', added the Weasel.

Aleksandr brought his hand down flat on the table. 'Comrade, you'll be my guest for dinner tomorrow before I go. I like the way you drink.'

The weasel face contorted into a grin. 'Don't come in uniform, uncle.'

''Promise', replied Aleksandr.

The Weasel giggled conspiratorially.

Later that evening, in a drunken haze, Aleksandr bemoaned the loss of his knife. He hoped through his stupor, the knife would be as effective a gift to a sober weasel as to a drunken one.

Rain kept Ryabov indoors for most of the following day. He lounged in the bar, read the papers and struggled with a crossword puzzle.

The Weasel appeared at eight. The waiter gave them the same table and the same nosey couple sat quietly by the swing doors. This time Aleksandr was out of uniform. The Weasel appeared marginally more relaxed. 'To the bar', said Aleksandr.

'Straight to the point, eh.' Dobrynin slunk out, tailed by Ryabov.

''Not eating, then?' called the waiter behind them.

The couple jumped from their table to follow. A chair fell.

'Vodka!' shouted Dobrynin at the barman.

Aleksandr laughed. 'Now who's straight to the point?'

The Weasel perched himself on a stool at the bar and fixed two small dark eyes on Aleksandr. 'The numbers correspond to the passports of a Nicholas Kostov of Pazardzik', he said, 'and of a Valko Potanin of Sofia. Both were issued legally, there has been no declaration of theft, and neither of these two has a police record.'

The bottle arrived. Dobrynin poured two shots. '*Do dna!*' he proclaimed, and the glass and his head snapped back together. Aleksandr followed suit: the freezing, syrupy liquid shot down his throat. Dobrynin produced the Swiss knife and used it to meticulously clean his fingernails. 'If you have time, Comrade, we could interview the owners.'

'All the time we need.'

'You need a travel visa and a car: Pazardzik is far.'

'We could see Potanin here in Sofia in the meanwhile.'

'That's not advisable.'

'Why not?'

'You will want to know about Kostov before we talk to Potanin.' The Weasel picked up the vodka bottle. 'Potanin may be an important link between your work and ours: he's the gardener at BAPTCo., the Bulgarian Agricultural Products Trading Commission in Orlof Square.'

The harbinger of bad news bore the sullen expression of the Kremlin Guard. Had he had his back to Ivan, the set of the shoulders, his height and the dark coat would have been enough to identify his regiment. Ivan cordially disliked the pompous Ninth: these officers were a law unto themselves; subject only to the whims of the Soviet inner *sancta*.

He stepped forward, a sealed envelope in his hands. 'For you, Comrade Colonel.' Ivan scanned the note. It was from Budhakin telling him to return with the Aeroflot Moscow flight the following day. 'I have come to accompany you, Comrade Colonel. I will collect you here at nine a.m. tomorrow. I have your ticket.'

Ivan nodded.

The Guard clicked his heels and strutted to the door. He stopped, turned, and added, 'And please be punctual.'

Ivan didn't like this arrogance; he didn't like the tone of the note; he didn't like being escorted like a criminal, and he didn't want to leave: so much was left to be done. And why the guard? Did Budhakin think he wouldn't come home? It was absurd!

He took the stairs back up to his room. Almost a month had passed since he had left Moscow. Budhakin was right of course, it was time to go home. The old dog didn't take chances with his personnel: defectors were bad publicity for an Area-Department Director.

He wrote to Aleksandr Ryabov to invite him to get back in touch as soon as he returned to the Soviet Union. *IF YOU CAN*, ended the note, *TRY TO LOCATE OTHER EMBASSY STAFF WHO KNEW NIKOLAEV IN ROME, AND HAVE SINCE RETURNED TO MOSCOW.* He mistrusted the contrived silence of the staff at the Rome Embassy.

He sealed the letter. How could he get it to Aleksandr Ryabov without the guards confiscating it? There was no guarantee Ryabov would return to the clinic and none that the letter would not be surrendered by Dr Puschner to the first Russian officer to ask for it.

With a sigh, he tore it up into small pieces and set fire to them each in the grate. Then he ground the ashes into a fine powder.

The phone rang. He didn't want to pick it up, but the bell wouldn't stop. He lifted the mouthpiece and croaked.

A woman's voice mentioned his name and added a few words in baby Russian. The handset clicked, and a man's voice addressed him. 'Comrade Colonel. The Embassy here. I know you've lost your voice, so I don't expect spoken answers.'

Ivan croaked again.

'What did you say.... ah! Yes, good! Well, Comrade Colonel, I have a request here from the Italians to interview you now you are well again. I have your clearance, and it's as well to cooperate: the culprits have been identified and the Italian Party thinks we should follow the course of justice. We are sending an interpreter: an Italian officer is driving up from Milan, and should be with you at about four.'

Even had he wished to, Ivan could not disagree.

'The interpreter is properly trained: you will be in excellent hands.'

Ivan had no doubt of that, and every word would get back to Moscow.

'Just write your answers and give them to him. If you understand and agree, please tap your earpiece.'

Ivan's eyes rolled to the ceiling: he tapped on the earpiece. 'Thank you, Comrade Colonel, he silently thought. There came a click at the other end and Ivan replaced the earpiece in its cradle.

The Italian officer had a large, kindly face and a generous moustache. His hazel eyes gazed at Ivan. Nino Glavina wondered who this exotic Russian could be to get himself shot in Rome and isolated in this conspiracy of silence. It had been impossible to get an interview in the hospital, even though the Russian was on sovereign Italian soil. Mademoiselle de Langeac had called him about two Russians she had met in a speech therapy clinic in Montreux. Nino had called a friend in the Italian Communist Party who had clout with the Russian Embassy in Berne to get the interview.

The interpreter waited for Nino to begin.

'Please ask this person to identify himself. I need his name, age, place of birth, and occupation.'

'Impossible', replied the interpreter in richly accented Italian.

'You haven't asked him', objected Nino.

'He is unauthorised to answer personal questions.'

Nino paused and frowned at Ivan. 'What may he talk about?'

'Questions confined to the incident, which have no bearing on our diplomatic relations. I am sure that, in return, he would be pleased to learn what your investigations have brought to light.'

'Ask him to recount what happened the day he was shot.'

'Only questions, officer, only questions.'

Nino's face reddened.

Ivan shifted uncomfortably in his seat. He knew what the Italian was going through: the interpreter was posturing to limit the flow of information.

'You may call this man, Grigoriy', added the interpreter.

'Ask Grigoriy to tell me whether he has ever seen the faces of the men in these photos.' Nino handed Ivan two photographs. Two bearded youths stared with the unfocused look of the dead. Ivan assumed they were the faces of his aggressors. He had never seen them before and shook his head.

'Grigoriy believes he does not recognise the faces.'

'Thank you', said Nino, irony in his voice. 'Did he see the faces of his attackers?'

The interpreter asked the question in Russian, and Ivan shook his head again. 'Grigoriy believes not.'

'Did he feel he was followed in Rome?'

The interpreter asked the question, and Ivan shook his head.

'Did he get any threats?'

'He believes not', answered the interpreter.

'You didn't ask him.'

'I know the dossier, officer.'

'Ask him, please!'

The interpreter sighed and asked Ivan in Russian. Ivan shook his head. The interpreter raised his eyebrows at Nino and puckered his lips.

'Is he dumb?' asked the *Carabiniere* colonel. 'Bullet wound?'

'I know nothing of his medical history.'

'So far I have wasted my time coming here!' snapped Nino.

The interpreter thought for a few moments and turned to Ivan. 'They want to know why you're here.'

Ivan wrote a few words.

'It seems', said the interpreter, 'Grigoriy lost his voice in Rome.'

'Because of the shooting?'

'He believes that to be so. You see how cooperative we are: why do you lose your temper with us? Surely you have things to tell us too.'

'I need more information. Who knew Grigoriy's movements the day of the shooting?'

'Impossible!'

'Does he know anyone involved with Italian crime?'

'You want him to speculate on the morals of your fatherland?'

'Ask the question!'

The interpreter did so.

Ivan wrote, *EVEN IF I DID, I WOULDN'T TELL.*

The interpreter smiled on reading the note and said, 'Grigoriy believes not.'

'Something amusing?' asked Nino.

'Idiom: just a turn of phrase, nothing important. Now please be so kind as to tell us what you know.'

'Has he heard of Genaro Cagnotto.' Nino pronounced the name slowly, looking Ivan straight in the eyes.

The name came as a surprise: the *Carabiniere* must have noticed him start. Ivan had heard it from Brigitte de Langeac's lips. Nino looked closely at him, and the interpreter, unaware of this silent communication between his two clients, blandly asked the question.

This man is professional, thought Ivan. He wrote.

After some seconds the interpreter answered, 'He believes not, but he was startled by the name because it sounds very like the name of a Croatian cousin of his. Why do you ask?'

Nino whispered to one of the two officers with him. Both had a good knowledge of Russian, which had been of no use whatever. The officer nodded, and Nino Glavina turned to face Ivan. 'Anything else to add?'

'No.'

'Ask him', retorted Nino, pointing at Ivan.

The interpreter asked the question in Russian. Ivan shook his head. 'No, officer', he said.

Nino stood.

'Wait, our information!'

'We have wasted our precious time here: I don't see why we should waste our breath too.'

Ivan wrote on the notepad and thrust it at the interpreter.

'Grigoriy wants to know what this Cagnotto has to do with the murderous incident in Rome.'

Nino stared at Ivan. 'Why?'

'He has a right to know who tried to kill him.'

'Alright', said Nino. 'Because I come from the free world and I don't need a chaperone, I'm going to tell him. Translate that!'

The interpreter did so. Ivan scowled.

'The two thugs in the photos I showed tried to kill him: they were small-time drug peddlers we think associated with the Catanzaro Mafia family. Tell your friend it's not the first time this year this family has been involved in Eastern bloc crime: this Cagnotto, I spoke of, works for the Catanzaro family too: he was indicted last summer for illegally importing and laundering large sums of money from Switzerland. What surprised us was that the money had been sent by a Bulgarian trade commission, but I assume', sneered Nino, 'that the Bulgarian Socialist Republic is still a satellite state of the Soviet Union.'

The interpreter finished translating. Ivan made a few notes.

'Grigoriy would like your card, officer.'

'Can I have his?'

'Impossible.'

'Good-bye. Nice meeting you.' Nino strutted out, followed by his two colleagues.

The interpreter leapt to his feet.

Ivan drew him to a chair and sat him down. He wrote: *I WANT YOU TO REPEAT TO ME EVERY SINGLE WORD THAT WAS SAID*

The interpreter recounted all the conversation on both sides with astounding accuracy.

There was barely sufficient room in the Zastava for the three of them. Ryabov's heavy frame fitted poorly in the back seat of the little Yugoslavian car. The driver had met them at the train station in Pazardzik, and had driven them to a tiny village through brown fields silently awaiting the arrival of the winter freeze.

The Weasel had not wanted an official car for the peasant depths of his homeland, but expediency and Ryabov's hurry led him to change his mind.... besides, a little gross officialdom helped to loosen tongues.

They pulled up in the late morning before a small, wooden cottage slumbering below an overcast sky. Above, a wisp of smoke spiked the still air. A family of crows, perched high in an ancient elm, croaked reproachfully at the newcomers.

The driver's door slammed shut. A corner of a grimy curtain lifted at a window. Here and there, in the front yard, shrubs and vegetables still resisted the oncoming cold. Ryabov and the Weasel crossed to the door.

'Winter supplies', commented Dobrynin, 'they ought to take them to the cooperative.' He stopped at the door, straightened his uniform, and knocked loudly.

Inside, a bolt thudded into its stop, and the door creaked ajar. The rugged features of an old peasant woman appeared at the crack. 'What do you want?' Her accent was so thick, Ryabov didn't even try to understand her.

'Official business', answered Dobrynin, 'we have some questions. I'd like to come in.'

She pulled the door wider.

A voice issued from the bowels of the cottage. 'Who is it, mother?'

'Militia', she replied.

The ample frame of a younger woman appeared.

'Not quite', said the Weasel, 'but close enough.'

The old woman wrung her hands as the two uniformed officers marched into the cottage. Ryabov had no trouble understanding the pallor on their faces. He had seen fear in the eyes of civilians for most of his short professional life, and he still wasn't used to it. The book said he would get used to that look: it said that the day he joined State Security, he had cut himself off from the society of his co-nationals.

'You had better sit', said the younger woman, waving at two stools before the open hearth. Dobrynin and Ryabov removed their hats and topcoats and sat at the fire.

"Some tea?' asked the daughter.

'No', answered Dobrynin, more concerned with the standard of hygiene than his thirst. He didn't bother translating for Ryabov. He stood again, back to the flames, to address the women, crossing his hands behind his back where a warm sensation at the seat of his pants pumped feeling back into his buttocks. 'Which one of you is Comrade Kostova?'

The younger woman was quick to reply. 'Both of us are: my father was Igor Kostov, and this is my mother, Irena. I am Anna.' She looked down, wringing her hands in apprehension, and added, 'I look after my parents: I'm not married.'

'You have a nice place here', commented the Weasel.

'We work at the cooperative', said Anna, 'The State has been good to us. My parents also worked at the cooperative before the Great Patriotic War.'

Dobrynin took a pack of cigarettes from his pocket. 'Would you like one?' he asked.

'None of us smokes', answered Anna, fear pulling at her traits. She sat on the stool next to the old woman and straightened the hem of her thick woollen skirt. She folded her hands in her lap and waited.

Aleksandr Mikhailovich studied her wide, Slavic features, tanned from work in the fields and strained by punishing labour at the cooperative. Dobrynin lit his cigarette, looking casually at the old woman, rigid with fear on her stool. He made no effort to allay the tension. 'Tell me, Irena Kostova.'

The old woman waited.

'Tell you what?' asked Anna.

'I want your mother to tell me about Comrade Nicholas, who also lives here, and whose passport is of great interest to us.'

The old woman's chin trembled. 'Nicholas!' she whispered. 'You want to know about Nicholas.' Tears welled in Irena Kostova's eyes.

Unaware of the daughter's rising anger, Ryabov and the Weasel were surprised by Anna's snarl. 'Get out! Get out!'

The Weasel looked worried for the first time since Ryabov had met him. He raised a hand. 'Comrade, we came asking a civil question that requires a civil reply.'

'I don't care. Go away! Leave us alone!' She put her hand on her mother's shoulder. 'Now she will be ill again.'

Dobrynin drew on his cigarette. He spoke through fumes pouring from his nose and mouth: it relaxed him. 'We have done nothing to upset your mother.'

'I will tell you about him, then you must leave immediately.'

'That depends', said the Weasel, distinctly more in control, 'but we can probably leave you in peace for now: tell us where he can be found so we can speak to him.'

'I know exactly where he is, but you won't get much out of him.'

'That', said Dobrynin smugly, 'is for us to judge.'

Anna Kostova scoffed. 'You are wrong: Nicholas is buried: my brother was crushed by a tractor when he was five.'

The gardener glared at his questioners in a stony silence. He preferred to be outside, where the air was pure. Tending the roses in the courtyard of the Agricultural Trade Commission's elegant white building on Sofia's Orlov Square was more than just a job, it was a vocation.

Aleksandr Ryabov watched him patiently, waiting for the truth. He looked at the man's hands, hardened by years of labour and marked by the tar solution he used to cure his sores. He felt an almost paternal interest in the fate of this gardener: he was, after all, a Bulgarian, a friend of Russia. He felt a hidden pride that Russia had liberated Bulgaria from the Ottoman Turks. A bond of sympathy united him with these people, whose ancestors had governed Thrace, Macedonia, and Albania before succumbing to five centuries of Ottoman imperial Muslim rule. Surely Bulgarian gratitude to Russia, commonly thought to be the case in the streets of Moscow, would smooth the flow of understanding.

Dobrynin stood, walked around the desk, and pointed his snout at the gardener. 'Valko Potanin, you have our word that none of what you say will be used against you.'

Potanin continued to gaze sullenly out of the window.

'But if you don't cooperate, and we find against you, we will not obstruct the course of justice. If you tell us the truth, what would you have you to fear?'

Cool sunlight bathed the courtyard. He had wrapped straw around the stems after pruning. Little oil lamps on the hard earth would chase away the first frosts before the arrival of the snow. Valko Potanin fished out a wallet from a back pocket. He opened it and took out a faded photograph. He handed it to Dobrynin. 'Me and the boy.'

A younger and more vigorous Potanin stood next to a pale youth slumped in a wheelchair. The Weasel handed the snapshot to Ryabov. 'Polio', went on Potanin. 'He caught pneumonia when he was thirteen, and didn't survive the winter. I got the passport so I could take him to Vienna for treatment.'

'A lot of money, Comrade.'

Potanin raised his head proudly. 'I was a "Fighter Against Fascism": I have a military pension, and Comrade Secretary Petrovic promised the Trade Commission would make up what I couldn't pay.'

'Comrade Petrovic is no longer Secretary', pointed out the Weasel.

The gardener thrust his chin at him. 'He is a fine man and a patriot. I don't care what he has done: he has always been good to me.'

Dobrynin sat casually on the edge of the desk and leant forward towards the gardener. 'How much did he give you for it?' His tone was confidential, almost reassuring, yet mocking.

Valko Potanin's black eyes flashed with hatred. 'Money? Everything is money. There was friendship, loyalty!'

'You gave him the passport?'

'It was of no use after my boy had died.'

'Did he say why he wanted it?'

'No, and I didn't ask.'

'Did he ask you for anything else, to do something, to sign papers?'

'No.'

'Did you inform the Ministry of the Interior?'

'I assumed the Trade Commission would look after the formalities: I can't read or write.'

Dobrynin threw a questioning glance at Ryabov, who shook his head.

'You may go', said the Weasel.

The gardener stood, looked at Ryabov, and scowled. 'That uniform: I've seen it before: it's not one of ours, is it?'

Dobrynin stifled his surprise. 'No, Comrade, we don't see one often in Sofia.'

'Let me see the insignia.'

Ryabov, having a good idea of the gist of Potanin's conversation, took off his brown hat, and showed him the small star and dagger on a red and silver shield.

'That's the one, and it wasn't on the streets, it was right here in this courtyard. I will never forget that young fat-head: he just stood there, breaking stem after stem. I shouted at him, and he laughed as if he owned the place. He said he was taking the roses home. I said he couldn't, and he said to complain to the Comrade Secretary. I almost hit him. The little prick was wearing this uniform.'

Aleksandr Ryabov strained to catch what he could through the gardener's dialect.

'What was his name?' asked the Weasel.

'I don't know: his shoulder boards had a stripe and two stars, just like his', he replied, pointing at Aleksandr 'That makes them both lieutenants, I suppose.'

Wondering how much the Russian had understood, the Weasel said, 'It's an honour, Valko Potanin, to be visited by our Russian cousins, and a tribute to Bulgarian agriculture.'

Dobrynin's sarcasm merited a bark of laughter from the gardener and a scowl from Ryabov. 'Ask him when', said Aleksandr Mikhailovich.

Dobrynin looked at the gardener. 'Did you understand the question?'

'Springtime, a season ago.'

'Would you recognise this man if you saw him again?'

The gardener growled. 'I remember him.'

'We may ask for your help again, Comrade.'

Potanin, tired anyway of all this talk, was dismissed from the room.

Fury raged in Dobrynin's eyes. 'Why can't you people even communicate between yourselves? I want to know who else from Moscow Centre is involved apart from you and your dumb rowing partner.'

Ryabov controlled his urge to strangle the Weasel: Dobrynin was starting to rub on his nerves. 'Perhaps another directorate is involved, Comrade: Moscow sometimes fields investigations in parallel, as I am sure Sofia does.' But he was confused: he had understood from Ivan Promyslov that no one else from Moscow Centre was investigating this affair. 'But wait, Comrade, the BAPTCo transactions and the Antonov and Petrovic offences date from this year: this officer visited Petrovic before any of these crimes was even discovered.'

Dobrynin nodded slowly. His thin face ruptured into a grin. 'Before they were discovered, but not necessarily before they were committed?' Mercifully, the Weasel's face became serious again. 'If this Soviet lieutenant from state security was here on business, we must have a record: I will check with our security staff. Excuse me.' He left Ryabov alone to think over the gardener's story.

Only three Aeroflot flights arrived at Sheremetievo that day: a vast cloud of fog had enveloped Moscow, making the forty kilometres into the city slow and miserable. The driver had appeared with written instructions to accompany Colonel Ivan Dmitriyevich Promyslov directly to the Lubyanka complex, where he was to meet an officer in the Sixteenth. The driver seemed to know about Ivan's voice problem and showed no desire for discussion anyway.

There was time to think in the back of the dark green Moskvitch. Ivan peered through the grey fog for signs of the homeland he felt he had left an age ago. The driver speeded, confident there were few cars on the road: that was a sign he was home.

The Sixteenth Department of the First Chief Directorate dealt with routine personnel matters, and particularly with the recruitment of young people into the small international sections of State Security. Ivan had no idea why he was taken there: it seemed to him his first stop should be in the office of his remote and disinterested Area Department Director, Budhakin. Little had been accomplished, it was true, but it was his duty to talk over the laxity he had found in the Rome Embassy. On the rare occasions his boss had invited Ivan into his office, it was to get answers to questions asked by his own superiors. Budhakin was always in a hurry because General so-and-so wanted information by yesterday, never because he, Budhakin, needed it. The advantage was that Ivan could get on with his job: the disadvantage was that no one knew or cared enough about him to judge whether he was promotable.

Budhakin had one passion, the limelight. Fancying himself a scholar, nothing pleased him more than a periodic invitation to address the odd congress or institution where, before a captive audience, he could expound on his hackneyed views without fear of contradiction. His latest passion was the class on civil organisation at the M.V. Frunze Military Academy in Moscow. It was a rare privilege for State Security officers to be invited to address the Military. Ivan wondered how an *ignatz* like Budhakin had been picked for the job. The Military, jealous of its independence, surely had staff capable of explaining the fine balance of power existing between the Soviet troika of Party, Military, and State Security.

The car stopped at the barrier closing off the courtyard of two Dzerzhinsky Square. A guard peered through the window at Ivan and inspected the identity papers presented by the driver.

'He'll have to get out here', he said: 'only general staff vehicles are allowed in the courtyard.'

The driver stopped the engine, held open the door for Ivan, and delivered his suitcase into the blockhouse where guards kept jealous watch over a horizontal red and white pole.

'You can leave it here, Comrade Colonel', said a guard, careful to introduce a note of respect in his voice.

Ivan nodded, retrieved his papers, and walked across the freezing courtyard to a rear entrance. He wished he had put his uniform on; he looked bad in his cheap, crumpled suit.

Once through the door, he felt happy to be back in these corridors with their artificial marble floors and perpetual smell of cheap cigarettes. The red carpets and moulded cornices typified Chekist tastelessness, but to him, this was home. He followed the painted signs to the Sixteenth and took the written instruction from his pocket: he was not sure how a personnel officer might react to a mute in civilian clothes arriving unannounced in his office.

The young captain behind the desk looked up angrily at this individual proffering a typewritten sheet without the least smile or formality. Only high-ranking officers took such liberties. Scowling, the captain read the note without a word and nodded. 'Please sit down, Comrade Colonel.'

He crossed to his safe: the door was open. 'I have to draw your file. I hope you had a pleasant trip back.' He read through a dossier, flicking pages fastidiously. 'A wonderful career, Comrade Colonel, exceptional experience. Such a shame, this accident.' He sat at his desk and spread his fingers into a steeple below his chin.

This man loves to give bad news, thought Ivan.

'First, I am to wish you our sincerest wishes for a speedy recovery.'

Our?

'Your Area Department Director, Comrade General Budhakin, is especially preoccupied with your state of health: he insisted you should be cared for in Switzerland. It's wonderful, Comrade Colonel, how strong leaders look after their men.' He waited for a nod of approval.

Ivan gave none and listened patiently on.

The captain frowned. 'We have received a report from this Doctor....., ah', he consulted his file, '.... Puschner, on your progress.'

We? This man would kill his own mother, thought Ivan: no wonder they had chosen him to break the bad news.

'He seems satisfied there's little organic damage but is unable to say when and if you will be able to speak again.' The captain crossed his hands on the desk. 'That's why we need to talk, Comrade Colonel.' He hid, he thought, his sudden embarrassment at this unfortunate choice of words, and watched for alarm on Ivan's face. He was met by the neutral stare most long-term employees practised within the walls of Dzerzhinsky Square.

'An officer of your quality understands, of course, the inconvenience to General Staff of a colleague who is not able to contribute fully: you see, a speech impediment at your level poses an enormous problem here.'

Ivan remained icy. Not a hint of acceptance escaped him: nothing satisfied the captain that Ivan agreed with his statements. Inside, he was writhing; the coup de grace was yet to come.

'Put yourself in the Comrade General's position', the captain was struggling, 'and you will understand his difficulty in finding the right future for you. He has great loyalty to his people, but there are limits to such generosity if he is to serve the State: it must come before the individual, as you know.' He took a pack of cigarettes from his pocket and offered Ivan one.

Ivan showed a palm in refusal.

The captain noted with satisfaction he was getting through: Ivan's coolness had degenerated into a strained frown. The rest would be plain sailing. It was easier talking to a mute: there was no argument. He lit up, and relaxed. 'We must take good care of you, Comrade Colonel, and give due recognition to the remarkable services you have rendered State Security. We have prepared a package to suit your case.'

He leaned forward, a sheet from Ivan's file in his hands. 'Firstly, we have registered you as a privileged patient with the Neurology Department at the KGB Hospital. The consultant neurologist, who will take care of you, has called this Doctor Puschner. You will not be required to live in, so you can stay at home.'

He looked up with a bright smile as if Ivan should be overwhelmed with this special treatment. He was confronted with the neutral stare. The colonel had brought himself under control again. He continued, 'Of course you are to maintain your rank and all your privileges in State Security so richly deserved.... however, ...'

This was it.

The captain's eyes wandered to a spot on the wall behind Ivan. '.... we may have to reclaim your dacha. There is such a demand: we have young, talented officers promotable to your rank who have never known such luxury, and you have had use of our property for some years I believe.' He peered at the file. 'Yes, quite a number of years. I will confirm this point in writing later this month, and, who knows, we may find you something just as pleasant elsewhere.'

Siberia? thought Ivan.

The captain selected another page. 'Finally, there is the matter of your posting bearing in mind your inability to communicate effectively with others. Please understand the difficulty for us, once again, of finding a position appropriate to the talents of a man like you.' He paused to read the note. 'I have written confirmation of an important new appointment for you in the Fifteenth Department. You are to assume responsibility for the security of the archives. This is a new position of trust requiring the vast experience only an officer of your calibre and trustworthiness can provide.'

Ivan was overwhelmed with bitterness: this was the graveyard of his career.

'You can begin as soon as the hospital authorises it. In the meanwhile, you may wish to reunite with your family and take the necessary steps to free the dacha, by the end of this week, please. We will move your stuff for you. Have you any questions?' The grin crumbled into sudden embarrassment. 'Uh....you may wish to write them down.' He pushed a notepad at Ivan.

Ivan's mind was in a swell. Frustrated by his inability to vent his anger, his silence screamed within, yet on his face, he wore little more than a frown. *NO*, he wrote, *INFORM COMRADE GENERAL BUDHAKIN I WILL MAKE MY REPORT IN WRITING.* He stood.

'Oh, that reminds me, you are, of course, no longer permitted to go back to your office. Any personal items you have in your desk or in your safe will be returned through this office. We will issue new keys to your successor as soon as the seals have been broken and the locks changed.'

Ivan wrote, *WHO IS HE?*

'We are unauthorised to divulge the name, Comrade Colonel, but, in view of your rank and your knowledge of the individual, we can make an exception in your case. You will be delighted. It's your able assistant, Comrade 'Captain' Vassya Nikolaev.'

Captain? Vassya! So, the scoundrel had been promoted and was this character's pal.

Ivan turned and strutted into the corridor.

The captain rushed after him. 'Comrade Colonel, your instructions.'

Ivan took the dossier and marched on.

The captain stared after him, smugly convinced his own career would never end like this.

The cold air, damper than it would be later, made his face tingle. He stopped for a moment in the courtyard to catch his breath and looked up at the six floors surrounding him. Lights shone from most of the offices giving them an orange tint against the blue-grey of the sky. He stuck the file under his armpit and thrust his hands deep into his pockets. He made for the guard house.

In the warmth of the small hut by the red and white barrier, Ivan rubbed the condensation on the window pane. He peered through the glass expecting to find his car parked on the road. He found a scrap of paper, and wrote *WHERE IS MY CAR?* He gave it to the guard.

'What car? Who are you?'

Ivan wrote, *COLONEL PROMYSLOV: FIRST CHIEF DIRECTORATE.*

The guard made a slovenly salute, and lifted a telephone. He turned his back on Ivan, and spoke quietly into the mouthpiece, then waited an age. He replaced the handset. 'Comrade Colonel, there are no more cars today. Is this yours?' he asked, pointing at the suitcase.

Ivan nodded.

'You can take a bus or the metro.'

Humiliated, Ivan lifted his case and walked out into the cold.

Circling the building towards Marx Prospekt, he passed the Children's World Exhibition and made for the subway across the square. Within twenty minutes he was climbing subway stairs. He walked the final three hundred metres to the corner of the street leading to his apartment block.

He arrived frozen to the bone; his arms ached; his thoughts were in a spin. He felt humiliated; Olya now had a broken man for a mate. He mounted the three flights, and, with a final burst of effort, knocked heavily at his door.

'Who is it?' came Olga's voice.

In agony, he realised he couldn't answer her.

'Who is it? What do you want?'

Ivan sat on his suitcase. He put his head in his hands and sobbed like a child.

The door opened slightly. Olga cried out and rushed onto the landing to hug her broken man.

BUGS AND THE JUNGLE COTTAGE

Florie McKinley waited for the others to finish. The ladies had agreed to share three daily newspapers and to circulate them, starting each morning at a different bed. Today, she was last in line. She reached out stiffly for the first to arrive: there were still two hours to lights-out.

She looked forward to her read before each night of insomnia. A few of the women had suffered nightmares following the assassination, but Florie would gladly have traded one night of their troubled sleep for those long hours disturbed only by the occasional word of comfort from a night nurse. Sleeping drugs were too dangerous for her frail system, but a few articles could relax her and help fill her sleepless mind with thought.

She saw the man's photograph in the Chicago Tribune. Florie stared at it for a long time, wondering why none of the others had recognised him. 'I can't be the only one', she mumbled, glancing surreptitiously around the ward.

'What'd you say, Flo?' came a feeble voice from the next bed. The night nurse walked in and announced it was time to switch off the lights.

'Never mind, dear', said Florie, 'tell you in the morning.' She turned painfully onto her side and gazed wide-eyed at the dim light above the ward door through which the terrorist had come and gone the day of the murder. 'It's him', she whispered, 'I know it's him!'

He sat by the old lady's bedside. 'Hello, Florie, I'm Jim Curry.'

'How do you do, Mr Curry. They said you are from the FBI: is that true?'

'Yes, Florie, and we would like to thank you: your information on the Secretary of State's assassination was very helpful.'

'Oh, good', she said, thrilled the other ladies might overhear.

'They've changed your ward', said Jim looking around the new second-floor ward room.

'A few nightmares downstairs after the murder: they moved us up here. I miss the courtyard.'

'I've heard you have more information, Florie, but that you won't give it to anyone but me. Is that right?'

'It is, officer Curry. It's too important to get lost in your system.'

Jim smiled. 'Very wise! Now, here I am. Now, what do you want to tell me?'

Florie took a few moments to collect her thoughts. 'Do you remember a man was found dead in a car in Oakbrook? A suicide, they wrote, in the papers.'

'Yes, we know who he was.'

'There's probably one thing you don't know about him', said Florie, the glint of old pewter in her eyes. She paused for effect as the ladies in the other beds strained their ears to pick up snippets of the conversation. 'That man was the policeman who walked into the ward just after the murderer walked out. He was the one wearing gloves.'

Now it was Jim's turn to collect his thoughts. 'Is there any possibility, any at all, Florie, that you could be wrong?'

'None! I never forget a face, officer, ever!'

Jim tried to remember the jumble of facts the old lady had given in her deposition. 'Are you sure he wasn't the killer himself?'

'I told your people, officer, but they don't listen: he looked very much like him, but he wasn't! No! They were two different people.'

Bugs slept fitfully for most of the flight from Kennedy.

He sensed the fragrance of the sub-tropical climate from the moment he climbed down the aeroplane ramp onto the apron: the air swept over him holding a thousand smells. He loosened the knot in his tie before greeting his one-man reception committee. Rosen stepped forward as Bugs entered the milling arrivals lounge. The Israeli looked casual in his open-necked shirt, the humidity encouraging no one to overdress. His features distinguished him among the other dark faces in the dusty lounge. 'Mr Macpherson?'

'Yes', replied Bugs. 'Are you Mr Rosen?'

'How do you do', confirmed Rosen. 'Welcome to Asuncion. Please come this way. I'll get someone to pick up your luggage. You should give me your ticket stub.'

Bugs followed Rosen under sleepy ceiling fans to the baggage claim, where he identified his bags for the benefit of a large *mulatto*. He clambered thankfully into the back of a new Ford and waited with Rosen for the *mulatto* to load his bags into the trunk and to drive to the Israeli Delegation.

Progressing along dusty roads to the centre of the city, he gazed at the old Spanish architecture and at streets lined with exotic Jacaranda trees. Following his gaze, Rosen saw him admire the plazas drenched in colour by the blooming Lapachos.

After a check on the hotel reservation, Rosen invited Bugs to a cool office where he drew a file on Fatima Al-Othman. The name of Carmen Muñoz on the cover had been struck through. Rosen passed the file across the desk and watched as the American leafed through the documents, now and again whistling softly as he read.

Bugs noted the dates and times of Fatima's trips to Asuncion.

The woman's attempts at finding ex-Nazis and Nazi sympathisers in the wild Chaco area, where many had settled after the war, had been inept. A Mossad agent had presented himself as a go-between. She had claimed she was fund raising for the Al Fatah Revolutionary Council and had blatantly asked for a contribution of a million dollars giving an account number at a Syrian bank. This account contained *bona fide* Palestinian funds. It had been a significant find for Israeli intelligence.

Fatima had been photographed during her fund raising and a trace through Tel Aviv had revealed her identity. She had disclosed her home address in Santa Ana, and the folder contained a thinly-veiled suggestion that her apartment be searched.

She had always returned to California through Bogota. This intrigued Bugs: Jim had said she had a lover there, and Bugs asked Rosen if he knew. 'I believe she was photographed with a man once in Bogota. Ask the FBI, who probably know her as Carmen Muñoz. The Bureau has useful information on her: we have contributed to their file.'

'You seem well informed!' remarked Bugs, wondering how Rosen had concluded he was not from the FBI himself. Jim Curry would not have betrayed his identity.

'We're running a state under siege', said Rosen: 'we feel strongly about the quality of our intelligence. For example, Mr Macpherson, you may have thought you came here incognito: not so! Israel remembers well her visitors, official or not. I know you came in 1974 to study our work to avenge the victims of the 1972 Munich Olympics atrocity.'

Bugs smiled: the Israeli had answered his unasked question. 'Can I have a copy of this file?' he asked.

'I'm afraid no', answered Rosen, 'but take any notes you wish.'

Bugs thanked Rosen, took some notes, and was driven by the *mulatto* to the Excelsior hotel on the outskirts of town.

He retired to the pool to relax in the sun until evening and to think about Fatima Al-Othman. The file had described a reckless and naive woman, easily led into acts of violence. Unlike the painstaking professionals of crime and terrorism, she was too unstable and rash to survive long in the violent world she had chosen. A search of her Santa Ana apartment in early 1985 had unearthed photographs of her in para-military uniform, taken, it seemed, in a desert camp. Handwritten accounts confirmed she was active in drug traffic and ferrying illegal immigrants, both felonies aimed at undermining the fragile fabric of American society. Fatima was a simple-minded, blind, idealist, the living prey of the vultures of terrorism, and a part of their daily sacrifice.

Although the information from Paraguay had been sent to the FBI, the Bureau had opted to let her run wild against the wishes of the Mossad so that she could be tracked to more important game.

The sun set quickly. Bugs picked up his towel and went up to his room for a shower after booking a table by the pool. He would dine alone, Rosen and his wife having other engagements for the evening. The waiter said a band would be playing outside that night.

It took two hours to place his call: the waiter came to his table once the line was available. Jenny took the call on the night shift at NIH and promised to call Bugs' secretary,

Carol, with his message. He changed his ticket to arrive in Bogota the following morning. Carol would notify Sinclair of the early arrival by cable. Bugs had not wanted the resident CIA case officer in Bogota informed of his visit: he would be able to work more quickly without red tape. It was a risk: John Glenn's murder and Simona Grassi's movements through Coombes air traffic control and a Texan women's clinic were now Duval's prerogative and not his own. Company lore required the awareness of local Bogota personnel unless the Director had personally waived the instruction. It was not the first time Bugs had stuck his neck out in this way.

To begin with, he found landing between mountain peaks unnerving. Then, he had been unprepared for the altitude effects: he felt dizzy for hours after his arrival, and the swarming city and the noise did little to comfort his frayed nerves. On the slow, busy road to the hotel, he gazed from the cab at a sea of faces testifying to an unbroken spectrum of ethnic roots. The cynical, self-demeaning cab driver claimed in broken English that one's friends were more or less *negrito* or more or less *blanco* depending on the speaker's own skin colour and that it was no big deal: Bogota was like that!

The traffic jam in a narrow street in the old Candelaria district seemed hopeless: someone was going to have to back off, and no one intended to do so. The cabbie stopped the motor and strolled into a bar for a coffee. Returning some minutes later to calm the ruffled feathers of his impatient *blanco* customer, he spoke with passion of the birds and of the butterflies in his hometown of Buccamaranga. He thought that Bogota was no place for a tourist, on the other hand, it wasn't safe to travel inland either.

At last, the traffic lurched forward, and the long trip to the hotel was resumed.

Bugs wound down in the back of the cab, slowly absorbing the meaninglessness of time for his host. He did not want impatience to blind him to the beauty of a country whose mountains had enslaved the peoples settling her valleys since prehistory. Discouragement and superstition wove an insidious web around the cabbie's words: he loved birds and butterflies and feared the magnificence surrounding him.

They drew up in front of the hotel.

With a shrug of his shoulders, the cabbie ended a commentary on his countrymen. 'You see, *señor*, nothing can be done because ours is a backward country.' He derived solace from those few fatalistic words as if they justified the violence and superstition of Colombia and so consigned his fatherland's glorious ancient culture and majestic peaks to a gratuitous trick of nature.

Sinclair had left a note at the reception desk to say he was unavailable until the following morning, so Bugs spent the day of his arrival walking in the immediate vicinity of the hotel. More than once he checked his wallet as young scavengers harassed him in the streets. He took the funicular to Montserrat, where he could look down onto the intricate pattern of narrow streets cut between stately, colonial mansions of the old Spanish Candelaria quarter. Even in the clearer air of Montserrat, the bustle was more than he was used to: he cut short the tourism and returned to the hotel for peace and quiet. He would leave the pre-Colombian collection at the Gold Museum for a visit with Jenny: he was a lousy tourist on his own.

The night was cold for a town a mere five degrees North of the Equator, but understandable at eight thousand feet above sea level: he dined inside.

Sinclair came to the hotel the following morning and recommended that Bugs pack for a three-day trip.

Sinclair's preparations did not impress Bugs at all: he clearly knew little of the country despite the DEA's struggle to protect America's children from the Medellin cartel's traffic of cocaine and marijuana. Sinclair rarely visited the Cesar and Guajira Departments near the Sierra Nevada de Santa Marta, where the bulk of the illicit trade was to be found, arguing that it was dangerous and that the police had the problem 'in hand.' He had slid comfortably into the role of a powerless bureaucrat patiently awaiting the end of his foreign assignment to claim a safe desk job back home. He stressed that his hands were politically tied and that his functions were really 'diplomatic.' After all, argued Sinclair, Colombia was a sovereign state.

At the office, Bugs was greeted by a scowl from a large *mulatta* at the door. Sinclair brushed by her asking for two cans of cold pop.

Leaning back in his chair, his hands clamped behind his head and staring vacantly at something on the ceiling behind Bugs, Sinclair speculated that Simona X might be the Simona Grassi the Texas FBI was searching for after she had landed the Bonanza several times in Texan airspace. He had thought at first, she was a figment of drugged minds, but after extensive enquiries, he said, he had found records of such a woman living deep in the Magdalena River jungle valley on the route to Valledupar and Maicao. She did exist, and in an area, that was both very beautiful and very dangerous.

Sinclair wanted to avoid Maicao and Finca Martinez, both dirty towns at the hub of the narcotics trade, situated in the far North on the edge of an arid plain overlooked by the snow-capped peak of Cristobal Colon, the nineteen-thousand-foot peak of the Sierra Nevada de Santa Marta.

With nothing more to add, he ambled off to find the two cans of pop that hadn't arrived.

Lush jungle slid by the window of the old train toiling sleepily along the Magdalena valley towards Santa Marta.

Clear, blue sky and dark foliage lulled Bugs into a state of quiet contentment. Sinclair had at last fallen asleep rocked by the monotonous rhythm of the old carriage bumping from rail to rail. A half-drunk Indian had sprawled himself over most of one seat causing the other occupants of the compartment some discomfort during the long night: finding himself by the window, Bugs had settled calmly. It had been a different story for Sinclair, who had suffered bleary-eyed and wide-awake throughout the whole night.

It was strange that, in a country that had taken so ardently to the air, Sinclair had insisted on a thirty-hour train journey. The valley was a dangerous area, infested with hungry mosquitoes and bandits. Well into the second day, Sinclair spoke of his fear of air travel in Colombia, where high terrain made flight dangerous and where aeroplane accidents were frequent and so often fatal. Feeling guilty that he was wasting time, Bugs spent most of it gazing at the majestic Cordilleras on each side of the deep river valley.

From time to time green walls of vegetation receded to show the dark valley plunging down to the rapid waters of the Magdalena River. Now and then the train would cross a trembling steel bridge running hundreds of feet above the torrent, and, as the Sierra Nevada approached, sleepy Indian villages rushed by. Brown faces looked impassively out from under incongruous bowler hats at the pale faces from the city, their bright clothes painting streaks of colour against the luxuriant jungle backdrop.

Across the valley, Bugs could see the vast coffee plantations providing much of the livelihood of these poor villagers. Deep in the jungle, hidden everywhere in the hills, lay more sinister plantations fuelling seventy percent of the US hundred-billion-dollar drug market.

Sinclair had spoken of the apathy of the Indian peasants: of course, they were attracted to villages paying more than a mere subsistence wage! They had wives and families to feed. The agony of a drugged America was too remote. They were farmers. Who were these foreigners to question their skilful husbandry? Those tender shoots of coca and hashish growing in magnificent jungle were nothing if not nature in her innocence? Man was the culprit: nature was blameless. Poverty was the enemy: nature's fruits gave release from care: what was so special about distant America? Overwhelmed by poverty, the Indian preferred to chew coca in his quiet fields than to further complicate an already harsh existence.

Violent men in mountain fortresses, ruling from hills in the Medellin area outside the control of the Colombian authorities, accumulated wealth and power beyond imagination. Sinclair claimed that their power was absolute: like feudal lords, they ran private armies. Their contacts covered an international spectrum of politicians and of criminals ranging from advisors sent by Cuba's DGI, to senators and underworld figures controlling networks capable of supplying every individual American, and most Europeans, with narcotics.

Aware of these dangers, the army major welcoming them off the train took no chances. The very jungle had eyes: it was futile to try to hide the arrival of the Americans, so he provided a fully armed escort, hoping that the weight of authority would drive the weaker bandits into the cracks and the stronger ones to think twice before nosing around. Stepping from the wagon, Bugs sensed the tension: he saw fear and hostility in the eyes of those on the platform. Were these meddlesome *blancos* a threat to their livelihood or were they just afraid of the military?

'Major Carlos Aguirre at your service', said the officer, saluting smartly, and stepping forward from a small unit of infantry at ease on the platform.

'How do you do', said Bugs. 'I'm Macpherson: this is Sinclair.'

'I've taken the liberty, Mr Macpherson, of providing an escort to visit the cottage: an American does not pass unnoticed here: it's dangerous.'

'I would have preferred something less conspicuous.'

'Pointless, señor: your presence is impossible to hide: you are safer in our hands, even if we do stand out a little. We have a two-hour drive into the jungle: it's rough, but if you haven't seen tropical jungle before, you will find it enjoyable. We'll stay on the Valledupar road if we can, but we'll have to turn off into the undergrowth eventually.'

They left in four Jeeps, heading farther and farther into the green valley at the mouth of the Northern Cordilleras.

Bugs listened enchanted to the sounds of a thousand birds above the straining engines of the Jeeps. He watched the inquisitive antics of exotic beasts and laughed at furry hind quarters disappearing into the undergrowth. The warm, heady fragrance of the jungle elated him despite the unbearable humidity. Bright, iridescent feathers streaked colours at every turn against the speckled green and yellow backdrop. He watched for snakes but saw none, not even when, from time to time, the driver pointed at a bush, or giggled when a long sinuous form wriggled across the Jeep's path. Bugs hoped his journey would go on and on.

A clearing appeared through the trees widening into a plain totally encircled by jungle and overlooked by low hills. An airstrip ran the length of the clearing now carpeted with large green shoots as the jungle advanced inexorably upon the untended site. A cottage appeared and a makeshift hangar capable of protecting a small aircraft from torrential downpours.

They stopped at the edge of the jungle, and the major ordered two of his men to check the perimeter of the clearing. He sent two others with one of the Jeeps directly to the cottage, mandating the use of the mounted gun if necessary. The rest waited silently, tuned into the walky-talkies to keep in touch with the scouts.

They spent thirty minutes checking the clearing before the major permitted the rest of the party to advance to the cottage.

Once at the door, he posted lookouts and waited tensely with them as Bugs and Sinclair entered the cottage to begin their search.

On its sea of rich, green foliage, the cottage was no architectural miracle. Its only concessions to style were a veranda to better enjoy evenings in the jungle and stilts to offer protection from the creatures inhabiting the undergrowth. An armada of tiny beings, energetically crawling up and down them, proved just how ineffective the stilts were.

The interior was devastated: the floor was strewn with clothes, toilet articles, shoes, hairbrushes and broken mirrors.

"Strange', said the DEA agent, 'why didn't they just steal the stuff instead of breaking it? This junk's sellable to the peasants.'

'They were searching, not looting, and, by the look of those broken plants, not long ago.'

The step up to the bedroom served no obvious purpose. Bugs knocked on the floorboards confirming his suspicion of a false floor.

'I'll get a crowbar from the Jeep', said Sinclair, faintly jealous of Bugs' obvious competence.

'If we find anything down there, they were either very unprofessional or disturbed on the job', mumbled Bugs.

Sinclair left, and Bugs continued to search among the fragments. A man and a woman had lived in the cottage: they had shared the bedroom and the closet, which contained clothes not all cut for jungle life. A pair of Texan snakeskin boots lay in a corner.

The DEA agent returned, chose a loose-looking board and prized it up with a steel bar. It lifted easily. He removed the plank and peered down into the space.

Sinclair's fingers disappeared into the hole.

'Stop!' yelled Bugs.

Something hissed in the darkness below. Sinclair leapt into the air like a terrified monkey. By the time he landed, his feet were scrambling for safety.

Bugs had yelled in time to save his hand from the fangs of a nesting pit viper.

Sinclair's face drained of colour.

'You don't get out too much into the jungle then', said Bugs grinning at the trembling agent.

'Fucking evil!' panted Sinclair.

'I guess the beast in there feels much the same about you. You'd better get one of our military friends to chase it out: they live with snakes all the time.'

They beat the floor with rifle butts, and slowly lifted the boards. They found a bundle of rough sacking. The infantryman leading the snake hunt rolled it over with the end of his rifle before picking it up. The viper's unhatched eggs rolled off into the darkness as if in search of their parent.

The slim, brown-faced soldier became quite still and slowly lifted his head. 'Listen', he whispered.

Sinclair stiffened. 'What to?' the hint of a tremor in his voice, 'I don't hear anything.'

'Exactly: the jungle is quiet, señor.'

The soldier walked to where Major Aguirre was standing frowning. The officer lifted his walky-talky to his lips and ordered the Jeep at the far end of the airstrip into the undergrowth.

The wild, rhythmic beat of a helicopter exploded above the trees fifty yards from the cottage. For instants, the dark craft hovered menacingly above, its pilot close enough to see Aguirre's personnel rushing for the Jeeps. Heavy guns instantly pounded the vehicles. Two burst into flames. Petrol tanks and ammunition blew. The third made the cover of the hangar as the gunfire swung towards it. The fourth, following Aguirre's order, stayed hidden in the bush at the opposite end of the runway.

Aguirre tossed his carbine to Bugs telling him to defend himself. He would run for the Jeep in the hangar: the car was equipped with a shoulder-launched rocket which ought to, with luck, knock out the helicopter. The superior officer was the only one trained to use it. Aguirre yelled into the walky-talky.

The helicopter relaxed its fire and veered towards the centre of the airstrip.

The major sprinted for his life. Bugs shattered a pane in the bedroom window and, with the infantryman, fired at the hovering craft. Armed men dropped from its belly, and rushed for the undergrowth. Bugs counted six, but at least one fell as a military bullet found its target.

In an angry rush through the torrid air, the rocket's 'red eye' sought the helicopter's hot turbine. Its smoky trail disappeared as if in slow motion into a brilliant, yellow flash.

Bugs ducked. The blast hurled vegetation and broken glass into the room and flung Sinclair to the ground. Flames roared out on the strip, consuming the craft. A pall of thick black smoke wound its way up into the blue. The shooting stopped. The surviving bandits melted into the undergrowth, leaving an ominous calm behind broken only by the hiss of the flames surging from the wrecked helicopter.

The major ordered two men to drive the Jeep to high ground to transmit to Valledupar and coordinated his remaining men to flush the bandits from their jungle cover.

The vehicle hidden at the far end of the strip advanced slowly towards the hut. The soldiers found two of the bandits in the throes of death. The rest had disappeared.

Bugs and Sinclair helped to bring in the bodies. Five infantrymen had been killed: two were critically wounded and needed urgent attention. An Army helicopter arrived just before sunset to evacuate them. The valley was darkening when the radio crackled into life. The pilot asked for a talk-in for his goniometer. A soldier counted into the microphone. The craft came finally into view and homed with its powerful lights onto a torch beam.

Half a dozen fresh men arriving with the helicopter would drive the remaining vehicles to Valledupar at dawn. The surviving members of Major Aguirre's troop and the dead and wounded were taken aboard.

Bugs clutched the rough sack he had found below the cottage floor. He hadn't yet looked inside. Looking gloomily down at the glowing hulk of the burnt-out craft as the military helicopter lifted clear of the valley floor, he wondered whether the small brown snake's nest in his hands had been worth the lives of so many good men.

Bugs didn't get to keep the snake's nest: someone in the police and military reception committee waiting for the helicopter took it from him. The sack still contained a snake egg. Bugs handed it across a police-office counter to an officious, moustachioed superintendent, who didn't appreciate his humour.

The superintendent emptied the sack onto a counter at the police station. Dust and flock flew up into the torrid air. He sneezed violently and wiped his nose on the cuff of his jacket. The air cleared. He began his inventory. He pushed a book and three Italian passports aside to expose a bundle of documents and a wad of twenty-dollar bills. He gaped at Bugs. A small, taped box contained a woman's diamond pendant, and, under it all, explaining the thud when they hit the counter, lay two pistols and a box of bullets. The officer fussily placed the cash and the pendant in the police-station's safe.

Bugs shuddered to think at the fingerprints he was destroying. Surrendering the valuables had placed him on a more casual footing with the policeman, and he asked if he could at least keep the documents.

With a shrug, the cop replied, 'No! Cannot go: is principle. You copy: machine upstairs: maybe work, maybe no.'

Bugs lifted the bundle with his handkerchief and trotted upstairs. He made the photocopies carefully to avoid smudging any more fingerprints. He returned. The superintendent didn't notice him take the originals and leave the photocopies: it would look like a mistake. By the time the police noticed the error, the lab in Langley would have seen them, but he had to leave Colombia before the enquiry started. The documents could always be returned with apologies. It was a risk, but Bugs doubted, incorrectly as it happens, that it would return to haunt him.

Back in his hotel room, Bugs went carefully through the documents: they included statements of account from a Swiss bank in the name of a Lucia Sereni; two letters written in Italian; and a bonus, the photograph of a man in battle fatigues holding an automatic assault rifle.

The passports were in the names of women with the photos carefully removed.

As far as he could judge, the book was written in a Slavic language and, from the writing on the fly sheet, probably dedicated by its author. The dust cover showed a man, probably in his early fifties, with a youthful face and almost white hair: the power in his dark eyes belied a man of strength and conviction. Bugs hadn't even bothered to ask the cop's opinion: he had just pocketed the book.

If Sinclair's Simona X was the same as Fred Coombes's Simona Grassi, the Texan Bonanza pilot, he was possibly onto the scent of John Glenn's killers. If it was not the same woman, American forensic know-how would help to put the Colombian authorities on the track of a mountain gang. He didn't want his hopes to ride too high, but, after all, Simona wasn't such a common name, and how many flew aeroplanes into and out of jungle or desert airstrips?

On his return to Bogota, Gary Sinclair found himself in the thick of an investigation: a summons from the Embassy awaited him: the jungle fiasco made headline news:

SOLDIERS KILLED IN VALLEDUPAR RAID: AMERICANS INVOLVED.

Sinclair was in trouble: he hadn't used diplomatic channels to get the army escort, but the expensive favour of a military friend, claiming that Bugs was an important American journalist studying the cocaine problem.

Bugs had already booked a flight, leaving Sinclair to dig himself alone out of the flak: the DEA agent's political skill probably far outran his own anyway, and his presence would only heighten embarrassment in the local American community. Involvement of the Company in this type of mess led to the kind of publicity the Director abhorred, so he left before the locals understood he was not a journalist. The first available flight was at 6 a.m. on Avianca to Mexico City. He took it, hoping to get an onward connection to Dulles, and found himself with two hours to kill in Mexico City before its departure. His bags were forwarded, he wasn't hungry, and there was little more to see than pottery and kitsch memorabilia at the stands in the transit lounge.

He ambled over to the newsstand and found a Chicago Tribune a few days old: he bought it and sat down on a bench to read.

The leader announced a gang-land suicide and told of the discovery of a body in a car near Oakbrook: the corpse had been identified as that of a Pino Cremante, a suspected mobster: a photograph of the underworld thug showed a lean, dark face. Chicago police confirmed that the suicide weapon bore Cremante's fingerprints. Then came the twist in the tale: there was a rumour that the revolver found in the car had been stolen from a Chicago police officer, and was probably the one used to murder police officer Patrick O'Grady the day following the attempt on the President's life at Golan Memorial Hospital.

Bugs walked off in search of a telephone.

It was dark when he reached Washington. A blanket of smog had smothered Mexico City delaying all the flights.

She was waiting, waving and smiling at the customs gate where Bugs picked up his bag. Jenny had those aquiline features that give a woman an ageless elegance. Her large eyes were an exercise in seduction themselves: they were his real home, and soon, her love would soak away the tension of the past days, bringing order as she worked in her fashion on the jumble of ideas rushing through his mind.

Hardly through the gates, she skipped up and gave Bugs a lingering kiss: not for her the reserve of a mature marriage. Neither had permitted the years since their whirlwind wedding to alter their love for each other: Jenny and Bugs were as young lovers. Bugs smiled and muttered self-consciously that they could continue the welcome at home in greater comfort. Jenny handed over his raincoat, and they left for the car.

'Jim Curry called from Chicago', she said later, skilfully driving along the soaking Route 66 towards Georgetown. 'He said he was sorry he wasn't in when you called from Mexico, but that you can call him tonight at home at any time.'

'Did you get his number?'

'No', she replied. Bugs turned to look at her in surprise. 'I told him you weren't talking to anyone but me tonight!'

Bugs laughed and stroked her shoulder.

The apartment was warm. Bugs slid into a hot bath. He lay steeping in the water: his eyes closed: the muscles in his neck slowly relaxed, and memories of noise and confusion in a Colombian jungle faded gently away. Jenny knelt by the bathtub. 'Would you like me to wash your back, honey?' He leant forward. She soaped it gently. Little by little she moved her hands over the rest of his body.

'How about that!' said Mike MacTavish to no one in particular. The others looked up from their lists of names.

Leroy Corbin walked over to the young federal officer. 'Found something?' he asked.

'Yes: the same two names appear all the time: sometimes one on an incoming flight and the other on an outgoing one: at other times the order's reversed.'

'What are the names?' asked Leroy.

'R. Cowan and J. Derry: Mister in both cases', said Mike.

''You sure the dates and times tally?'

'Perfectly: I've checked. One flew 535 from Chicago, arriving at 10.05 a.m., and the other left at 11.09 a.m. on 180 back to O'Hare, like clockwork.'

'We'll check again together before we tell Bugs', said Leroy.

'How are you doing, Leroy?' asked Mike.

'Less luck than you', he replied: 'the Bonanza didn't open one single plan in flight. None of the controllers recalls communicating on those days with a female pilot except for a few women flying regular commercial lines. This Simona doesn't want anyone to know she's up there, nor where she's going, and she's willing to sacrifice her safety to ensure that.'

"This what you wanted, Doc?' asked Leroy Corbin tossing an envelope across the desk.

The gynaecologist stifled his anger at his visitor's bad manners and read through the court order in silence. From time to time he looked up and glared pure poison at the two feds.

Leroy's irritation showed. 'Nothing's too sacred to bring federal officer murderers to justice, not even your ethics, doctor. You wanted a court order: you've got one; now you owe us!'

Leroy and Mike sat uninvited.

The physician read on: the tension slackened. At length, he put down the order and took off his glasses. 'What do you want to know?' His voice was terse.

'All about Simona Grassi, a woman who landed her plane locally a number of times.'

'I don't know all about Miss Grassi', he replied sarcastically.

'Then tell us what you do know, doc', said Mike, trying to defuse the antagonism growing again between them.

'There's nothing to tell you. I treat her for a medical complaint. I don't know anything else about her. She always pays cash.'

'When did you last see her?' asked Leroy.

'Late summer.'

'What's her trouble, Doc?'

The doctor hesitated and looked again at the court injunction. 'She comes for hormonal ovarian stimulation: Miss Grassi has an unexplained sterility.'

Leroy Corbin opened the letter from the French Foreign Office. It read: -

Dear Sirs, Following your recent enquiry into a private pilot's license and log book issued in 1976 in Tripoli, Libya, we questioned the Libyan mission here in Paris on your behalf. We regret to inform you that the People's Arab Republic of Libya refuses to confirm or to deny details to

*other states of its own internal official documents.
Unofficially, however, we have good reason to believe that
no such pilot's license has been traced under the name of
Simona Grassi. Yours faithfully, J. Lefebvre.*

'Could be this: could be that: they're the same the world
over!' He sighed. 'Precious bunch!' He stuffed the letter into
an envelope addressed to Bugs in Washington.

Bugs found the English-language translation of the book
from the jungle cottage among the papers Carol had left for
him. The Central Reference Service had found the
translation at the British Museum Library under the name
'Albania Shall Conquer.' The book's author was a Mehemet
Shkoder.

Albania stood, a pearl of anachronism among its Adriatic
neighbours: an Ottoman Muslim country among Orthodox
Christians; a Stalinist among progressive Communist states;
a Maoist society in the heart of the Mediterranean. Albania,
an allegedly atheist, yet profoundly Muslim, Balkan state,
had introduced Chinese Communist orthodoxy in 1961
following a row with Moscow. Free of Soviet influence, the
country paid faithful lip service to the Chinese way for more
than a decade, but the ways of Mao did not meet with
widespread enthusiasm locally: the Albanians were, after all,
Mediterraneans, who neither relished nor understood Slavic
stoicism: theirs was a different flavour of peasant struggle.

Published in Sofia at the height of the ideological war,
Shkoder wrote the book to attack Party comrades voting
against alignment with Red China: he had backed the wrong
horse: not above savage liquidation of their opposition, his
enemies, much to his chagrin, invited him to leave the
country within twenty-four hours of the final vote. Shkoder
considered himself a patriot; many thought him an
intellectual; a dangerous few found him a damned nuisance.
He was an ascetic from the North, and, as professor of
politics at the University of Tirana, held to be an authority
on urban revolutionary war throughout the Eastern Bloc
despite Albania's compulsive isolationism.

Jenny sat down at the small table in the bedroom after
dinner to review her patient files. Bugs sprawled on the bed
to read Shkoder's book.

According to the translator's preface, Shkoder had fled to Bulgaria in 1977 where he had joined a son finishing a doctoral thesis at the University of Sofia. His first act on reaching Bulgaria had been to write the book, an outrageous amalgam of communism and Islam. With every page, Bugs became more and more dismayed by the writer's dangerous rhetoric somewhere between Jihad and revolutionary civil war. In trying to woo the Muslim from his doctrinal aversion to communism, Shkoder painted the infidel and the bourgeois with the same brush.

Bugs sat on the edge of the bed.

Jenny had finished her files and was sewing.

'Listen to this, Jen.' He read: -

The determinant of armed revolutionary struggle against American decadence is a strong peoples' army capable of introducing the joy of true socialism to the proletariat. But imperialism and bureaucratic capitalism are not eradicated until the urban guerrilla awakens the masses: once awake, they overrun the bourgeoisie by weight of numbers in the teeth of its genocidal attempts to defend itself. The urban guerrilla is the root of a peoples' army: he is like the holy martyr giving his life to crush the infidel. He attacks the bourgeois in his cities where he is weakest: the impersonality of the capitalist city provides excellent cover. His brand of war strikes at the soft underbelly of capitalist institutions. Their corrupt militia is no match for him. His urban war destroys the confidence of the bourgeoisie in its society and its pathetic craving for security. His war accelerates corruption and downfall. He inspires the young and gives them just cause: under the tutelage of a people's army, children's' lives are not broken by the corruption of a capitalist bourgeoisie. His blow is terrible and unforeseen: when he fades into the grey of the city, they cannot find him.'

Bugs folded the translation, picked up the original, and flipped through its pages. 'It's a game of peasants and feudal overlords.'

Jenny sewed on. 'It sounds like the ravings of a lunatic! You've dropped something, honey.'

A torn blue slip had fallen from the original book. It was a used ticket to the Chicago International Agricultural Commodities Fair earlier that year.

Bugs looked again at the jungle papers in his office.

'June 79' had been written in Arabic on the back of the photograph. The Kalashnikov intrigued Bugs, the trooper cradling the weapon like a professional with no hint of macho brandish. His fatigues showed no insignia. He looked at the camera with black, sinister eyes. The sun was directly overhead. Dark hair, a young, lean face, and the fatigues gave him the look of a Middle-Eastern military cadet.

Where had Bugs seen a face like that? He frowned at the bright haze outside the window. Carol entered with coffee.

That afternoon, he thumbed through Lucia Sereni's Swiss account, also found among the jungle papers. The balance early that summer had been twenty thousand Francs. Before 1983, monthly credits from the Libyan Arab Bank had varied between four and five thousand Dollars.

He stared gloomily over his coffee cup at the large white dome of Langley's 'Bubble' and asked Carol to run a trace on the funds. The transfers had been made years ago, and the bank would not be helpful.

And why did the face of that sun-tanned trooper look so familiar?

The two Italian love letters were filled with sexual overtone and dreams of peasant bliss: they were signed, *Victor*, and dated, *Rome, June 1980*. They began, *Amore mio,* My love. Despite his limited knowledge, Bugs thought that, with the crossings out, the Italian was poor, although the handwriting was strong and confident. Here and there a word was written in the Arabic alphabet.

He put the letters carefully in an envelope addressed to Bill Jones at the graphological laboratory and added a note asking for a fingerprint check.

It was too late to call Glavina. He penned a long cable to the Italian giving details of Glenn's murder and asking for records on the three passports. Nino would have a six-hour start before Bugs placed his call the next morning.

He arrived at Langley early the following day. He wanted quiet to talk to Nino, and he wanted to get to him before noon local time: lunch made afternoon concentration tough for all but the hardest Italian stomachs.

'*Pronto*', came a voice at the other end.

'Nino, it's Bugs Macpherson in Washington.'

'*Santo cielo*, good heavens, Bugs! How are you? How nice to hear your voice again. How's Jenny?'

Bugs plodded through the preliminaries. 'Did you get my cable?' he asked. Units ticked expensively in the handset.

'Indeed, and I have information for you.'

'Go ahead.'

'You have found yourself a real live Red-Brigade terrorist in your jungle cottage! Lucia Sereni is dangerous: she was imprisoned in 1982 but escaped in April 1983 during a transfer from Bologna to Rome. We lost her. I think the Mafia helped her break free, but don't quote me. The Libyan income is useful information, but not a surprise.'

'So, who was this pilot, Simona Grassi? And what about the three other passports?'

'Four women's passports were stolen together from the Bolognese I.D. Office in January 1983. The spare photographs we keep in our records were clipped to them and were taken at the same time. Three had the names you gave in your cable: the fourth belongs to a Simona Grassi who can't be found in the Bologna region of Emilia, but we are searching for her elsewhere in Italy. If the documents were found with Sereni's bank account, we could be talking of the two being the same woman, no?'

'Lucia Sereni and the pilot, Simona Grassi?'

'It's a hypothesis, of course; but there's more: Sereni is an accomplished pilot, just like Simona Grassi: she started as a student in 1969 when studying at Urbino. After graduation, she went to the Lebanon and then on to Libya. She may have trained with the Libyan Air Force. Her Italian license and log book were confiscated and sent back to us by the Lebanese in 1975 at the beginning of the trouble in Beirut when they discovered she was a Palestinian Liberation Organisation activist.'

'That might explain the Arabic characters in the log book.'

'But the passports were stolen in '83: you say in the cable the log book was issued in 1976, so it would probably be in the Sereni name.'

'The writing's in Arabic, Nino: no one reads Arabic in Texas! She could have over-written 'Simona Grassi' later.'

'There have been Texan oilmen in Saudi Arabia for years, Bugs', laughed Nino, 'some learnt Arabic. I think you can test the idea that the pilot was indeed Lucia Sereni, that she has been living since 1983 under the name of Simona Grassi, and that she lived at one time in the Colombian cottage you visited.'

'I guess I wanted to hear someone else say that.'

'Where is she? I want her.'

'No idea. I doubt we'll find her back at the cottage now.'

'She'll go underground.'

'Nino, do you have identity photographs of Lucia Sereni?'

'All you need!'

'I need one good one.'

'Anything else?'

'Yes. I'm sending you one in return of a man wearing fatigues and holding a Kalashnikov. I want to know if you recognise him. I found it in the cottage.'

'I'll work on it as soon as it arrives. Why don't you come to Italy: you'll find useful material here.'

'I may do that. Thanks for your help, Nino.'

'*Arrivederci*, Bugs.'

Bugs thought that Rosen, his Mossad contact in Asuncion, had forgotten about his visit until a photo arrived with a short note. It looked like a useless shot, showing Fatima Al-Othman's face in full view and the back of a man's head: his hair was dark; he was slim, square-shouldered, youthful. Through a magnifying glass, Bugs found a mark on his right ear: it looked like a large wart or a birthmark. Nothing else distinguished him. Bugs smiled at the irony: look for a man with a wart on his right ear and laughed.

Fatima appeared radiant in the shot. Rosen's letter explained that the two had kissed, and left too skilfully to be followed through the crowded airport at Bogota. Bugs called Carol and asked her to send Fatima's photo and Rosen's cover letter to Jim Curry at the FBI. Then he asked for a day-return ticket to Chicago.

Jim picked up the cable. It read: -

ATT J. CURRY. MILITARY BERETTA ASSAULT RIFLES TWO OF FIVE STOLEN 6/81 CASERNA DI BOLOGNA STOP THREE RECOVERED BY GLAVINA 12/83 BRIGATISTA HIDEOUT TURIN STOP BRIGATISTA TERNI IN ASCOLI PICENO JAIL STOP REGARDS, CARABINIERI, ROMA

He walked into Duval's office and sat down facing the CIA case officer. 'Look at this, Ed.'

The man from the Company took the sheet, read it quickly, and returned it with a 'so-what' look. Jim had disturbed his train of thought. 'I guess they filed down the serial numbers on the stock: you can show them up with light etching and ultraviolet.'

'Could we use your people in Italy to follow up on this?'

'Thousands of weapons stolen each year', replied Duval. ''Black market for 'em: you can buy a Kalashnikov for less than two hundred bucks in Beirut. I need more than this to mobilise our people. Expensive; pointless.'

'Maybe 'your people' can phone this Glavina guy in Italy.'

' 'Probably doesn't speak English, and I don't know anyone who speaks Italian. Look, you're running this case: you call him. I'm not telling you how to do your job. I'm here as an observer, not as free labour for the Bureau.'

'That's not what I'm saying', said Jim, infuriated: 'I'm asking for help from your Italian locals: the Bureau doesn't have your resources abroad. This is a lead on two important weapons, and this cable's in English, isn't it? Someone over there speaks our language!'

'It's not usable. Our job's here in Chicago. I can't make recommendations incurring unnecessary cost for the Company: it's more than my job's worth!'

Jim stood and strutted out. Back in his office he called Bugs Macpherson.

The report on Florie's identification tests fell on Jim's desk the following day. Her judgment was unerring: Cremante's mug shots were mixed with others of men resembling him, and the old lady had picked out the Italian with unswerving accuracy.

One or two of the other ladies concurred she was probably right, though none seemed blessed with her powers of observation.

Carmen Muñoz's file was also on his desk. Since his conversation with Levine, he had only been able to access the Muñoz file by terminal, and he preferred to work with paper. Had she lived, there was more than enough material to put her behind bars including photographs of her dealing with drug pushers and a report on her collections from illegal immigrants in Santa Ana. A Bureau decision allowed her to continue: she was not operating alone: she could lead to bigger game.

The Muñoz apartment had been searched by Israeli agents. Every corner had been photographed including the hiding place under the water heater where she had kept her accounts. Every document had been replaced exactly as it had been found.

The report gave serial numbers of bank notes and an inventory of the documents found under the water heater. The Israelis found a stolen French identification card, a few ounces of marijuana, a 1979 Student Card from the Libyan University of Tripoli, and a photograph of a smiling Fatima Al-Othman wearing fatigues and a military beret, set at a coquettish rake.

Jim had played few rounds that year: all had been in the bright summer sunlight of early spring when fair weather golfers come out of hibernation. Now that the November morning sky bathed the course in a flat, grey light, he missed the dark shadows of great oaks over peaceful greens. 'At least the fairways aren't snow-bound?' he said, carefully lining up his drive.

No enthusiast of early-morning games, Bugs yawned, waiting for his friend to drive off from the seventh.

To a lusty oath, Jim's orange ball curved gracefully into the rough on the right. He grinned sheepishly at Bugs and retrieved the tee. 'If I keep this up, Bugsy, I won't even break a hundred.'

'That's surprising with your ancestry, Jim, most Scots break seventy-five before they can walk: it's in their blood.'

Jim laughed. Bugs drove a strong two hundred and forty yards down the centre. They walked towards the balls towing their golf carts.

Jim continued his description of Cremante's record. 'All we have on him is a minor assault charge. He arrived on a tourist visa in late eighty-three and was arrested within six weeks on the Southside for mauling a card player. He was treated leniently by a Chicago Judge known on the circuit for a light hand and should have been sent home to Italy after his detention. He travelled frequently to Italy and had no apparent means of financial support, but, by the look of his home in Evanston, he was a big spender. We've searched the house.'

'So, where did he get his money?'

'Don't know. We can't find any bank accounts in his name.'

'And you believe he was a mobster?'

'Yes, I do. He was Italian; he was well treated by a dishonest judge; he had money, lots of it, and we don't know where it came from. He forgot to destroy a box of stolen passports hidden in his home. We found nothing else: perhaps he cleaned everything else up before the suicide.'

'Did he own his place?' asked Bugs.

'Yes: the settlement agent remembers the closing: Cremante appeared with a briefcase-full of Hundred-Dollar bills. The title company went bananas and almost refused to accept them. Cremante went bananas too when they refused.'

Jim split off to search for his ball. He found it, chopped desperately, and sliced right of the fairway. It curved into the rough fifty yards ahead of the green. He walked glumly back.

'Are you sure the lady at the hospital really recognised him and not someone else?' asked Bugs.

'Positive: she recognised his face time and again among a hundred mug shots.'

'And she says he wasn't the killer.'

'"Insists on it, but he looked, and I quote, "just like the terrorist".'

'Like the terrorist?' asked Bugs.

'Yes, but I think that the old lady lost her cool during the murder and was as confused as the rest of them. Cremante had to be the killer.'

'Has she been wrong yet?'

'No', admitted Jim, 'except about that.'

Bugs chose a nine iron and lobbed the small white ball onto the green. It stopped four yards short of the hole.

'Nice shot', said Jim.

'Let's assume Cremante was the hit man', said Bugs: 'would the Mob take a contract on a top politician?'

'Maybe, but not with fuss like this. Terrorist tactics bring bad publicity, and they're unprofessional. Anyway, the politicians who interest the Mob are easy prey to money, sex, cocaine, you name it: they're more useful alive than dead!'

Bugs pursed his lips in thought. They approached the green. 'We're at sea, Jim: the Mob struck anyway at a Secretary of State, and did so during a nation-wide broadcast, but it's strange because the assassination of the President would have made a weightier statement.'

Jim chipped a lucky shot back onto the fairway and followed with a high lob into a bunker. 'Sometimes, Bugsy, I wonder whether the Good Lord intended me for this game.' They walked onto the green. Bugs putted the ball in for a birdie. Jim got down the hole in seven. There was a line for the departure at the next tee. The two sat on a bench to await their turn.

'Have you checked Cremante's Italian record?' asked Bugs.

'Not yet: I was hoping for support from the Company through Duval, but he's unhelpful. I'm not wasting any more time on him. You were over in Italy once, weren't you?'

'I have a contact. Give me a week or so, and I may just find a way to go over and bring his record back myself if I can get it.' Jim watched the other golfers' antics at the tee. 'It's wrong, Jim: a hardened hood gets depressed and takes his life with the most dangerous 357 in Chicago: any cop, finding him with it, would have torn his eyes and shot him in the street.'

'It doesn't necessarily mean that Cremante was the one who killed O'Grady.'

'It's still crazy!'

The two men fell silent, then Bugs asked, 'How many Mob families have you in Chicago?'

'Just one. The new gangs in the ethnic areas on the Southside don't speak Sicilian. Catanzaro holds the rich end of town. He lives less than a mile from where Cremante's body was found.'

'That was careless!'

Their turn came to tee off. Jim aimed left: the ball stayed mercifully out of the rough. Bugs sent his own down the middle. It flew two hundred yards, bounced, and rolled thirty more along the ground. There was no point in hurrying: a slow foursome ahead stolidly blocked the following players.

'So, what's happened to the O'Grady woman?' asked Bugs.

'Her pa's death was a shock. Her evidence is useless. She wants to join the Chicago Police if they'll have her. She'll certainly be motivated.'

'Any progress in identifying the woman with the disfigured face?'

'None, Bugsy: the corpse is in a temporary grave. We've got a few weeks to find someone to claim the body, otherwise, it gets cremated by the City at the taxpayers' expense.'

'Tell me when Jim: I want to go.'

'You'll be the only one there if you go.'

'What about the analysis of that dirt under her fingernails?'

Jim looked at Bugs surprised. 'You asked for one?'

'The pathologist at the hospital promised to send samples to the Chicago Crime Lab.'

'I'll try to trace it', said Jim.

'I've sent you a report on Fatima Al-Othman's movements in Asuncion, and a photo of her taken in Bogota.'

'They arrived', said Jim. 'She looks pleased to see her boyfriend, but we only get to see the back of his head: he's going to be hard to find if that's all we have to go on.'

'Finding anything at all in Bogota is a nightmare. Try to get Duval interested in a search. Time in Colombia might straighten him out.'

'The Israeli's report says the boyfriend and Fatima disappeared quite skilfully: there may be local police records on them', said Jim.

'Yes, Duval could get himself fully involved over there,' Bugs winked, 'and leave us to get on with the job.'

'Us?' Jim smiled.

The slow foursome moved on. Jim lunged, and cheered, as, still on the fairway and running uncomfortably close to a bunker, the ball rolled towards the green. They walked to Bugs' ball. His short iron swept it gracefully into the air, and it landed on the edge of the green too.

'Los Angeles agents from the Bureau went to the Carmen Muñoz apartment in Santa Ana, Bugsy. It was gutted: a hidey-hole under the water heater was bare. The neighbours won't talk, and we don't know what's happened to her things. Fingerprints were obviously wiped. The landlord said rent had been paid in cash to the end of the year.'

'Drugs?'

'The place reeked of them, but I'm not sure whether any were found.'

Bugs got down for the par in two putts, and Jim got down in five. He was smiling brightly as they joined the line for the next hole.

There was still no break in the clouds.

The ninth was a par three. Jim landed on a different fairway, leading to the tenth. Bugs lobbed his ball neatly onto the green, and diplomatically stifled a smile. They stopped at the ninth and retired to the clubhouse bar for a coffee in front of a log fire. The sky became more and more overcast as they sipped at their hot mugs. 'If I get to go to Italy, Jim, I'll find some background on the Beretta assault rifles. The *Carabiniere* who was mentioned in the cable, the one who arrested the hood in Turin with the other three assault rifles, is a friend of mine.'

'He's military, not a cop, right?'

'He's both: the *Carabinieri* are a military corps but they do police work.'

'Military police for a civilian population?'

'They're not military police, but they are organised as a military corps. They handle violent crime and work in controlled competition with road police, public security police, financial police, municipal police and I guess a few others. They're a national insurance policy protecting the constitution: other police come under local influence and can be manipulated by unscrupulous politicians. Machiavelli was an Italian, Jim.'

They watched flames lick the back of the fireplace and relaxed in their chairs. Jim felt particularly virtuous after the morning's exercise.

'I want you to do me a favour.'

'Shit! I was just beginning to relax', answered Jim.

'Sorry, it's important.'

'You won the first nine holes.'

'Can you get me the list of exhibitors and visitors to the International Agricultural Commodities Fair at McCormick Place last April.'

'I'll see what I can do', said Jim. 'I've done you one favour already this week: I've had Mao Tse Tung's little red book on people's war released back to you. It smells of garbage, but that won't bother you, will it?'

'Were the fingerprints identified?'

'Catanzaro touched it, and we're checking a second set. I'm more and more pessimistic of pinning anything on Catanzaro through his garbage, and, now, one of his contracting companies is installing an incinerator in his grounds. The old fox must suspect what we're up to. Maybe we can get at him through this Cremante suicide.'

Don Hailsham sat with his back to the window. The Director of Central Intelligence picked up his notes and sat at the head of the table one seat down from his subordinate. He would have preferred Hailsham to face the window so he could see his eyes.

'Don', said the Director, 'you know my style. I believe the earlier you get a problem into the open, the earlier you solve it.'

'Yes, Sir.'

'I'm concerned about your lack of progress. It has been more than a month since the Secretary of State's assassination in October, and the White House is getting restless. I need some results, or the case gets turned over officially to the Bureau. That would be an embarrassment for me, Don.'

'There has been progress, Sir: Duval identified one of the women in the shoot-out, and he's finalising a report claiming this was a Mafia killing.'

'Cosa Nostra doesn't like televised sensationalism: it's bad for business. The Secretary of State was an acquaintance of mine, Don: he was a man of integrity; not the type the Mob would risk interfering with. He's barking up the wrong tree in my view.'

'Duval's comfortable with the idea, Sir.'

'You know, Don, it wasn't Duval who discovered the Palestinian woman's identity, but Mossad analysts: they called the FBI.'

Hailsham's pupils in his pale blue eyes became pin points under the shadow of his brow. 'Really, Sir? I had no idea.'

'I had cocktails at the Israeli Embassy last night: the information was issued in answer to a Bureau alert. Duval's parked in the Fed offices in Chicago Hoover building, isn't he?'

Hailsham shifted uncomfortably in his chair. The Director continued. 'Don, I've been through his cost sheets: he spends a fortune on forensic testing. I'm sure it's useful, but I would expect more field expense as well as some results.'

'He's following a lead in South America, Sir.'

'What's the lead?'

'I think it's a photo, Sir.'

'When you have the details, come and see me. How's the Glenn case progressing.'

'Not very well, Sir, not well at all.'

'Is Macpherson having trouble?'

'He flies around a lot but always comes back empty-handed.'

'That's not like him. Anything wrong?'

'We haven't managed to find the problem, Sir. It could be anything: women; drink; middle-age; narcotics. You know, of course, he has no children.'

'Yes, of course', said the Director slowly, intent on Hailsham's face. He should have switched on the lights before sitting down: Hailsham's eyes remained hidden. 'But talent like his is difficult to replace. What has he done?'

'We had a serious incident in Colombia involving him last week, Sir.'

'I thought that was the DEA.'

'No, Sir. Macpherson is involved: in fact, he caused the crisis.' Hailsham watched his superior's eyes narrow.

'Why do you believe that Don?' he asked quietly.

'An American journalist answering Macpherson's description stole documents from the Colombian police.'

'That was not necessarily Macpherson.'

'That's what I had hoped, Sir until the documents appeared in our lab. If you have a few moments, I'll explain the background. Then you'll understand why I'm recommending his suspension.'

Lucia Sereni, the Italian *brigatista's* prison photos arrived that morning with her police file from Nino Glavina in Rome. Bugs gazed at them for an age before ordering copies for Leroy Corbin in Dallas. They had been taken in 1982 after her arrest, a board hanging from her neck displaying her name and number. Nino had pinned a note saying the photos had been sent to the Attorney General's Office with her fingerprints after her jail break in 1983. A phone call confirmed that this record had not been kept, and Bugs asked it be kept on file this time.

Lucia had none of the doe-eyed beauty of the classical Italian woman. Her eyes sparkled with a black fire that devoured the weaker features of an otherwise-unremarkable face. They flashed with disdain and defiance. They were savage. Were they the eyes of John Glenn's executioner?

Nino Glavina had penned a few words saying he had not managed to identify the man in fatigues holding a Kalashnikov in the photo Bugs had sent, and that he recommended a search by Israeli Intelligence. The cut and camouflage indicated probable Soviet desert issue. Similar clothing had been traced in Italy to Libyan guerrilla training camps.

His note ended: *Lucia Sereni has a lover called Mischa who is among the most dangerous of the brigatisti. We have not found him yet. He may not be Italian, and he is more than just a hot head. His disappearance has worried me since 1983. Regards, Nino.*

Bugs liked the Director: a professional, he walked the razor's edge between politics and intelligence with integrity. Secure in that knowledge, he entered the large, austere office feeling no apprehension whatever. His mood changed when he saw Hailsham. 'Good morning, Sir', he said.

''Morning, John. Take a seat. I've asked Don to sit in on our conversation.'

He sat opposite Hailsham, who looked up and replied a peremptory, 'Good morning', to Bugs' greeting.

The Director sat at the end of the table. 'The new Secretary of State has been asked by the Colombian Government to return some documents it seems you took from them. What's going on, John?'

Bugs had expected this meeting and regretted that Hailsham was at it. 'I was following a lead on Glenn's murderers and switched an envelope containing documents with one containing photocopies, Sir. I've more faith in our own lab, so I brought back the originals. We can return them.'

The Director suppressed a smile. 'There are ways of doing that without stealing, John: that's why we have agents in Bogota. What do they think of your international incident?'

'They weren't aware of my visit, Sir.'

'But you had permission from Langley.'

'No, Sir.'

A dangerous dullness crossed the Director's eyes.

Hailsham bent his head over his notes. 'Did you know that Don?' asked the Director.

'No, I'm afraid not, Sir', Hailsham replied: he turned on Bugs, 'You contravened instructions, John!'

Bugs had no wish to reply.

'Don, here, directs Central and South American Operations, and he's your boss. What would it have taken to get clearance from him? Why didn't you at least inform the locals.'

'I wanted to move quickly, Sir.'

'You left debris: the sacking of a DEA officer; the indictment of a Colombian Army officer; a minor international scandal; seven dead military.'

'Seven?'

'Yes, seven!'

Bugs ran a hand through his grey hair. 'I was trying to do my job, Sir, sometimes I have to take risks.'

The Director's voice was steely. 'That's no excuse for chaos.' He stood to calm his rising anger. The Director of Central Intelligence turned his back on the table and walked to the window. He addressed Bugs without turning. 'I am suspending you from duties until Christmas. The terms will be in a letter you shall countersign if you wish to keep your employment. Pass your material on Glenn to your superior. Questions?'

'No Sir.'

'Don, kindly leave me with Mister Macpherson.'

'Of course, Sir', said Hailsham and left the room.

Bugs stared at the table top. He felt numb, humiliated. He loathed the idea of turning his work on Glenn's murder over to Hailsham.

The Director still had his back to him. 'What's going on? You're getting sloppy. Why?'

'That's not true, Sir. I took a risk and blew it. It's not the first I've taken, and I doubt it's the last.'

'That's not the point!' The Director turned from the window and went back to his seat at the table. He sat facing Bugs. 'What's stopping you from performing?'

'I don't understand, Sir.'

'You were doing fine in Europe.'

'I enjoyed the field work, Sir.'

The Director hesitated. 'Are you leading a, uh, … full home life, John?'

He eyed the Director warily. The older man was off limits now. 'I don't have much time for that, Sir.'

'There are doubts about your teamwork in the department.'

'I don't have that problem, Sir.'

'John, are you communicating well with Don Hailsham?'

'I'd rather not answer that.'

'He doesn't think you enjoy your work.'

'That's opinion, Sir, not fact.'

'There's no mileage in harbouring dislike of a superior. It's dangerous: subordinates don't win against a hostile boss.'

'I don't intend to criticise Mister Hailsham, if that's what you mean, Sir.'

The Director walked to his desk.

Bugs looked outside: orange leaves were falling, their tints warm against the silver-grey of the lawn.

The older man sat in thought, then spoke. 'You haven't taken a vacation since you got back, and this suspension would be a good time to take one. The Senate Intelligence Committee wants local research done on a mobster called 'Cremante' in liaison with Italian police to find if he's connected with the Secretary of State's murder, and it seems to me your background and command of the language are suited to the assignment. I've had the Illinois State Governor on the phone a dozen times about this thug: it seems he shot a Chicago-Irish cop, and then took his own life with the same pistol. Have you heard of him?'

'I read about the suicide, Sir.'

'You can contact Ed Duval for the details at the Hoover Building in Chicago, and bring him up to speed when you return. I suggest you and Jennifer take a few weeks in Italy. My office will pick up the expense. There's no need to talk of this to your colleagues: just say you're taking a vacation.'

Bugs struggled between conflicting messages: the trip was a privilege, the suspension, a sanction. 'Well, John, what do you think?' asked the Director.

'I'd like that very much, Sir. My wife's a doctor, she may not be able to get away.'

A flicker of irritation crossed the Director's eyes. 'I can't give you more than a day to confirm. Talk to her tonight, and call me back in the morning. Your suspension is effective from Monday.'

'Yes, Sir.' Bugs left in bewilderment.

'Are you sending the papers back to Colombia, honey?' asked Jenny, gingerly wiping away remnants of eye shadow.

'Tomorrow. Hailsham will want to check the fingerprints and send samples of the letters to Italy.' Sitting on the edge of the bed, Bugs tugged at an uncooperative shoe-lace. 'He claims it's a waste of time, but he'll do it.' He attacked the tie knot. 'How did you manage to reschedule your patients so quickly?'

'Priorities! We need a break. They'll survive the few days I'm away: I'm not the only medical heroine at NIH! Besides, how could I resist those buggy rides along the Via Appia or warm evening strolls over the Ponte Rialto?'

'It's winter, Jen. Rome will be foggy and Venice flooded.'

'Then we'll pretend it's summer, and anyway, we'll be the two of us under the rain.'

When Bugs slipped into bed, Jenny was leafing through the translation of Mehemet Shkoder's book, found in the jungle cottage, Albania Shall Conquer. 'Jen', he said, folding his hands on the pillow behind his head, 'what I did was wrong, but I'm not being punished at all: I got a suspension and a disciplinary letter, but that will be thrown out with my next pay increase, and the suspension is an expenses-paid vacation for two in Italy courtesy of the Senate Intelligence Committee. What's more, I've wanted this case from the start.'

'He did that because you're the best, honey. He knows it.'

'You're a lovable liar.'

'Not so! And no husband of mine is getting licked by scheming bureaucrats.'

Bugs laughed.

Don Hailsham loved action. The three acolytes attending him in his office at Langley looked paralysed with fear. 'And I want a stop put on the surveillance of the Esperanza airstrip', he went on.

'Yes, Sir.' A chorus.

'There's been no more movement there since Glenn's murder in September?' he asked.

'No, Sir.'

These characters were sheep. 'You people have to understand round-the-clock watches are out. We are living, gentlemen, a time of severe budgetary contraction.'

'Bugs Macpherson wanted to wait a few more days before disbanding them, Sir.'

Hailsham was in no mood to listen. He needed them to understand who was in charge. 'I want the strip destroyed. I want it done now. I want the contents of the hut impounded, and get me those documents from the lab.'

He would show these people how to operate within a budget. He would close the case out quickly himself before Macpherson's reinstatement.

The major sat in the belly of an army helicopter taking the valleys North from Bogota. A police officer slouched by him, staring gloomily through an open hatch at acre upon acre of green jungle hissing past below.

'A hell of a business. 'Got court-marshalled, didn't he?'

'What?' yelled Aguirre, wishing he'd shut up.

'Court-marshalled!'

The major nodded, and went back to his brooding. The prosecution and dismissal of his superior officer had rattled him.

'They say it was M19 guerrillas. 'That true, Major?'

Carlos Aguirre hadn't heard a word, but he nodded again to keep the policeman quiet. The loss of seven of his men had hit him like a thunderbolt: two of the servicemen wounded during the attack had been hospitalised too late to be saved. None of the bandits had been identified, not even the dead ones taken back to Valledupar. They might have been M19, they might have been from the drug cartel; he didn't know.

He had taken the Americanos into the jungle under orders, so his own career had survived the court martial, but his superior officer's career had certainly not. The American DEA's claim of a bribe had been damning. It was right that the idiot Sinclair had been dismissed for paying it.

'And that sonofabitch reporter who stole documents from us. It's humiliating!' yelled the cop.

Aguirre didn't bother to reply. The Americano with the grey hair had handled himself too well to be a journalist, and he had surrendered the cash instead of the documents: he had even turned in a diamond pendant. Who's mad enough to exchange useless paper like that for valuables? That was no journalist!

Aguirre felt bitter: these Americans had no right to humiliate his countrymen like this. Colombia was a sovereign state but still suffered imperialism at the hands of these foreigners, who couldn't understand the towering majesty of his country nor the dignity of its people.

'Almost there', yelled the pilot above the din.

His mission was to protect the police sent to search the cottage. The rest of his unit would join him over land. They intended to airlift various remains of the burnt-out helicopter to Valledupar for inspection.

The craft circled and began its descent. Aguirre could see the charred patch on the airstrip, where his small shoulder-launched missile had hit the attacking helicopter.

He gasped.

The cottage and the hangar had been burned to the ground: nothing remained of them. The bandit's craft had disappeared. The strip had become a charred offering to a jungle soon to reclaim its heritage: in a few weeks, the disappearance of Simona X's Colombian hideaway under the jungle would be complete.

The airfield was deserted, and the door at the foot of the tower stairs was open.

Leroy Corbin fetched two cups of coffee from the club house, crossed the apron in the night, and walked up the steps of the tower at Addison Field to the dark, glass-panelled room where the Texan kept his vigil. Little was left in the cups by the time he arrived, and his sticky fingers burning, he elbowed the door into the sombre green glow of the observation room.

'I brought you a cup of coffee, Fred', he said.

Fred Coombes's dim outline trembled in the pulsating light of a radar screen. 'Who's that? No one ain't allowed here.' He peered at the door and picked out Leroy's dark features.

'Stay cool, man, I'm Leroy Corbin. This is an official visit.'

'I don't care who you are. You can't come in, an' that's official too.'

'I won't stay long, Fred. I just need you to look at some snapshots. We met last month about that lady pilot. Remember?'

'Sure I do, but I'm on duty. I can't put the lights on, or I lose my night vision. Go to the club house, Sir, an' I'll come over at sun up.'

'OK, buddy', said Leroy, thankfully depositing one of the warm, sticky cups on a table. 'Wake me up when you arrive. Enjoy the coffee.'

When Coombes appeared at the club house, a timid dawn was already drawing a grey streak across the horizon. He prodded a snoring bundle.

Leroy started. Massaging the stiffness in his neck, he rose slowly from the bench.

'My turn to bring the coffee', said Fred brightly, handing the sleepy CIA officer a warm cup. 'What can I do for you, Sir?'

Leroy rubbed his eyes, yawned, and sipped. He opened his briefcase and took out a wad of photos. 'Go through these, Fred. Take your time. Tell me if you recognise anyone.'

Coombes shuffled over to a bench under a light bulb and came back ten minutes later holding three photos including Lucia Sereni's.

'The Grassi woman could be any one of them', he said.

'Which one, Fred?'

'Difficult to say. Could be that one', he said, pointing at Lucia Sereni's shot, 'but she didn't look so mad.... well, maybe she did, when I asked all them questions about her log book. Yeah, I guess that's her.'

'OK, Fred, thanks.' Leroy stood to go.

'Did I get it right, Sir?'

''Hard to say, for now, Fred. Thanks. I'll be in touch: we may have to do this again.' Leroy left.

Two hours later he was standing at a telephone in a Dallas bar. 'Pretty good identification, chief.'

'How good, Leroy?' asked Bugs, gently swinging his chair from side to side.

'Coombes hedged but chose the right one. Young Phil at Quality Limousines last night didn't even go through the rest of the shots, just stopped at the Sereni photo, and said, 'That's her!' He says she scowled that way each time he dropped her off at the clinic.'

'Good work, buddy', said Bugs. 'Now we're sure Lucia Sereni flew that Bonanza under the alias of Simona Grassi.'

'The pilot on the video tapes fits her build too, though we can't identify her features and the sound was inoperative.'

Bugs hesitated and then plunged. 'I'd like you to do me a favour, Leroy.'

'What can I do for you, Chief?'

'I'm on vacation until Christmas. I want you to report progress to Don Hailsham on this mission until I get back. Call him yourself now, and tell him what you've told me.'

Leroy struggled to understand Bugs' disappearance at this point in the investigation. As hard as he tried, he couldn't hide the disillusionment from his voice. 'That's your prerogative, boss', he said quietly. 'I guess I'm disappointed for Glenn's family and for the rest of us you want to leave the team right now.'

'I'll bring Don up to speed personally before I leave, Leroy'.

'If you don't mind, chief, I'd rather wait and report to you when you get back.'

'Just do as I say, and keep Don fully informed, OK?'

'If that's the way you want it.'

'Affirmative, Leroy.' Bugs hung up. He felt humiliated. He continued to clear his desk.

LUCIA

The 747 was rerouted to Milan's Malpensa airport because of thick fog. Armed troops patrolled the lounges. Since the Amal Shi'ite Militia hijacking of a TWA jet in Beirut in June, and with the Fatah Revolutionary Council's renewed activity, airport terminals throughout Europe were taking extraordinary measures against terrorism. A *Carabiniere* holding a card saying *Sig Macpherson* met the couple at passport control. He had instructions to expedite their luggage through customs and to drive them to the Hotel Cavour.

At eight-thirty, Nino and his wife, Edda, welcomed them for dinner to a table in the glass-enclosed terrace in the *Galleria Vittorio Emanuele II*, where Milan's chic browsed expensive boutiques for Christmas ideas.

They were well into the second bottle of *Barolo* before Nino mentioned Lucia Sereni. 'She's another of these middle-class kids seduced by the ultra-left at university. Italy swarms with young anarchists. They believe they know Italy's needs better than anyone else, and reject all forms of authority. Her father's a lawyer and used to be highly respected, but his reputation hasn't survived his daughter's. The family's from Bologna.'

'A Communist city', remarked Bugs.

'Indeed', replied Nino, 'and for many years the best-run in the country; a real showpiece for the Party.' Edda nodded her head gently, 'The Apennine hills between Emilia and Tuscany were home to Communist resistance during the war, first against the Fascists, and then against the Nazis. Many families lost relatives, shot as suspected resistants. It's in our republican blood to resist absolute power. Communist councils get support in these towns even though there's probably not a single dyed-in-the-wool Marxist among the voters.'

'The Apennines have brought us many revolutionaries', added Nino, 'since Garibaldi, who helped to unify our country in 1861. It's ironic when you think that Italy and Germany are younger states than your U.S.A. Communism', he paused to swallow, 'is a bit avant-garde. Convent-school educations muddle peasant poverty with saintliness. The Latins have none of the capitalist, Protestant work ethic on which your country was built. Sereni's parents had certainly been Young Fascists, proud of *'la Patria'*, the fatherland: so many Italians of their generation were.'

'Their marching song was *Giovinezza* which means Youth', said Edda.

'The young of Fascist Italy were proud then, but the pendulum swung all the way back for this post-war generation after the Axis with Berlin. Sereni's generation feels rather more humiliated by Fascism:' added Nino, 'we have been governed since the war by a Christian Democracy terrified of professing right-wing politics, and in power with Vatican support.'

'Don't pay any attention to him', laughed Edda, 'Nino's anti-clerical.'

Bugs and Jenny smiled politely, terrified of being drawn into this political discussion.

Nino added, 'Marshall aid and government paralysis since the war have given us the freedom to recreate small businesses....and to enrich the Mafia. We overheated for thirty years and made money, but when the young arrived to claim their heritage, we faced the Palestinian question, two oil crises, rampant inflation, and severe unemployment. Many of our children felt cheated and turned to anarchism. Government has had to manage both left-wing anarchy and right-wing Freemasonry, the Mafia, the Camorra and N'drangheta, and it has not had the stomach to challenge political graft and corruption.' Nino loaded a fork-full of pasta and daintily dabbed traces of red sauce from corners of his mouth. He looked up with a satisfied grin.

'Was Sereni a good student?' asked Bugs, getting back to the subject.

'Not really.' Nino attacked his teeth with a toothpick, drawing an irritated scowl from Edda. He snapped it with a sigh and threw it into the ashtray. 'She studied philosophy at Bologna from 1969 under a left-wing assistant professor: they took their interests to bed together. I often visit him now for information, but not at the university: he's behind bars in a high-security wing at *Bad 'e Carros in Nuoro* for strafing the legs of Milanese businessmen. He believes he did it all for the good of his country. Misguided like all the *brigatisti!* A man called Curcio founded them in Milan in 1970 but we started to take his obscure Maoist group seriously only in 1973, the year Lucia left for the Lebanon. If her Mossad record is right, she disappeared into the Palestinian refugee settlements around Beirut. She was out of the country during the hot years. By 1980, she had spent four years in Libya too. She published in Tripoli, mainly on the theme of the Arabs and communism: her articles are dated. You want to read them?'

'No thanks', answered Bugs.

'She would have trained as a guerrilla: I believe she has a good military mind worthy of Red Brigade interest.'

'So why would she have come back to Italy?' asked Bugs.

'I suspect to support the Red Brigades, maybe not. She may have had a love affair: she moved in with an elusive *brigatista* called Mischa. She may have been outraged by the explosion at Bologna that August: eighty-five were killed and two hundred injured by a bomb in the railway station.'

'I would have thought a terrorist bombing is music to the ears of a Lucia Sereni', said Jenny.

'No. That bomb was planted by the right wing, who picked Bologna because it's a Communist city! The following year showed the extent of left-wing outrage: they followed the Bologna massacre with the abduction of The American Brigadier General James Lee Dozier by the Red Brigades, which led to Bugs' first visit to Italy, right, Bugs?'

They ended the evening with a tight espresso in a bar facing the Duomo, Milan's Renaissance cathedral. Brassy Christmas music filled the piazza from a brightly lit department store in one corner. The air was cool and moist, and Bugs and Jenny felt almost on vacation.

Bugs arrived at Nino's Milan office at 2 p.m. the following day. Nino invited him to take a seat, and ordered coffee: his hazel eyes could be as cutting as they could be warm. An enormous moustache set off their sparkle, folding at times into an infectious grin, but flattening quite often into menacing dislike. He was overweight and didn't care, besides, that was part of his image: dieting made his face a cadaverous olive-green. He was happy with the way he was: at home, he boasted a loving family, and, at work, a brilliant career. He dressed in jackets which were a little too tight and wore his hair a little too long, probably to compensate for the shine spreading imperturbably under his black curls. No one said anything about it because he didn't view his impending baldness with humour.

'Nino, the official invitation says I'm here to research the assassination attempt on the President last October. Officially, that means I need to talk about the Beretta automatic assault rifles used on the President and about a thug called Cremante probably connected with the Catanzaro Mafia family. Unofficially, I want to locate Lucia Sereni.'

'Yes, I've heard of a Cremante linked with the Catanzaros. I will do what I can to help you', said Nino, 'but let's start with the Beretta assault rifles used in the Chicago assassination.' Nino opened a folder on his desk and ran his eye down a page. 'The weapons were stolen with thirty-round magazines from a barracks in Bologna in 1981. The thieves got help from left-wing sympathisers among the younger conscripts, and five of these AR-70's taken found their way into the hands of the Red Brigades. In late '83 we were tipped off by a young man who had joined them through bad luck rather than bad judgment: he claimed his brother, a *brigatista*, had press-ganged him into the ranks. The kid didn't find much out, but he did visit a flat in Turin belonging to a man called Terni. When the elder brother was executed by his column for "ideological deviationism," the boy came to us and talked: that's how we got the address. Terni ended up in jail at Ascoli Piceno, and the rest of the weapons were sent to the *Museo* in *Venezia*. There's a lot of interesting material there. We have tape recordings of *brigatista* interrogations: there's even one of Sereni, would you like to hear it?'

'Yes, I would.'

'I'll arrange it for this weekend', said Nino, 'and I'll show you our collection of bullets dug out of Red Brigade victims. Frankly, I find the place depressing.'

'So, this kid led you to the weapons', prompted Bugs.

'Not directly: first he led us to this "Terni", a weak-minded creature with an appetite for guns, who maintained a *brigatista* armoury in Turin. He's in for life now: in any other country, he would have been hanged, garrotted or guillotined. I've exchanged information with him for minor privileges. He's unsavoury, but he knew people in the columns, and he has a loose tongue. Terni swore he had only three of the five stolen rifles, the three we found in his apartment and didn't know where the other two were. It took a few weeks to claw the rest of the truth out of him: a mobster called Genaro Cagnotto, who was prepared to pay cash for two military-standard semiautomatics, contacted him in January 1983. Terni needed cash, took the deal, and this Cagnotto left with the Beretta AR-70 assault rifles. Had his *brigatista* comrades discovered this, they would have shot Terni.'

'So, the Mafia knew the Red Brigades had weapons to sell?'

'Not the Red Brigades, Terni sold them personally for the money. But the question has always baffled us: we simply don't know how they knew. Cagnotto, who's in jail, says he was told by telephone to buy them from Terni. He always got his orders by phone, and has no idea who called him.'

'So now that Cagnotto has the assault rifles, what does he do with them?' asked Bugs.

'He kept them in his apartment until August fifteenth last summer. That's a national holiday, *Ferragosto*, when Italy sleeps on the beach or dozes in the city heat. We had been watching him since May for laundering funds through a Mafia casino in the North. We expected he would lead us to bigger game, and kept a watch on his apartment. At noon, someone left it carrying a suitcase and vanished. Our lookout was literally caught with his pants down. By the time we went into the flat, we were too late and saved our honour by taking Cagnotto in on an old warrant. We questioned him, but he knew nothing.'

'Did he know his customer?' asked Bugs.

'No: he described him as dark, and Cagnotto thought he had an accent. Someone had called him ten minutes before and told him to deliver the guns at noon. We checked our tapes: our listener in the basement admitted he had dozed off in the heat. We fired him as a precaution: it doesn't happen often, but, you see, the basement was cool, and we continually suspect Mafia infiltration in our ranks.'

'Did you say Cagnotto laundered funds?'

'Yes. In June, an informer told us of a Swiss man regularly losing massive amounts of money in a casino in St. Charles in the *Val d'Aosta*. We followed this gambler with the help of the French customs police, the *Douaniers* because the casino is close to the triple frontier between Italy, France and Switzerland. He crossed into France through the Mont Blanc tunnel and then into Switzerland at Geneva. Not counting on much help from the Swiss, the *Douaniers* followed him themselves as far as Lausanne, taking with them a Swiss woman called de Langeac working as a private investigator. The gambler, who was, in fact, Cagnotto, went to a bank to pick up a million Dollars in cash, and the Swiss private investigator got a job there straight after. She didn't find anything for a few weeks: all she had to go on was Cagnotto's passport number: he left it on a counter, where she saw it. He wasn't Swiss at all, of course, but Italian.'

'So, they didn't arrest him?'

'No, we had a deal with the French: our own Customs Police would have a fit if they knew. As *Carabinieri*, we were, as you say, pissing across the fence.' Bugs laughed. 'Besides, if an Italian brings in a few million from rich Switzerland, who are we to stop him?' continued Nino with a shrug, his hands splayed in the ultimate gesture of Latin fatalism. 'We did, of course, watch him, but he was only small potatoes.'

'And this investigator?'

'She found no foreign exchange movements of that size and assumed the cash had come from a lock box. One morning, the employee looking after the safe didn't appear, and so de Langeac looked after it. She found a card showing Cagnotto's passport number, and took a photocopy. She sent it to the French. Bugs, you should use this information carefully: our Ministry of the Interior is quite sensitive about it being generally known.' He went on. 'The holder of the lock box was BAPTCo, the "Bulgarian Agricultural Produce Trading Company".'

'The Mafia was doing business with the Communist bloc!'

'We were surprised too! And the second Ali Agca trial had just begun: he claimed the idea to kill the Pope had come from Bulgaria, and here we had evidence of the transfer of millions of Dollars between Bulgaria and the Mafia. We found ourselves in a political hush-up, and have been there ever since.'

Bugs whistled softly.

'The Mafia's half of Italy suffers from poverty, the Swiss are so rich, and the money came from the Communists: who were we to stop such generosity? Journalists would have swarmed us for months and the Mafia closed its ranks had we talked. We have let things take their course, but the casino remains under surveillance.'

'I assume a Mafia family operates the casino.'

'They're on your shopping list: the Catanzaro family.'

Small engineering and masonry yards lined the *autostrada*. Petrochemical towers surrounding Venice's polluted lagoon jutted black into a hazy sky. The limousine consumed the final kilometres of viaduct leading to the island city's massive car parks. A thick, late-morning mist lost its hold to a bright if opaque sky. Nino had booked a launch, avoiding them the toil of heaving luggage onto one of the public canal boats. The boatman and the driver loaded while a timid sun peeped through the rising mist, giving the lagoon its cool, winter, silver and violet bloom.

Bugs and Jenny gazed at the Renaissance facades lining the *Canal Grande*, their ornate facings evoking once-powerful merchant families. The Rialto bridge slid into view, and Bugs mused that this architecture of almost feminine beauty found its origins in a warrior community. Venice had retained political and military independence for a thousand years, and though this glory of the Renaissance had been financed by feudal overlords, it had been nurtured by the Church: more than a hundred chapels adorned the city. Authority over men's souls and fortunes was the muscle behind its power.

The launch drew up at the blue-and-gold mooring pylons of the Palazzo Gritti, and the couple disembarked.

In the room, Jenny swung open the blinds to reveal a soul-stirring view along the *Canal Grande*. 'It's timeworn and beautiful, like an old princess: not one block of concrete has spoiled the old lady's majesty.'

'The *Piazza San Marco* is flooded.'

'Cut the excuses, Macpherson. We're going for a walk.'

They retired after dinner to the floating terrace, where, in summer, boatmen pass singing to their passengers, all of them mellow with wine and the gentle sway of the gondolas.

Bugs met Nino off the train. The launch carried them both to the *Calle de Carmini*, where the *Museo* was housed in a hidden *palazzo* surrendered to the state by a wealthy Venetian family in lieu of inheritance taxes. The family had made it a condition that the *Carabinieri* assist in getting some of the funds collected world-wide to save their ancient city back. The cash had fallen into the hands of bogus architects and unscrupulous bureaucrats: little of it remained to engineer the city's protection, and that part was kept in Roman coffers, in a way true to the centuries-old rivalry between Italy's ancient cities. Venice's people suffered from the organised dishonesty, financial opportunism, and bureaucratic apathy of the state.

An officer guided them through vast stuccoed rooms of photographs, documents and hardware. Exhibits varied from extreme right movements to extreme left, but the bulk of the material concerned the Red Brigades.

Bugs was astonished by the ages of the young who had murdered. Photos showed scenes of violence; of eminent Italians gunned down in anarchical fury. There were volumes of depositions and transcripts of trials. The *brigatista* captains themselves, photographed sitting and laughing together in cages at their trials, looked for all the world like normal Italian youth. The virulent cases shouted from their bars at a society they despised, caring not for the anguish it suffered at their hands. He was beyond trying to understand the *brigatista* plague: he struggled to maintain a sense of balance between the open anarchy of these young people and the manipulation of Italy's heritage by greedy, powerful men practising a quieter form of terrorism.

A steel cabinet lined with hundreds of small, flat drawers, held deformed bullets taken from the bodies of terrorist victims. 'We keep them here with a peripheral photo of the bore marks to identify slugs shot from the same barrel. Some *brigatisti* use a favourite weapon, helping us to secure several convictions for earlier crimes when we catch up with the killer,' said the guide. He led them to another room looking like a library. 'This is where we keep tape-recordings of interrogations.'

'We can listen to the Sereni tape here; you'll have no trouble with her Italian I think', said Nino. He picked one and read the label. 'This is the last interrogation. Being a tough subject, she spent time in solitary. I'll spare you the earlier tapes with all the harassment and name-calling, when she shouted slogans and even threatened her investigating magistrates personally. She was a handful. She's a different person here from the pig-headed revolutionary we started with. By now she was weakened and careless; a woman alone led to believe she had been betrayed by her lover. It's a credit to her that she tried to protect the man we claimed had betrayed her, the elusive Mischa. It wasn't true, of course.'

'That was a hateful trick, Nino.'

'You know those were tough years! People were murdered every week by the *brigatisti*. The magistrates brave enough to risk their lives to stop terrorism used tough tactics: they were in the front line, some were killed. This was war, Bugs; urban war, but war nonetheless. These magistrates traded privileges with weaker terrorists in return for information. They used solitary confinement to break down the more stubborn elements. We suspected Lucia Sereni of murdering Andrea Castelli, a prominent Italian businessman a few months previously. Italy was outraged; Rome wanted a quick conviction, and now, here she was, alone, her hands chained and standing in the centre of a cold interrogation room. She had waited for more than four hours facing bright lights, watched by guards.'

'This sounds like something out of a Gestapo manual.'

'Lucia is a killer, trained to defend herself and to use weapons. She was trained in Libya, probably by the East-German Stasi, and isn't amenable to tea-party interrogation.' Nino glanced at the transcript. 'The magistrates started questioning her at the first signs of tension, and, by the time she started to talk, she was weakened. Lucia is the first to speak. All three of the magistrates were women', said Nino. 'You'll hear the voices of only two interrogators. The third magistrate was there to represent the state and to testify that the prisoner was not subjected to violence. Listen to this.' He turned on the tape player.

'You disgust me. Look at me, damn you. Show yourself! What are you afraid of?' There were footsteps. A door opened and closed. 'Bring me a stool so I can sit down.' No answer. 'You bitches, we've been working all this time for your kind. Damned sadistic bitches.'

Footsteps. A woman's harsh voice, 'Silence! We will continue until we are satisfied you have answered us truthfully, Sereni.'

'Go to the devil!'

'And you will not leave this place until I am satisfied.'

'I want to pee.'

'When you have answered our questions.'

'Is this your justice?'

'Cooperate, Sereni, and you can go back to your cell.'

'Go to hell.'

A gentler voice interjected. 'Are you cold dear? It is cold in here.'

'You're sadists', shouted Lucia.

'Cooperate, Sereni, and everything will be fine.'

'It's cold. If you don't warm this hole up, I won't talk to you.'

'As you wish.'

Lucia's hoarse laughter sounded more like a sob.

'Aren't you tired, dear, standing like that all this time?'

'If she wants to sit down, she can answer my questions.'

'I'm not answering that bitch.'

'I'm sure her questions aren't difficult. You must be so tired, dear.' The gentler voice again.

Lucia's shivering moan turned to sobs.

'Please answer them, Lucia.'

'I won't answer her, and don't tell me what to do.'

'*Lucia, I don't like seeing you like this.*'

The tougher magistrate broke in. '*There's no point in hiding anything, Sereni. You're a murderer. I have an affidavit saying so.*'

'*That's not true.*'

'*Your fancy boy has betrayed you.*'

'*Crap!*'

'*Yes, your Mischa betrayed you to us. He's here on the same murder charge. He's more intelligent than you: he knows how to cooperate. You'll never see him again. Does he make love well?*'

Lucia screamed, '*You old bitch!*'

'*These men aren't to be trusted you know*', *came the softer voice.*

'*Sereni, did you kill Commendatore Andrea Castelli in Bologna on November 3rd, 1981? Speak up so we can hear you.*'

Lucia cried out her reply, '*This is not justice.*'

'*Nonsense, Sereni. I can do what I like with a criminal like you. No one can get you out of here: you're going to live caged like an animal. In a way, Sereni, you're already dead. Did you murder Castelli?*'

'*I won't answer her.*'

'*I'm extending your solitary confinement for three more months: no privileges, no books, no mail; strict diet. Let's go, we're wasting our time.*' *A chair scraped against the floor.*

The soft voice interjected. '*Lucia, you know there's no escape.*'

The hard voice added, '*I have all the time I need, time that will drag unbearably for you.*'

'*Poor dear, you must be very cold and tired*', *came the friendlier voice.* '*Answer her. It's such an easy question. If you didn't kill him, just say so. You're going to have to answer in the end anyway. Be wise; save yourself now from all that loneliness: you'll have nothing to read, no light, and that crushing boredom for months! If you answer, Lucia, maybe she'll let you off more lightly. It's so cold.*'

'*I won't answer her.*'

'Then tell me, Lucia, not her. Just say yes or no. Poor Lucia, you are as headstrong as my own child.'

Lucia moaned.

'All you have to do is answer yes or no, my dear, is it true that you shot Commendatore Castelli?'

Lucia sobbed, and then, quietly, answered, 'Yes', then she screamed, 'YES!!!'

Nino stopped the tape. 'Two *brigatisti* present at the scene of the crime later attested that it was, in fact, Mischa, and not Lucia Sereni, who gunned down Castelli. Lucia was there, but the slugs found in the victim's skull came we now know from a Walther pistol known to belong to him, not to her.'

'Then why did she admit to the murder?'

'To protect him, I suppose. This story about his being in captivity was a hoax, he was still very much a free man.'

Bugs felt moved by this passionate woman with her savage, lover's honour. She had been chained like a wild animal, a non-being isolated from the rest of humanity. He felt cross at the way she had been tricked. This woman, willing to make such personal sacrifice to protect her lover, had she murdered in cold blood? 'Is there more on the tape, Nino?' he asked.

'Much more. The questioning lasted two hours. The magistrates had to continue while she was weakened. She gave us useful material negotiated in return for lenient terms for Mischa. Her information was more useful than she probably thought: Lucia Sereni was one of the few who had been admitted to the inner sancta of the Red Brigade executive committees, and she knew most of the columns. Now she had...how do you say?... "spilt the beans" on her comrades, she had broken the code of silence.'

'How did you capture her?' asked Bugs.

'In 1982, our information was improving: we netted a character called Paolo Ferraresi, a motor scooter driver for the hit teams. He knew where some of the column captains lived. We put out eighteen squads to round up suspects within an hour of his deposition and three hours of his arrest. The word hadn't got around yet when we swooped. We had emergency powers: we could hold suspects twenty-four hours before allowing them legal aid. We had the tools to get the job done.'

'And I assume one of these teams raided Mischa's hideout where you found Sereni.'

'Exactly.'

'Do you think I could meet this Ferraresi?'

''No problem. I'll see whether you can meet some of the tougher cases too at Ascoli Piceno jail.'

'This Mischa turns up everywhere!'

'We don't know much about him. The name is certainly an alias. He's a cool murderer, a careful planner, and possibly not Italian. He appears an *eminence grise*: planning operations; stiffening the ideological backbone. He knows a lot about Marxism, enough to talk on the subject, and has disappeared for now, but we'll find him. Maybe, Bugs, where you find Sereni, you will find him too, and when you do, we will help you bring them both to justice. We have enough in the *Museo* to nail Mischa. We found Sereni asleep in his flat. We brought her in and searched the apartment. One officer needed stitches for a bitten hand.'

Bugs chuckled, 'She's a lioness.'

Nino seemed unamused. 'We got to her Browning automatic before she did: it's here in the Museo. Mischa kept the apartment clean: he's a professional.'

'I suppose you found fingerprints.'

'Oh yes. We have a good set we believe are his. In April 1983, we moved Sereni to Rome to stand trial after consolidating our evidence on the Castelli murder. It's not clear how she escaped. A guard claims Lucia overpowered her, took her uniform, and locked her in the cell. Even dressed as a guard, she couldn't have escaped without help: she had to know which time card to punch out, which keys to use in the prison and how to cross security barriers without being recognised. She had to avoid attracting attention for two hours until the end of the shift in a prison she didn't know and to be sure during that time that no one would discover the guard she had overpowered and left in her cell. Why wasn't the alarm raised? I tell you, Lucia Sereni's escape was the work of the Mafia. She was helped. No other organisation has a reach this long.'

'Did you question the guards?'

'The prison service in Rome is not my responsibility; it's under the justice department, not the police. They shrugged off the case.'

'The thought of a link between the Mafia and the Red Brigades is as disturbing as their penetration of the department of justice.'

'They complement each other: the Mafia nurtures violence; the Red Brigades use it to promote anarchy. Both are closed societies outside the law, with strict codes of silence. Death awaits betrayal of trust by a member of either movement. How useful it is to overlook the ends of each organisation, and to join their resources now and again for a cause considered to be to the advantage of each, though not necessarily in their common interest. The justice department is a bigger problem.'

Bugs' look seemed slightly out of focus.

'Bugs, you look strange. Would you like a glass of water?'

'What? .... I'm fine. I read a similar idea in a copy of Mao's Little Red Book with a dedication given to the Catanzaro family Mafia don in Chicago: let me try to remember: it said something like, *our means of slitting America's soft underbelly may be one, but our ends will be forever opposed.*'

THE TAPES AND THE BOAT HOUSE

Ivan Promyslov continued his therapy in a square, grey building off Lenin Prospekt, a far cry from the lovely chateau at Geneva overlooking Lake Leman. The results were excruciatingly slow, and, with each day of frustration, Ivan felt less and less like an officer of the Soviet State. His depression deepened with the dawning that he would finish his broken career as just another of the sullen Muscovites he crossed every day now in the Metro.

Then, improvement stopped altogether. The relaxed, individual treatment he had received in Switzerland had made progress easy: now his mind was in turmoil: the dacha was gone, and his most human means of communication had been destroyed by a bullet from the pistol of an unknown foreigner.

Behind his personal tragedy loomed Nikolaev, the young man who had taken his job. Olga tried repeatedly to jerk him out of his apathy. He sat around the apartment in silence, and, the more she tried to draw him from his reverie, the more the memories of the vigorous man she had known, drove her to the verge of despair. The silence oppressed her very soul: she felt thoroughly alone despite his presence. Communication became one-way, her husband abandoning the burden of writing his replies or thoughts. The man she loved, her Vanya, was becoming someone different.

The week following his return, she invited Tatiana Demicheva to dinner, sure that seeing her would help him relax. He felt a fatherly tenderness towards the young woman, and Olga saw immediately from her eyes that the woman was feeling lonely since Aleksandr Mikhailovich Ryabov's departure for Rome. Tanya arrived with wine and flowers. Embarrassed by Ivan's dumbness, she talked to Olga during dinner, not even venturing a glance at him. When the time came to clear the table, Olga insisted she stay with Ivan to talk about her work, and, sitting by his feet on the floor, Tanya's own curled under her, she looked up at him through her wide, blue eyes. 'I am so sorry about your accident, Comrade Colonel.'

He looked around, stood, and walked over to a desk. He returned to his chair with a sheet of paper on which he wrote, *IVAN!*

She giggled nervously, 'Ivan!' An embarrassed silence, she turned serious: 'I'm sure you'll get better soon. You'll think back to these times one day, and smile.'

He nodded, his face serious, riddled with doubt.

'I thought you would like to know what's happening at the Centre.'

Anxiety lined his features.

She had to tell him. 'Comrade Nikolaev has your office. He was promoted to Captain.'

Ivan looked gravely at her.

'Everyone is so tense: they all despise him. One woman in Communications heard him shouting two days ago, because no one had opened your safe yet. I suppose he'll ask for your keys soon, and open it himself.' Tanya hesitated and reddened. 'I hope you don't mind me asking, but, ... those tapes I lent you?'

He didn't mind; he had thought of little else. Once they were found in his safe, he would be imprisoned, no questions asked: it was only a matter of when.

Tanya understood the worst. Tears welled in her eyes: it meant dishonour to her father; cancellation of her marriage; even prison.

Ivan wrote, *I WILL TRY TO EMPTY THE SAFE: DON'T WORRY. IF THE DEPARTMENT GETS THEM FIRST, THEY WON'T KNOW THEY CAME FROM YOU.*

'Oh, thank you', she sobbed, 'I've been so worried.'

At that moment, Olga brought in the coffee. Instead of two smiling faces, she saw the woman in tears and Ivan as pale as a wraith. She felt disheartened: nothing she did seemed to remove the pain around her, and she burst into tears too.

Later, during a sleepless night, Ivan tried to think of a way of getting into his office: he had managed to walk straight into the personnel section without being stopped. He traced the steps in his mind: there would be no problem at the gate, but access to area departments and to the special operations sections of the First Chief Directorate was gained through checkpoints held by Guards. Lists of authorised personnel were modified daily and, even if Ivan still had his building pass, his name was no longer listed. He knew most of the guards by sight: they would probably recognise him, so he couldn't risk trying to impersonate another officer. Ryabov could get past, but he was somewhere in Bulgaria, and Ivan was not about to expose Tanya's future to further risk.

Perhaps the Administrative staff would empty the safe, and bring its content to his desk at the archives, but they would first make a security audit: only a miracle would avoid the discovery of those tapes, and, despite his mother's religious fervour, Ivan was not about to believe in miracles.

There was no doubt in Captain Vassily Nikolaev's mind that he had Moscow by the tail. A uniformed driver had appeared again that morning to accompany the young officer to his new office overlooking Dzerzhinsky Square. Racing down the Chaika lane, he had looked down his nose at the rush-hour crowds. He craved those looks and was shocked to find only hostility and disinterest in the ill-tempered faces glaring back at him.

At the office, he demanded efficiency, and was critical of colleagues who were slow to respond or showed no initiative: he would make change his special priority, starting with the idiots in Administration who had not yet produced the keys to Promyslov's safe.

He was delighted Promyslov had been kicked into the archives. He would have liked to teach the old fool a lesson himself, but that Italian bullet to his head was good enough for now: he wondered how his father had persuaded, Ovarev, the GRU resident in Rome to so efficiently neutralise Promyslov at least for the time being; it was sad about Kapalkin, the cipher officer, though. On the other hand, Vassily Nikolaev was worried that Kapalkin might have discovered by now his theft of the transmitter and the cipher machines he had sent to Milk: it would be dangerous if that information fell into Promyslov or Ryabov's hands.

He picked up the telephone and dialled an internal line.

A female voice. 'Victor Department.'

'General Budhakin's staff: I need Promyslov's safe opened.'

''Lost the key?'

'Do you have someone?'

'Have you got authorisation?'

'Yes. I want it done now?'

'There's an instructor free in ten minutes, but we won't touch the safe without written permission. Is it still sealed?'

Nikolaev hit the phone hook and let it spring back. Of course, it was still damned well sealed! He dialled Major General Budhakin's secretary. 'Raya, I'm dictating an authorisation I want the General to sign: I want it in ten minutes.'

'But, I....'

'No arguments, Raya, I know he's there. Ten minutes!'

When the training officer from the Executive-Action school arrived, Nikolaev thrust the authorisation under his nose.

He crossed to the club at building twelve across the street for a coffee and returned twenty minutes later.

The safe door was open, a neat hole drilled through the lock.

The instructor stood by a guard. 'We preferred to wait for you, Comrade Captain. I insisted on the presence of this guard as a witness: I have not disturbed the contents of the safe since I opened the door. We must now wait here while you complete an inventory of the contents, and allow us to leave with a photocopy.'

Nikolaev peered past the instructor into the safe.

The contents were neatly stacked. He found a pile of dossiers, a few hundred rubles, a brown envelope, and a pistol. Duplicate keys to the desk lay in one corner. The envelope was unsealed: he tipped its contents onto the desk and whistled. What was the old fool doing with tapes in his safe? They could not be taken from the Communications and Ciphers Department: there were written procedures that he, and everyone else, had to read every year, threatening dire consequences if they were not respected.

He thumbed through the dossiers. The third was entitled simply, 'Ahmet.' The colour drained from Nikolaev's face as he read it.

He waited for both the instructor and the guard to leave the office with a copy of his inventory and phoned for a new lock to be put on.

Minutes later he called Major General Budhakin personally. 'May I come and see you, Comrade General? I am going through the contents of my predecessor's safe, and I believe he left items requiring your personal attention. This could be very serious.'

'Of course, my boy', answered Budhakin, 'come straight up.'

Ivan Promyslov's flat was carefully suited to his station, not quite located where it could be, but equipped with a second bedroom. He had never felt completely at home in the apartment block, populated with austere, uniformed men from State Security and by their wary families. Little of the milk of human kindness flowed in these corridors, surveyed day and night by video cameras and patrolled hourly by guards with dogs. The overwhelming advantage in his eyes was that it was close to the river, where it meandered East of Moscow around the promontory of Terechovo.

The evening following Tanya's visit, he went for a stroll through Fili Park as far as the river, hoping to think of a way of getting into his safe. Returning along the railway tracks to Kuncevo station, and approaching the corner of his street, he stopped. A black Zhiguli, its engine running in the cold, waited at the entrance of his apartment block.

'If there's ever trouble, Olya', he had told her, 'draw one bedroom curtain and not the other, and leave the light on.'

The blue-grey of the sky threw the orange window lights into sharp contrast. Now light shone from one-half of the bedroom window: one curtain was drawn open, the other, closed.

He crossed and kept walking. At the end of the street, where it runs into Zitormirskaya, there is a telephone box: a man was inside, phoning; another, dressed like the first, stomped around outside trying to keep warm.

Ivan turned into Kastanayevskaya and walked through the yard of a building giving onto an alleyway running parallel with his own street. He peered over the gate into the garden surrounding his home: someone in the alley giving onto the rear entrance was lighting a cigarette. In the yard behind, was a garden shed, its door unlocked. He crept in. A sack of straw lay on the floor ready to be wound around rose branches before the arrival of the winter frosts. He sat on it and leant his head against the wooden wall behind him. An hour later he drifted into a cold, troubled sleep.

Ivan awoke with a start. Dawn's first half-light peeped shyly through the shed window. His back ached, and he felt frozen half to death. He arose stiffly and stepped across to the door. He crept into the alleyway and looked over the gate at the rear entrance: a guard was patrolling some thirty metres away. He walked down the alley to where he could see the bedroom: the light was still on, and still only one curtain was drawn. He walked around the block into Kurina Gerasima, and back along the railroad tracks. The Zhiguli was still there, otherwise, the street was deserted.

He returned to the garden shed, took off his coat, put it back on inside-out, and picked up a bundle of sticks. Balancing the load on his shoulder, he walked down the alleyway and out through the garden gate of another apartment building into Rublovskoye. He walked on towards the station. The telephone box was empty.

At Kuncevo station two men in a parked Zaporozhets saw a hunched, elderly-looking man walking towards them with a bunch of sticks on his shoulder. 'Maybe that's him!' said one of the men in the car. He shook his companion. 'Quick! Show me the photo.' The other yawned and fished in his pocket for the shot. 'I can't find it.' He yawned again and rubbed his eyes. 'If that's who you mean, you're wrong! Promyslov isn't that old: I doubt anyone who rows for State Security walks with a stoop like that.' He burst into laughter.

'Maybe it's on the floor. Come on, hurry!'

The man with the sticks walked towards them. He took no notice of the car and limped slowly along: clouds of vapour billowed from his lips as he struggled on below his load.

'Look, I can't find it, and he looks like a bloody gardener: I doubt one of our colonels is going to walk around Moscow at this time in the morning looking like that tramp; he's even got a bit of a beard from the little I can see. Get out, and ask him who he is.'

The guard gripped the door handle and turned it. Cold air streamed into the warm compartment. He hesitated, closed the door, and wound the window down instead. The man with the sticks had turned the corner and, with his back to them now, walked towards Kastanayevskaya. It was a wide back, but bent, as if by age. He thought of shouting as the old boy shuffled off. He was probably half deaf anyway. 'Those sticks must be damned heavy. I bet the old buffer wishes he were doing our job.' He wound the window back up and rubbed his hands. 'He's not heading for the apartment block anyway. It's so damned cold.'

'Old Father Frost is preparing winter', said the other. He took out the logbook, and noted, *0715: GROUNDSMAN PASSES WITH FIREWOOD: HEADS NORTH TOWARDS FILI-MAZILOVO.*

Out of the line of sight of the Zaporozhets, Ivan dropped the sticks behind a hedgerow. The stiffness in his back made him walk slowly: it wasn't so difficult after a night in a cold shed to walk like an old man.

A truck fumed North along the M25 watched by a militia officer outside the Kuncevskaya Metro station. Ivan walked to the entrance of the Fili amusement park and followed a path to the riverside looking for a tea-stall. He would walk as far as the boat house. Yuri Berzin, the boat keeper, had known Ivan since his university days when the river had been a bus ride away down Lomonosovsky Prospekt. The gruff, veteran sculler, who now barely had the strength left to lift an oar, lived for the sport. He lived in the boat house, heated by an old, stinking, oil stove. Perhaps he would let Ivan hide there until he could make some sense out of his problems: a few rubles might help to persuade him.

Close to the river bank, a stout woman was taking a wooden panel down from the facing of her stall, revealing the blue glow of a paraffin lamp inside. Its pungent smell reached out to him through the damp air.

Wrapped in layers of clothes, capped with a blue shawl, she turned to Ivan and smiled. 'No snow yet: that's good: but the frosts must start sooner if we want an easier winter this year.'

Ivan nodded. She didn't wait for his opinion, carried the panel inside, locked the door, and stood to face him. She crossed her arms under a voluminous bosom and leant on the counter. In one corner were stacked loaves of black bread, cheese and ham. In the other bubbled a samovar.

'Black tea? Cold's late this year, I said.'

Ivan nodded, and smiled again, making sure, this time, she saw his face.

'Trouble talking, or a weirdo, are we?'

Ivan pointed at his mouth and shook his head.

The woman looked closely at him. 'You have a disability card? The tea's cheaper if you do.'

Ivan nodded and drew his wallet: for once, his red KGB card was of no use to him here.

'Nice wallet. I can lend you a razor, dear: 'don't want to walk around in the park looking like that at this time in the morning, do we? The militia will run you in, no questions asked. Have a shave: you'll look as though you're out for a walk. And, for heaven's sake, that coat!'

A shave would be a good idea, and he still had his coat on inside out.

The woman laughed at a private joke and thrust a cracked porcelain cup under the samovar's tap.

Hot, rich tea warmed his belly. The woman cut thin slices of black bread and started making cheese and ham sandwiches. Ivan ate one, then another.

She poured him a second tea. 'You want that razor then, dear?'

Ivan nodded. She produced a bar of soap, a bowl of cold water, an old razor, and the fragment of a mirror. 'Do it around the back: they won't see you in the bushes. You'll find a comb hanging from a piece of string tied to the tree. That'll be thirteen kopeks in all.'

Rarely had he suffered so using a razor: not an adept of the cut-throat variety, Ivan left blood all over his face. The soap burned, and the water was icy. He found a filthy comb hanging from a branch and, with the help of the cracked mirror, tried to pick the straw out of his hair. Admittedly, he looked better, if bloodied after his battle with the blunt blade. He put his coat back on the right way and looked less of a tramp now. He strolled back through the damp bushes to the tea stall.

The two uniformed militia officers at the counter did not see the shock on his face, but the woman recognised his fear instantly. She took the shaving gear from his hands, and said, with a wink, 'Well, Comrade, we are off to work early this morning.' She turned to the militia, 'Black tea?'

They broke from their conversation and watched Ivan. He waved at the woman, grunted, and walked off towards the river.

She shouted, 'See you tomorrow, Comrade', and turned to the officers. 'Lovely man', she said, 'totally dumb, you know.'

'He isn't here often', said one: 'I've never seen him before.'

'Quite often, but not so early.'

They returned to their conversation.

Ivan would have been stopped had he been unshaven, uncombed, walking around with his coat inside out and straw in his hair. He was in debt to this woman. Never had he savoured the affinity he suddenly felt with this workaday Muscovite: a strange feeling of affection for his countrymen unexpectedly touched his soul.

He reached the riverside. The boat house loomed darkly in the mist behind the trees. He stepped onto the slipway and looked at the fast-flowing waters of the swollen Moskva: they beckoned him with a lure of peace. He shivered and turned his back on them.

A dim light flickered through drawn curtains at Yuri Berzin's attic window. Ivan tried to open the huge, boathouse doors, but they were locked. He walked to the path and picked up a handful of pebbles. Returning to the slipway, he threw them at the boat keeper's window, hoping his advancing years had not made him totally deaf.

Yuri's face appeared at the curtains. He opened the window and peered at the slipway. 'Who's that?' he growled. He wasn't deaf, but he was short sighted.

Ivan waved frantically.

'Go away!' scolded Yuri. 'If you want breakfast, try working for a living.' He closed the window with a bang.

Ivan turned and walked glumly back through the mist to the riverside. He sat on the slipway and shivered. Grey water swirled under his feet. He could see the *Krylatskoye* Water-Sports Complex from here on a clear day: it had been the focus of his youth, and would soon be the venue for the all-Moscow regatta he had trained his colleagues so hard for. Somewhere, through the trees and the eddying mist to the right, were the golden 'onion' cupolas of the *Cerkov Pokrova Filach*, the church of Our Lady. His mother had found something in all that church going.

Ivan thrust his hands deep in his pockets. The damp wooden planks he was sitting on warmed a fraction.

He was sure they had found the tapes. Reception committees like that outside one's home were reserved for special cases: he could have expected more than 'just a few simple questions:' there was caffeine to make him talkative; sodium barbital to suppress his resistance. He had been wise to give Olga a sign, fortunate to spot the Zhiguli, and surprised to be helped past the militia by that woman in the tea stall. He counted on his luck holding. Yet, this affair of Tanya's tapes had cost him his career. He cradled his chin in his hands and stared gloomily at the water.

Bringing in Ahmet ought to have been uncomplicated enough for a man like Fedorenko. He hoped that both Fedorenko and Ahmet were back in their 'Wet Affairs' offices by now. If they weren't, they could be in deep trouble: the West would be on Fedorenko's trail, because, if French and Italian police already knew of the BAPTCo deal, Ivan had to assume the link with Ahmet would be discovered. If they were caught and tried in public, it would set the Soviet General Secretary's dreams of détente back years to the height of the Cold War. The consequences would be disastrous for the new leadership. Besides he liked this young politician, who could move mountains with his will and charisma and be a real father to a progressive Soviet Union, able to face change confidently.

It was as well the American President had been unharmed: if Konstantin Strugatski's theories were right, that old lion, Marshall Sergei Borisovich Volkov would have discredited his young Party opponent, the General Secretary, and crippled competing KGB influence in the Politburo. Ivan was impressed: Volkov had contracted Ahmet, a KGB illegal, to make the attempt on the American President's life rather than compromising one of his own GRU agents: had the plan misfired, the fault would have devolved on State Security, removing any suspicion of blame from the Military. But the Marshall hadn't counted on the weak link snapping: Kimon Antonov, Volkov's Bulgarian-Party protégé, had been incompetent for that kind of intrigue.

And now it was said that Volkov no longer attended Politburo meetings, in fact, he had completely disappeared. In the middle of all this mess, was young Nikolaev! Kapalkin, the Cipher Officer murdered in Rome, might have helped indict Nikolaev for stealing the transmitter he had stolen to give to Milk, but would there have been enough to nail this young officer?

Running Cremante, this GRU agent codenamed 'Milk', was too weighty a responsibility for one so green and impulsive: there was no doubt that Nikolaev had only succeeded because of his father's military clout and support from the Rome GRU Resident, Ovarev, who was, like Nikolaev, a Kiev-Tank-School alumnus. Today, the key to Vassily Nikolaev's success at State Security was his record in Rome and Ivan's boss, Budhakin's, ambition. Nikolaev's father must have weighed in with so much support that the family clout was still feared at the Embassy. Ovarev was not alone under Nikolaev influence: Ivan thought about the trap he had laid for Khotulev, the KGB Resident: he had written he wanted Milk's file to be sent by Ryabov to Ilya Fedorenko via the Direccion General de Inteligencia in Havana; but Khotulev had not told Ryabov the file was for Fedorenko and, as a result, Ryabov had mistakenly sent it to Garcia. Officers of Khotulev's grade didn't make that kind of mistake unintentionally. He had told Khotulev to say nothing to Nikolaev or to anyone in Military Intelligence, so Ivan would now have to work on the counter-assumption that both Ovarev and Nikolaev well knew now that Ivan had sent an Executive-Action agent to trail Milk in America. Ivan had no doubt now that Nikolaev would do everything to create trouble for him when the KGB bloodhounds closed in.

And what had that 'special mission' been that Nikolaev had spoken of to Ovarev in Rome?

It was said that Nikolaev had left the Military for State Security because he didn't like the trappings of war, yet he ran Milk as a deep sabotage agent, exactly the way the GRU ran their *Spetsnaz*. This was military style, not KGB, and the Nikolaevs had been, by tradition, warrior princes under the Tsars. What was he up to at State Security? Had he resigned his military commission? He was mysteriously playing down a brilliant military education at the Kiev Tank School and the Military Diplomatic Academy. His move to the KGB was completely incomprehensible: a promising start in the Red Army, and an influential General in the GRU for a father opened an obvious military career, not one in State Security. What was young Vassily Nikolaev up to?

Ryabov's comment had been perceptive: he had said, 'Maybe Milk wasn't working for us at all.' At first, Ivan had thought that Ryabov, who detested Nikolaev for maltreating his fiancée, had been sowing the seeds of intrigue. But Nikolaev's manoeuvres really had made Ryabov suspicious, especially his clumsiness as Snow in hiding his dispatches from others at Dzerzhinsky Square and the peculiar way he paid Milk. Even if Nikolaev had successfully hidden payments to Cremante through the complex tricks the Moscow Centre auditor had explained over lunch, Ivan wasn't sure that such tricks would be enough to incriminate Nikolaev: KGB money was always available to get things done.

The Italian police officer had said that the thugs, who had tried to kill Ivan in Rome, belonged to the same Mafia gang as the one laundering the BAPTCo money from Switzerland. Coincidence had no place in these events: Ivan was convinced that someone in the Embassy had hired them precisely because he had been there; someone such as Ovarev or even Nikolaev himself. Such terrorist-style killings occurred almost daily on Italy's streets but they were never aimed at staff from the diplomatic missions.

He shifted uncomfortably and rubbed his back. Mist shrouded the dark building behind him. He stared at the dark swirls of the Moskva and broke again into reverie.

The Cipher Officer, Kapalkin, had mentioned a name. It was so hard to remember. He held his head between his hands. What name had he spoken of before the shooting? Ivan closed his eyes and concentrated on each letter of the alphabet until he arrived at M....Mischa! Yes, Mischa: a Moscow Centre illegal, it seems, involved with the Red Brigades through a woman, and with the Mafia through 'Milk.' The Mafia had broken his girlfriend out of jail, otherwise, the Red Brigades would have murdered this 'Mischa.' Why? Who was he? And, like Ahmet, this 'Mischa's' real name would appear to have been Muslim: Kapalkin had said so. An illegal from State Security with a Muslim name was an unlikely Russian, yet, Ahmet was one.

The wind rustled gently through the trees. He heard the soft crackle of the first heavy drops of freezing rain. He would have preferred snow. Two or three large drops fell on his head. He jogged back along the slipway to where the boathouse roof protruded sufficiently to keep the rain off the wooden boards below: he sat on them and leant his back against the wall.

Kostya Strugatski's story, about Marshall Volkov wanting to discredit the Party General Secretary before the summit fitted in well with an attempted American assassination: it had been a BAPTCo employee, this Traicho Botev, under orders from the trading company's Secretary, Anatoly Petrovic, who had passed Ahmet his letter of introduction to this Chicago gang. Through Petrovic's boss, Kimon Antonov, Marshall Volkov had paid them with BAPTCo foreign exchange through Switzerland. Very clever!

Shortly after, someone had killed the American Secretary of State during a terrorist attempt on the US President, which was not in the same class as assassinating the President. If indeed Ahmet had mounted this killing, he would have needed help, and who better than a local gang to provide it? It seemed unthinkable that a highly-trained illegal such as Ahmet would have shot the wrong target. Ivan might have mounted the same scenario himself in any one of the Soviet republics, though no Soviet mob would have agreed to go after such an important political target: politicians were taboo, expensive, and dangerous. But in America, who had killed Kennedy? Money was king over there, and Volkov had some in Bulgaria to spend. He decided to work on the idea that Marshall Volkov had indeed financed Ahmet, Milk and this gang to mount an assassination in the United States, which would have normally targeted the President; and that Nikolaev was somehow involved in all of this up to his proud young neck.

Ivan thought back to the TV report of the assassination attempt in Chicago: two motorcyclists had gone after the President with a fanaticism he had rarely seen: a Russian transcript, circulated at Moscow Centre shortly after, had confirmed that both had attacked in total disregard for their own safety. Suicidal operations did not carry the silent stamp of the Executive-Action Group, nor even, frankly, the professionalism of the Mafia. An analysts' report speculated that, because of their size, build, and the way they moved both were possibly women!

His wallet formed an uncomfortable lump in his back pocket. He fished it out and drew his red KGB card. How proud he had been the day he had got it: he had felt admitted to the table of the masters. The insignia had lost the outline of the shield and dagger, but the colour was enough. They had told him it could open any door. Who were they trying to fool? The comradeship, which the woman at the tea stall had shown him that morning, was firmly closed against it: to her, and to the rest of the Soviet people, he well knew his card spelt state terror rather than state security.

Nikolaev probably considered himself by now at the table of the masters too. He was aggressive: he had set up Ahmet and Cremante, run this illegal, Mischa, and penetrated the notoriously difficult Red Brigade movement. But he was also a hot-head: he had cheated the KGB, using its funds to pay an   agent; he had lied to Ryabov at the Italian desk claiming he couldn't remember 'Milk', and carelessly terrorised Ryabov's fiancée.

Ivan stood and stretched his legs. Rain poured down furiously, freezing as it hit the ground. He crouched, pulling his coat tightly across his shoulders to try to stop shivering.

How was Ryabov doing? Were the numbers on the Swiss account card really Bulgarian passport numbers? He would have liked to see Ryabov. The bank was the key. Nikolaev's angry reaction to the closure of the BAPTCo account by the auditors had been curious: what interest could he possibly have had in a facility with a foreign bank, unless he needed money abroad to...but that seemed a preposterous idea! Yet what had the auditor said? The revolving letter of credit allowed virtually unlimited transfer of funds out of BAPTCo. Perhaps, thought Ivan, Kostov and Potanin's Bulgarian passports allowed BAPTCo funds to be withdrawn from the Swiss account and not only deposited, a useful asset for defectors as much as for paying the Mafia.

The sputter of icy rain drowned his thoughts. A stream of gutter water fell from a stalactite of ice forming at a roof corner and splashed onto the wooden planks below. The temperature increased a degree or so. Ivan raised his collar and dug his hands deep into his pockets. The night had been short: he felt exhausted: he closed his eyes, and dozed off.

A firm, gnarled hand gripped his shoulder and shook it. Ivan awoke with a start. It was still raining.

'How can I open the damned door with you leaning against it?'

Ivan stood, rubbing his eyes.

The old man walked to the centre of the boathouse's river wall and unlocked the heavy doors. He swung them open to a groan of hinges. Yuri Berzin had not recognised his squatter.

Ivan faced the old man and smiled.

Yuri peered at Ivan's face. 'Well, I'll be! It's young Promyslov.'

Ivan nodded.

''You the one who threw stones at my window this morning.'

Ivan nodded again.

'Why don't you answer me?'

Ivan pointed at his mouth and shook his head.

'Lost your voice, eh? It's cold out: come in and have some hot, black tea: it may free up your vocal chords.' He giggled and led the way.

Ivan followed the bent old frame of a once-powerful oarsman into the depths of the boathouse. A small door opened onto wooden steps leading up to Yuri's garret room. An oil stove burned in one corner, heating the base of a small copper samovar. Ivan sat on the narrow bed, and gratefully took the small cup of hot tea from Yuri's hands. He sipped the dark liquid, shivering convulsively in the damp heat of the attic.

'I don't know what you're doing out in this weather: this dampness is bad for the bones.' The old man scratched his ribs. 'Have you come to use the boats?'

Ivan shook his head.

'Then you came to see me', said the old man with a triumphant chuckle.

Ivan nodded seriously.

Yuri looked surprised. 'Me?' he repeated and peered at Ivan, who nodded again. 'Ivan Dmitriyevich, isn't it. What do you want?'

From the tone of his voice, he did not like being imposed upon. Ivan moved his hand as if writing.

'That's no use, I can't read.'

Ivan put both hands to one side of his head and pointed at the floor.

'Of course, you can sleep here.'

Ivan took ten rubles from his wallet and placed them on the small log table.

'It's not for the money, young Promyslov. I'm not in the hotel business. Anyway, there's not enough space here in my room, so you'll have to rough it in the changing rooms, but at least they're heated, and, here, take your money.'

Ivan pointed at his open mouth.

'To eat!' said Yuri, 'You'll be my guest!'

They took the steps down to the changing room. There were shower heads in one corner, and the doors to the toilets in another. The concrete floor was covered with rough sacking; closets were fitted along the walls. A long wooden bench lay diagonally across the room. It did not make an inviting bedroom, but Ivan felt he would be relatively secure there at night.

'Not so bad, eh! You have a built-in shower and toilet. I can put some sacks on the floor to make it more comfortable to sleep on. You won't be able to sleep here during the day: people use the boats. Come back up, and we'll have some lunch.'

The samovar lost its place over the stove to a blackened saucepan, into which Berzin poured a jar of red beet broth, and dropped two lumps of pickled pork.

'You can take a skiff out this afternoon if the weather clears.'

Ivan smiled gratefully. It would be cold and wet, but the exercise would pump some of the depression out of his system. Yuri stirred his pot thoughtfully, and Ivan picked up two heavy books sitting in the corner of the watchman's room.

'That's the membership register; it goes back almost to the Glorious Revolution.' The old man chuckled. 'There are some famous names in there they tell me. You'll find your name too in there somewhere; teams are listed at the end of each year, along with the trophies.'

Grateful for something to read, Ivan sat on the floor under the small window. He opened the first volume. He made out the club's first statutes, laboriously written in faded ink and post-revolutionary doubletalk. The language had been chosen, no doubt, to avoid the embarrassing fact that rowing was a sport widely considered outside the reach of the proletariat. But every sport has its lovers, and, in 1925, the young Soviet Union still boasted a few fine oarsmen.

'I'll put yours in the cup, and eat mine out of the saucepan', said Yuri.

Ivan took the cup and ate hungrily.

'Do you want me to tell anyone you're here', asked Yuri.

Ivan shook his head vigorously.

'I can telephone your home: I can handle numbers.'

Ivan shook his head again, and the two ate in silence.

'Send a letter?'

Ivan looked thoughtfully up at the window and nodded his head slowly.

'I'll get you some paper and an envelope. I have a stamp', said Yuri, almost with pride.

After lunch, Ivan returned to the membership book while Yuri tended to half a dozen children sent by a Moscow school for an afternoon's recreation. Ivan would await the youngsters' return before taking out a skiff: children's memories of faces were too good to risk being seen by them. By mid-afternoon, he had read through to 1938. He heard young voices singing children's songs in the changing rooms. They would be gone in a few minutes.

At the end of that year, he found an inscription that read: *The double skulls championship was won by two military officers rowing on behalf of our club. At the annual dinner, the Chairman thanked these two fine sportsmen, Lieutenant Felix Pavlovich Nikolaev and Captain Sergei Borisovich Volkov, both of the Military Diplomatic Academy, for their remarkable achievement and contribution. Received: one engraved cup for the club room.*

So, the elder Nikolaev, Lieutenant Vassily's father, and Marshall Volkov, the member of the Politburo who had disappeared, had rowed together: that made them friends for life; and all, including Lieutenant Vassily, had gone to the Military Academy. He sat at the small, log table and looked for a long time at the pencil between his fingers; then he wrote: *DEAR KOSTYA, I THINK THAT THERE IS TO BE A DEFECTION. IF IT ACTS WITHOUT MILITARY SUPPORT, THE PARTY CAN STOP IT. I AM POWERLESS. DO YOU REMEMBER THE YARD AT THE ANDRONIKOV MONASTERY WHERE WE PLAYED AS CHILDREN? I NEED TO SEE YOU THERE AT 1730 THIS COMING MONDAY.*

He dated the note, and signed it, *VANYA P.*

Captain George Kevorkian was more than worried: a month had passed since his rowing-team coach had convinced him to keep quiet about the text of the cable using the obscure GRU cipher: now time was passing, a feeling of impending danger gnawed at his entrails. He would feel more comfortable getting his duty over and done with, but that would be disloyal to Ivan: he would either have to lie to his boss or find a damned good reason for hiding this information for over a month.

It was the morning George Kevorkian had decided to talk things over with his superior officer that Major General Budhakin's new aide appeared at his office door. Kevorkian's own boss was standing by his side.

'I don't know what you're doing, George', said his superior officer, 'but could you get these tapes quickly transcribed? They've never seen the cipher in the offices.' He turned to Budhakin's aide. 'Comrade Captain Kevorkian will take the transcript personally to the General once he has found the code. Of course, we must keep a copy for our files, if you don't mind.'

The aide turned his back on George's boss and strutted off.

'Who's he?' asked George.

''Name's Nikolaev: Budhakin's new aide. 'Takes himself very seriously indeed!' He left George to the tapes.

George fed them through the printer and saw similar groupings to those using the old GRU cipher on Ivan's cable. After five hours of labour, he had reconstructed the series of broken words into a language looking much like Italian. From his safe, he drew a copy of the tape he had deciphered for Ivan. 'The same code names: "Neve" and "Latte": Snow and Milk', he muttered. 'My friend Ivan Dmitriyevich would be interested in these. I wonder what the hell that Lieutenant Nikolaev, is doing with them.'

He locked copies in his safe and set off with his transcript for the offices of the First Chief Directorate. An aide hustled him into Budhakin's office; and left, closing the door behind him.

Budhakin looked up from a clear desk. 'Yes?' Irritation tinged his voice.

'I have a transcript of your tapes, Comrade General.'

'Where's Nikolaev?'

'Your aide left, Sir.'

'Aide?'

George stared stupidly. 'You did ask for tapes to be transcribed, Comrade General?'

'Well? What do they say?'

He felt an idiot: he should have had them translated first. 'They're severely garbled, Sir. I....'

'Then reconstruct them, Captain.'

'Of course, Sir. I will pass them on to your staff: we can do little more with them in Communications.'

'Show me', ordered Budhakin, extending his hand towards George's notepad. He flipped testily through the pages. 'Spanish: may be Havana.'

'Italian, Comrade General.'

'Get it translated.'

'Yes, Sir.'

Budhakin compared a few pages. 'What does 'Neve' mean?'

'Snow, I believe, Sir: I think it's a code name.'

Budhakin glared at George. 'You speak Italian? What's your accent?'

'I'm Armenian, Comrade General. I don't speak Italian, but I checked the dictionary for that word; I saw it repeated too.'

'Very clever, Captain', snapped Budhakin. He lifted a phone. 'Get Nikolaev. Who's at the Italian desk?'

There came a moment's pause.

'Wasn't he the one who went to get Promyslov in Rome? 'Engaged to the Demicheva woman.'

Another pause.

'....in Sofia? What the hell was he doing there? What about Promyslov?'

He looked up at George, surprised the big Cipher Officer was still standing in his office. He cupped his hand over the mouthpiece. 'You're dismissed.'

George turned and walked to the door.

'Then get the fucking dogs out after him!' snapped Budhakin into the handset, and banged it down.

Nikolaev rushed past George into the office. George turned into the corridor, and stopped out of sight of Budhakin's desk, and listened.

'First, Promyslov disappears, and now his damned friend Ryabov goes gallivanting all over Europe. Get him will you, Vassya. Let him cool his heels in quarantine.'

George Kevorkian gasped, and quietly slipped off.

'Close the door, Vassya', went on Budhakin. 'A cigar?'

'No thank you, Comrade General.'

Budhakin opened the humidor on his desk and rolled a cigar fastidiously to his ear. He lounged back in his vast, leather chair, leaving Nikolaev standing.

'Tell me, my boy, how is that charming father of yours?'

'The General is very well, Sir. He was delighted with your lectures at the Funze Academy.'

'Good of him to invite me. He's a clever chap, your father, and very young: you could find yourself one day the son of a top military brass.'

'I believe he already is, Sir.'

Budhakin blustered through blue smoke. 'Yes, of course, my boy: I meant he could be promoted again; 'could be quite soon, actually.'

'Yes, Sir.'

'A bad business about the Marshall', said Budhakin with a wink.

Nikolaev was aghast at this familiarity. 'Yes, Sir.'

Budhakin sighed. 'I wish it were all.'

'Sir?'

'Those tapes you found in Promyslov's safe....'

Nikolaev waited in silence: he felt the thrill of Promyslov's impending downfall. What had his grandfather always said? 'Remember, little Vassya, revenge is a dish to be savoured cold.'

'He's a fool to keep tapes in his safe. Heavens knows where he got them.'

'Have they been deciphered, Comrade General?'

'Not yet, my boy.'

'Would you like me to handle the enquiry once I lock up Ryabov?'

'It's difficult; what with Promyslov your predecessor, and his years of service. He's disappeared, you know: someone must have tipped him off.'

'I don't see who, Comrade General. The Ninth Directorate is very discrete, and who else knew?'

The major general scowled at his cigar. 'I don't understand it: he didn't come home; he wasn't at the hospital;

he just disappeared. His wife said he'd gone for a walk. I've got the militia looking for him all over Moscow.'

Nikolaev stroked at the stubble on his chin. 'He'll appear, Comrade General; it's only a question of time.'

'Yes, of course', said Budhakin, ''strange, those tapes, though.'

'Why, Sir?' asked Nikolaev.

'In Italian.' Budhakin laughed. 'Either they were about the weather, or our code names are becoming more stupid every year.'

'Sir?' A film of perspiration appeared on Nikolaev's forehead.

'Snow, my boy. Someone has been talking about snow in Italy.'

Nikolaev felt his throat tighten.

''You alright, Nikolaev?'

'Yes, Sir', he stammered. 'I'm tired: I've been up all night going through the section files.'

Budhakin peered at the young officer. ''Don't know anything about this 'snow', do you?'

'Certainly not, Sir', he lied. Then he regretted his stupidity. 'But....'

Budhakin went on heedless. 'Another thing I want you to look into. You'll find documents in the files on an illegal called Fedorenko from the Executive-Action group who, according to Havana, has got himself into a mess. Promyslov sent him West against my better judgement.'

'I'm aware of the case, Sir.'

'Damned embarrassing. Promyslov's been dithering. I want this cleared up quickly.'

The colour returned to Nikolaev's brow. 'You can rely on me, Comrade General.'

'Ah! That's what I like to hear, my boy; that's the Nikolaev fibre. Carry on.'

'Thank you, Sir.' Nikolaev saluted smartly and left.

From Ivan Promyslov's old office, now Nikolaev's, he placed a call to the DGI in Havana. In clear, slow Russian he gave instructions to a liaison officer called Garcia and agreed to confirm his orders over the satellite link. Later that evening, the spurt of radio messages bouncing off a sophisticated assembly of light alloys and silicon somewhere beyond the ionosphere between Moscow and Havana, contained Moscow Centre's explicit instruction to liquidate special agent Fedorenko; it was signed Colonel Ivan Dmitriyevich Promyslov.

Nikolaev waited in the corridor between two guards. Aleksandr Mikhailovich Ryabov's startled look sent a ripple of tension through the party waiting to escort him to the cell block.

'I am to put you into quarantine, Comrade Lieutenant', stated Nikolaev. He tried to hide the thrill in his voice. This was the first time he had made an arrest.

'Why?' stammered Ryabov.

'You will be informed in due course. Please come with us. From now on you are to talk to no one but to me.'

Minutes later, Aleksandr Ryabov, in full officer's uniform, found himself in a Lubyanka quarantine cell.

That evening, George Kevorkian rowed alone in the tank. Promyslov had disappeared, and now Ryabov was in quarantine. He had heard a lot about the pretty, blue-eyed Demicheva woman from Aleksandr Mikhailovich. She would be worried about her fiancée's disappearance so soon after his return from Sofia. Seeing her would be easy enough because both she, and George, worked in the same wing housing the 13th Department. He would invite her for a drink, but first, he had to find out what she looked like.

Life on the river is sluggish when the Moskva river is not in swell; that's the way the barge people like it; it's why they lead the life they do; a varied life from one Soviet republic to another, and vodka is cheaper a long way from Moscow.

The Moskva takes a hairpin around the Lenin Central Stadium; passes the ski jump on the left bank; and continues upriver, past the church of St. Nicholas, on to the Kremlin's mighty walls. Barges glide ponderously from bridge to bridge along this stretch.

The Likhachev was a heavy vessel, specially built in the German Democratic Republic for transporting Zils from the auto factory in Moscow to a warehouse North of the city; and its captain was a small, rotund fellow with rosy cheeks and reeking breath. The militia could catch him easily on this stretch in their launches, so he ate raw onions to hide the smell of alcohol. The vodka was rarely flushed from his system before late afternoon when it took a clearer head to navigate the Moskva's chicanes through the Soviet capital, and, especially, to avoid the stone uprights of its venerable bridges.

He was inching gingerly through the swell under the Luznikowsky bridge below Komsomol Prospekt. The vessel was wide of its course, but the Likhachev would have no trouble clearing the uprights under the expert, if slightly drunken, control of its rubicund captain. The bow was well clear now, but the bearded Czech responsible for the bow ramps was jumping up and down like a kangaroo, waving his arms at the bridge.

The captain scanned the river for a skiff his subconscious had registered travelling towards them not fifteen seconds earlier, and in sickening realisation, rammed the throttle into full reverse. The barge shuddered and drifted dangerously skew on the current towards one of the Luznikowsky bridge's pillars. The Czech spun two lifebelts into the river where the skiff had capsized under the bow wave. An oar had hit the side of the barge, ejecting the sculler; the Czech was terrified it had hit his head; he searched anxiously for a sign of him in the turbulent waters. A hand surfaced briefly.

The Czech kicked off his clogs and leapt in after it. His thick, sodden clothes weighed heavily in the freezing waters. Go with the current, his senses told him; don't fight it; go at his speed, whoever he was. He surfaced, gasped, and squinted around through dripping eyebrows for the hand. He saw the massive steel hull of the Likhachev towering above him. A lifebelt hovered downstream. He swam towards it and clutched its smooth, reassuring form.

An arm pointed downstream over the edge of the barge; a face mouthed at him hysterically. 'Over there!' The Czech pushed the lifebelt ahead of him in the arm's general direction. Then he saw the hand again, raised limply as if in a final farewell.

His lungs bursting, his muscles at breaking point, the Czech lunged after the hand, and grabbed it. Was there a pulse of recognition in those cold fingers? He clutched at the arm, kicking furiously in his sodden clothes to keep his head above water. The rower was wearing a cotton tracksuit; the Czech seized it in one hand and grasped the lifebelt with the other.

Now another swimmer was beside them in the water, helping to pull up the lone sculler. A small rubber craft was lowered from the barge. Someone gripped the Czech: another took the drowning man. The strength flowed from his limbs. Strong hands lifted him from the water into the rubber craft, and, in a daze, he watched the dripping body of the oarsman dragged out of the water and laid beside him on the raft's floor. The rower's torso was bare, his head hidden inside the track-suit jacket, pulled up around his ears in the effort to drag him out of the water.

A colleague was on his knees, freeing the head, tilting it back, holding the nose and blowing into the mouth. Another felt the drowned man's pulse for a heartbeat.

The Czech trembled. Minutes passed; he was freezing. No signs of revival came from the still body beside him. Far above, faces stared down from the bridge. He heard the faint sound of a siren. A militia launch raced towards them: the barge was sitting sickeningly across the bridge uprights.

In the distance, the hull of a small, polished wooden skiff smashed against a pillar and disappeared around a chicane on its long journey to the river plain.

The oarsman's limp body was lifted onto the launch. A tube was thrust down his throat while the militia officer listened for breathing; another rolled up his sleeves to give heart massage.

Seconds later, one stood and shouted. 'He's alive!'

The bearded Czech sobbed. Strong hands ruffled his hair, and he lay down alongside the oarsman's trembling form.

The last person Aleksandr Mikhailovich Ryabov would have expected to visit him was the man who had him flung in jail in the first place, Major General Leonid Budhakin. The general strutted into the cell, a mirthless grin hovering at the edges of his mouth.

Ryabov jerked awkwardly to attention.

'Well, young man, how do you feel after a few days of quarantine?'

Ryabov felt afraid and dirty; his uniform was crushed, and he suspected the cell smelt strongly of the latrine in the corner. 'Confused, Comrade General.'

Budhakin laughed and sat on the bed.

Ryabov hesitated, then asked, 'Why am I here, Sir?'

'Because nobody in the First Chief Directorate goes anywhere in Moscow without my permission, and you go gallivanting all over Europe without even informing us!'

'But Sofia is....'

'You did not inform your superiors!'

Aleksandr did not feel like saying that Colonel Promyslov, had not only been aware of the trip but had given his permission. 'Yes, Sir, of course.'

Budhakin pointed at the wooden stool. 'Sit!'

'Thank you, Sir.'

'Why were you so keen to see Promyslov in Italy?'

'Haven't you received his report, Sir?'

'I'm in a better position to ask the questions!'

'Yes, Sir.' Aleksandr Mikhailovich wanted to cross his legs but thought it disrespectful.

The general adopted a listening expression, anxious to control his impatience with this 'know-it-all.'

'The Colonel asked for me from his hospital bed, Sir. He indicated he mistrusted local embassy staff and needed someone to be, as it were, his voice after he was shot in the head.'

'A mere glancing blow. Why did he mistrust them?'

'He didn't say, Comrade General.'

'What do you think?'

'I'm not aware of the details, Sir, but I believe the Colonel suspects links with Italian organised crime.'

''Nonsense, Ryabov: I'm surprised someone of your calibre would fall for that. Promyslov's future is behind him: when a man fails in middle age, he makes up cock-and-bull stories to regain his self-esteem. He's an unhealthy companion; make friends with officers likely to make something of their careers.'

'Yes, Sir.' Ryabov waited.

'Well? What else?'

'What else do you wish to know, Sir?'

'Switzerland.'

'Moscow Centre sent him there for treatment, Sir.'

'The translator; the Italian militia?'

'I don't know, Sir.'

'Weren't you there?'

'Where, Sir?'

'Damn it, Ryabov: the interview!'

'The colonel can't speak, Sir.'

Budhakin made a mental note to check the transcript of the interview with the *Carabinieri* to see whether Ryabov had indeed been absent. 'Why has he gone missing, Ryabov?'

It came as such a shock to Aleksandr Mikhailovich that he could only think of feigning more stupidity. 'Who, Sir?'

Budhakin reddened. His fists clenched tight, his knuckles whitened, and he yelled at Ryabov, 'On your feet boy! Guard! Guard!'

The door was unlocked. A frightened, armed guard opened it.

'Take this man's clothes: all of them!'

Ryabov could hardly believe his ears. He looked at the general.

'Eyes front!' yelled Budhakin.

Aleksandr Mikhailovich's hands went to his buttons.

Budhakin screamed at him, 'Attention!' He turned to the guard. 'Undress him!'

Every vestige of clothing was stripped from Ryabov's muscular body. He would have loved to cross his hands over his genitals, but that was not the way you stand to attention in the Soviet Union.

Budhakin sat and watched. His eyes blazed with anger. He waited for the guard to go to the door. 'And get them washed!' he ordered, 'This place stinks.' He turned to Ryabov. 'I don't care who you are, nor whom you know; the only person who can get you out of here is me. Now, answer me truthfully.'

'I had no idea the Colonel is missing, Comrade General.'

'Why were you in Bulgaria?'

'I was tracing passport numbers, Sir.'

'Why?'

'They're evidence in the Antonov/BAPTCo case, Sir.'

'Did you find what you were looking for?'

'Yes, Sir: it's in my report.'

'Listen, I'll ask when I want to know something: your report is of no interest. Understood?'

'Yes, Sir.'

'Do you believe Promyslov's activities unpatriotic or suspect in any way?'

'No, Sir. He loves his country; almost naively so.'

Budhakin's eyes narrowed to slits. 'What does that mean?'

'He goes too far in obeying the rules, Sir: had he been more political, he might have made his life ten times easier.'

Budhakin fell into silence, then asked, ''You at the Italian desk, Ryabov?'

'Yes, Sir.'

'What does N-E-V-E mean?'

'Snow, Sir; I think.'

'Good. Does it mean anything to you professionally?'

'We have an agent-runner couple, Sir, called Milk and Snow.'

'Tell me more, Lieutenant.'

'Colonel Promyslov suspects agent Milk to be a contact between our Rome embassy and the Mafia, Sir. In reality, he is a GRU agent, but Lieutenant Nikolaev paid him using KGB funds while he was on assignment in Italy.'

There! He had said it: now that insufferable idiot was in the shit too and deserved it. He hesitated: Budhakin hadn't uttered a word. Ryabov cocked an eye at the bed where the general was sitting.

Budhakin's face had turned scarlet. 'Comrade Nikolaev has been promoted to Captain. What the hell has he got to do with this? This could be the end of your career, Lieutenant, falsely accusing a fellow officer.'

'Excuse me, Comrade General, I thought you knew.' And if the old fart didn't, it was going to be Aleksandr Mikhailovich's pleasure to tell him.

'Knew what?' Budhakin hissed.

'That Comrade Captain Nikolaev, in his last posting, ran, not only this GRU agent, Milk but also the KGB Executive-Action illegal, Ahmet, whom Colonel Promyslov was instructed to bring home after the Antonov affair in Bulgaria.'

'Impossible!'

Ryabov was surprised at the old fool's vehemence, but he went on. 'And Snow, or Neve, as he is called, is Comrade Captain Nikolaev's codename, Sir.'

Budhakin leapt to his feet. His hand swept a wide arc, the back hitting Aleksandr Mikhailovich squarely in the mouth. Unprepared for the blow, Ryabov staggered back.

'Get up', screamed Budhakin. 'Nikolaev is a fellow officer, boy: don't forget it! Attention!'

Ryabov stood; blood trickled from his lower lip. 'Everything I have said is verifiable, Comrade General.'

Budhakin sat down on the bed again. 'You are in deep trouble, officer.'

'Yes, Sir.'

'Explain this unforgivable calumny.'

'Comrade Colonel Promyslov's investigations, and my own have uncovered independent witnesses who will attest to Captain Nikolaev's involvement. You may find that the facts, when they are made known, will require an official investigation, Sir.'

'Into what?'

Ryabov detected a note of hysteria in the general's voice. 'Irregular Moscow-Centre activities in the Antonov/BAPTCo affair.'

'That investigation is being handled by Sofia.'

'Colonel Promyslov was about to extend the work to include Russian citizens, Sir.'

'You insist on sticking your neck out, you young idiot. I suggest you rethink your position before subscribing to Promyslov's fantasies.'

'Yes, Sir.'

'In the meanwhile, I will read through the garbage in your report. You should count on a long stay in this place: it's cold without clothes.'

Ryabov hung his head.

Budhakin yelled at the cell door that he wanted to be let out.

A neon tube winked sporadically from the ceiling of the emergency room, and a hand clutched his forearm. His stomach contracted violently, and he vomited over the side of the bed.

'That's a good sign', came a voice.

'Have you seen that scar? It looks like a bullet wound. I'll get someone to clean up this mess. Where did he crawl out of?' came another.

Ivan relaxed on his bed.

'I don't know. He appeared at the club a few days ago, slept in the changing rooms, and spent most of his time on the river. He's been a member for years; 'a champion sculler when he was a lad.'

'What did you say his name is?' asked the doctor.

'I don't remember', said the old boat keeper. 'What is the militia doing by the door?'

'They're the ones who brought him in.'

'Why haven't they gone?'

'An identity check, I suppose. They want to talk to you.'

'By the black marks on his fingers, they'll know his quite soon.'

'That's routine, they say: as soon as they fish anyone out of the water, dead or alive, they take his fingerprints.'

Ivan groaned.

Yuri blinked at him in surprise.

'I thought you said he's mute.'

'He is.'

The doctor left through the swing doors.

Yuri Berzin glowered after him. When he turned to look at Ivan, he saw him looking back. 'Hey, old son, it's me, Yuri.' He laughed. 'You look as though you've seen a ghost.'

Ivan opened his mouth, and said, 'Yuri, thank you.' He coughed violently, lay back, and stared at the ceiling.

'It's alright now, Vanya', he said, and tears flooded into his eyes. He felt like a fool. 'It's OK old son.' He sniffed.

'They've put the barge captain inside: too much vodka! The fellow who pulled you out deserves a bloody medal, but he's a Czech. They sent him back to the barge. What's left of the skiff has gone to the bottom.'

Ivan listened in disbelief. 'I was hit by a barge?'

'That will teach you to turn and look where you're going! You can't hear those barges sometimes until the motor section clears the bridge. Why did you spin me this line about not being able to talk?'

'Because I couldn't. It's our secret now that I can, Yuri.' Ivan coughed.

The old man thought it was a stupid joke, and changed the subject. 'Maybe I should call someone from your family, but you've been so secretive I've been afraid of doing something wrong.'

'Don't call anyone, Yuri, just get me away from here.'

'I can't: the militia's outside the door. They have your prints, you know: look at your fingers.'

'Damn!'

'And you've got no identity papers on you.'

Ivan reflected. 'Yuri, did you send the letter?'

'No, I took it personally to the address you wrote down; one of the lads read it and told me where to go.'

'If anyone takes me out of here, call my wife, Olga Sergeyevna, on 43524 at my home. Tell her what happened, but don't say I can talk.'

'43524: I'll remember.'

'Say to her I want Kostya to find me, nothing more: she'll know who I mean.'

Yuri's eyebrows arched. 'I need friends like that.'

'Do you have money to make the call.'

Yuri forced a thin smile. 'I'm rolling in rubles, Comrade.'

'Now help me into my clothes.'

'Are you joking? They're soaking wet.'

A nurse walked into the room and swabbed the vomit.

A minute later, two black-coated characters followed her in. 'My compliments, Comrade Colonel, you had a narrow escape from death', said one. 'If your friend would like to leave us now, you can get dressed and come with us; we have dry clothes for you.'

Yuri stood, squeezed Ivan's arm, and left the room.

The rear gates of the Lubyanka compound opened and closed immediately behind them. Ivan, sandwiched between the two black-coated individuals from the Ninth Directorate, shivered in the back of the limousine. Once in the courtyard, he was escorted to the entrance of the cell block. He had never suspected such depths of despair could exist. He had opened these same doors in the past as a jailer, but now, they opened to him as a prisoner, and he felt utterly wretched.

Barred steel gates slid open and clanged shut behind. He passed into the bowels of the building. They took him to the political wing. Before him, an ashen-faced guard held folded, grey garments. 'Get into these.' He pointed at an open cubicle. 'In there; all your belongings in the basket.' Ivan changed into the grey, rough cotton shirt and trousers. The tracksuit he wore was the property of State Security, and his rowing strip was still drying at the hospital. He handed the basket back, empty.

'Nothing?'

Ivan shook his head.

'Well?'

Ivan pointed at his mouth and shook his head again.

It finally dawned on the jailer he was a mute. 'Stand over there.'

He stood with his back to the grid.

'Hands above your head.'

The guard performed a thorough body check: no square centimetre of his body was left untouched. The guard then photographed his face, in full, three-quarters, and profile, and took a full set of fingerprints. Satisfied the formalities were complete, the two black-coated men from the Ninth left and the guard marched Ivan through more steel into the heart of the cell block. 'Stop', he said. 'Prisoner face right.'

Prisoner? He had called him prisoner!

He opened a steel door, pushed Ivan in, and slammed it shut behind him.

The guards patrolling the apartment block disappeared one day. Returning from the store at the officers' club, Olga found the limousines fuming in the cold, gone; and the hall and alleyway, behind the block, empty of its bored, foot-stamping, uniformed sentries. She should have felt relieved; instead she felt a cold panic: had they found Vanya?

The idea of having a husband on the run shocked her; yet she was sure there had been a mistake, and that, in the end, he would triumph.

When the phone rang, it would have been for Ivan: neither her own family nor his, had one. She hesitated, hoping the ringing would stop; it didn't; she lifted the handset.

'Is that 43524?' An old man's voice.

'Yes. Who are you?'

'A sporting friend of your husband's.'

Olga wanted news; she was afraid. 'Where is he?'

'Tell Kostya to come and find him.'

'Where is he?'

'At the hospital, but I think he's gone now.'

'He's hurt!' she cried.

'A sporting accident; but he's alright.'

Olga sobbed. The caller waited patiently for her to stop. She heard rapid clicks; they stopped; he had put more coins into the phone box.

'Don't cry. He's alive. Can you call this Kostya? Do you have his number?'

She regained her composure. 'In Vanya's diary, I think.'

'Don't waste time. I have no more coins.' The receiver clicked rapidly, and the line went dead.

Yuri's rough tones swum in her mind. She took a handkerchief from her cardigan sleeve and blew her nose. The diary would be on the dressing table. Oh, please don't let them have taken that too. She searched everywhere; in the bedroom, then in the rest of the flat; but the diary had gone, as had his wallet, keys, and identity papers. She burst into tears, and sat on the edge of the bed, hugging her husband's photograph; the one he was the proudest of; the one taken after his last promotion to Colonel showing him in full dress uniform. Her suffering husband could not even rely on her to make a simple phone call.

That same evening, George Kevorkian walked into the basement club feeling ready to introduce himself. He had seen the blonde in the cafeteria one evening as she came on duty. It was going to be difficult to keep his head: Tanya Demicheva's eyes troubled the soul of the most platonic of men. He pulled a comb through his hair, picked up a tray, and joined the queue of diners arriving on the night shift. Peering beyond the till he saw her sitting with her girlfriends at their usual table. He walked up and sat almost opposite Tanya. George bit into his liver sausage and swallowed some tea. He caught Tanya's eye and smiled. She nodded coolly; she had seen him in the corridors of the 13th Communications Department but had no idea who he was.

He approached and said, 'I'd like to talk about Sasha', in quiet, Armenian tones.

Tanya's eyes flashed to meet his. Her lips opened a fraction. 'Where is he?'

'Can we speak alone?'

Tanya looked pleadingly at her two girlfriends, who picked up their trays and moved to another table.

'Where is he?'

'Budhakin had him quarantined.'

Her hand shot to her mouth. She stared at George.

'Act calmly here, Comrade: people watch. Try not to frown like that, please.'

Tanya removed her hand. 'Why Sasha?'

'He got himself into some intrigue with Ivan Promyslov: your fiancée's friend, and mine.'

Tanya blinked at the table: she looked as though she was going to cry.

'For pity's sake, not here!' smiled George.

She swallowed hard.

'Ivan Promyslov was investigating some communications tapes before he left; they were found in his safe. It was a foolish thing to do.'

'They were mine', stammered the girl.

'You knew about them?'

'He took them to help me.'

'Are you serious? This is worth your job, at least; you could find yourself the next one in jail.'

'That's why the Colonel was trying to help me.'

George frowned. 'We've more talking to do than I thought, Tatiana Demicheva. Maybe we should save time, and include the boss.'

Tanya dropped her gaze. 'Yes, with Sasha in prison, I think the time has come.'

'Are you prepared to lose your job?'

'If it gets Sasha out of trouble, yes.'

The two left the cafeteria together and knocked at the door of the Assistant Director of Communications, 13th Department of the First Chief Directorate. He was coming to the end of a long day, or so he thought: he was wrong, the two members of his staff, who walked in, kept him talking until well past midnight.

The cell's white walls reflected a stark light. No window let in the softer light of day. The small space allowed no exercise, and he felt cold. A steel-framed bed stretched along one wall. A latrine, a stool, and a wash basin took the other. An issue of Pravda and a copy of Marx's *Das Kapital* lay on the small table occupying remaining precious space.

He had uttered no sound since his parting with Yuri. The cells in the Lubyanka had microphones, and though he would have liked to experience the thrill of hearing himself speak again, the time was not right for others to know he had regained his power of speech. He put his head under the blanket and softly, very softly, hummed to himself. He opened his mouth and quietly said, 'Olya.' He repeated the alphabet in a whisper. The relief of rediscovering normal speech helped him fight off his depression.

He surfaced, picked up the Pravda, and spent two hours reading it from cover to cover. He would have liked to do the crossword, but he had no pen. He managed about half of it in his head and attacked the chess problem. He lifted Marx's monumental thesis, and read a few pages, remembering his early Komsomol lectures on Dialectic Materialism. The book was heavy going: he dropped it on the floor and stared at the ceiling.

Little by little, the despair returned. Before his imprisonment, Budhakin could at least have shown the courtesy of informing him that the tapes had been discovered. How long would he be in the cell? Had Yuri got through to Olya?

Self-pity swept over him; even death had refused him, twice now. The joy he had felt in recovering the use of his voice was swept into darkness, and, exhausted, he fell asleep under the glare of the cell lights.

CREMANTE AND BALAIAN

The driver negotiated ancient, narrow streets towards Padua's Via Pindemonte, where, in January 1982, the American Brigadier General James Lee Dozier had escaped the clutches of his captors. Ten 'Leatherheads' of Italy's 'Central Operational Security Nucleus' had released him in a ninety-second operation.

Bugs thought back to that foggy, London morning in December 1981 when the cable had arrived with his new posting. He was to present himself within hours to the Defence Department coordinator in Rome to join a team of two thousand investigators searching for the kidnapped American general. Every lead, even the most minute, had to be thoroughly investigated. A communiqué issued by the captors claimed the kidnap would promote the Red Brigades' international unity with the West-German Red Army Faction, the Irish Republican Army, and the Basque ETA movement. Every scrap of American investigative talent available in Europe was rushed to Italy to help in the search. After the humiliation of Aldo Moro's murder in May 1978, Italy was anxious to show its worried NATO allies a new spirit of cooperation and a vast improvement in police techniques.

Nino's thoughts turned to his country's lonely battle against terrorism. 'You know, Bugs, I used to get really cross when they showed those snapshots on television of unshaven kidnap victims under the five-pointed star of the Red Brigades. Curcio is in his early forties now: he was twenty-five then, so young to launch a cult of terror. When he finally leaves prison a free man, he'll find a different Italy. His old allies may not be so ready to help him.' Nino looked gloomily through the windshield.

'I remember the Red Brigades described themselves as an "armed proletarian vanguard, a political group recognising neither God nor master": they styled themselves as the "revolutionary strength of the 'exploited classes'", said Bugs, 'Their philosophy is well explained in a book I found in

Colombia written by an Islamist Albanian writer called Mehemet Shkoder. Have you heard of him?'

'No', replied Nino.

Jenny said, 'Tell me about Curcio'.

Nino drew his gaze from the car window and quickly warmed to his subject. 'He married a woman called Margarita Cagol in 1969, and the two settled in Milan. She became known as Comrade Mara. Curcio was arrested for arson and kidnapping in September 1974 and was sprung from jail in 1975 in a dare-devil attempt successfully led by Margarita. She was killed a few months later in a shoot-out. Curcio was recaptured in January 1976, and he's been inside ever since.'

'So, the Brigades survived Curcio's captivity', interjected Jenny.

'Yes, sadly;' continued Nino, 'they brutally murdered Aldo Moro two years after Curcio's recapture. What a black year! Moro was a law professor, had been Chairman of the Christian Democrats, and five-times Italian premier. His captors dubbed him as his party's "political godfather" and as an "anti-proletarian criminal". It was very hard!'

'And the culprits?'

'They're in jail now; he died, they live on. They murdered him after a so-called 'peoples' trial.' Twelve shots, as if each individual member of his jury were his executioner; and all the slugs, except one, coming from the same Czechoslovakian pistol. The government had just refused the kidnappers' ultimatum to release thirteen detainees. They found him, Jenny, a pathetic corpse huddled in the trunk of an old red Renault, parked mid-way between the Christian-Democrat headquarters and that of the Communist Party.' He was still dressed in the blue suit he had been wearing when captured. My country had not suffered such humiliation for forty years. I saw grown men with tears in their eyes in the streets of Rome, as though the murder had occurred in their own family. I believe the cause of the Red Brigades, even among their own ranks, suffered more on that day than any other, before, or since. I believe the outrage of that brutal murder led ultimately to their destruction. Even wild young people, who might otherwise have been attracted to them, were sickened.'

'Why did they want Moro?' asked Jenny.

'They needed big game to satisfy their megalomania; to free their comrades from jail; and, as usual, to discredit the government. They were well trained: they kidnapped Moro professionally and handled their arms with skill. They prepared for months, following his movements; practising every contingency. The kidnap was as premeditated as the murder itself.'

The driver stopped beside an eight-floor building. Nino beckoned Jenny to the other side of the street, where they could see the outside of a second-floor apartment. 'In that apartment, Jenny, a twenty-one-year-old doctor's daughter played host in late 1981 to an unwilling James Lee Dozier and his kidnappers. It belonged to her father, as did a yacht she used for arms running. His beloved boat was impounded by the Italian authorities. It must have come as quite a shock: he thought his daughter was studying history at Venice University.

'And do you see that supermarket?' asked Nino, pointing at a store on the ground floor. 'We locked the shoppers in when we freed the General. We ran a bulldozer outside to give our 'Leatherheads' noise cover: we call them that because they wear leather masks to avoid recognition. They strike with extreme force against insurgents in the same way as your Delta Force, the Special Air Service, or Grenzschutzgruppe 9. They did a fine job. Not a shot was fired. Despite that, three of them were subsequently prosecuted for using excessive "extreme force" against the terrorists; one of them even served a jail sentence.'

Jenny gasped in surprise.

'Those, my dear Jenny', continued Nino, 'are our contradictions. The main issue is that, after forty-two days of captivity, General Dozier was freed. He had borne intolerable stress like a true soldier.'

'And his kidnappers?' asked Jenny.

'The leader, Antonio Savasta, had been personally involved in Moro's abduction. Another week and the General would have spent as much time in captivity as Aldo Moro when he was "executed."'

'How did you find him?'

'Has Bugs never told you?' asked Nino.

'He never discusses his work with me. I only get to see the steam when the safety valve blows.'

'Ah, I understand. It's difficult at times to know how much to tell one's family.'

Jenny smiled.

Nino went on. 'The investigation led to one hundred and fifty arrests, and to the discovery of almost forty hideouts. We worked on weaker sympathisers to get leads on hard-core activists, the *'irreducibili.'* The break came when we interrogated two characters called Petrella and Galati. Both were arrested for drug running. We flew one up from Rome to confront his testimony with the others in Padua. That was how we found the hideout.' Nino looked up at the windows of the apartment across the street. 'The success of that operation, Jenny, led to a new-found confidence in Italy's legal institutions.'

Bugs had been walking around the building lost in thought. Nino and Jenny crossed the street to join him.

'It brings back memories doesn't it, Nino.'

'Yes, of anguish and joy.'

They returned to the waiting car.

Nino turned to his silent guests in the rear. 'Weren't you saying, Bugs, that someone in Chicago was kept in captivity the same way as General Dozier?'

'A girl called Corinne O'Grady. Her dad was a cop, gunned down after the assassination attempt on the President. She was abducted and chained to a platform inside a pup tent, mounted, she thinks, inside a room. She had just enough light to read, and the bulb was replaced with a blue one when she was expected to sleep.'

'Did they force her to listen to music through a headset?' asked Nino. 'The General's kidnappers did that to him: the music was so loud he had ear trouble for a long time after.'

'Of course,' interjected Bugs. 'I had forgotten; Corinne O'Grady had had to listen to music through a headset too. All of it as if her abductors had learnt from the Red Brigades.'

As the car sped on to Milan, the three lapsed anew into silence.

The following morning, they flew to Ascoli Piceno, where Bugs wanted to interview Paolo Ferraresi in jail, as he was the *brigatista* whose interrogation had led to the raid on Mischa's apartment, and to Lucia Sereni's arrest. Nino had tried unsuccessfully to secure Bugs' clearance to enter the jail's top-security wing, where all the *irreducibili* were imprisoned.A guard led him to the visitors' cubicles. Ferraresi hadn't wanted to see anyone at first.

Bugs was surprised at his boyish face. Over the speaker, the terrorist's voice sounded remote and detached from the lips mouthing into the microphone behind the bullet-proof glass screens. A guard patrolled the corridor between them: a no man's land; a final separation between society and its undesirables. Now and then he verified tapes recording their conversation.

Bugs lied about being an American sociologist researching the Red Brigade movement. Ferraresi's humour turned: he seemed almost pleased to be selected for questioning. Bugs could see that he was relieved to break the crushing boredom and loneliness of his jail sentence. The Italian promised to answer as well as he could. He asked Ferraresi to describe *brigatista* doctrine in an Italian he could understand.

The boy replied carefully. He had had time in his cell to question the opinions of his past. 'We used urban warfare to provoke a repressive response from government. We thought that strong government reaction would alienate the masses and underscore the futility of our institutions.'

'Do you believe you succeeded?' asked Bugs.

'We made fools of them for a long time: government couldn't handle us.'

'And did government reaction alienate Italians, as you predicted?'

'I think we failed: we lost control of public opinion in 1978 with Moro's execution. The clamp-down led to a law limiting *habeas corpus*; we could now be held for twenty-four hours without legal aid. A law like that would never have been voted before.' He paused. 'I'm not sure our ideals were completely wrong; I prefer to think Italian society wasn't ready for us. We were going too fast for the proletariat to understand: our motto was, *'vogliamo tutto, e subito!'* which translates to 'we want it all, now!' but society changes slowly unless it's ripe for revolution.'

'So you were ahead of your time.'

'Yes, that's it; ahead of our time.'

'Did you have any rules in the columns?'

'Did we have rules?! We followed them rigorously too; reading only approved revolutionary literature; carefully organising our cover; looking and acting like bourgeois students. We kept regular hours; made no noise after ten; had no wild parties. The code was ascetic, allowing us to blend into urban life without arousing suspicion.'

'Did you know a woman called Lucia Sereni?'

'I knew of a Comrade Lucy. It could be the same woman.'

'Tell me about her.'

The *brigatista* told what little he knew of Comrade Lucy. He had heard she was a top activist's lover. Comrade Lucy could well have been Lucia herself, but Bugs learnt nothing new from the terrorist's statements. He had worked on the fringe of the movement as a driver and had never been near any of the inner committees.

When Paolo volunteered more opinion, Bugs decided there was no point in staying. His allotted time was up, and he felt the claustrophobic gloom he suffered every time he passed a prison gate closing on him. The locked, steel bars, dark green gloss walls, and flickering, stark neon lights deepened his suppressed panic. How could inmates tolerate this anguish for decades on end?

He stood. Ferraresi's eyes widened. A guard stepped forward to escort the boy back into the depths of the high-security block.

Bugs hesitated, remembering something. 'Paolo', he called. The boy spoke into his microphone. 'Yes;' he replied in a voice belying clear tones of strain.

'I almost forgot. I can send you some books if you want.'

'I'd like that', said the boy, brightening. 'You could write to me too; I'd like that.'

'What can I send you?'

Ferraresi thought for a few seconds. 'I'd like two books, but you'll have trouble finding one of them.'

'Shoot', said Bugs. He suddenly regretted his choice of words, but Ferraresi showed no sign of embarrassment. 'I'd like an Italian/English dictionary: I want to read about your American, military-industrial, capitalist complex, in English.'

'No problem', said Bugs.

'I'd also like a book with a title about, as far as I can remember, Albania winning. I don't know who wrote it, and I've no idea where you'll find it, nor in what language.'

Bugs' eyes flickered: he invited Paolo Ferraresi to sit down again and made a sign at the guard requesting more time. The guard looked importantly at his watch, held up five fingers, and returned to his post behind the prisoner.

'Paolo', said Bugs, 'I can even find an English edition to help you with your language studies. I know exactly where to find it, but I can't guarantee the prison authorities will approve you having it in your cell. Tell me why you want it.'

'I want to review my ideals. Sometimes I feel confused: I had assumed them to be self-evident; now I'm not so sure.'

'Where did you hear about this book?'

'At the Balaian summer school in 1981', replied Ferraresi.

'The what?'

''A seminar held by an Armenian intellectual called Victor Balaian in a farm house outside Riccione. Most of the columns sent at least one representative.'

'Wasn't it risky meeting like that?'

'Certainly, but Balaian's talks were worth it.'

'What did he talk about?'

'About adapting Maoism to the Western, urban context with the least ideological deviation. Balaian quoted extensively from the book and claimed it was the only text successfully adapting a doctrine developed for an oriental, rural society, to Western ways. I think the author had intended to align Islam with Marxist thought, and that's a question that really interests me.'

'Did you attend the talks, Paolo.'

'Some of them.'

'So you met Balaian.'

'I saw him. I drove him around once or twice, but he never said much.'

'Tell me about him.'

'He was foreign.'

'And where is he now?'

'No idea, and I doubt anyone knows in here. He disappeared at the end of 1982.'

'Why?'

'There's a story, but I don't know how true it is.'

'Tell me; I'll use it in my chapter on Red-Brigade mythology.'

'From memory, Balaian had claimed he was Armenian; his column accepted it without question because many Armenian names end in -an; but we had Armenian comrades learning our ways so that they could attract attention to the 1915 Turkish massacres. One of them, a person called Dekermenjian, was invited to meet Victor Balaian at a committee meeting. The story goes that it ended in acrimony: Dekermenjian insisted Balaian was not Armenian at all: not only could he not speak the language, but he had not even heard of Mount Ararat, the mountain that reputedly harbours the remains of Noah's Ark, and separates Soviet, from Turkish Armenia. Balaian claimed, I remember, that he had spent his youth in Syria because his grandparents had fled the Turks: for this reason, he couldn't speak the language, and produced a Syrian passport.'

'What's wrong with that?'

'Absolute trust was essential. He had created a doubt, and it had to be resolved: the columns were paranoid about penetration of their ranks.'

'So, his column had him meet a Syrian, right?'

'Absolutely, and he failed that test too: the Syrian claimed Balaian's Arabic was North African; though he could quote texts from the Koran like any Moslem, the Syrian swore that, with that accent, Balaian could not have spent his childhood in his country. Then someone claimed that the Armenians Turkey persecuted in 1915 had been Orthodox Christians and not Muslims.'

'So, if Victor Balaian was neither Armenian nor Syrian and possibly Muslim, where was he really from?'

'I don't think anyone ever found out. He fled the movement and completely vanished. Oh, yes, and someone at the Riccione seminars told me he thought he looked a lot like Comrade Lucy's lover too.'

They were preparing for dinner when the call came. Bugs suggested Jenny go down to the lobby to meet Nino and Edda while he took the call in the room. She walked out as it came through.

'You're a hard man to track down', came Jim Curry's jovial voice.

'This can of worms keeps me on the move, Jim. Now you've found me, what can I do for you?'

'Negative, Bugsy, I've got something for you.'

'It's dinner time in Rome, Jim.'

'Oh, yes, sorry. It's only lunchtime here. Are you sitting down?'

'Jim!'

'We've found your Bonanza.'

So, the Feds, and not the Company, had found the aeroplane. That would be an embarrassment for Hailsham. 'How and where, Jim?'

'We got a call from the FAA at Meigs Field asking us to trace the owner of a Bonanza that had been sitting out there on the apron for a few months. When they tried, they found the registration was bogus. They called the Hoover Building just as the plane was beginning to disappear under the snow. As Meigs Field is the airstrip built onto the Lake Michigan shoreline in downtown Chicago, I think you'd do well to look for Glenn's killers in the Windy City, Bugsy.'

'Who owns the Bonanza?'

'We don't know yet; we're checking the frame number with the manufacturer.'

Bugs strolled into the venerable library of the University of Rome's School of Sociology and Political Philosophy. A librarian sleepily rubber-stamped cards at the end of a hallway decorated with massive, dark tempera attributed to an obscure, Renaissance artist. Bugs asked in a forced whisper where the index file was kept. The lady directed him fussily to a small wood-panelled room near the back of a vast study area overlooked by a Baroque gallery.

It took some time to find the name: so many cards were out of strict alphabetical order. He noted the references and asked the librarian for copies of the documents. In no hurry, the woman reappeared twenty minutes later, and Bugs retired to read them at one of the large tables in the centre of the study hall.

'Well, well', he said to himself, opening the first one. A few heads lifted. Bugs forced himself to keep quiet. The essay was entitled 'Islam and Communism;' written in 1979. More than the content of the paper, Bugs' attention was drawn to the academic pedigree of its author: Victor Balaian claimed a doctorate from the University of Sofia, and, at the time of writing the paper, was reputed to be an associate professor at the University of Tripoli in Libya.

Back in the hotel room overlooking the Trevi Fountain in the heart of the historical city, Bugs lifted the handset and dialled a local number. At the sound of a tone, he fitted the scrambler he had taken from his room safe. He identified himself and asked that all available information on Victor Balaian be sent to the Director's office in Langley, Virginia to await Bugs' return from Europe.

Nino was summoned to a public commission, giving him an excuse to bring Edda to the Eternal City; an event that always thrilled her, despite her haughty, Northern-Italian views. Besides, he looked forward to another long dinner with the Americans; his polite, captive audience seeming to well understand his need for catharsis. He liked their race: they had welcomed his forefathers and showed 'Marshall' understanding after the war. Their diplomacy could be pedestrian, he thought, but they acted, in general, honestly and responsibly.

After the fog in the North, the Roman climate was warmer and drier; the more athletic had not yet taken to their overcoats.

He proposed they dine in a trattoria; Bugs and Jenny were finding the heavier food in the pretentious restaurants more and more difficult to digest, and neither was used to eating so much so late in the evening. Inside, the trattoria was warm and bright. Long tables accommodated noisy family dinners of ten or twenty. Chattering children; ringing plates, and guffaws between mouthfuls of pasta; wild gestures, and the musical lilt of the Roman accent, gave the illusion that the entire world was having fun in that room.

The owner gushed up to Nino. He called the officer, *Commendatore*, and led his party to a quieter corner, where a table lay covered with a red, plaid, plastic tablecloth. With evident pride, he recited the day's delicacies. After ten minutes of haggling, the man disappeared, satisfied that the *Commendatore's* party had made the right choice. 'In our country, Jenny, and, especially in our venerable capital, you never order food, you negotiate it! The owner does his own buying, often travelling to the coast or into the countryside to find fresh produce, and he knows what's special today. He knows where his cook's strengths lie; and if he fusses over his customers, and shows he wants them completely satisfied, they will be loyal, and help him make his fortune.'

'Sound business sense', said Jenny.

'No Italian enters an empty restaurant, but he will fight like a tiger to get into a full one. The more elbows per square metre, the better he expects the food to be. I suppose you have the same habits in the United States, no?'

'It's not such a cult back home', volunteered Bugs.

'That, *amico mio*, is uncivilised! Good food is one of our great sensual pleasures; it compares with sex, and is probably less sinful.' He winked at Edda. 'The legion of pasta samples I have ordered will prove this.'

'I'll burst', laughed Bugs.

'If you do, I shall consider our hospitality adequate.'

They were served by a matronly figure with a red face and teeth permanently on show. Delicious smells torpedoed all prudence, and conversation was simply ignored. At last, Bugs refused a dish: Nino, still in full gastric orgy, listened as he told of the jailed *brigatista*, Paolo Ferraresi's, obvious psychological vulnerability.

'They change behind bars', replied Nino, delicately wiping the corners of his moustache, 'only the real bone heads don't soften up. The rest take the time to think: they feel sorry for themselves, especially if they're bright. The hard-core consider themselves martyrs; they'll be dangerous when they're free again unless old-age slow-down gets to them first!'

'I'm surprised your government didn't try any undercover operations against the Red Brigades.'

'Easy to say, Jenny, and tough to do. In the seventies, Police intelligence was not coordinated. Petty rivalries blocked consolidation of information, and we had to fight the political unacceptability on the far left, of a crackdown. Our excessive liberalism helps us forget the ghosts of our past, keeping us on the wrong side of this thin line separating civil rights from civil security. Italian institutions have imprisoned lawmakers for getting tough with crime; you can't expect these same people to risk their lives and careers if even the law doesn't support them, let alone the politicians.'

'But a mole in the ranks might have been useful.'

'We tried undercover work, but the *brigatisti* used a clever idea to frustrate us: they insisted that all new recruits perform criminal acts as proof of their political convictions. Serious crime is doable for the weak under supervision, but out of the question for any normal person believing in the cause of justice.'

'What kind of criminal acts?' asked Jenny.

'Kidnapping a local personality or businessman for ransom; theft to finance the movement. In the three months, between January 1978, and Moro's abduction in March, anarchists killed seventeen Italians, maimed two hundred more, and planted nine hundred bombs; it took the tragic death of a statesman to reverse our slide into chaos.'

They ate quietly for a while, the hubbub in the restaurant providing a backdrop to their silence; then Bugs spoke of Ferraresi's request for a copy of Mehemet Shkoder's book, 'Albania Shall Conquer.'

'If this book inspired the Red Brigades, *amico mio*, would Lucia Sereni not have her own copy? Everything you found in that Colombian jungle cottage is probably hers!'

'Maybe, Nino, but it's published in a language she doesn't understand.'

'You have no proof she can't read Albanian. It could be a keepsake. There's a dedication; what does it say?'

'More or less, as I remember: *I dedicate this work to you, the one I love, the one who understands, the one who will continue my work when I am gone.* The author certainly thought highly of the book's owner! Some of the pages are earmarked, and I found a ticket to a Chicago exhibition inside, probably used as a book mark.'

'There's nothing in our records to say she speaks Albanian. She speaks Palestinian and Libyan Arabic, a little English, and she must have picked up some Spanish in Colombia.'

'And her lover?' asked Bugs.

'No idea. This 'Mischa' has disappeared like a wraith: it's irritating.'

'You've nothing at all on him?'

'Only hearsay', replied Nino, 'our records speculate that he attended the Patrice Lumumba University in Moscow, widely suspected as a recruiting station for foreign terrorists, and he may have coached subversives in Libya. That kind of work is done by Khaddafi's *Staatssicherheitsdienst* support staff, leading us to speculate that Mischa may be an East German himself, but I'm not convinced. That's all we know, except for his affair with Lucia Sereni. Oh, and he had a favourite pistol, a Walther, I think.'

'And what of Victor Balaian?'

'I've never heard of him Bugs. Is he another revolutionary, another third-world academic? You say he has published?'

'Yes, in Tripoli.'

'You may know that in July 1970, Khaddafi expelled fifteen thousand Italians, and nationalised their assets, causing a lot of movement between the two countries and haggling over ownership rights. It's normal to admit Libyans into Italy, but I can check that summer's immigration lists, if you insist.'

'If you two would like to stop talking shop, Edda and I want a buggy ride around Rome', said Jenny.

'It's too cold outside', said Bugs.

'Don't worry about us, we'll snuggle up, won't we Edda?'

Edda forced a half-enthusiastic smile and eyed Nino for approval.

They took a horse and buggy ride along the Via Appia, Nino securing a bargain Christmas price to the Catacombs of St. Calixtus and back. The carriage was covered, and, though it was too dark to see outside, the rhythmic noise of hooves on cobblestones and the gentle sway of the rig provided an altogether more soothing setting than the trattoria.

Edda and Jenny spoke of the Italian couple's children, and the two men waited patiently for the ladies to become engrossed in their conversation before resuming their own.

'The way they held the O'Grady girl was too like the way General Dozier had been kept, to be pure coincidence', said Bugs.

'The Dozier case was in all the papers; anyone could have read about the details.' Nino's thoughts drifted elsewhere: the two women were well into a conversation concerning the elder son's disappointing school grades.

Bugs listened to them with limited interest. 'Nino, ...'The Italian turned to him. 'This *mafioso*, Cremante, was recognised by a hospital inmate during the assassination attempt last October. She swears he wasn't the killer, but that Cremante appeared right after, dressed as a cop. She says the real murderer looked almost exactly like him, like a twin, so the FBI are promoting the idea that the killer was, in fact, Cremante himself: they want to discount her evidence because she is an old lady. Whether they're right or not, his being there means the attempt almost certainly implicates the Chicago Mafia; and you confirm that the Mob bought the two AR-70 Beretta assault rifles used on the Presidential party. The problem with this scenario is that it disregards eyewitness testimony. Either way, I need to bring back Cremante's record from Italy.'

'You'll need an extra suitcase to take Pino Cremante's record back with you; this man's a Mafia lieutenant. What's happened to him?'

'Police found him dead in a car in a Chicago suburb.'

'He must have put up one hell of a fight: Cremante was quite a thug.'

'It looks like a suicide. He blew his brains out.'

'Suicide? Come on! Are you sure?'

Bugs described the death scene as he had read about it, and ended, 'He shot himself with the same 357 used on

O'Grady, the Chicago cop whose daughter was kidnapped. His brains blew out through the window into the field by the car. If that, along with eyewitness identification, doesn't compromise Cremante in the Secretary of State's assassination and the attempt on the President, then I don't know what could.'

'If I remember Cremante's file correctly, I have a very serious doubt about what you say; if I'm right, he may not have committed suicide at all. Let's meet at the barracks at eight tomorrow. I'll have a copy of his record for you.'

Nino was in fine spirits the following morning at the *Carabiniere* barracks. 'I was right about Cremante being a Catanzaro lieutenant. My memory is not so bad; the probability that Cremante committed suicide is about zero', said Nino.

'How on earth do you know that?'

'You were right to ask for his record. Look at what I have underlined, it says, *'Mancino: poco pratico della mano destra.'* That means he was left-handed; his right was almost useless. From what you said, the bullet penetrated the right temple, as the shot blew his head out of the window.'

'Yes.'

'Then someone in the passenger seat shot him. Had he shot himself, he would have held the pistol in his left hand, the slug would have entered the left side of his skull, and the body would have collapsed onto the passenger seat leaving a lot of him in the car. Nobody committing suicide would go to the trouble of using the wrong hand to hold a gun!'

'Leaving the corpse's prints on the weapon would have been easy, and the killer could have left the revolver on the car floor', said Bugs.

'As for Cremante using terrorist methods against a political target, surely not. Incidentally, the file reminded me that Cremante knew the Red Brigades well. He's named in at least two depositions as a middle-man for exchanging stolen goods against weapons. He may even have helped organise an operation or two; but a televised, terrorist-style assassination attempt on the American President, no: that's not the Mafia's way; there has been too much speculation since Kennedy was assassinated.'

'So he may just have helped.'

'If it led to drug sales; to big money; to the discrete elimination of an able or honest, and dangerous, magistrate, or to something of that nature, why not!'

'He could have been aware of how General Dozier was held and organised Corinne O'Grady's captivity in the same way.'

Nino thought for some seconds. 'Everyone read the newspapers.'

'And, if he knew the Red Brigades so well, he could have been the middle-man who organised the purchase of the AR-70 Berettas for the women who went after the President', said Bugs.

'Maybe; maybe not. I don't know.' The *Carabiniere* colonel took a call, leaving Bugs to stir his coffee. The espresso was warm and strong enough to give his sleepy, morning brain a wake-up jolt. Nino replaced the earpiece on the phone cradle.

'Anything else I should know?' asked Bugs.

'No. I'll give you a copy of the file, but it's in Italian.'

'We'll manage.'

'Oh, there's one more thing, an idiosyncrasy of Cremante's. He collected stolen passports, just as people collect stamps. He loved to pose as a British man it seems, though he was dark, and spoke poor English.'

Christmastide arrived in America, with its gentle values of goodwill and peace. Back in the commercial sterility of suburbia, they missed the ancient stone adorning dwellings in Europe and the abrupt change in time zone would cause them a week of sleepless nights. Bugs left directly for Chicago, where he would spend the Monday and Christmas Eve briefing Jim Curry while the Italian trip was still fresh in his mind. The snow at O'Hare came as a shock after the temperate climate of Tuscany. Hearing that the Streeterville pad was occupied, Bugs took a cab downtown to the Hyatt, where he had made a reservation from Washington National. He carried a pile of magazines up to his room to while away the sleepless early-morning hours, and went straight to bed.

He had been awake four hours by the time Jim Curry arrived at his breakfast table in the glass-domed lobby. The FBI Deputy Assistant Director sat and listened intently. Bugs took care not to colour his account with the ideas which had begun to form during his early-morning sleeplessness.

Silently, Jim took notes on a paper napkin.

'I'd like a copy of your report, Bugsy.'

'Sure, it's because of the Chicago investigation I went to Italy in the first place: it wasn't even my idea. I was going to ask for permission to go, Jim, but almost got myself fired before I could.'

'Yes, I heard. You had bad luck, Bugsy. We all take that kind of chance from time to time. We wouldn't be in this business if we didn't.'

'You heard what? Who told you?'

'Ed Duval did before he left for South America. It's common knowledge you got yourself and the Director into trouble. He was personally challenged at the Senate Select Committee on Intelligence for sending you to Italy. Things have been happening during your absence. You've got your heart in field work; you shouldn't be an analyst. The way I read it if the Director decided to send you and Jenny on a paid vacation to Italy, he wasn't interested in firing you.'

They walked to the Hoover Building in Dearborn. The windshield factor was almost minus thirty by the high-rise offices, and, in his thin raincoat, Bugs shivered all the way. Store windows in the Loop were decorated with the warm, yuletide glow of Christmas trappings in a cold winter light reflected by the snow-covered streets.

'I'm inviting you to dinner with my new girlfriend at the Water Tower', said Jim. 'I want you to remember how we live over here; it's my duty to knock that Europhilia out of you before you turn native!'

'So what's Ed Duval up to in Colombia?' asked Bugs.

'We haven't heard from him. That photo of Fatima Al-Othman's boyfriend was lousy material to build his research on, especially in a country already swimming in crime. A good shot of the back of a man's head doesn't leave a lot of scope for success, even with Duval's 'buttons-and-bells' techniques!'

'He was different; he had something like a wart on one ear', said Bugs.

Jim burst into laughter.

Bugs borrowed Duval's office and called Washington. The review session with Jim Curry and his team would take the rest of the day, and Bugs wanted to lay some groundwork in Langley before the vacation. Carol promised to arrange the meetings and confirmed she would get a second copy of the Shkoder translation from a London publisher to send to Paolo Ferraresi in jail.

She sounded remote. She said that Hailsham had only just asked for the tests Bugs had recommended before his departure, and read a letter over the telephone from the Swiss police, in which they refused to give any details about funds transferred to Lucia Sereni's bank account unless an approach was made through their embassy as part of a criminal investigation.

Jim walked in as Bugs was replacing the handset. The session was due to begin in five minutes. The federal officer slid a report from the over-worked Chicago Crime Laboratory across the desk. 'It's arrived at last', he said. 'That cute secretary brought it in while you were on the phone.'

'What's in there?'

'An errant analysis report of dirt under one of the dead women's fingernails. Friedman, the Pathologist at Golan Memorial Hospital, asked for the report but forgot to say where to send it. We found it on the desk of a Chicago Police-District detective who'd been taken off the case. Read it; I think they've got themselves confused with motorcycle oil: the two terrorist women were riding motorbikes.'

Bugs opened the folder and read the summary: *Analysis of hydrocarbons found under subject fingernails confirms aircraft- engine-oil additives.* He stood up in excitement. 'This is it!' he said. 'A link! She must be Lucia Sereni. Was the Bonanza checked for fingerprints?'

'Of course, Bugs, and it's still impounded at Meigs Field.'

'Can you compare the fingerprints from the joystick and the throttle with those of the dead woman? I'll get the Italians to send another set of prints overnight. I'll wager you they're the same. If we needed to go further, we could check the Bonanza's sump oil with what we found under her fingernails.'

'So, you think Lucia Sereni was the second woman terrorist brought down outside the hospital, eh? I'll get onto it right away, Bugsy.'

'If we're right, we have the identities now of both dead women: Fatima Al-Othman and Lucia Sereni.'

Bugs was impressed with the openness and quality of Jim's staff. They agreed on a plan of action with a reasonable chance of success of flushing out the killer, though Bugs had doubts about the cowboy tactics the younger feds advocated. 'Thanks for listening to my doubts about Cremante being the murderer; and I realise this could be a dangerous venture for Florie McKinley, but if I'm right, I see no other way of flushing our terrorist out into the open.'

'If I talk to Florie personally, Bugs, I'm sure she'll cooperate; besides, she's only lending her name, it's the press doing the real work; we shall move her away from any potential trouble.'

'If we fail, and the killer wasn't Cremante, as I still believe, she'll be in great danger as the only person able to identify him. Are you sure the press hasn't spoken about her up to now?'

''Pretty sure, but I'll check', replied Jim.

'Let's time the article for the twenty-seventh, with a follow up on January second. Hospital staff should have been thoroughly briefed by then. Can that be done?'

'Yes, they'll cooperate: we have the clout of a potential federal grant. It should run smoothly, providing that this man exists, that he hasn't flown the coop and that he reads Chicago papers. Not much to ask for a foreigner!'

'We may have a real problem if he passes the operation to the Chicago Mafia', said Bugs.

'Catanzaro won't help Cremante's killer if it's true his prime lieutenant didn't commit suicide', remarked Jim; 'our terrorist will do the job himself: it's no one else's problem.'

Late on Christmas Eve, last-minute visitors flying in and out to family suppers crowded Washington National. Bugs drove straight to Langley, wanting to go through his mail in peace and quiet; it was too late now for duty staff to be around. Once past the Virginia State Troopers at the gate, a security guard he vaguely recognised asked how the Italian vacation had gone. He uncharacteristically checked Bugs' clearance before releasing the turnstile to his magnetic card.

Before starting on the pile on his desk, he reread the Coroner's report Jim had given him at the review session. He stared gloomily at the phrase which had touched him so deeply: *Subject hormone autopsy reveals six-week pregnancy.*

So, Lucia Sereni, as he was now sure she was, after months of disappointment, had finally conceived, and the child in her womb had died with her mother in her suicidal attempt on the US President.

Fingerprints taken from the Bonanza's cockpit tallied with the set provided by Nino overnight, proving that she had indeed piloted the Bonanza, and had probably been a key accessory to John Glenn's murder. Her corpse now lay with the Bonanza's aircraft oil under her fingernails in a temporary municipal grave in Chicago, a long way from the ancient land of her forefathers and from her Colombian jungle cottage, where she had probably lived with her man.

Nino promised to contact the woman's parents to claim the body. Soon, a grieving Italian lawyer and his wife would come to take away the remains of a daughter who had slid far into the depths of international terrorism, crowning her dubious career with an attempt on the life of the most powerful politician in the world. How different their dreams for their child must have been, when, as an innocent, Lucia had probably filled a father's heart with tenderness, and a mother's with the anticipation of a white wedding and grandchildren.

Bugs threw the report onto his desk and picked up the photo he had found in Lucia's jungle cottage of a man in military fatigues. He had already seen that dark, intent gaze elsewhere, but where? Were you the father? He thought. If so, do you know your child is dead? And its mother too? Who are you? Are you the Red Brigade, Mischa? Some

Colombian guerrilla? Could you be the Marxist intellectual Balaian, even? From his briefcase, he drew the bore-mark photos he had brought back from the *Museo* in Venice and sent them to the ballistics department asking to check them against the P.38 Parabellum bullets taken from the dead Secretary of State's skull. He added a copy of a set of Mischa's fingerprints, also brought back from Venice.

His secretary, Carol, had left a note saying that Hailsham had received a report from Duval claiming that a burnt-out helicopter hull found in Northern Colombia had been ultimately traced to joint drug cartel and Mafia interests. She added that the analysis Bugs had asked for following the Colombian incident, would not be concluded before early January.

Jim had sent Bugs a list of exhibitors and visitors to the Chicago Agricultural Commodities Fair: Bugs would go through it on Christmas day in the comfort of his apartment, and he dumped the printout in his briefcase.

Deep under papers in a desk drawer, he found Mao's Little Red Book on People's War retrieved from Don Carlo Catanzaro's garbage on Chicago's Southside. He read the dedication again: *To C.C. Our means of slitting America's soft underbelly may be one, but our ends will be forever opposed. With thanks, M.*

He dropped the red, plastic-covered book into an envelope with a short, hand-written note to Bill Jones, the manager of the graphology laboratory. Bill had been a wise and competent ally in cracking several cases and could be counted on to overlook absolutely nothing on a sheet of paper. Bugs asked for a handwriting comparison between the book and the Colombian love letters. He was sure Bill would work as quickly as he could as a special favour.

Finally, Bugs wrote a note to Carol asking for the report on the search of Pino Cremante's house following his murder.

When he had finished, he picked up the telephone and called Jenny to say he was coming home.

The return from the European time zone took its toll: awake at 3 a.m., he got up as gently as he could to avoid disturbing Jenny and walked through the dark apartment to the sitting room overlooking the street. Christmas had been a quiet affair, Jenny's sister unable to come with the children, so the two had celebrated quietly in front of the fire. He sat by the little tree Jenny had prepared for the kids. Outside, sodium lamps shone down onto the snow-covered street, reflecting their yellow light onto the walls of the room. Bugs touched one of the baubles on the tree, and thought sadly that the following Christmas would again be spent as a twosome at the Macpherson home, and not as the threesome Jenny's lateness had headily led them to believe. What a Christmas gift her pregnancy would have been.

Lucia Sereni had died a pregnant woman. She too had struggled with infertility and had finally overcome it, only to die months before giving birth to the child that would have transformed her desperate existence. This was a cruel destiny. She must have known she was pregnant but had she told the father; and who was he? Lucia must have known several men in her life, yet Mischa was the only one to recur as a constant lover. She may have had an affair with Victor Balaian too, the intellectual, described by Paolo Ferraresi in his jail, who had given the Riccione summer school on Marx; unless there was another 'Victor' to sign her jungle-cottage love letters.

Balaian had played a dangerous game; he must have realised that, in a society as closed as that of the *brigatista* columns, anything less than total trust would lead to execution to protect the integrity of the movement. He had disappeared quickly after the columns had discovered he was not an Armenian. At about the same time, Lucia and Mischa disappeared too after she had been sprung from jail. Balaian might certainly have been liquidated by *brigatisti* frightened of a traitor in their ranks, and perhaps this was the reason for his sudden disappearance.

Yet this line of reasoning didn't satisfy Bugs: Balaian served the cause, and must have known the rules; he had been invited to address the whole movement in the summer of 1981 at the old Adriatic fishing village of Riccione; he was an important man, and, as a purported academic, unlikely to be stupid.

Then something suddenly occurred to Bugs that had been staring him in the face all along. 'Why hadn't I noticed that before?' He whooped in the night, turned on a reading lamp, and reached for notepaper and a ballpoint. He wrote down the name. 'It fits! There had to be a touch of bravado, didn't there? An attempt at immortality. And your dark face; yes, and your eyes, of course! Where's that book? Now I know who you are, Victor Balaian! It was in your name all along!'

The looming depression of meeting Hailsham left him as he concentrated on completing his report with the results of the tests he had asked for on Christmas Eve. Her eyes betraying unusual anxiety, Carol confirmed she had scheduled a meeting with the Director to present the Italian conclusions. Bugs asked outright what was wrong.

'I've been here since eight trying to start on what you left me, but everywhere I go people give me the put off; it's a conspiracy! Even Mr Hailsham's secretary rang five minutes ago to cancel this morning's appointment; he's never done that before.'

'Did you take the Little Red book down to Bill Jones at the graphology lab?'

'Yes.'

'Did you get the same put offs?'

'No, but I got the impression Bill Jones was doing you a mighty favour.'

'OK, Carol, put anything you can't get done on my desk, and I'll handle it myself.'

She left the office with a look of relief.

Bugs closed the door and picked up the telephone. He dialled a number and waited for a reply.

'This is Bill Jones.'

'Bill, Bugs Macpherson. I'm back and I need to talk to you. How about coffee.'

'My place or yours, Bugsy?'

'Yours, I invited you last time.'

'Come on down. I have your results right here.'

Bugs left for the corridors of the Scientific and Technology Department, where technical staff plied their dark crafts. A few tables cluttered with papers and magnifying lenses furnished Bill Jones's laboratory. Filing cabinets lined an entire wall; another was panelled with frosted glass, transmitting grey, morning light. Bill led Bugs to the tranquillity of a small office in a far corner.

'Sit down, Bugsy. No coffee near the documents.' He grinned apologetically. 'It's a positive identification.'

'I thought it would be. Were Catanzaro's fingerprints on the book too?'

'Yes, I'm surprised the FBI let you keep it.'

'You'd better keep it locked in your safe. It's not often you get to corner a Mafia don. I'll sign any papers you need.'

'Good of you, Bugsy, but I can't accept that.'

'What do you mean, Bill?'

He shifted uneasily and stared into the depths of his coffee mug. 'It's difficult; have you seen Hailsham recently?'

'No, why?'

'You ought to.'

'Bill, we've known each other a long time, and I've always respected you for being square. What the devil's going on?'

Bill Jones looked over his half-moon glasses like a Victorian uncle. 'Langley staff have instructions not to release information to you until further notice. The note hit the desks on Christmas Eve, and took us all by surprise this morning.'

'Hailsham?'

'Yep.'

'Does the note say why?'

'No, Bugsy, but it's common knowledge you had the Agency dragged through the shit after a "situation" in South America; we know why you've not been around.'

'I see', said Bugs, quietly. 'I appreciate your sincerity, old friend. I guess I have some cleaning up to do, right?'

'I guess so.'

Bill went on to describe the identical features between the handwriting on the love letters and that in the dedication on Mao's booklet: the same hand had written both. Lucia Sereni's lover had dedicated Chairman Mao's booklet to Catanzaro, the Chicago Mafia godfather. Bugs waited until Bill had finished and took the stairwell to the Director's office, carrying his dossier under his arm. He asked for an immediate appointment. The Director' secretary replied that Bugs' own meeting had been organised for 2 p.m., and that the Director was tied up.

Bugs insisted he needed to see the Director of Central Intelligence straight away.

She disappeared into the Intelligence Chief's office and returned moments later. 'If you'd like to wait, Mr Macpherson, he'll see you as soon as he's finished, but only for ten minutes. He has asked me to call Mr Hailsham so you can speak to them together.'

'Don't do that please.'

'But, those are my instructions, Mr Macpherson.'

'Then go back in the office, and tell him I want to see him alone.'

She went back in and returned instants later.

'Very good, Sir, please take a seat. He has almost finished.'

That meeting lasted two hours. In near panic, the Director's secretary cancelled a lunch appointment and rescheduled the afternoon, a rare occurrence for one so punctilious as her boss. She put two calls through to the White House to the new Secretary of State. She wondered what Macpherson had said to win such attention, especially after his star had fallen so low? When he surfaced from the intelligence chief's office, the lines of worry clouding his features a few hours earlier had given way to his usual look of assertiveness. He strode past the secretary, the faintest shadow of a grin dancing on his pursed lips, and disappeared down the stairwell into the depths of the Langley complex. On the way down, Bugs took another look at the photograph that had been waiting for him in the Director's office: the archives had found a photo of Balaian in a 1978 Libyan newspaper. From the moment, the Director compared it with the rest of Bugs' material, he gave him clearance to finalise the investigation.

The first article appeared in the Chicago Tribune that same morning; Bugs bought a copy over lunch. The press had done a fine job describing the investigation, and revealing to an excited Chicago public the facts outlined at a restricted press conference at the Federal Building. It was a scoop for the newspaper: in return, it had run an in-depth focus on Florie McKinley. The paper developed this human-interest theme almost to the point of boredom, which suited the FBI perfectly. The leader read: *CHICAGO WOMAN RECOGNISES SECRETARY OF STATE'S KILLER*

A spread like that was difficult to miss. Florie McKinley was portrayed as a frail, glistening heroine, rather than the shrewd old lady she was, but the article would serve the purpose very well indeed. Now all Bugs could do was wait, and hope the gamble would pay off.

The Director intervened to speed up the analyses Hailsham had dragged his feet over, but Science and Technology whined it could only work so fast because of the budget cuts. Bugs would have to wait a few days more, and he decided he might as well do so in Chicago, where the action, if any, would be.

Ed Duval had got back from Colombia to spend Christmas with his family. Except for information about joint drug cartel and Mafia ownership of a burnt-out helicopter frame in Maicao, his research had been fruitless. No one knew or was willing to admit to any knowledge of a Carmen Muñoz, let alone to that of a Fatima Al-Othman or of her boyfriend. Ed was ridiculed when he presented the photograph of the passionate couple. The man had a wart on his ear: so, what? Half of Colombia's male population had black hair and many, probably, warts on their ears! Disillusioned, and tired of the streets of Bogota, Ed had been relieved by the permission to go home, albeit empty handed, for Christmas. Don Hailsham had some material for his report, promising he would have some results to present anyway at the meeting scheduled with the Director on the Saturday morning of the twenty-eighth. The two worked late into the night to integrate Hailsham's information into a credible scenario.

When Duval finally stood before Hailsham and the Director, he was smiling despite the spate of nerves that had almost driven him to call off sick that morning. The Director switched on his office lights and sat with his back to the window. He listened carefully to the plot Duval started to develop.

'We are convinced, Sir, the Secretary of State's assassination was organised by the Mafia and discharged by a Mob lieutenant called especially over from Italy. The suspect later committed suicide with a revolver he had stolen along with a police uniform he wore at the shooting.'

'I suppose you are referring to Cremante', said the Director.

'Affirmative, Sir. The suspect worked with an Italian and a Palestinian woman; both were terrorists, brought down outside the hospital while trying to attack the Presidential party. The Palestinian has been identified as a Ms Al-Othman, and we're pleased to say we've identified the Italian as a Red Brigade terrorist called Sereni, despite disfigurement of her face by explosive impact of a police bullet. We're....ah.... working on the idea that Cremante and the Italian woman knew each other, were involved in drugs and teamed up with this Palestinian who had contacts in Colombia. We believe they attempted to frame a third party who was Sereni's lover, trying to deflect the blame on him for the Secretary of State's murder.'

'Why do you think that Ed?' asked the Director

'Because we've identified this third party's fingerprints from love letters found in a Colombian jungle cottage and probably addressed to Sereni with those found on the Secretary of State's murder weapon, Sir.'

'So you're sure Cremante shot him.'

'Yes, Sir; it's why Cremante was wearing gloves the day of the shooting; to avoid smudging the third party's prints already on the pistol. He left the pistol behind so that we would go after Sereni's boyfriend.'

'Ed, have you reviewed the file recently?'

'We went through it again quickly last night, Sir.'

'I think you will find the testimony claims plainly that the person who shot the Secretary of State last October was not wearing gloves.'

'We prefer to disregard that, Sir. The old lady who said that probably made a mistake.'

'Your idea also contradicts her sworn statement that Cremante was not the killer, Ed. She even recognised his face from a press photograph. Don't you think you should take account of the McKinley evidence?'

Duval turned to Hailsham in embarrassed silence. In their haste to develop their theory, they had chosen to disregard the old lady's testimony.

Hailsham stared back stonily. Duval was out on a limb; he was better ou there on his own.

The Director turned to Hailsham. 'Don?'

'I think you're right, Sir. Duval should go back and do his homework.' An embarrassed silence followed.

'There are positive aspects to your scenario, Ed; tell me how you identified the Sereni woman.'

Duval felt in deep enough trouble already and had no wish to make his poor performance any worse. 'I have to thank Don here for providing this information from fingerprint work performed in the lab, Sir.'

Hailsham's eyes narrowed.

'Is that right, Don? Did this information come from your work on the case?'

'Not exactly, Sir.'

'What do you mean by, "not exactly"?'

'It comes from a lead Macpherson was following on the John Glenn case.'

'Are you claiming a link between Glenn's murder in an aeroplane over Texas and the presidential assassination attempt in Chicago last October?'

'Possibly, Sir.'

'Have you spoken to Macpherson about this?'

'No, Sir.'

'Why not, Don?'

'I haven't seen him since he got back, Sir.'

'I thought you had a meeting with him on the 26th.'

'I had to cancel it, Sir.'

'He would have seen the laboratory reports by now, I suppose.'

'Probably not, Sir.'

'Why not?'

'I saw no reason to keep him informed, Sir.'

The Director, a note of eerie calm entering his voice, addressed Duval once more. 'You say, Ed, the prints on the P.38 found at the hospital correspond to fingerprints on love letters very probably addressed to the Sereni woman and found in a Colombian jungle cottage, correct?'

'Affirmative, Sir.'

The Director turned again to Hailsham. 'Do I assume, Don, that Macpherson is unaware of that too?'

'Yes, Sir.'

The Director stood and walked to his desk where he read some notes. 'What else doesn't he know?' he asked, without lifting his head.

'We found the same fingerprints on a Chinese book given to a Chicago Mafia boss', answered Hailsham.

'Catanzaro's Little Red Maoist book?'

'Yes.'

'So we have evidence that the terrorist, Sereni's, Colombian lover held the pistol which shot the Secretary of State and that he knows the Mafia Don, Catanzaro, well enough to provoke him with an anarchist dedication in a burning Chinese manifesto.' Without waiting for an answer, the Director addressed Duval. 'Ed, thanks for your presentation, I think you'll agree it needs more work.'

'Yes, Sir.'

'And Ed, please inform Macpherson immediately of the laboratory results; you will find him with the Chicago FBI. That's all.'

'Yes, Sir.' Ed Duval gratefully left the room.

The Director walked to the window and looked out over the snow.

Don Hailsham shifted in his seat and cleared his throat.

The Director turned to face his subordinate. 'Macpherson came to my office the day before yesterday to complain about the time the laboratory was taking to produce these results. Because his Italian trip was so successful, I decided to help him, and to expedite them myself; that's when I discovered you already had the results and had issued instructions on Christmas Eve to keep him in the dark.'

'I saw no reason to inform a suspended employee of progress on a case you gave to me, Sir: it's a question of security.'

'Quite so, Don, but we had agreed before his disciplinary interview that it would be counter-productive to inform

Langley staff of his suspension. I had counted on you respecting this decision.'

'I had to justify cutting Macpherson off from information pertinent to the Glenn case, Sir, so I informed one or two key people confidentially.'

'You informed them in writing, Don. I have a copy of your memo; more than just 'one or two' people got it. Were you aware I sent Macpherson on assignment to Italy following a request made by the Senate Committee?'

'Not until recently, Sir.'

'How did you find out?'

'I heard the committee questioned the choice of Macpherson for the job, and that this led to some embarrassment for the Company, Sir.'

'News travels fast in Washington, Don. I was personally embarrassed, not the Company, and the committee didn't learn about his peccadillo from me: as you were the only other person informed in the intelligence community, and Macpherson had already left for Italy, I suspect word got out because you failed to comply with my instruction to keep his suspension quiet. Would that be so?'

'I think I acted in the best interests of security, Sir.'

'Furthermore, Don, you had no need to justify cutting him off from information: he even reports to you.'

'Yes, Sir.'

'But this does not change your failure to comply with a direct instruction I gave you personally.'

'Yes, Sir.'

'I find this to be extremely serious; I can't afford a man in your position who doesn't know how to respect orders unquestioningly.'

'What do you mean, Sir?'

'I mean I can't keep you in your current position any longer: it's a question of trust, but you're a young and valuable man, so I'd like to see what other openings I can find you in the Agency. The problem is I don't have anything I can offer you at the same level.'

Don Hailsham paled.

'I will ask for a security guard to accompany you to the reception area; you can await your personal effects down there while security brings them down to you. The personnel people will be in touch to arrange interviews for another position.'

Hailsham trembled.

The Director went to his desk to call a security guard. He returned to the table and sat down. 'You know, Don, with your background you could make a wonderful career in the private sector; or why not stand for office? The money's better out there; test your worth on the open market'

'Yes, Sir.'

'Look upon this as a fine opportunity to find out what's going on out there in the real world: this could be a very exciting time for you, especially if what the Company finds for you doesn't meet your personal goals.'

A knock came at the door, and a sentry walked in.

'Escort Mister Hailsham to the reception area. Then collect his personal effects from his office and help him get them home or put them in storage. The usual drill. He will surrender his badge and pistol to you before he leaves the premises.'

'Yes, Sir.'

The Director stood and held out his hand. Hailsham seemed to struggle to leave his own chair.

'Goodbye, Don. Keep in touch: I'll be very interested to learn what you decide to do.'

Don Hailsham shook the Director's hand and followed the security guard out.

ILYA AND AHMET

Ivan Promyslov did not keep his appointment at the Andronikov Monastery. His letter lay open on Konstantin Strugatski's desk in his office inside the Kremlin. A transcript of Olga Promyslova's telephone conversation with Yuri Berzin was beside it. He wondered why Olga Sergeyevna had not called him as her husband had asked. He folded the letter and walked out into the long, marbled corridor leading to the Politburo executive offices. A tall, young Kremlin Guard snapped to attention as Konstantin ambled by, absorbed in thought. Vanya was a dear and honest friend, but trouble-prone. He didn't have the smoothness to handle conflict: he was a man of passion, of action; there was something endearing, of the rough peasant about him, and that, of course, was totally out of place in the kind of position Vanya ought to have occupied at his age, whether a convinced Party man or not!

Konstantin asked to see the cabinet secretary, and was ushered into a marble-floored office. An urbane, silver-haired man of distinguished bearing greeted him.

'My dear Kostya, how good of you to come and see me.'

'It's always a pleasure, Vladimir Vasilevich.'

'Come and sit down. Some tea?'

'No thank you. You are very kind.'

Konstantin sat. The cabinet secretary was in a good mood, yet the more pleasant he seemed, the more dangerous he could be. He frowned, hoping to move him quickly off the pleasantries.

Vladimir Vasilevich's eyes hardened a fraction. Not a muscle of his smiling face moved. Come on! thought Konstantin.

'What can I do for you, my friend.'

'You are always a great help, Vladimir Vasilevich, in helping me resolve issues I bring before State Security from the Party apparatus.'

Vladimir Vasilevich remained quite still.

'An urgent matter has come to my attention concerning a possible serious defection to the West.'

Vladimir Vasilevich sat forward, the smile gone.

'The coming defection was discovered by an old-school friend of mine who seems to have disappeared. I fear he has got himself in over his head.'

'I'll get someone from the Second Chief Directorate to consider the problem immediately.'

'It's not so simple; unfortunately, you see, my old-school friend is himself a Colonel in State Security.'

The atmosphere became brittle. Vladimir Vasilevich, seemed frozen.

Konstantin went on. 'I'm talking of my friend, Colonel Ivan Dmitriyevich Promyslov. His recent investigations involved this sordid business in Bulgaria following Marshall Volkov's stupid trick on the General Secretary.'

''Hardly a trick; more like treason!' Vladimir Vasilevich wrote down Ivan Promyslov's name. 'I'll consider the problem personally.' His eyes seemed to bore into Konstantin's. 'Promyslov; wasn't he the one who...?' He opened a desk drawer, and took out a file from within. 'Yes; that's the one who got shot in Rome. According to Budhakin, he's mute; it seems he disappeared after the First Chief Directorate discovered an indiscretion: tapes or something.'

'Ivan Dmitriyevich is incapable of committing indiscretions', said Konstantin. 'He's such a ponderous fellow, that he's compulsively honest.'

The phone rang. Konstantin stood to leave, but Vladimir Vasilevich waved him back to the chair. Konstantin managed to hear little of what the cabinet secretary said. 'That was the Communications Directorate at Dzerzhinsky Square: your friend, Promyslov, is spinning in the eye of a hurricane. I think I had better fish him out of State Security's hands for a while, and find out what the hell's going on. I would invite you to join me in debriefing him, but as he's your friend, Kostya, it may be as well....'

'I'm flattered, Vladimir Vasilevich, but I am first and foremost a servant of the Party and hopefully in your trust.'

The cabinet secretary beamed. 'I'll see to it straight away.'

Nothing in his cell distinguished day from night. The ceiling light came on brightly for long periods, and then dimmed for a time. Disorientation was the first trick in the book: Ivan grimly wondered how they would handle a mute; yet the periods seemed regular enough, and the food was more edible than the gruel he had expected. The worst problem was the boredom: the guards refused him books. He exercised on the bed, the floor space not enough for the swings and bends making up his normal routine. When he couldn't sleep, he exercised his memory, retracing the smells of flowers, nursery rhymes, Olga's face, names of school pals, anything at all. He tried to remember the exact wording of Milk's message to Snow that George Kevorkian had deciphered more than a month ago, yet he could only remember its gist. George's time would be up by now; he would be in the State Prosecutor's line pointing an accusing finger at Ivan for his indiscretion over the communications tapes. That month of grace was long past, and George had a family to support.

The sound of heavy, military steps came from the corridor: this was it; the first stage in questioning was about to begin. Ivan faced the door. He preferred to be standing when they came for him; he braced himself for the worst. The steps came to a halt outside his cell. A key turned in the lock. The door opened wide. Outside, stood two uniformed sentries wearing the royal-blue arm-of-service shoulder boards of the Kremlin Guard, and flanking a ramrod-stiff officer in coat and fedora.

'Good morning, Colonel Promyslov. You are required to change into uniform and to come with me. You are now under my custody, and no longer under that of State Security.'

Ivan stared, open-mouthed, dirty and unshaven. He shuffled in his grey shirt and trousers to the door, and turned to look at the cell.

The appearance of the elite Kremlin Guard focused the attention of Ivan's captors wonderfully: he was shown into a shower room, where he washed and shaved; a new colonel's walking-out uniform appeared, and by the time he stepped into the searing morning light, he looked, and almost felt, like his old self, albeit far thinner and paler than before.

The officer slipped a handcuff around Ivan's wrist and secured the other to his own. Though of inferior grade to Ivan, he assumed that almost mocking bearing peculiar to his corps. They sped the few hundred metres to the Kremlin, the Chaika passing under the Kutafya tower, and stopping beside the Armoury, a small building dwarfed by the Grand Palace. They marched him to a room with barred windows and took his handcuffs off. The officer saluted pompously and left, locking the door behind him.

How much more comfortable he felt in uniform; he felt he had recovered a part of his lost dignity. He was shocked by the thinness and pallor of the face that looked back at him from the mirror hanging over the fireplace: thankfully, the uniform made up in style for what he had lost in bearing. A key grated in the lock, and the door swung open. Ivan turned to find himself face-to-face with a man of regal stature and silver hair. The cut and quality of his shoes and clothes put him into a class Ivan was never likely to cross in a Moscow street; he felt he should know this face, yet he had never seen it before.

'My dear Colonel', he said, 'please accept my apologies for the vulgar way you have been brought here. I hope you were not kept waiting too long.'

'No, thank you, ... uh....' stammered Ivan.

The man looked at him strangely. 'I hope you won't mind my own manners, Colonel, but I'd rather not introduce myself: we can't be too careful during this time of change, can we? I'm on the administrative side. But, Colonel, more importantly, tell me; I thought you had lost your voice.'

'I had, but after a recent accident on the river it seems to have come back.'

'Wonderful!' The silver-haired gentleman smiled through mirthless eyes. 'Please sit down. Perhaps you would like some tea. Vodka? I believe we even have some Scotch somewhere.'

'A tea would be fine, Comrade....Sir.'

The door opened, and a white-gloved waiter walked in. The gentleman ordered teas, and turned back to face Ivan. 'What a pleasure to meet you after such a distinguished career, Colonel.'

Yes, thought Ivan; it's a shame it's finished. 'Thank you, Sir.'

''Such an awful accident in Rome.'

'I'm not sure it was an accident, Sir.'

His eyes hardened to blue steel; the urbane smile lingered at his lips. 'Colonel, this may sound impolite, but have you really been mute since the accident or was it, how shall I say, ... necessary to act a part?'

'I really did lose my voice, Sir. What part do you mean, Sir?'

'That's wonderful', said the cabinet secretary, feigning excitement, 'I am pleased we can talk without resorting to nods and notes. Your accident on the river was not serious, I hope.'

'No, Sir', lied Ivan.

'Who else knows you can talk?'

'Only a boat keeper on the Moskva.'

'How quaint. It may be useful for now not to show you can talk again, Colonel.'

'If you wish, Sir.'

'Excellent! Now, down to business.' Vladimir Vasilevich clasped his hands under his nose, and paused as if to collect his thoughts.

The tea arrived, and the waiter poured two cups.

The cabinet secretary walked to the window and looked outside, biding his time until the waiter left, then, his back to Ivan, said, 'I am aware of a few of the circumstances surrounding your attempted murder in Rome, Colonel, and because you will be fully implicated in an enquiry I have been asked to head, you should know now that you were shot on orders from an officer working locally in Rome for the GRU, Military Intelligence.'

If the cabinet secretary was expecting a gasp of surprise, he was disappointed. He turned to Ivan. 'This doesn't surprise you?'

'No, Sir.'

The steely eyes flickered. 'Why not?'

'I suspected it, Sir.'

'Would you care to try to name the individual who ordered you shot?'

'I assume it was Colonel Ovarev, Sir, Rome Resident of the GRU.'

'Acting on whose orders?'

'I suspect General Felix Pavlovich Nikolaev's, Sir, from Moscow.'

Vladimir Vasilevich appraised this 'Promyslov' through new eyes. 'Excellent, Colonel. You know about the GRU?'

'Few people at Dzerzhinsky Square don't, Sir.'

'They went to a lot of trouble to eliminate you, Colonel.'

Ivan assumed this was meant as a compliment.

'Luckily', went on Vladimir Vasilevich, 'you survived, and can fit in pieces missing from this puzzle.'

'If you wish, Sir, however, I fear I may be forced to mention a member of the Politburo itself.'

'Who?'

Ivan hesitated. 'Marshall Volkov, Sir.'

'The Marshall disappeared over a month ago, Colonel; for that matter, now, so has General Nikolaev.'

Ivan could hardly believe his ears. 'And his son?'

'Your ex-assistant has vanished too; two Nikolaevs within twenty-four hours; an intriguing coincidence after Volkov's disappearance, isn't it!'

'They can't just vanish, Sir', said Ivan, conscious of the vast resources of the Second Chief Directorate.

'It seems they can, and they have. Now, let's see if we can make some sense of all this. Would you start by telling me why you were charged with an investigation in Italy: it's not your area of responsibility, is it?'

'No, Sir, but I was the first to interview a certain Bulgarian, Kimon Antonov, when he was brought in; I believe I was the first to learn that someone in our Rome embassy had sent a KGB illegal, called Ahmet, to America to kill their President and had sent money through Switzerland to an Italian crime syndicate to help. Because of all this, General Budhakin instructed me to send an Executive-Action agent, Ilya Fedorenko, to pull Ahmet out of America before he did any harm.'

'So, you believe that Marshall Volkov, one of the highest-ranking military officers of the Supreme Soviet, manoeuvred a KGB agent, instead of one of his own GRU agents, to do this "wet work".'

'I hoped Fedorenko, would get to Ahmet before the assassination, but he started the search under difficult conditions and arrived too late to stop an assassination attempt: just, we don't know how he got the American Secretary of State instead.'

'And you followed up in Italy.'

'Yes, Sir.'

The cabinet secretary smiled.

'Have I said something to amuse you, Sir?'

'No, Colonel. I am smiling because I know more about this business than you think, and your circumspection amuses me: your style is charmingly prudent.'

Ivan felt humiliated: this man was playing with him. 'Sir, if there's little I can add to your knowledge of events, perhaps I would do better to listen than to talk.'

The silver mane flew back, and the cabinet secretary laughed lustily at the ceiling. 'I like your spirit, Colonel. Yes! You should know some of what I have heard: that way we shall both gain time.'

Ivan coughed, and swallowed a mouthful of tea.

'Colonel, following a conversation with our mutual friend, Kostya Strugatski, I called a few people I know at State Security, and discovered some startling facts. Not only had you, a Colonel of impeccable credentials, been incarcerated, but also had your colleague, one Lieutenant Ryabov, and this on orders of your department chief, Budhakin, with minimal justification.' Vladimir Vasilevich confirmed with satisfaction the shock in Ivan's eyes. He went on, 'It was linked to some ridiculous story about not getting permission to visit Sofia; but for you it was more serious: you had hidden in your safe tapes you were not expected to remove from the Communications Department.'

'Yes', whispered Ivan, 'I thought they would find them.'

'Imagine my surprise when, a few hours later, I got a call from my illustrious friend and colleague, Secretary Kirill Fedorovich Demichev, First Secretary of the Central Secretariat, to say that his daughter, Tatiana, had been fired from State Security over a cock-and-bull story about a few tapes. I put two and two together, dear Colonel, and decided that your demise was linked to that of the young Demicheva, who, I later learnt, is Lieutenant Ryabov's fiancée.' He laughed. 'How anyone can be so stupid as to suspect such an obviously Russian trio to be involved in anti-state activity, is quite beyond me!'

He drank a mouthful of tea. 'I had the young Demicheva, a charming creature, in my Lubyanka office along with a big Armenian fellow with a cordial moustache.'

My "Lubyanka" office! Thought Ivan.

'He gave me a pile of deciphered, transcribed, and translated messages off these same tapes addressed to a certain 'Snow' by someone called 'Milk.' Then I sent for Ryabov who shed some light on this business, and advised me to talk to you. That's when I had you brought here.'

'Those tapes are vitally important, Sir; they trace the management of a GRU agent, Milk, by General Nikolaev's son, who is Snow, before and during his assignment to me in Dzerzhinsky Square. They may give clues to how the American assassination was organised.'

'They most certainly do, although the text is often disjointed; there's more than enough to nail Nikolaev and probably his father too, when we find them!'

'Do you remember any details on those tapes, Sir?'

The steel-blue eyes showed sudden irritation. 'Colonel, we are here so you can inform me, scarcely the other way around!'

'Yes, Sir.' Ivan waited.

'I seem to remember a description of arrangements between our KGB illegal, Ahmet, and this Milk. Two women were involved as an insurance against failure. The final messages claim that Ahmet tricked them, I believe, and there is talk of conflict between Ahmet and Milk. The text is so broken; we're probably reading more into the messages than we ought to.'

'Have the messages stopped?'

'They have.'

'There are opposing interests, Sir.'

'What the devil do you mean by that, Colonel?'

'Milk is a GRU agent, and Ahmet our KGB illegal. There could be an order that one or the other should be liquidated after the operation, Sir.'

The cabinet secretary stroked his chin.

'I think', continued Ivan, 'that Marshall Volkov placed Milk as an observer and as field support, but contracted for our KGB illegal to assassinate the American President: that way, as you say, the Military could deflect any blame onto State Security.'

'Is that why you asked Kostya Strugatski, who is a Party man, to help you?'

'How could I be sure that anyone I called at the Lubyanka was not involved in all this Sir? And I don't know anyone in Military Intelligence.'

The two men fell silent. Vladimir Vasilevich lifted the phone. 'Get me the Moscow State Prosecutor's office.' He arranged for Ivan's testimony to be recorded later that afternoon.

'Depositions are so tedious, Colonel: you have to stick to facts and leave speculation to the committees. We must get back to the groundwork. Later, based on your statement and my recommendations, the State Prosecutor will drop the charges against you; however, certain powerful individuals, who are currently free, consider you, and some of your colleagues, as targets. You are today possibly their most dangerous enemy, and if they had no hesitation in Rome to try to kill you, they will have none in Moscow either. This is why I am confining you to these walls until we find them or until the matter blows over. I think you will find your stay agreeable, as indeed will your wife, Olga Sergeyevna, whom I have taken the liberty of inviting to join you in the guest wing.'

Vladimir Vasilevich stood and with no further ado glided towards the door. Ivan didn't even have the time to say thank you. Vasilevich turned at the door: 'I believe that your work during this difficult time will have been critical to the support of our General Secretary and to the protection of our Soviet… but I never said this to you, Comrade Colonel.'

Ilya Fedorenko despaired of cruising Chicago's hot quarters looking for a white hooker with a bruised face. He had no other lead on Ahmet. He had not seen the woman well enough at Catanzaro's North-side safe house to recognise her, but he knew her face was bruised. He patrolled the singles bars and began to get dangerously noticed by the pimps.

In desperation, he contacted the Cuban. They met at the park bench. The sad eyes smirked during Ilya's account. 'You don't have what it takes. Go home, and we'll find them. We'll call you when we find your friend.'

'I'm not going until I've finished, and he's not my "friend".'

'Then relax, Comrade, and leave the job to us. You have photos of your friend?'

'I said he's not my friend. You can get one from Havana.'

'Run along, and we'll get on with the job. We know this town. You can finish your job when we find him.'

'What if you don't?'

The brown face cracked into an ugly smile. 'Then we have phial for you too: you can end your days here.'

Ilya scowled.

'You lost him, not us', continued the Cuban.

'Go to hell', hissed the Soviet illegal.

The Cuban resumed his sad look. 'What a way to talk to a comrade of the revolution. Be grateful for the help we give you. You see you cannot do this alone. You're sure your friend's still in Chicago.'

'He's here, and you have ten days to find him, or I'll use another track', said Ilya standing.

'The Italians?'

Ilya walked off.

The sad Cuban jumped up and ran after him. He spluttered, 'They want to kill him, you know. They won't help you, and Moscow Centre wouldn't agree.'

'Ten days', repeated Ilya leaving the small figure behind.

'So, it took fifteen days, and not ten, to find him. So what? Thanks to me you get to finish the job and to go home.... alive', said the Cuban.

'Where is he?' asked Ilya.

'I shall take you.'

'You shall show me the place, and go!'

'Such gratitude, Comrade, after all I have done for you.'

'Is he with the woman?'

'No, but we found him through her.'

Ilya waited for further explanation, his irritation mounting as the Cuban maintained a pointed silence. 'How?' he growled.

'We know the white pimps. She was easy to find. It was just a matter of following her around until she led us to your friend.'

'He's not my friend. Let's go.' Ilya stood and marched towards a waiting youth. To the Cuban's surprise, Ilya barked, 'Get the car!' The youth gave a terrified look and rushed off to the underground parking lot in Grant Park.

The two sat side by side in the car. It was dark outside, and so cold that neither Ilya nor the sad Cuban felt like getting out, though the Russian was torn between staying in the heat, where the Cuban's personal freshness reached ad standards and breathing something sweeter. Ilya wound down the window in fury when the Cuban lit a cigar stub.

He insisted on leaving the radio off, claiming that a watch required continual concentration. The real reason was that the music was too loud and that the publicity irritated him. The Cuban had sulkily kept his mouth shut ever since.

Many figures came and went through the filthy, brown doorway. Ilya doubted Ahmet would have chosen such a dingy hideaway, yet this area was too racially mixed to be patrolled by the Italians, and so, safer than most.

Ahmet appeared walking down the other side of the street. He eyed the car.

'Move!' hissed Ilya.

The sad Cuban had kept the engine running. He pulled the stick into drive. Ilya watched from the vanity mirror. Once around the corner at the end of the street, he got out and told the Cuban to park out of sight.

Ilya saw Ahmet continue some yards down the street before crossing and doubling back to the dirty doorway.

Ilya smiled and walked back to the waiting car. He wanted to meet Ahmet as if in friendship and to slip the deadly contents of the sad Cuban's phial into his food or drink. He moved into an apartment across the street, where he could watch Ahmet's occasional walk to the corner store and the hooker's suspicious looks each time she entered the dirty downstairs hallway leading to the studio flats.

At Christmas, he had thought of using this strange feast to approach Ahmet, but his quarry had disappeared with the hooker on Christmas Eve, not to return until the twenty seventh. Ilya had spent a worrying few days not knowing whether Ahmet would return.

On New-Year's Eve, a cab stopped in front of the dingy hallway. Ilya reached for his riding gear and pulled on his boots. His man appeared; he grabbed his pistol and raced downstairs to the motorcycle.

He pulled into the street just in time to see the cab turn North and followed it at a safe distance into the city. Ilya waited fifty metres behind when it stopped outside a store while Ahmet bought some flowers. He then got back into the cab, which continued North towards the yellow haze of the Chicago lights. As it crossed into North Michigan Avenue, it stopped again. His man paid off the taxi driver, and walked into a telephone booth. Ilya continued a short way down the avenue and parked the motorcycle in a quiet adjoining lot. He strolled back in time to see Ahmet marching along Clark Street towards Golan Memorial Hospital.

The registration desk took the call at about 7.30 p.m. on New Year's Eve. The duty clerk replied, 'Women's wing.'

'Flowers for McKinley', came a man's foreign voice.

'Drop them off at registration, Sir. We'll see she gets them.'

'Personal delivery.'

The clerk glanced at a note on her desk. 'OK, Sir, please wait a moment, I'll check her room number; she's been moved.' She picked up the telephone again a minute later. 'Sir, she has a single room now, number 405, but it's too late to deliver them now, visitors leave at 7.45p.m.'

'OK, tomorrow. A surprise.' The caller hung up.

A dark-haired man with a bunch of flowers, stepped from the elevator into the fourth-floor corridor. He listened intently. The irritating patter of a television set came from one room, its door slightly ajar; from another came low voices and the clink of cutlery. He started off down the corridor.

Ilya Fedorenko watched the elevator dial from the ground floor, and then took the stairwell up. Slipping through a safety door, he saw a man behind a curtain screen across a turn in the corridor: Ilya could see Ahmet, seemingly unaware he was being watched, walking silently along, reading room numbers.

There was an open office to his left; Ilya slipped inside, removed his riding clothes, and put on a blue operating-theatre smock and cap; he clipped a stethoscope around his neck, and sat at a glass panel from where he could see the hallway without being in the line of vision of the man behind the curtain screen.

A nurse appeared from one of the rooms and walked towards Ahmet. 'It's too late to visit now, Sir. If you're looking for the exit, it's along the hall, there.' She pointed at the elevators.

Ahmet flashed a smile. 'I leave flowers for.... lady.'

'No flowers in the rooms overnight, Sir.'

'OK, I say good-bye and go, yes?'

The nurse walked on; Ahmet did not see the fright in her eyes. He realised he was too tense; he thought too much; he should relax and concentrate on what he had to do.

Another door opened further down the corridor. A worried looking man with grey hair stepped out holding a bag; he ran his fingers through his hair, and walked towards him. 'Hi', he said, almost brushing him and walking on. Those grey eyes had looked at him closely, too closely; the grey-haired man was looking for something in his face, as if peering into Ahmet's very soul.

At first, he shuddered, then relaxed a little; there was too much movement; he was too nervous: he had to calm down; he was spooked by his own nerves.

His senses on edge, he found room 405.

Movement stopped in the corridor; he could still hear television patter from an open door; it reassured him.

He knocked softly on the door to 405, turned the handle, and crept in.

Ilya watched the man steal furtively around the screen; he had a pistol. He felt an impulse to rush to the help of his colleague, realising Ahmet's life was as much in danger with his friends as with his enemies. He froze: two more armed men, one with a machine pistol, joined the first from behind the curtain and walked off in pursuit. What if they caught him alive? Ahmet was a grave security risk. Ilya knew he must intervene now: Ahmet had to be eliminated on Soviet terms, and no one else's.

He got up, and reached below the blue smock for the automatic. He heard a movement behind him as his hand clasped the stock. Ilya spun around.

As he entered the room, Ahmet attempted a smile.

'Florence', he whispered.

The reading lamp was on, and magazines lay over the bed. What appeared to be a shock of thin, grey hair was all he saw of the motionless form huddled under the sheets.

He crept up to the bed, leaving the flowers on the floor. He took a loaded syringe from his pocket, removed the plastic cap covering the hypodermic needle, and drove the needle through the bedclothes deep into where he had expected flesh.

He found only bedding. The door burst open.

Two figures rolled along the floor, one to each wall; another rushed through, pointing a rapid-fire automatic pistol.

Ahmet jerked out the needle, and turned.

'Freeze', yelled the figure at the door.

Cornered like an animal, Ahmet drove the needle into his own arm, and injected the remaining fluid. Under the stupefied gaze of the Feds, his face contorted in pain: in seconds, he fell to the floor gasping.

Jim Curry shot forward from the doorway where he had covered his two more-athletic colleagues. 'Get a doctor!' he yelled.

Ahmet's frantic gasps became a gurgle deep in his throat; the writhing turned to convulsion. The skin around his eyes darkened against the grey of his face. His limbs stopped jerking, leaving the merciful release of death.

One federal officer ran out for a doctor, bumping heavily into Bugs, who was sure the killer had noticed his efforts to recognise him. There was no doubt, this was the same man as in the photograph, Victor Balaian, the intellectual, and Mischa, the *brigatista*. Bugs had given Jim and his two feds the thumbs up to pursue the killer into Florie McKinley's room.

Jim picked up the broken syringe and wafted it under his nose. He drew back at the pungent, distinctive smell of almonds. 'Cyanide', he said. 'Can't do anything for him now; it takes seconds.'

The woman agent, who had impersonated the nurse, walked into the room, and immediately turned on her heel at the sight of the corpse, saying she had to inform the duty clerk that patients could be moved back into the wing the next morning.

Bugs looked down at the contorted figure on the floor. He knelt beside it and pressed closed the eyelids to hide the glare of agony. He gently rolled the head to the left, and ran his finger behind the right ear: as in the photo, he found a prominent wart. This corpse was very probably that of Fatima Al-Othman's Paraguayan boyfriend, their relationship going back possibly to terrorist training in the Libyan desert, and, thought Bugs, also of one and the same Balaian and Mischa.

In the office, Ilya spun around to find a red-haired Chicago cop staring at him in surprise.

'You shouldn't be here, doc!' he exclaimed. 'This wing's out of bounds. Don't you read notice boards?'

He relaxed his grip on the pistol, and slid his hand into his pocket to get a handkerchief. 'Yes. I forget. Excuse.'

The policeman looked closely at him. ''Not from these parts, are you, doc?'

Ilya made no reply.

The policeman frowned. 'There's lots of police on their way. We've got a dangerous situation here. I'll have to escort you out.'

They heard running steps in the corridor. A federal officer rushed into the room. 'Come with me, doc', he shouted, 'now!'

Ilya was pulled away by the arm before he could say anything. The red-haired policeman followed. He had to follow the agent to avoid arousing suspicion. He had to act like a physician, or risk being caught. His fear was rapidly mounting. He instinctively recoiled from the ugly contorted form on the floor. The federal officer was surprised, expecting the doctor to surge to its aid. Controlling an impulse to vomit, Ilya stepped up to the corpse and knelt. A man was already kneeling on the other side: with a strangely fierce expression, he seemed to be rubbing the dead man's ears. Ilya felt like hitting him for disrespect. He pretended to listen through the stethoscope, and pulled back an eyelid as he had seen medics do on television. He gave a dozen beats of heart massage, and listened again through the stethoscope.

Then he arose, as did the man facing him. 'Is he dead?'

'Yes'

'He injected himself with something; can you tell what it was from the symptoms?'

'Later', replied Ilya. 'We take body away now.'

Bugs looked closely at the physician. 'We need a stiff drink; 'you join us?'

'I cannot', stammered the Soviet agent.

Two orderlies stood in the corridor with a wheeled, stainless-steel cart.

'Where are you from, doc?' asked Bugs.

'Europe; I just arrive.'

'That's a big place, doc.'

Jim Curry beckoned Bugs to a spot where they could not be overheard, and began a whispered conversation with him.

Ilya looked carefully around. No one was taking much notice of him. He walked purposefully towards the office where he had left his riding gear. The red-haired policeman had left to join others. Ilya stuffed the riding gear into a plastic garbage bag and returned as orderlies were lifting the corpse. He tossed the bag onto a shelf under the cart and helped to draw a cotton sheet over Ahmet's body. He walked behind them as they pushed it towards the group of police guarding the access to the elevators and to the stairwell.

'You taking him to the morgue?' asked the red-haired policeman recognising Ilya.

'Yes,' replied an orderly.

The policeman wondered whether he should check the cart.

'You want see?' asked Ilya. He stepped forward and pulled back the sheet from the dead man's face as the cops grouped around. He felt pity for the form that had been his companion for a short time. He felt like shouting, Look! This is what you have done to him! The policemen stepped back, then, white-faced, Ilya said, 'We go now.'

In the elevator, he retrieved his garbage bag, and got out at the first floor. The orderlies continued with Ahmet's remains to the hospital morgue in the basement.

Minutes later Ilya Fedorenko breathed bitterly cold air, riding his motorcycle through the dark streets of Chicago. He thought compassionately of the lonely, ugly corpse that could once have been a comrade, to be buried un-mourned, so far from its native land.

Ilya's mind raced: the trap sprung on Ahmet clearly meant that he himself was in danger. He should leave the country before it closed on him. He would contact the fat Cuban in the morning: in the meanwhile, he would pack his belongings and leave the apartment the following day.

THE DENOUEMENT

Empty corridors at Langley echoed to his footsteps when Bugs returned on New-Year's day to compile his report in the calm of the vacation morning. An envelope with the Director's insignia lay in the office safe. He opened it; inside, a note authorised him to complete investigations both into the Glenn case and into the Chicago assassination. Ed Duval would report to him on his work in Chicago. Bugs was puzzled: how would Hailsham react to that?

He dialled an outside line. A woman answered; children laughed in the background.

'Ed Duval, please.'

'One moment', she answered. It was a gentle voice. A child giggled with joy, and asked daddy to 'do it again.' He had never thought of Ed as a family man. The child was told to wait, and the laughter subsided. There were footsteps.

'Hello.' Ed's voice sounded relaxed and expectant.

'Ed, it's Bugs Macpherson.'

A moment of silence: Ed's voice turned professionally dull. 'Happy new year.'

'I'm at the office. I need to see you.'

'Now?'

'I'm afraid so, Ed.'

'Stay on the line.' He heard the low, hollow sound of voices behind a cupped mouthpiece. 'Come over for cocktails this evening. Bring your wife. We can get together in the study.'

'No thanks, Ed. I appreciate the invitation, but we need to talk in the office. Have you seen the Director's note?'

A growl in his voice, Ed murmured, 'I'll be there in an hour.'

Bugs replaced the handset and glanced through the documents Carol, his secretary, had left in the safe awaiting his return.

The ballistics department had addressed its report to Hailsham, but the document had been redirected through the CIA Director's office to Bugs: the slim document affirmed that the bore marks on the slug which had killed the

Secretary of State were identical with the ones on a photograph Bugs had brought back from the *Carabiniere 'Museo'* in Venice.

A second report confirmed that a set of fingerprints he had sent the lab perfectly matched those found on the P.38. Bugs felt satisfied: the photograph was that of the bore marks coming from a Walther P.38 Parabellum considered by the Italians to be Mischa's personal weapon, and the prints were a set lifted from Mischa's apartment after Lucia's arrest.

'It's you: Mischa *and* Ahmet', he whispered.

He pencilled a note asking that these same fingerprints be compared with those of the corpse of the man in the custody of the FBI who had injected himself with poison the previous evening at Golan Memorial Hospital in Chicago.

He glanced through a Chicago FBI report confirming that Lucia Sereni's fingerprints had indeed been found on the controls of the Bonanza left in the snow at Meigs airfield in Chicago and that the trace quantities of engine oil under the fingernails of Lucia's disfigured corpse had indeed come from the Bonanza's engine. Bugs lifted the printout of visitors and exhibitors at the last Chicago Agricultural Commodities Fair from his briefcase and put it on his desk with the other documents. It reminded him of the ticket to that fair he had found hidden as a bookmark in Mehemet Shkoder's book, *Albania shall Conquer* in the Colombian jungle. Remembering Nino's description of the Catanzaro link with Bulgaria, he had marked a red circle around one of the delegates' names: the BAPTCo organisation, represented by a Mr Traicho Botev.

It was 5 p.m. in Milan when Nino lifted the phone and heard Bugs' relaxed voice wishing him and his family a prosperous New Year. Nino returned the wishes, and complained about a humid, throat-catching fog engulfing the city; he came rapidly to the point; 'Both Ferraresi and Cagnotto recognised the man in your photograph.'

'Who did they say he was?' asked Bugs.

'Ferraresi wouldn't talk until I told him it was for you; you must have impressed him. He was surprised; he said he would never have expected Victor Balaian, a reputed intellectual, to be wearing fatigues and holding a

Kalashnikov! I pressed him on the possibility of a mistake, but he was adamant: the man in the photo is definitely Balaian.'

'What about Cagnotto?'

'He stated the man in the photo was the one who picked up the AR-70 Berettas from his Turin flat last August fifteenth.'

'Is he sure?'

'Absolutely positive; Balaian himself picked up the assault rifles.'

'What about the paper and ink tests on the love letters?'

'That's a tough one, Bugs, do you really want us to continue?'

'No; drop that one for now, Nino. You should get in touch with the Colombian police; they still have the pistols I found in Lucia Sereni's jungle cottage. You may find some useful pointers cross-checking their bore marks with your *Museo* records.'

The exchange finished rapidly, and Bugs continued to read through the numerous reports that had suddenly found their way into his safe: what had happened to provoke this avalanche of information? He left an account of the search of Cremante's house on the pile and wandered off down the hall towards the coffee machine. Everything was quiet, making him feel strangely virtuous working while others were home watching TV; then he thought of Jenny waiting alone for him to return and hoped Duval would be quick.

He sat to read about the largely-useless outcome of the search. An appendix listed the names and numbers of Cremante's passport collection. In the interests of thoroughness, he thought he ought to read through them, although it seemed a waste of time. He stretched, gazed thoughtfully at the wall for a few moments, sipping and chewing on the plastic cup; then put it on the desk.

The names were in alphabetical order; most of the passports, long since surrendered to the consulates of the issuing countries, were European. 'Cowan?' he mumbled. 'Cowan!' He opened a drawer in his desk and removed a sheaf of hand-written notes marked, 'John Glenn.' Inside he found a note from Mike MacTavish claiming that a Mr R. Cowan and a Mister J. Derry had alternately flown in and out of Dallas from Chicago on days Lucia was known to be there, either from records of her flights into Addison Field or of her attendance at the gynaecology clinic.

'The other man was called J. Derry.'

Sure enough, next in alphabetical order of the names in the appendix, Bugs found Mr J. Derry.

He got up from his chair and strolled around his desk engrossed in thought. Could Cremante have used that identification himself to liaise with Lucia in Texas? But why? A passport wasn't necessary for a mainland destination, although a false ID always came in handy for a crook. And what could Cremante and Sereni have had to talk about to see each other so regularly?

A meeting with Hailsham was now necessary: he wrote a memo asking for one. Hailsham could hardly refuse a written request. He took it down to the entrance hall. The security guard was a shrewd old timer, though not quite shrewd enough to escape New-Year's-day duty. He smiled through the bullet-proof glass and tossed his head at the two sentries standing outside the lobby. 'Morning, Sir. Looks cold outside. The boys must be freezing.'

'Yes, it does. Happy New Year.' Bugs slid the envelope through a slit in the glass. 'I'd like this delivered to Mr Hailsham; it's urgent.'

'Should I send it to his home, Sir?' He seemed flustered.

Bugs was surprised at the question. 'There's no point in disturbing him at home today, as long as he gets it first thing tomorrow.'

'Is he coming back tomorrow, Sir?'

'I guess he'll be in after the vacation.'

'Very good; we understood he wouldn't be back, you see.'

'Why not?' asked Bugs.

'When I escorted him from the Director's office, it seemed to me he was, well...er…leaving...if you see what I mean, Sir.'

'You had better give me back that envelope. I'll deliver it myself.'

'Very good', said the guard, sliding it back.

A blast of chilled air wheezed through the lobby doors, and Ed Duval walked in. The glass doors closed with a pneumatic snort and a scrape. Looking pale and annoyed, clutching a briefcase and dressed in jeans and a jacket, Ed addressed Bugs a humourless 'Hi.'

'Thanks for coming in, Ed; if you'd like to come up to my office, we'll get our meeting over with so you can get back to your folks. How did it go in Colombia?'

'Useless', replied Ed sourly. He stopped at the coffee machine, walked into Bugs' office, pulled up a chair, and sat tensely on the edge leaving his unopened briefcase at his feet.

'Are you OK, Ed?'

'You don't have any kids, do you Bugs.'

'No, Ed. My wife's waiting home alone.'

Ed relaxed.

'Come on, Ed; we've a case to settle, and we're almost there. Let's try to get out of here before sundown.'

Duval picked up his briefcase. 'What do you need to know?'

'I want to compare notes: we can help each other.'

'I have some information on the John Glenn investigation. The Colombian Military found a burnt-out helicopter frame with the registration numbers ground off sitting in a breaker's yard in Maicao; there aren't many like it registered in Colombia, so it was easily traced to a Colombian shell corporation clearing international money orders for the drug cartel; the interesting point is that it runs a joint venture with a Chicago trading company owned by the Mafia.'

'Catanzaro?'

'Right.'

'His name comes up all the time, Ed.' Duval raised his head and, for the first time that afternoon, looked Bugs in the eye. 'Catanzaro was a contractor and paymaster for the Golan Hospital assassination', went on Bugs. He explained his findings in Italy. Ed listened, ever more engrossed, until, at length, Bugs closed his narrative.

'You're saying Bulgarian Reds used the Mafia to mount the operation?'

'Who else could they use? They needed an international organisation with the resources to organise an assassination and they paid five million bucks to get the job done. It was paid in cash through a Swiss account, the money laundered through a casino belonging to the Catanzaro family in Italy.'

'Surely Catanzaro would never involve the Mob in trying to assassinate a US President. After the Kennedy shooting, they would steer clear of anything like that.'

'Wrong, Ed. He's in up to his neck: look at the support he has given: I'm sure it was Cremante who kidnapped Corinne O'Grady in mid-August: the operation had the stamp of the Red Brigades all over it. Cremante kept her in a tent the way he knew that the Red Brigades had confined General Dozier. Balaian, who was in Italy at the time of the kidnap, picked up the assault rifles from Cagnotto, a small-time Catanzaro mobster and it was Cagnotto who imported the cash from Switzerland. I have the Justice Department checking whether Mafia influence got the Chicago cop, O'Grady, the job of protecting the Presidential party: his kidnapped daughter made him a clearly obvious security risk. Mafia money got another cop baseball tickets so the Mob could steal his weapon and uniforms, one for the killer, and one for Cremante. $125,000 of Mafia money provided the bail to get O'Grady out to where he could be murdered. Need I go on?'

'So Cremante was a go-between.'

'I'm pretty sure he was running this show for the Catanzaros. Cremante probably met Balaian in Italy and used Mafia help to spring his girlfriend, Lucia Sereni, from jail in 1983. Balaian needed her out; he was about to get himself shot for giving a false, Armenian identity, and she could have pleaded on his behalf; but why did the Mafia help? Ed, the more I think about it, the more it seems to me that they were under contract to a Soviet client. If this was so, it would link Balaian to a Bulgarian, agricultural-products trading company, and would mean that he was acting under the control of the Eastern Bloc!'

Ed laughed for the first time since he had arrived. 'Bugs! That's outrageous and very far-fetched! What about this Mischa? He might have sprung her from jail himself. You don't even know whether Lucia Sereni knew Balaian.'

'Excuse me, Ed, but we know that Balaian shot the Secretary of State with the P.38; we know that the fingerprints on it correspond to those thought by the Italians to be Mischa's, and we know that its bore marks identified it as Mischa's personal pistol. Mischa was known to be Lucia Sereni's lover, but we found her love letters in bad Italian signed, "Victor", which was Balaian's name, not Mischa's. Lucia, Mischa and Balaian all disappeared at the same time: not three persons, Ed, but two, because Mischa and Balaian were almost certainly one and the same person.'

'Oh, OK.'

'And remember that Cremante and the killer, Balaian, looked almost like twins. I think that suited both the Mafia and Balaian using similar men to make the hit, and I think it's this that led to Cremante's murder, but I'm still working on that theory. Incidentally, I discovered that Cremante, travelling under false names, met Lucia Sereni regularly in Dallas to pay her probably for flying drugs, crooks, illegal immigrants, or whatever out of Colombia.'

'If that's so', remarked Duval, 'he may have paid her for the assassination attempt too, but, you know, Bugs, when I look at the video footage of her suicidal tactics, I doubt she wanted to get out alive.'

'She was pregnant, and had every reason to live.'

'And you think that the Mob cleaned up Fatima's apartment in Santa Ana?'

'Yes, and Cremante's place after his murder, carelessly missing his box of stolen passports; and I believe the drug cartel searched Lucia's jungle cottage immediately after her death in Chicago. I think the cartel wanted it burnt down, and when their apes came to do it, they found me, Sinclair, the Bogota DEA resident, and a small platoon of troops. I got a book, some love letters and a photograph before it burned, and brought it all back. I guess you know about that.'

'Yes, I do.'

'You may wish to know that Balaian, whose real name was not that at all, killed himself biting a cyanide phial in Chicago last night as we closed in on him. It's getting dark outside. I propose we outline our next steps together tomorrow.'

Ed Duval stood to go. 'OK, Bugs.' On the stairs, he remembered he had other information. 'You recall you asked for a cross-check of the fingerprints on those love letters; well Hailsham gave me the results.'

'The prints match those on the P.38 and on Mao's Little Red Book on People's War given to Catanzaro, right?'

Ed nodded.

'And soon, Ed, the lab will confirm that the handwriting on the love letters and on the Little Red Book comes from the same hand.'

Ed walked thoughtfully off to the car park.

Bugs thought to himself....and that, John Glenn, neatly identifies your killers too.

Jenny gazed sadly at the log fire and snuggled closer. She brought his hand up to her burning cheek and pondered the story he had told her during their warm evening together.

'How could he have been so callous?' she asked.

'He was a killer, Jen: he would have learnt his trade in Moscow after his recruitment from the Patrice Lumumba University, and perfected it in Libya with Stasi training; as a terrorist in Italy he would have learnt to handle guilt.'

'But to coolly plan the death of two women who loved him was inhuman.'

'His love for Lucia may have worn thin: she may have been a complication; from their difficulty together shown on the desert video, Lucia was probably jealous of Fatima, pregnant, and in need of a father for her child. It was probably her only hope of breaking her violent lifestyle: thirty-five is a tough age for a woman to find herself a lonely outlaw and a mother.'

'Could he have known he was going to be a father? Do you think even a man like that would plan his own infant's death in its mother's womb; his own flesh?'

'She was six weeks pregnant; I doubt he knew. I even wonder whether he was aware of her visits to the Dallas gynaecological clinic each time she flew into Addison Field to pick up their payments from Cremante.'

'A woman can hide those things from her man, honey', whispered Jenny, glancing uneasily at him.

Bugs was too engrossed in his own thoughts to notice Jenny's look: he went on, 'Fatima was a problem too; she was naive; careless. Her outings to Asuncion on behalf of Al Fatah attracted half of the South American intelligence community's attention. Balaian probably noticed they were being followed when they met during her return trips through Bogota.'

'He must have underestimated the difficulty of running separate love affairs with women like those. Lucia must have been furious with Fatima if she wanted him as the father of her child. How could she trust Victor Balaian, when he lusted after Fatima? She may even have discovered he left her alone in the jungle at times to meet Fatima secretly in Bogota.'

'Or openly, Jen; we don't know what the relationship was, though there was a video taken of the desert airstrip: the two women pointedly ignored each other, but we think we see Balaian walking up to Fatima, and embracing her.

'They had known each other at least since 1979 when he was supposedly an academic in Libya, but probably training terrorists too. Lucia went to the Lebanon in 1973 to work in the Palestinian refugee camps, so it's possible the two women had known each other since then, although Fatima would have just turned fourteen that year. Both Balaian and Fatima were photographed in the desert wearing the same Soviet cut and pattern of military desert fatigues. The shots were taken in the Sahara in June 1979; he was probably working with the East-German Stasi in Libya; he might have trained both Lucia and Fatima. Few of the Stasi's instructors would have been as highly trained as he if it's true he had been recruited by the GRU or the KGB through the Patrice Lumumba school. He spoke well; he was, after all, an academic; he wouldn't have had much trouble attracting fanatics like Lucia and Fatima to his ideals, and why not to his bed? It gets cold in the desert at night.'

'Why bother with Lucia?'

'She had more to offer than Fatima at a certain point: she could introduce him to the Red Brigades; a movement so independent that Eastern-bloc intelligence surely found them too tough to penetrate.'

'So he used her!'

'He used everyone! Lucia wasn't that naive. She was paid by the Libyan Arab Bank through a Swiss bank account: could that not have been for the help she gave Balaian? It may be due to him she was sprung from jail in 1983. Some bond united them at some point: after all, they did live together on her return to Italy in 1980.' For a few moments in silence, they pondered bright yellow tongues of flame whose light flickered off the walls of the dark room around them.

Bugs went on: 'He probably took the name Mischa soon after his arrival in Italy. He used the Victor Balaian identity in the summer of 1981, addressing the movement on Maoism, quoting from *Albania Shall Conquer*. I'm surprised he took such a risk: maybe he was trying to publicise the book! From then on, he could be recognised as Balaian even if he used the Mischa identity. The Mischa name was intended, I suppose, to be an alias for his more violent persona.'

'And no-one you met in Italy understood that Victor Balaian and Mischa were one and the same person?'

Bugs stretched: his feet were becoming uncomfortably hot before the roaring flames. 'No. But although one and the same, he was neither one nor the other, Jen. I do know now who he is: his name gives him away.

'His identity trouble started in 1982 when his cover as an Armenian was blown. Lucia was in jail, where she couldn't speak for him; his life was in danger because his column would rather shoot him than trust an Armenian who wasn't, and who claimed he was raised in Syria, but wasn't, as he spoke Arabic with a Libyan dialect?

'I have no idea how Balaian succeeded contracting with the Mafia to get Lucia sprung from jail: that's when he met Cremante I suppose, who, as a Catanzaro lieutenant, worked on his behalf with terrorists. Once Lucia was free, I suspect they both fled to Colombia. Lucia, a good pilot, put her skill to use with the drug cartel, and, in ferrying drugs into the United States, she used the desert refuelling stop near the Rio Grande. Balaian somehow brought Fatima into a trio with Lucia. The Palestinian woman's drug business in Santa Ana domiciled her in the US, where she could drive fuel to the airstrip.

Ivan lifted the newspaper cutting and read the translation clipped to it once again. Deep in the bowels of the Lubyanka building, deft minds had cross-referenced facts and sent the article to the operations room of the First Chief Directorate. It was old news now: it said that an Italian called Cremante had committed suicide in a car somewhere near Chicago. That evening, the Russian Embassy in Washington called to say that a second article had appeared in the Chicago press since the twenty-seventh of the month claiming that an old lady was able to recognise the Secretary of State's assassin. Ivan had more than a gnawing conviction that she must have seen Ahmet.

'You've become something of a celebrity, Vanya', said Konstantin Strugatski. He made himself comfortable and accepted a Cognac.

Ivan owed him a debt of gratitude, but Kostya's manners irritated him. He had nowhere near the class of the silver-maned gentleman who had headed the enquiry. 'Who was he?' he asked Konstantin.

'One of the cabinet secretaries: he's from a breed with roots hundreds of years old at the time of the October Revolution. I can't tell you his name, and he's allergic to publicity because of his responsibilities in security.'

'Impressive!'

'Yes, very', said Strugatski, the faintest envy tinged his voice.

Ivan put down the cutting.

'Do you like it here?' asked Konstantin.

'Olya loves it.'

'And you?'

'It feels like a golden prison, but still a prison. I'd rather be back in my old office. Frankly, Kostya, I want to go home. I want to see the dacha again before they take it away from me.'

Konstantin laughed. 'Don't worry about that, Vanya: it was one of the first things our silver-haired friend took care of. With his clout, you're in there for life! Maybe you'll get something bigger!'

Ivan's brow cleared. 'No: the one I have is the one I want. I'm grateful, Kostya, but when can I get out of here?'

'Not until they find Volkov and the two Nikolaevs. You're far too valuable to lose before the trial: if those three are guilty of treason, they'll be dropped alive and screaming into the cremation oven before they're dead, and you're the State Prosecutor's star witness, Vanya. These people are your enemies now, and they would kill you if they could find you: if they managed an attempt on the American President using third-parties, just imagine what they could do to you on the streets of Moscow.'

Konstantin laughed again, but Ivan couldn't see the humour. 'I've read your depositions', he continued; 'do you really believe all this adds up to rivalry between the KGB and the GRU?'

'That's not the point', snapped Ivan, wary of Konstantin's politics.

'Then, what is the point?' he asked coldly.

Ivan stood. A few days of good food and rest had filled the hollows in his cheeks. His uniform was regularly pressed by an aide-de-camp. He turned to warm his seat at the open log fire.

'Incidentally', added Strugatski, 'you're looking much better.'

Ivan settled his brown eyes on his old-school friend. 'The point, Kostya, is that Volkov wanted to discredit the General Secretary: you yourself told me that months ago. The point is, he organised an international incident before the summit to try to sabotage it; and used our apparatus in State Security so that the KGB, rather than the GRU, Military Intelligence, would be accused by the General Secretary at the Politburo if things went wrong. The point is, this old bastard got a colleague's son to join the KGB, and to do the dirty work for him.'

'I checked that', interrupted Strugatski; 'your Captain Vassily Nikolaev was secretly promoted to Lieutenant-Colonel of his old regiment at Volkov's personal request in July of this year. Your assistant was, in effect, still a full-time, professional officer on assignment to Military Intelligence. Frankly, Vanya, I don't find he's that competent.'

'Nikolaev is still inexperienced. His plan was sound, but his cover lousy. He takes stupid risks.'

'No finesse.'

Ivan walked up and down in front of the fire. 'If I'd had a son, I'd never have sacrificed him like that. His father got him into State Security using his contacts: he got him a foreign posting through contacts and set up his career using the GRU Resident in Rome. I don't see how that boy could have survived before someone questioned his abilities sooner or later.'

'He did set up Ahmet and Milk to assassinate the American President.'

'Yes, that was clever', admitted Ivan, 'but I believe the operation was planned by his father, or even by Volkov himself.'

'Do you think Milk knew what Nikolaev was up to?'

'No. Cremante was instructed to be nothing more than Ahmet's support: even if he was a GRU agent, I suspect he neither knew nor cared whether the Military or the KGB was paying him. Cremante's role was to involve his gang in America and to procure back-up. When Milk brought Nikolaev his shopping list, Marshall Volkov used his distant Party protégé, Kimon Antonov, to get cash to him through Sofia: Bulgaria is far away! Once Cremante had taken his cut, the money was transferred to the Catanzaro gang through Switzerland, and laundered in an Italian casino.' Ivan smiled. 'An attractive Swiss investigator told me all about that.'

'Your only trip abroad, my friend, has been more eventful than any one of the fifty I have taken myself! You may like to know that Colonel Ovarev owned up to organising the attempt on your life through his friends in Italian crime. He's being escorted back from Rome tomorrow. He's willing to testify against General Nikolaev, who gave the original order....' Konstantin smiled an evil smile. '.... probably given at the request of his son. Oh, and while I remember, you may wish to know that your boss, Budhakin, has decided to take his retirement, although I'm not sure that he's aware of this yet.'

Turning his back on Konstantin, Ivan scowled into the fire. His school friend had become as bad as the others.

'Either you were getting uncomfortably close to the truth, or Nikolaev had some reason to.... well.... dislike you.'

The silence of the room was broken only by the crackle of the fire and the peal of Kremlin bells striking nine p.m. The large room was warm despite the below-freezing temperature outside. 'I've missed something', said Ivan: 'something unaccounted for.'

'You're on the way to closing the case, old friend. Soon everything will be cleared up.'

'No, there's something urgent: I'm sure! And then, the Resident at the Rome Embassy mentioned another name, Mischa: I must follow it up: he may have been trained by us. I have to get back to the office soon!'

'Soon enough.'

'And I'm worried about Ahmet and Fedorenko. They're still out there. European border guards had a lead on the Swiss account: who knows how close they have come to our men in their American investigation.'

'Don't worry.'

Ivan stared through the window at the dark night, then turned in horror. 'Konstantin! Nikolaev ran my office for more than a week: he got into my safe: he knew about Fedorenko. One call to Havana, and....I must get back to my office. Help me!'

'I can't.'

'Then get Ryabov. Please! Quickly!'

Konstantin lifted the phone.

It was six a.m. when Aleksandr Mikhailovich Ryabov strode grinning into Ivan's golden prison. He marched up to the Colonel and looked him in the eyes. ''Wonderful to see you, Coach. You look well enough to make us suffer again in the rowing tank.'

'You're putting on weight Ryabov: you need me!' retorted Ivan with a laugh. 'Ask for some tea at the door, and come and sit down.'

Ryabov gasped.

'Yes, Aleksandr Mikhailovich, I can talk again.'

Ryabov whooped and slapped Ivan on the back. He opened the door and called for some tea.

'How's your pretty bride-to-be?' asked Ivan.

''Looking for a job.'

'She should never have been allowed to leave: the Komitet needs people like Tanya.'

''Too late now, Coach.'

'Maybe not: we'll see. So, what did Strugatski's calls unearth last night?'

'He has a long reach! Budhakin met George Kevorkian and me at midnight at the main entrance. George went through all the dispatches from your office over the past month. One left your office for Havana signed by you some weeks ago ordering Ilya Fedorenko to liquidate Ahmet, and a second left only last week instructing Garcia to finish off Ilya Fedorenko! That one was signed by you too. Either it was an out-of-mind miracle that you signed them or someone else signed for you; we suspect Nikolaev.'

'We can catch Garcia at home. It's strange Budhakin was with you: it seems he's retiring.'

'If he is, he doesn't seem to know it, although he looked personally embarrassed to discover your forged signatures: that's not like him at all. I've already spoken to Garcia: he was at dinner. He's afraid we're too late for Ilya Fedorenko, but he'll try. Ahmet has disappeared: Garcia thinks he may already have been liquidated by Fedorenko.'

Ivan fell silent. Bleary-eyed, he looked into the fire. 'Two good men, for nothing.'

Aleksandr Mikhailovich walked over to the window and watched large, soft snowflakes fall in the light of the old lamps illuminating the Kremlin paths. He waited a little and came back to sit in front of Ivan. 'Coach! Perhaps I should tell you about Sofia.'

'Yes of course', answered Ivan, his brows clear again.

Ryabov talked about the Weasel and the discovery that both Bulgarian passports were of dead people under the names of Kostov and Potanin. 'The gardener spoke of someone from State Security visiting the Agricultural Directorate: a young fellow in a uniform like mine.'

'Who could that have been?' asked Ivan.

Ryabov saw a twinkle in his eye and laughed. 'I sent a photo yesterday morning to the Weasel by courier. He called back yesterday evening to confirm.'

'Nikolaev!'

'Yes.'

'Sofia's a good stopping-off point between Rome and Moscow. Wouldn't you say, Aleksandr Mikhailovich?'

'Yes, Coach.'

'So another piece of the puzzle fits, pushing Vassily Nikolaev closer and closer to the edge of treason.'

The tea arrived. The two officers waited in silence for it to be served. The hot, sweet fluid loosened Ivan's vocal chords, that hadn't had so much exercise in more than a month. The waiter left the room.

'Where is Nikolaev?' asked Aleksandr Mikhailovich. 'I spent most of yesterday looking for him to ask about this Mischa fellow.'

'He has disappeared.'

'Disappeared? I'll bet no one in the Department knows.'

'Budhakin surely knows by now', corrected Ivan.

'Then no one does below the General staff level. I wonder where he's gone?'

'Nikolaev appears to have vanished at the same time as two very senior military officers.'

'And one's a relation?'

'No comment.'

'I doubt they'll get far', said Ryabov: 'if they're recognised they'll be stopped, and if they're not, the militia will find them during an identity check.'

Ivan clapped a hand to his forehead. 'But of course,' his eyes met Ryabov's in a blaze of agitation. 'Get on that telephone: get me the Director of the Border Guards. If he's still in bed, get him out: keep him on the line. Tell him you're calling from the Kremlin. I'm calling an internal line first, then I want to talk to him, and Aleksandr Mikhailovich?'

'Yes, Coach?'

'Get those Kostov and Potanin passport numbers too: we need to send them quickly to the border guards?'

He stopped well short of the block and quietly pushed the motorbike into the yard. He parked it and took the iron fire escape in the dark leading up to the rear door of his flat. He stopped close to the top of the stairs; a faint light glimmered in the darkness through the kitchen door's frosted glass panels. He waited. The light moved. Someone inside the apartment was smoking. He crept up to the door and found it ajar. There was a shuffle inside. Ilya backed up to the wall under the window. The door opened, and a small figure emerged holding a cigarette.

Ilya slid up behind the figure and clutched the neck tightly from behind cutting off all blood through the carotid arteries. Within seconds the figure slumped to the floor of the fire-escape landing. Ilya lit a match and peered down at the face; he saw the pale, unconscious features of the fat Cuban. He dragged him into the kitchen, pulled down the blinds, and turned on the light. He was unarmed: there was a small pill box in his pocket, but it was light and too small to hold anything dangerous, and yet....

The Cuban came to and frowned weakly. His hands moved up to his head. Ilya stopped his search, and slid the small box, unopened, back into the Cuban's pocket.

'You do that well, sonofabitch. I think I'm gonna throw up.'

Ilya poured a glass of water and threw it in the Cuban's face.

The fat man retched. 'Ah, that's much better.'

'Why are you here?'

'I came for a talk', answered the Cuban. He propped himself up on one elbow and wiped his dripping face on his sleeve. He grinned and pointed at a brown paper bag on the table. 'See, I even brought dinner.'

Ilya relaxed and took off his jacket.

The Cuban came shakily to his feet and reached into his pocket for the small box. Ilya turned to see him staring pale-faced at the floor.

'You want coffee?' asked Ilya filling the kettle without waiting for the Cuban's answer.

'Look', said the fat man, 'I want to help you. No hard feelings. OK?'

Ilya plugged in the kettle and turned to face him.

'Come on, let's shake hands and be friends', said the Cuban; 'we need each other.' He held out his right hand, palm upwards.

Ilya hesitated. This man was obnoxious, but his only link with home. His dependence would be better served in friendship. He took the hand in his own.

The Cuban laughed and slapped the Russian on the arm with his free left hand. He must have hit quite hard: Ilya felt a pain in his shoulder. He moved his left hand up to rub it, his features freezing as he touched a small, hard object lodged in his flesh.

The Cuban backed away, terror in his eyes.

Ilya felt suddenly weak. He pulled. The four short needles embedded in his muscle came away with a tug. He slumped to his knees. The kitchen went into a spin, like the flying lessons at the Executive-Action school. He reached for the Cuban, fancying the fat man's frightened stare had turned into a grin.

He fell forward on his face, feeling no pain despite the force with which his head hit the floor.

The Cuban searched the apartment, collecting every trace belonging to Ilya Fedorenko. He softly bolted the front door to the flat and broke the glass seal of a chemical detonator in the bottom of the brown bag. He opened the gas valve in the oven, and dragged the Russian's limp body to its open door, then, taking Ilya's belongings, he walked out into the night, carefully closing the fire escape entrance behind him.

'Happy New Year, gringo', he laughed.

The explosion blew out three floors of the building.

In the rubble, the following day, the police found the remains of two decimated families, and, forced into an oven, the body of an unidentified male whose blood plasma held a murderously high concentration of barbiturates. It was an obvious case of a gas explosion following a suicide: the smallest spark could have caused it.

The Director liked early starts and had asked Bugs to be in his office at 6 a.m. to answer any questions he still had after reading the file on the Presidential assassination attempt.

'You've done a fine job, John.' The Director ushered Bugs to the chair in front of his desk. 'Before we make the presentation to the Select Committee on Intelligence, I need clarification of a few facts.'

'What do you need to know, Sir?'

'First, seeing as the President has talked about sitting in on this afternoon's meeting, he's going to want to know why this fellow killed the Secretary of State, and not the President himself?'

'I never spoke to Balaian, Sir, so it's tough to judge what kind of a character we were dealing with, but my bet is that he thought he had a better chance of escaping alive if he went after the wrong man; I think his plan was to frame Cremante for the Secretary of State's murder, and the women for the President's: he could count on their terrorist fanaticism to get themselves killed.'

'Are you saying the man was a coward?'

'He was certainly a manipulator.'

'Why on earth would he want the women killed? Both had been his lovers it seems!'

'I think his relations had become complicated, Sir. They probably knew more about him than he thought healthy.'

'And you don't think he was a terrorist himself.'

'Both Lucia and Fatima were prepared to die for a cause: the rebuilding of Italian society; the Palestinian homeland. I don't believe Balaian was driven by a cause in that sense. He may have been a political activist, but my feeling is that he was primarily a trained killer; unwilling to take risks others could take in his place; a professional doing a professional's job.'

'Soviet?'

'Eastern bloc, Sir.'

'He must have been good to convince those two women to commit virtual suicide.'

'He didn't have to: Lucia Sereni outside the hospital the day of the murder anxiously awaited some pre-arranged signal after the assassination; she hears shots; the President himself appears, so he's alive and there's no sign of Balaian.

Her nerves break. She assumes the father of the infant she carries has been killed. Blind with hatred, she sets their contingency plan in motion.'

'Yes, I see', said the Director; 'distaste for society and a lust for vengeance of her mate's presumed death would be powerful motives; but how was the other woman involved?'

'Fatima was known to be impressionable and naive. She had also had an affair with Balaian, and was surely under stress. A person of Lucia's strength of character would have had no trouble forcing her to join in an armed attack despite their apparent dislike for each other.'

'Presumably, the contingency plan involved both women anyway.'

'Yes: in Italy, Balaian took delivery of two Beretta assault rifles, not one. The women were there to back him in the event of failure; the question is what did he intend by failure? He probably succeeded in his own objectives quite well: he saved his own skin by killing a poorly protected but important target, leaving the heavily protected one of the US President to the women. This way, he safeguarded his credibility; he would claim he had killed the wrong man in error. And it was only bad luck his contingency plan for the two women to murder the President by a terrorist attack misfired: it did almost work! His professionalism could not be doubted by his principals; he had planned the operation with adequate resources and foresight; they would never suspect cowardice as a motive for failing to attain the objective.'

'Had the women known he had not even tried to assassinate the President, things may have been different.'

'Especially if they had known he was still alive, Sir.'

'How did you arrive at these theories, John?'

'Jim Curry of the Chicago FBI and I were surprised by Florie McKinley's stubbornness: she stuck to her testimony like a limpet, so we accepted her account as factual; the next step was to find a scenario to fit it. For example, do you remember the movements of the officer who entered the ward right after the shooting? He appeared instants later; had he not seen Balaian rushing from the ward? Balaian made a quick change in the laundry room across the corridor; a long, straight, echoing, empty corridor, cleared of personnel in the interests of security: you have to be deaf and blind not to notice an escape like Balaian's in a place like that.'

The Director added, 'Possibly: her testimony affirms this policeman made no attempt to check whether the victims were still alive. He made no exclamation of shock; he calmly walked to the window, looked outside, and returned to the door, where he disappeared with "another policeman", she said, "looking just like the terrorist himself". I admit those details surprised me too. This man showed exemplary calm.'

'Florie McKinley's evidence points clearly to the fact that this man was Cremante; the other policeman was Balaian, the killer, Sir. Both he and Balaian prepared the assassination together and got out dressed as police after Balaian dropped his white coat in the laundry room. If you remember, the Irish cop, O'Grady, said he had to wait for a signal from a policeman standing at a corridor window overlooking the courtyard before kicking up his rumpus. Without being at the door of the ward, Balaian couldn't choose the exact moment for the hit, yet that moment was perfectly chosen because the Secretary of State was within range. Had Balaian been alone, signalling O'Grady would have lost him precious seconds. Balaian could choose his moment by signalling to Cremante, who was at a window where he could signal O'Grady to start his antics in the yard. All Cremante had to do was to stay in full view of both Balaian and O'Grady, and wait for Balaian to signal him.'

'So Balaian saw the bodyguard leave to see what was happening in the yard, and chose that moment to make his kill.'

'Exactly, Sir. That second bodyguard should never have left the Secretary of State's side.'

'Then he crossed back to the laundry room, took off the white coat, and stupidly left his pistol behind?'

'I believe he gave the P.38 to Cremante, who was waiting by the window as he left the ward. It's clear that Cremante took the automatic with gloved hands, and we believe he was the one who left it on the window sill, and not Balaian.'

'Why?'

'Because it was the murder weapon and because it had Balaian's prints over it. I suspect Cremante wanted to frame Balaian. Suppose these two characters had been caught: they looked like twins and were both disguised as cops. The prints on the P.38 were the only evidence able to save Cremante from the Gas Chamber, and to convict Balaian? I'm sure Cremante left it purposely where the police would find it. He wisely wore gloves with the pistol probably suspecting Balaian wanted the Italian's fingerprints to cover his own on the pistol: Balaian must have been furious.'

'Yes, that is one theory, I suppose.'

Bugs looked in surprise at the Director. 'Sir?'

'It occurred to me, John, that framing Balaian would suit the Mafia anyway. After all, they have very little interest in being involved in the murder of an American politician through one of their own men, have they?'

'So, you think Cremante left the pistol behind because Catanzaro told him to.'

'There's no evidence Balaian ever worked for the Mob; his fingerprints over that pistol would take it nicely off the hook.'

'You may be right, Sir: Cremante acted with forethought. Leaving a murder weapon behind for the police on the spur of the moment would have been one hell of an initiative!'

'Yes, in my view, his move must have been premeditated. Cremante was wearing gloves, and had a motive to plant a weapon with Balaian's fingerprints.' The Director thought for a few seconds and then resumed. 'A nasty type, this Balaian; not only was he prepared to sacrifice the women outside but his accomplice too. Cremante must have suspected treachery from the outset; he was too experienced to be so easily tricked and prepared to meet Balaian's treachery with his own.

'I believe, Sir, that Victor Balaian planned with the care we might have expected of the Red Brigades. He must have chosen Cremante because they looked alike, and witnesses would confuse the two, one with the other. Balaian didn't wear a mask or gloves because he wanted to frame Cremante, but the Italian was smart. I suspect that Victor Balaian was outraged that Cremante did, in fact, think of wearing gloves and that's why he murdered him shortly after. We can add, Sir, that Cremante would have been the only one to understand that Balaian may intentionally have murdered the wrong man inside the hospital; a man who was less protected than the President. What could stop him reporting Balaian for cowardice?'

'Yes, John, that would have made Cremante very dangerous indeed, especially if he felt outraged at the way Balaian's treachery got the women killed. I understand that Lucia Sereni and Cremante met at times in Dallas, where he paid her for her work; maybe they were more than just friends.'

'Perhaps, Sir: both were expatriate Italians; he had organised her jail break; perhaps he even knew about her pregnancy.'

'John, how can you be sure that Balaian was the father of Lucia's infant and not, for example, Cremante himself?'

Bugs murmured, 'I can't, Sir.'

'Please go on with your account.'

Bugs looked for some seconds at the Director and then continued. 'After the murder, Cremante entered the ward dressed as a cop; the appearance of authority helping to deflate the tension a little. He wasn't concerned with the two victims, but very interested in O'Grady and the second bodyguard arresting him in the yard: that's why he walked to the window and looked outside.'

'He then joined Balaian waiting at the door, now dressed as a policeman, correct?'

'Yes, Sir. Balaian would have worn the uniform under the white physician's coat; recovered his hat from the laundry room across the corridor; dumped the white coat there; and then probably forgot or neglected to give a pre-arranged signal to the women meaning he was safe: that committed them to the contingency plan to assassinate the President, putting them in mortal danger. We have an observant witness in Florie McKinley, stating clearly that the killer was not wearing gloves, and that Cremante was.'

'And surely the P.38 would have been identified as Balaian's pistol in the end.'

'Yes. The bullets dug out of the Secretary of State and his bodyguard were compared with those of Mischa's Red Brigade victims in Italy: all were fired from the same pistol. Cremante's prints and physical resemblance with Balaian could well have incriminated Cremante himself as Mischa; he was, after all, an Italian. That's what Balaian, no doubt, hoped, but Cremante took precautions. Balaian possibly didn't know the Italian police already had a set of his prints taken from the apartment where they arrested Lucia Sereni.'

'So, had his plan turned out correctly, Balaian could have withdrawn incognito, leaving Cremante alone responsible in the eyes of the law: and this both for his crimes in Italy under the Mischa alias, and for the Chicago assassination attempt. That's quite a plan!'

'Which makes me believe Balaian was preparing his retirement.'

'He wouldn't have left any trace of his existence; all blame would have fallen on Cremante, possibly, on the Mafia and on the women!'

'Yes, Sir.'

'That's clever! But are you sure Balaian and Mischa are the same man?'

'The pistol and the fingerprints are conclusive evidence, Sir. The rest is circumstantial: for example, Balaian and Mischa disappeared at about the same time from Italy, and, although Lucia's lover was known to be called Mischa, the two love letters found in the jungle cottage were signed, Victor, which is Balaian's forename. He probably assumed Mischa as a revolutionary name, and was called this by the Red Brigades: however, the Executive Committee knew of the Balaian identity, so he had trouble defending his nationality as an Armenian although their names often end in -an. The hand that wrote the love letters wrote the dedication in Mao's Little Red Book given to Catanzaro, and provides us the link between Balaian and the Mafia.'

'And why would Catanzaro have used Balaian to try to assassinate the President instead of Cremante, for example?'

'The contract with the Bulgarians may have specified they provide their own hit man: it avoided the Mob the embarrassment of committing a very un-American crime. We believe that Victor Balaian contacted a Bulgarian trader at a Chicago agricultural fair last spring and visited Catanzaro himself, leaving him a dedicated copy of Chairman Mao's Little Red Book on People's War. The Mafia boss threw it out, ironically leaving himself wide open to criminal proceedings: thanks to the handwriting in that book, the Justice Department has a warrant out on

Catanzaro. The FBI believes the Mafia used influence with the police department to get O'Grady into the Presidential protection group, and put up the bail to get the Irish cop out to where he could be shot walking his dog.'

'I suppose Balaian murdered O'Grady himself.'

'Possibly, Sir. O'Grady was told to walk his dog at a set time, no doubt expecting to get his kidnapped daughter back. Instead, he got a bullet in the head from the stolen police revolver. Balaian would have liquidated O'Grady because the cop had seen him face to face, and could recognise him again. We assumed Balaian would try to murder the old lady in the hospital, Florie McKinley, for the same reason, and that's how we trapped him.'

'And he murdered Cremante too?'

'Yes, making it look like a suicide, and cleverly using the stolen police weapon to make us believe it had been Cremante all along who had killed O'Grady. It could have been competent work had he not overlooked Cremante's left-handedness.'

'Catanzaro must have been wild at the loss of a prime lieutenant.'

'Probably, Sir. If Catanzaro breaks under FBI questioning, we should know more.'

'And what of John Glenn in all this?'

'Sadly, Sir, John's plane got in Balaian's way. He was unwittingly on the trail of the Chicago assassination attempt before it happened. With Lucia as the pilot, I guess it was Balaian who fired the high-calibre, tipped, tracer shells from the Bonanza at John's plane. You know the rest.'

'So you're ready for today's presentation.'

'Yes, Sir.'

The Director arose from his desk and strolled to the window. He spoke with his back to Bugs. 'Excuse me if I interrupt you there, John, but I have a meeting in five minutes. It may interest you to know that we are expecting a very important Soviet defection tomorrow in Turkey: seeing that you have a lot of European experience, would you like to fly over there and handle the debriefing?'

'I'd like that very much, Sir, but the Middle East isn't my area; why....'

'In that case', interrupted the Director, 'I'll have my secretary call you. The dossier will be delivered to you in the plane tonight.'

'Very good, Sir', said Bugs, and walked off, surprised by the Director's latest strange offer.

The archives held intelligence material forming the daily diet of Langley analysts. Bugs had always taken special care over his relationship with the talented librarians, who watched over them with loving care.

A be-spectacled lady glared up from a reading lamp and smiled at Bugs, who, she knew, had a healthy respect for her encyclopaedic knowledge. 'Mr Macpherson, how are you, Sir. I hear you've been on vacation in Italy.'

'Yes, Leslie, and now I'm back, I need your help.'

'What can I do for you, Sir?'

'What do you have on Albania?'

'A nice little section on Enver Hodja and the post-revolutionary period, Mr Macpherson; it's not consulted very often, so it's a bit difficult to access. Is there anything I can get for you? Oh, and I should tell you I have a note asking me to get authorisation from Mr Hailsham first. Will that be a problem?'

'No, Leslie, and I'll go through whatever you have myself.'

The nightmare of an untrained person among the archives was anathema to this Cerberus of the CIA basement, and then, where was Hailsham's authorisation? 'I can't allow that, Sir. You would need permission from the Director himself.'

'Of course, Leslie, that's why I asked him to write me this', said Bugs, handing over a note.

Cerberus read it, scowling and growling quietly under her reading light, and, with a sigh of resignation, pressed the switch to the electrically-operated, safety doors protecting her precious documents from a hostile world.

'I'm going to need coffee, Leslie', said Bugs, amusing himself a little more at the expense of the flustered librarian.

"Gracious, Sir, no coffee near the documents, in case you spill it.'

'And, when do you close for lunch?'

'We never close, Sir. Twenty-four-hour service', she said, proudly.

'Then send in some sandwiches.'

Cerberus smiled thinly.

Bugs penetrated the dry interior and burrowed his way through corridors of material until he reached the remote section he was looking for. He pulled up a stool and settled down to look through tedious page after tedious page. Much of it was not translated.

A few hours later, hungry and happier, he found what he needed in a youth magazine dated July 1968. In his excitement, he almost left the archives with the original; but, ever watchful, the duty librarian stopped Bugs' headlong rush for the door with a firm smile, and made him wait for a copy.

'....and the Director said he would like to invite you and Mrs Macpherson to dinner next Saturday to introduce your new boss to her', said the secretary.

Bugs was surprised that the Director had said nothing to him. 'Who is it? Why just to her?'

'He didn't say, Sir. He just told me to give you the message: to introduce your new boss to her.'

'Anything else?'

'Just that a car will collect you from the White House to take you to Dulles at 4 p.m. for the red-eye to Ankara, Sir. The driver will have the papers with him concerning the Soviet defection.'

'Thank you.'

Bugs collected up the dossier on his desk and mentally ran through the outline of his presentation once more. He ran a comb through his tousled hair before taking the stairs, realising half-way down that he had left the all-important slides on his desk, and ran back up to get them.

The car was waiting in the snow, and he was five minutes late. Stony-faced, the driver pulled away. Bugs snatched a look at his watch. It would be OK. The White House was only a short drive along the Washington Memorial Parkway from Langley.

Bugs drank some water. The initial spate of nerves had given way to a confident presentation, the deceptively amiable manners of the President doing much to allay his stress. Most of the members of the Select Committee had appeared and were seated around the conference table. Bugs recognised many of the faces from press photos.

Taking advantage of the pause, the Director added a few comments of his own. 'You may wish, Mr President, Senator, ladies and gentlemen, to know what has become of this Victor Balaian. I'm pleased to say that thanks to exemplary cooperation between the Central Intelligence Agency, and the Department of Justice, we successfully laid a trap for this criminal at the Golan Memorial Hospital in Chicago. A patient there, a certain Ms McKinley, kindly allowed us to use her name in press articles which claimed that, as a witness to the crime, she was perfectly able to identify the killer. Balaian rose to the bait, and was caught by special agents on New-Year's eve. Naturally, the lady was never in any danger because a dummy had been left in her bed. Balaian committed suicide when we closed in on him. Now, John, perhaps you would conclude your remarks.' The Director of Central Intelligence sat down.

'Yes, Sir. Our conclusion is that an Eastern-bloc power, acting through a Bulgarian trading company, commissioned the assassination attempt on you, Mr President, using Mafia resources. For the reasons, I have explained, the attempt misfired. We could speculate why it was made at all, and this question needs political analysis, however, it may be significant it was made to look like a terrorist act: your administration has done much to fight the growth of anarchism and to champion freedom and democracy in countries prey to left-wing extremism: according to political analysts, an attempt like this could be interpreted as a warning shot across our boughs from behind the Iron Curtain.'

The wizened senator sitting at the corner of the conference table lifted his white mane, and interrupted, 'Of course, Mr President, you may know that not all the Russkies agreed to your meeting with the General Secretary.'

There was a murmur of assent.

'Maybe not, Senator', agreed the President, 'but I met him anyway, and I think the future will prove that summit to have been a turning point in our relations with Moscow.' He turned back to Bugs. 'Now, Mr Macpherson, can you identify this man, Balaian, for us?'

'We believe Balaian was one of a breed of Soviet agents specialised in terrorism, Mr President. The Red Army's military intelligence organisation, the GRU, call these highly-trained, deep penetration agents, Spetsnaz. We believe the KGB also field similar specialists as illegal foreign residents after training in their Executive-Action department, charmingly called, Wet Affairs. Balaian was well educated, because, beyond the callousness to prepare and commit cold-blooded murder, he had the intellectual preparation to preach urban guerrilla ideals to an audience of Italian anarchists. It's an intriguing combination of scholar and killer.

'At first sight, his background appears confused. He came to Italy from Libya, he was not Armenian, Syrian or Italian, and he was run by Bulgarians possibly for the benefit of the Russians. Fortunately, he left us the clue to his ream identity in his name. Look at this picture of him taken in 1968 when he was only fourteen years old.'

Bugs turned to the screen on the wall behind him. The photo of a serious-looking boy in uniform appeared in one corner. A few instants later, he projected the photograph that had been waiting in the Director's office on his return from Italy on a second corner of the screen. 'This second photo was taken ten years later by the Arab press when Balaian, a young Ph.D. from the Bulgarian University of Sofia, accepted a post at the Libyan University of Tripoli.'

In a third corner, Bugs projected the photo found in the Colombian jungle cottage of the man wearing fatigues and holding a Kalashnikov. 'This third shot of him was taken at a Libyan guerrilla training camp in 1979. One of Fatima Al-Othman wearing Soviet issue fatigues of identical cut and pattern, and taken on photographic paper from the same batch, links Balaian with Fatima in Libya.'

Bugs' voice deepened and underwent a change in tone. 'For a long time, I couldn't understand why the look in his eyes, the same intense gaze you see on all three of these photographs, seemed so familiar. I thought it was due to his resemblance to Cremante, but it wasn't that. Now I know the reason: look at his father's eyes: they have the same, intense gaze.'

Completing the fourth corner of the screen, he projected a photograph of a white-haired gentleman with the same ferocity in his dark eyes. The features of the two men were so strikingly similar that the relation of father to son was immediately obvious.

'Victor's name holds his identity', continued Bugs. 'Rearranging the letters in "Balaian" to the word "Albania", and recalling the meaning of the Latin word *Victor* as *conqueror*, we get the name of his father's book, *Albania Shall Conquer*. In the Colombian jungle, I found a copy dedicated by the writer, Mehemet Shkoder, to his son, Ahmet Shkoder; this photo of the father is taken from the dust cover of the book. Inside, an inscription confides the future of his work to his son, Ahmet. Mehemet must have had great regard for his son to write such an inscription: 'I dedicate this work to you, the one I love, the one who understands, the one who will continue my work when I am gone.'

'The first photo I projected was taken in Tirana, Albania, when Ahmet Shkoder was an Albanian youth-league leader responsible for the political orthodoxy of the youth journal. As you can see, his simple, Chinese-style uniform does nothing to dilute that passion in his young eyes. He went on to study for a doctorate in Bulgaria, and was later joined by his father, who fled Albania. It was probably shortly after, that Ahmet was targeted as a potential subversive at the Patrice Lumumba school in Moscow; the Soviets would certainly have recruited him there.

'He moved to Libya, ostensibly as an academic, but in reality, to help in Khaddafi's desert training of subversives; his schools are run by the East German Stasi; the Staatssicherheitsdienst, or State Security Service. He may have expected to infiltrate an Arab terrorist organisation there, such as Black September or the Fatah Revolutionary Council, but, when the opportunity arose through Lucia Sereni of joining the Red Brigades, he took it. It was pure fate: Ahmet Shkoder, as Balaian, might have ended up in the Irish Republican Army, the Basque ETA movement, the German Red Army Faction, or any one of several such organisations.

'He fled Italy when his false identity was blown, and, by that time, had gained enough experience to be trusted with an attempt on your life, Mr President. He gave the hit a flavour of fanatical terrorism, and expected to escape without compromising his cover, simply by implicating a dead crook, Cremante and two ex-girlfriends. It shows the quality of Ahmet Shkoder's training that he almost succeeded in escaping the free world as a total unknown, with the responsibility for all his past crimes falling on the shoulders of a dead Mafia lieutenant and two dead fanatical women. I believe we can assume he had intended the operation to be his last in the free world for now.'

The old senator lifted his eyes from the doodles filling his notepad. 'Maybe that Cremante fella was a Russky agent too, Mr Macpherson.'

Laughter filled the room.

Bugs smiled, then frowned at the senator, and returned to his seat amid applause.

The President walked over to thank him personally.

The members of the Select Committee dispersed, some leaving before the press conference.

Bugs had never been the centre of such attention before, and, for the first time in his career, he enjoyed the light-headedness of public acclaim. Committee members walked up to compliment him on his presentation, the Director, hovering close by, introducing him from time to time with the self-satisfied smile, and patronising pat on the back, of a mentor. Finally, he too left for the press conference.

Jenny walked across the lobby with Jim Curry. She was flushed with the excitement of meeting the First Lady. Watching her walk towards him with the elegance of a cat, her smile radiant, his reputation soaring, Bugs had rarely felt so happy.

Jim shook his hand warmly and invited them both to dinner. 'How about Saturday?'

'No thanks, Jim. The Director has invited us both to his home so, it seems, Jen can meet my new boss.'

Jim smiled at Jenny. 'You've never met the Director before?'

'Jim', protested Bugs: 'I didn't say the DCI himself was my new boss.'

Jim pumped his hand. 'Congratulations, Bugsy: I always said you were the greatest.... outside the Bureau, of course.'

'You're jumping to conclusions. The Director doesn't have that kind of sense of humour.'

'We'll see. You call me Sunday morning: I'll wager you now you'll tell me you've got Hailsham's job.'

'No way.'

'Bugs. Did you hear that this Ahmet injected himself with pure hydrocyanic acid? And do you remember the medic who gave him heart massage and pronounced him dead?'

'The guy with the accent?'

'Disappeared! Not a trace! Vanished! Nobody at the hospital knows him.'

'He said he was European.'

'Maybe he was in cahoots with Ahmet: there is a Europe East of the Iron Curtain. But whoever he was, he's long gone.'

'Yes', mused Bugs, 'whoever he was', and left to catch his plane for Turkey.

Not far South of Aktopol, an ancient city basking on the Western shore of the Black Sea, the road following the shoreline to the Bosporus takes a gentle turn into the red and white barriers of a frontier post. On one side, Bulgarian guards patrol the uneasy perimeter, and, on the other, Turkish police wait drowsily in the sun. Not many people cross the frontier at this point: from time to time, privileged Bulgarians passing the summer months on the coast go for a drive to Istanbul, but few have that kind of clearance. Trucks bearing fruit and industrial machinery often cross each other, but, in general, the frontier is quiet. The Turkish police expect no trouble from their Bulgarian counterparts, and the

Bulgarian border guards are clever enough to mind their own business: in private, they hate each other.

It was evening and getting dark when a blue Polski FIAT on the road down from Aktopol drew up at the Bulgarian customs post. The junior lieutenant, who asked for the passports and visas, was afterwards to claim that the two elderly gentlemen inside had given him their documents without betraying any signs of emotion at all: they had not even spoken a word. He assumed that these Bulgarians, called Kostov and Potanin, were businessmen: they wouldn't be tourists at this time of the year.

The reason he took their documents to check them inside the frontier post lay, he later claimed, in two facts: first, the car was completely empty: there wasn't even a briefcase on the back seat: second, the cut of their clothes was so good that these fine gentlemen were either crooks or Nomenklatura: if he stopped them, in the first case he would get a promotion, and in the second he would get noticed. In any event, the formality of stamping the visas broke the boredom. He saw the gentleman on the passenger side open the door and get out, but they all did that on these long drives to stretch their legs, or to use the toilet. Besides, whatever happened, they would have to await their documents.

The problem was that the lights in the office were so strong that anything on the outside was almost invisible at night through the reflection in the glass, and the procedure, when properly applied, was so long: the exit-visa details had to be laboriously copied down, and, of course, the passport signatures had to be checked.

And there was that daily list of names and numbers sent out from Sofia.

His heart ground to a halt: not one, but both numbers were on the list: Kostov and Potanin were hot. This meant a sure promotion. He felt like yelling for help, but he sat and tried to remember what it said in the manual. He had to stay calm: he had to find two more officers to accompany him, and take the presumed offenders into custody until Sofia took charge. He looked out of the window again, but the wall light reflected at him. He couldn't see the car very well, but they wouldn't know, and they couldn't go very far.

He walked into the mess room and quickly explained the problem to two guards having a languid smoke. The two straightened up and marched officiously out with him to the waiting car.

It was empty: both front doors were open. The junior lieutenant's head jerked towards the barrier. He saw them break into a pathetic fifty-metre sprint. A bell split the silence. A battery of halogen floods turned the dark stretch of no man's land into an arena as bright as the Super Bowl. 'Get them!' he yelled.

The guards ran to the barrier and knelt, lifting their Kalashnikovs to their shoulders.

'Mind the fucking Turks!'

The heavier man came down at thirty yards: he was so slow; it was child's play. The lighter, younger, one, who had been the driver, got five yards further. Both assault rifles hit him almost simultaneously, almost lifting his smaller frame off the ground.

They were left to bleed while the junior lieutenant telephoned for instructions.

From time to time the heavier man groaned.

The Turks didn't move a muscle, terrified they might get a salvo themselves.

An escorted ambulance arrived more than two hours after the incident. It was driven onto the brightly lit stretch and surrounded by armed militia. The groans had stopped more than an hour before. Two lifeless bodies were lifted inside, and the cortege returned to Bulgarian territory.

At that moment two men drove up to the frontier on the Turkish side. As their car came to a halt, the halogen lamps were extinguished.

The ambulance left slowly, its siren quiet.

One of the men, an American, asked a Turkish officer what had happened.

Minutes later, the political refugee in his car learnt that his father, General Felix Pavlovich Nikolaev, and his father's good friend, the eminent Marshall Sergei Borisovich Volkov, sometime member of the Russian Politburo, had just been shot by Bulgarian border guards while making a dash across the frontier.

Vassily Nikolaev broke down and cried like a baby.

Bugs Macpherson, who was driving, turned his deep-set, eyes to look in sympathy at the young Russian. He frowned and ran a hand through his prematurely greying hair.

Ivan relaxed in his chair and looked out at the early-morning snow. 'Olya', he said, 'do you want to come for a walk in Fili Park?'

'Are you mad, dear?' she answered, laughing.

'Tomorrow we must get a dog.'

'Vanya! No!'

'A short walk, just to have a cup of tea.'

'You mean at one of those filthy stalls?'

Ivan paused. 'Yes.'

'You never know what you might catch: they never wash the cups.' Olga waited for an answer, but Ivan continued to stare out of the window. There was an intensity in his gaze she had not seen before. 'Vanya, why?'

'I want to see someone, Olya: I owe her a debt of gratitude: she's out there in the real Moscow. Will you come? I want you to meet her: she serves tea in the park....and there's someone else....an old man I used to know well and who looks after rowing boats. Please come.'

EPILOGUE: 10th NOVEMBER 1989

I walk with a stoop now. Gone are my straight back and the dark gaze that had held so many of my students in spell: now my eyes are softer. Now and again I am told they seem strangely vacant, as if my thoughts leave for times long past, in some distant land. My hair has become completely white: it gives me an air of frailty and of benevolence, they say. The students come to visit me all the time because I am alone in my dacha, apart from a woman paid for by the Party who comes to clean once a week. She says I have been distant ever since the visit from Promyslov: I go to the window and look outside at the snow for long periods, in a dream, as if waiting for someone to appear, she says. She swears she has seen tears in my eyes, and when she asks what's wrong, I say, 'nothing'.

She says I have a thick accent. My walls are hidden by rows and rows of books. Here and there proudly hang innumerable honours and diplomas, both studied for, and honorary.

She was away on the day the visitor from Sofia came. He told me he had almost turned back, overwhelmed by the grandiose gardens surrounding the dachas and the guarded entry to this walled-in, golden prison: it seems that an aimless, compulsive fear haunting his entire being had driven him nonetheless to knock at my door, but, of course, the gate guard had phoned through first.

He must have taken me for a servant. He gave his name with a vacuous self-importance. Times had been rough for him after the Agricultural Directorate scandal: he said that Promyslov had helped to get him off the hook, and that now he was back in his old job.

He said, 'Please tell the professor I'm here.' His accent was thick with the intonations of a Bulgarian to which I had become attuned during my years in Sophia.

'Pleased to meet you, Comrade Botev. Come in please and sit down.' I said.

He shook my hand daintily, a look of doubt in his eye.

'Vodka?' I asked and disappeared into the kitchen when he replied, ''Please.'

I sat in an armchair facing him, and offered him a glass: the liquid was syrupy, frozen, clear. I raised it, 'To loved ones who have left us', and relaxed.

He seemed suddenly frightened. My students used to say that I get the 'look' when I focus on people

'What can I do for you, Professor?' he stammered; he crossed his legs.

'I asked Promyslov whether you could tell me something of your experience in America, oh, it must be almost four years ago, now. I fear the probable breakdown of our Soviet won't allow me such privileges very soon from now. Did you hear what happened yesterday in Berlin?'

'Professor, I'm flattered you thought of contacting me: I do have personal experience of the mid-western states in America, though I could probably answer questions on other areas too.' He put his empty glass on the table by his side.

'More vodka?'

'Please.'

I came back from the kitchen with the bottle this time, and refilled his glass. 'I believe your trip was to Chicago.'

'Ah, Chicago! What a disgrace: such poverty and crime!'

'Were you not there for an exhibition?'

'Yes indeed: it must have been ... in April 1985.'

'I'm told you handled a matter of great sensitivity with the utmost skill, but.... had a little bad luck.'

His knuckles whitened over the armchair grip. He uncrossed his legs, and re-crossed them the other way. 'I am not free to discuss the matter, Comrade Professor.'

'No, of course not, and I would never dream of embarrassing you with questions of national security.'

'That is most understanding of you, Comrade Professor.'

'There is one thing, however, I would like to discuss that is of a...less delicate nature.'

'What is that?' he asked. He clutched his vodka.

'I would like you to tell me about someone you met. A man: you gave him a letter. Do you remember?'

He trembled. It was not that warm in the dacha. 'Would you like to sit closer to the stove?' I reached over to fill his glass.

'What about him?'

Then I almost couldn't say it. I felt my years and stared for some seconds bleary-eyed at the floor beyond my knees, my lips trembling, before my eyes a spectral procession of children, of a smiling mother, of my dear dead wife and my poor dead boy. I reached into my pocket and took out the briar pipe my son had given me in Sofia. I filled it with black Balkan tobacco and turned my head to blow my nose. 'I would like you to remember all you can about him: what he said; how he looked; what he wore: everything. I believe you were the last to see him: I had not seen him for so many years. We argued, you see: he was my son.'

'Ah, Comrade Professor', he started, 'what a fine man, but you speak of him as if he were dead.'

'I believe he is, Comrade', I replied.

'What a loss! Such a fine, strong young man.' I smiled, encouraging him to go on. 'Let me tell you how he looked when we had a drink together: I remember well now: it was at the McCormick Hotel during the fair. I tell you, he looked...well...did you not resemble each other?'

Bob Gillespie has worked and lived in the U.K., the U.S.A., Italy and France. His interest in comparative Western European cultures brought him to author *Machiavelli and The Mayflower* in 2009. He started writing *Brutes for Kin* under the title *The Angry Sky* in 1985 and finished a researched first draft shortly after the fall of the Berlin Wall in 1989, which more-or-less sabotaged the whole Northern-Hemisphere, Cold-War thriller genre. With the return of complexity in Russian relations with the West, and with the encouragement of a M.A. in Critical and Creative Writing at the University of Sussex to be completed in 2018, he has rewritten and republished his novel as *Brutes for Kin*. Bob currently oscillates between Paris, Brighton and a few other places.

Also by Bob Gillespie at La Remige Publishers:

Machiavelli and The Mayflower – How to understand the Europeans – © 2009
ISBN 978-2-9533867-0-7   UK English Paperback Edition
The Lourdes Carer Guide – © 2012
ISBN 978-2-9533867-1-4   UK English Edition